21

THE CHATEAU

WILLIAM MAXWELL was born in 1908 in Illinois. He is the author of a distinguished body of work: six novels, three short story collections, an autobiographical memoir and a collection of literary essays and reviews. A *New Yorker* editor for forty years, he helped to shape the prose and careers of John Updike, John Cheever, John O'Hara and Eudora Welty. His novel, *So Long, See You Tomorrow* (1980), won the American Book Award, and he received the 1995 PEN/Malamud Award. He lives in New York City.

So Long, See You Tomorrow, Time Will Darken It, All the Days and Nights: Collected Stories, The Folded Leaf and *The Château* are now made available in Britain by The Harvill Press.

Also by William Maxwell and published by Harvill

SO LONG, SEE YOU TOMORROW

TIME WILL DARKEN IT

ALL THE DAYS AND NIGHTS:
COLLECTED STORIES

THE FOLDED LEAF

Other books by William Maxwell

BILLIE DYER AND OTHER STORIES

THE OUTERMOST DREAM

OVER BY THE RIVER AND OTHER STORIES

ANCESTORS

THE OLD MAN AND THE RAILROAD CROSSING
AND OTHER TALES

HEAVENLY TENANTS

THEY CAME LIKE SWALLOWS

BRIGHT CENTER OF HEAVEN

William Maxwell

THE CHATEAU

THE HARVILL PRESS
LONDON

First published by Alfred A. Knopf, New York, 1961

First published in Britain in 2000 by
The Harvill Press
2 Aztec Row, Berners Road,
London N1 0PW

www.harvill.com

1 3 5 7 9 8 6 4 2

Copyright © William Maxwell, 1961

Acknowledgement for the epigraphs is made to Alfred A. Knopf Inc., for the quotation from *A World of Love* by Elizabeth Bowen and to W. W. Norton and Company Inc., for the quotations from *The Letters of Rainer Maria Rilke 1892–1910.*

William Maxwell asserts the moral right to be identified as the author of this work

A CIP catalogue record for this book is available from the British Library

ISBN 1 86046 577 3

Printed and bound in Great Britain by Butler & Tanner Ltd
at Selwood Printing, Burgess Hill

CONDITIONS OF SALE

All rights reserved. No part of this publication may be reproduced, stored in a retrieval system, or transmitted in any form or by any means, electronic, mechanical, photocopying, recording or otherwise, without the prior permission of the publisher

This book is sold subject to the condition that it shall not, by way of trade or otherwise, be lent, re-sold, hired out or otherwise circulated without the publisher's prior consent in any form of binding or cover other than that in which it is published and without a similar condition including this condition being imposed on the subsequent purchaser

For

E. B.

E. C.

M. O'D.

F. S.

W. S.

" . . . wherever one looks twice there is some mystery"

ELIZABETH BOWEN, *A World of Love*

"And there stand those stupid languages, helpless as two bridges that go over the same river side by side but are separated from each other by an abyss. It is a mere bagatelle, an accident, and yet it separates . . ."

RAINER MARIA RILKE, *letter to his wife, September 2, 1902, from Paris*

". . . a chestnut that we find, a stone, a shell in the gravel, everything speaks as though it had been in the wilderness and had meditated and fasted. And we have almost nothing to do but listen . . ."

RILKE, *letter to his friend Arthur Holitscher, December 13, 1905, from Meudon-Val-Fleury*

THE CHATEAU

Part I

Leo and Virgo

Chapter 1

THE BIG OCEAN LINER, snow white, with two red and black slanting funnels, lay at anchor, attracting sea gulls. The sea was calm, the lens of the sky was set at infinity. The coastline—low green hills and the dim outlines of stone houses lying in pockets of mist—was in three pale French colors, a brocade borrowed from some museum. The pink was daybreak. So beautiful, and no one to see it.

And on C Deck: Something had happened but what he did not know, and it might be years before he found out, and then it might be too late to do anything about it. . . . Something was wrong, but it was more than the mechanism of dreaming could cope with. His eyelids opened and he saw that he was on shipboard, and what was wrong was that he was not being lifted by the berth under him or cradled unpleasantly from side to side. He listened. The ship's engines had stopped. The straining and creaking of the plywood walls had given way to an immense silence. He sat up and looked through the porthole and there it was, across the open water, a fact, in plain sight, a real place, a part of him because he could say he had seen it. The pink light was spreading, in the sky and on the water. Cherbourg was hidden behind a long stone breakwater—an abstraction. He put his head clear out into the beautiful morning and smelled land.

His lungs expanding took in the air of creation, of the beginning of everything.

He drew his head back in and turned to look at the other berth. How still she was, in her nest of covers. Lost to the world.

He put his head out again and watched a fishing boat with a red sail come slowly around the end of a rocky promontory. He studied the stone houses. They were more distinct now. The mist was rising. Who lives in those houses, he thought, whose hand is at the tiller of that little boat, I have no way of knowing, now or ever. . . .

He felt a weight on his heart, he felt like sighing, he felt wide open and vulnerable to the gulls' cree-cree-creeing and the light on the water and the brightness in the air.

The light splintered and the hills and houses were rainbow-edged, as though a prism had been placed in front of his eyes. The prism was tears. Some anonymous ancestor, preserved in his bloodstream or assigned to cramped quarters somewhere in the accumulation of inherited identities that went by his name, had suddenly taken over; somebody looking out of the porthole of a ship on a July morning and recognizing certain characteristic features of his homeland, of a place that is Europe and not America, wept at all he did not know he remembered.

THE CABIN STEWARD knocking on their door woke her.

"Thank you," he called. Then to his wife: "We're in France. Come look. You can see houses." He was half dressed and shaving.

They stood at the porthole talking excitedly, but what they saw now was not quite what he had seen. The mist was gone. The sky was growing much brighter. And they had been noticed; two tenders were already on their way out to the liner, bringing more gulls, hundreds of them.

I: *Leo and Virgo*

"So beautiful!" she said.

"You should have seen it a few minutes ago."

"I wish you'd wakened me."

"I thought you needed the sleep," he said.

Though they had the same coloring and were sometimes mistaken for brother and sister, the resemblance was entirely a matter of expression. There was nothing out of the ordinary about his features, nothing ordinary about hers. Because she came of a family that seemed to produce handsomeness no matter what hereditary strains it was crossed with, the turn of the forehead, the coloring, the carving of the eyelids, the fine bones, the beautiful carriage could all be accounted for by people with long memories. But it was the eyes that you noticed. They were dark brown, and widely spaced, and very large, and full of light, the way children's eyes are, the eyebrows naturally arched, the upper eyelids wide but not heavy, not weighted, the whites a blue white. If all her other features had been bad, she still would have seemed beautiful because of them. They were the eyes of someone of another Age, their expression now gentle and direct, now remote, so far from calculating, and yet intelligent, perceptive, pessimistic, without guile, and without coquetry.

"I don't remember it at all," she said.

"You probably landed at Le Havre."

"I mean I don't remember seeing France for the first time."

"It could have been night," he said, knowing that it bothered her not to be able to remember things.

Mr. and Mrs. Harold Rhodes, the tags on their luggage read.

A few minutes later, hearing the sound of chains, he went to the porthole again. The tenders were alongside, and the gulls came in closer and closer on the air above the tenders and then drifted down like snow. He heard shouting and snatches of conversation. French it had to be, but it was slurred and unintelligible. A round face appeared, filling the porthole: a man in a blue beret. The eyes stared solemnly, unblinking, without recognition as the face on the magic-lantern slide moved slowly to the left and out of sight.

ON SHORE, in the customs shed at seven thirty, they waited their turn under the letter R. She had on a wheat-colored traveling suit and the short black cloth coat that was fashionable that year and black gloves but no hat. He was wearing a wrinkled seersucker suit, a white broadcloth shirt, a foulard tie, and dusty white shoes. He needed a haircut. The gray felt hat he held in his hand was worn and sweat-stained, and in some mysterious way it looked like him. One would have said that, day in and day out, the hat was cheerful, truthful, even-tempered, anxious to do what is right.

How she looked was, Barbara Rhodes sincerely thought, not very important to her. She did not look like the person she felt herself to be. It was important to him. He would not have fallen in love with and married a plain girl. To do that you have to be reasonably well satisfied with your own appearance or else have no choice.

He was thin, flat-chested, narrow-faced, pale from lack of sleep, and tense in his movements. A whole generation of loud, confident Middle-Western voices saying: *Harold, sit up straight . . . Harold, hold your shoulders back . . . Harold, you need a haircut, you look like a violinist* had had no effect whatever. Confidence had slipped through his fingers. He had failed to be like other people.

On the counter in front of them were two large suitcases, three smaller ones, a dressing case, and a huge plaid dufflebag.

"Are you sure everything is unlocked?" she asked.

Once more he made all the catches fly open. The seven pieces of luggage represented a triumph of packing on her part and the full weight of a moral compromise: it was in his nature to provide against every conceivable situation and want, and she, who had totally escaped from the tyranny of objects when he married her, caught the disease from him.

They stood and waited while a female customs inspector went through the two battered suitcases of an elderly Frenchwoman. Everything the inspector opened or unfolded was worn, shabby, mended, and embarrassingly personal, and the old woman's face cried out that this was no way to treat someone who was coming home, but the customs inspector did not hear, did not believe her, did not care. There was the book of regulations, which one learned, and then one applied the regulations. Her spinsterish face darkened by suspicion, by anger, by the authority that had been vested in her, she searched and searched.

"What shall I tell her if she asks me about the nylon stockings?" Barbara Rhodes said.

"She probably won't say anything about them," he answered. "If she does, tell her they're yours."

"Nobody has twelve pairs of unused nylon stockings. She'll think I'm crazy."

"Well, then, tell her the truth—tell her they're to give to the chambermaid in hotels in place of a tip."

"But then we'll have to pay duty on them!"

He didn't answer. A boy of sixteen or seventeen was plucking at his coat sleeve and saying: "Taxi? Taxi?"

"No," he said firmly. "We don't want a taxi. One thing at a time, for God's sake."

The wind was off the harbor and the air was fresh and stimulating. The confusion in the tin-roofed customs shed had an element of social excitement in it, as if this were the big affair of the season which everybody had been looking forward to, and to which everybody had been asked. More often than not, people seemed pleased to have some responsible party pawing through their luggage. In the early spring of 1948 it had seemed to be a question of how long Europe would be here—that is, in a way that was recognizable and worth coming over to see. Before the Italian elections the eastbound boats were half empty. After the elections, which turned out so much better than anybody expected, it took wire-pulling of a sustained and anxious sort to get passage on any eastbound boat of no matter what size or kind or degree of comfort. But they had made it. They were here.

"Taxi?"

"I wish I hadn't brought them now," she whispered.

Tired of hearing the word "taxi," he turned and drove the boy away. Turning back to her, he said: "I think it would probably look better if we talked out loud. . . . What has she got against that poor woman?"

"Nothing. What makes you think exactly the same thing wouldn't be happening if the shoe were on the other foot?"

"Yes?" he said, surprised and pleased by this idea.

He deferred to her judgments about people, which were not infallible—sometimes instead of seeing people she saw through them. But he knew that his own judgment was never to be trusted. He persisted in thinking that all people are thin-skinned, even though it had been demonstrated to him time and time again that they are not.

In the end, the female customs inspector made angry chalk marks on the two cheap suitcases. The old woman's guilt was not proved, but that was not to say that she was innocent; nobody is innocent.

When their turn came, the inspector was a man, quick and pleasant with them, and the inspection was cursory. The question of how many pairs of stockings a woman travels with didn't come up. They were the last ones through the customs. When they got outside, Harold looked around for a taxi, saw that there weren't any, and remembered with a pang of remorse the boy who had plucked at his coat sleeve. He looked for the boy, and didn't see him either. A hundred yards from the tin customs shed, the boat train stood ready to depart for Paris; but they weren't going to Paris.

I: *Leo and Virgo*

Two dubious characters in dark-blue denim—two comedians—saw them standing helplessly beside their monumental pile of luggage and took them in charge, made telephone calls (they said), received messages (perhaps) from the taxi stand at the railroad station, and helped them pass the time by alternately raising and discouraging their hopes. It was over an hour before a taxi finally drew up and stopped beside the pile of luggage, and Harold was not at all sure it hadn't arrived by accident. Tired and bewildered, he paid the two comedians what they asked, exorbitant though it seemed.

The taxi ride was through miles of ruined buildings, and at the railway station they discovered that there was no provision in the timetables of the S.N.C.F. for a train journey due south from Cherbourg to Mont-Saint-Michel. The best the station agent could offer was a local at noon that would take them southeast to Carentan. At Carentan they would have to change trains. They would have to change again at Coutances, and at Pontorson. At Pontorson there would be a bus that would take them the remaining five miles to Mont-Saint-Michel.

They checked their luggage at the station and went for a walk. Most of the buildings they saw were ugly and pockmarked by shellfire, but Cherbourg was French, it had sidewalk cafés, and the signs on the awnings read *Volailles & Gibier* and *Spontex* and *Tabac* and *Charcuterie*, and they looked at it as carefully as they would have looked at Paris. They had coffee at a sidewalk café. They inquired in half a dozen likely places and in none of them was there a public toilet. The people they asked could not even tell them where to go to find one. He went into a stationery store and bought a tiny pocket dictionary, to make sure they were using the right word; also a little notebook, to keep a record of their expenses in. Two blocks farther on, they came to a school and stood looking at the children in the schoolyard, so pale and thin-legged in their black smocks. Was it the war? If they had come to Europe before the war, would the children have had rosy cheeks?

He looked at his wrist watch and said: "I think we'd better not walk too far. We might not be able to find our way back to the station."

She saw a traveling iron in a shop window and they went in and bought it. They tried once more—they tried a tearoom with faded chintz curtains and little round tables. The woman at the cashier's desk got up and ushered Barbara to a lavatory in the rear. When they were out on the sidewalk again, she said: "You should have seen what I just saw!"

"What was it like?"

"It was filthy. And instead of a toilet there was a stinking hole in the floor. I couldn't believe it."

"I guess if you are a stranger, and homeless, you aren't supposed to go to the bathroom in France. Are you all right?"

"Yes, I'm perfectly all right. But it's so shocking. When you think that women with high heels have to go in there and stand or squat on two wooden boards. . . ."

They stopped to look in the window of a bookstore. It was full of copies of "Gone With the Wind" in French.

THE LOCAL TRAIN was three coaches long. At the last minute, driven by his suspicions, he stepped out onto the platform, looked at the coach they were in, and saw the number 3. They were in third class, with second-class tickets. The fat, good-natured old robber who had charged them five hundred francs for putting them and their luggage in the wrong car was nowhere in sight, and so he moved the luggage himself. His head felt hollow from lack of sleep, and at the same time he was excited, and so full of nervous energy that nothing required any exertion.

The train began to move. Cherbourg was left behind.

The coach was not divided into compartments but open, like

an American railway car. Looking out of the train window, they saw that the sky was now overcast. They saw hedgerows enclosing triangular meadows and orchards that were continually at a slant and spinning with the speed of the train. House after house had been shelled, had no windows or roof, had been abandoned; and then suddenly a village seemed to be intact. They saw poppies growing wild on the railroad embankment and could hardly believe their eyes. That wonderful intense color! They were so glad they had seen them. They saw a few more. Then they saw red poppies growing all through a field of wheat—or was it rye? They saw (as if seeing were an art and the end that everything is working toward) a barn with a sign painted on it: *Rasurel.*

Their eyes met, searching for some relief from looking so intently at the outside world. "We're in France," he said, and let his hand rest lightly in hers. The train came to a stop. They looked for the name on the station: *Valognes.* They saw flower beds along the station platform. Blue pansies. "*Pensées,*" it said in the pocket dictionary. They saw a big blond man with blue eyes and bright pink cheeks. They saw a nice motherly woman. They saw a building with a sign on it: *Café de la Gare.* The station was new. In a moment this tiny world-in-itself was left behind. He looked at his watch.

"What time do we change?" she asked, smothering a yawn.

"At two. It's now seventeen minutes of one."

"We'd better not fall asleep."

He felt his right side and was reassured; his wallet and their passports were in his inside coat pocket, making a considerable bulge. "Is it the way you remembered it?" he asked anxiously. "I know there weren't any ruined buildings, but otherwise?"

"Yes. Except that we were in a car."

That other time, she was with her father and mother and two brothers. They went to England first. They saw Anne Hathaway's cottage, and Arlington Row in Bibury, and Oxford, and Tintern Abbey. And because she was sick in bed with a cold, they left her alone in the hotel in London while they went sight-seeing, and she had a wonderful afternoon. The chambermaid brought her hot lemonade with whisky in it, and it was the first time she had ever had any whisky, and the chambermaid took a liking for her and gave her a gold locket, which she still had, at home in her blue leather jewel case.

After England, they crossed the Channel and spent two weeks in Paris, and then they drove to Concarneau, which they loved. In her snapshot album there was a picture of them all, walking along a battlement at Carcassonne. That was in 1933. The hem of her skirt came halfway to her ankles, and she was twelve years old.

"What is Cinzano?" she asked.

"An apéritif. Or else it's an automobile."

. . . five, six, seven. Knowing that nothing had been left behind, he nevertheless could not keep from insanely counting the luggage. He looked out of the train window and saw roads (leading where?) and fields. He saw more poppies, more orchards, a church steeple in the distance, a big white house. Could it be a château?

The yawn was contagious, as usual.

"Where do you suppose the Boultons are now?"

"Southampton," he said. "Or they might even be home. They didn't have far to go."

"It was funny our not speaking until the last day—"

"The last afternoon."

"And then discovering that we liked them so much. If only we'd discovered them sooner." Another yawn.

"I have their address, if we should go to England."

"But we're not."

She yawned again and again, helplessly.

They no longer had to look at each hedgerow, orchard, field, burning poppy, stone house, barn, steeple. The landscape, like any landscape seen from a train window, was repetitious. Just when he thought he had it all by heart, he saw one of Van Gogh's little bridges.

Her chin sank and sank. He drew her over against him and put her head on his shoulder, without waking her. His eyes met the blue eyes of the priest across the aisle. The priest smiled. He asked the priest, in French, to tell him when they got to Carentan, and the priest promised to. Miles inland, with his eyes closed, he saw the gulls gliding and smelled salt water.

His eyelids felt gritty. He roused himself and then dozed off again, not daring to fall sound asleep because they had to change trains. He tried willing himself to stay awake, and when that didn't work, he tried various experiments, such as opening his eyes and shutting them for a few seconds and then opening them again immediately. The conductor came through the car examining tickets, and promised to tell him when the train got to Carentan. Though the conductor seemed to understand his French, how can you be sure, speaking in a foreign language, that people really have understood you? . . . The conductor did come to tell them, when the train was slowing down, on the outskirts of Carentan, but by that time the luggage was in a pile blocking the front of the coach, and they were standing beside it, ready to alight.

What should have been a station platform was, instead, a long, long rock pile. Looking up and down it as the train drew to a stop he saw that one of his fears, at least, was justified: there were no porters. He jumped down and she handed him the lighter suitcases, but the two big ones she could not even lift. The other passengers tried to get by her, and then turned and went toward the other end of the coach—all except a red-headed man, who saw that they were in trouble and without saying a word took over, just as Harold was about to climb back on the train.

What a nice, kind, *human* face . . .

All around them, people were stepping from rock to rock, or leaping, and it was less like changing trains than like a catastrophe of some kind—like a shipwreck. The red-haired man swung the dufflebag down expertly and then jumped down from the train himself and hurried off before they could thank him. Until that moment it had not occurred to Harold to wonder how much time they would have between trains.

He stopped a man with a light straw suitcase. "Le train à Coutances?"

"Voie D!" the man shouted over his shoulder, and when they didn't understand, he pointed to the entrance to an underpass, far down the rock pile. "De ce côté-là."

"Oh my God!"

"Why aren't there any porters?" she asked, looking around. "There were porters in Cherbourg."

"I don't know!" he said, exasperated at her for being logical when they were faced with a crisis and action was what was called for. "We'll have to do it in stages." He picked up the big brown suitcase, and then, to balance it, two smaller ones. "You stay here and watch the rest of the luggage until I get back."

"Who is going to watch those?" she demanded, pointing at the suitcases he had just picked up. "What if somebody takes them while you are coming back for more?"

"We'll just have to hope they don't."

"I'm coming with you." She picked up two more suitcases.

"No, don't!" he exclaimed, furious at not being allowed to manage the crisis in his own way. "They're too heavy for you!"

"So are those too heavy for you."

Leaving the big white suitcase and the dufflebag (two thousand cigarettes, safety matches, soap, sanitary napkins, Kleenex, razor blades, cold cream, cleaning fluid, lighter fluid, shoe polish, tea bags, penicillin, powdered coffee, cube sugar, etc.—a four months' supply of all the things they had been told they couldn't get in Europe so soon after the war) behind and unguarded, they stumbled along in the wake of the other passengers, some of whom were now running, and reached the underpass at last, and went down into it and then up another long flight of steps onto Track D, where their train was waiting.

"How *can* they expect people to do this?" she exclaimed indignantly.

Track D was an ordinary station platform, not another rock pile, and all up and down the train the doors of compartments were slamming shut. "It's like a bad dream," he said.

He left her standing with the luggage beside a second-class carriage and ran back down into the underpass, his footsteps echoing against the cold concrete walls. When he emerged onto Track A again, the train from Cherbourg was gone. Far down the deserted rock pile he saw the big white suitcase and the dufflebag; they hadn't been stolen. From that moment it was not merely France he loved.

He swung the dufflebag onto his shoulder and picked up the suitcase. It weighed a ton. The traveling iron, he thought. And Christ knows what else . . . His heart was pounding, and he had a stitch in his side. As he staggered up the steps of the underpass out onto Track D again, he saw that she was the only person left on the platform, beside the last open compartment door.

"Hurry!" she called. (As if he weren't!)

He thought surely the train would start without them, not realizing that it was full of ardent excitable people who would have thrown themselves in front of the engine if it had. They leaned out of all the windows all up and down the train, shouting encouragement to the American tourists, shouting to the conductor and the brakeman that Monsieur was here, finally, but still had to get the luggage on.

When the luggage had been stowed away in the overhead racks, they sat trembling and exhausted and knee to knee with six people who did not speak a word of English but whom they could not under the circumstances regard as strangers. A well-dressed woman with a little boy smiled at them over the child's head, and they loved her. They loved her little boy, too. Looking out of the train window, they saw the same triangular meadows and orchards as before, the same tall hedgerows, and poppies without number growing in the wheat.

"It was very nice of that man to hand the suitcases down to you," she said.

"Wasn't it."

"I don't know what we'd have done without him."

"I don't either."

"What an experience."

Conscious that by speaking English to each other they were separating themselves from the other people in the compartment, and not wanting to be separated from them, they lapsed into silence. He made himself stop counting the luggage. After a time, the man directly across from them—a farmer or a laborer, judging by his clothes and his big, misshapen, callused hands—took down a small cardboard suitcase. They saw that it contained a change of underwear, a clean shirt, a clean pair of socks, a loaf of bread, a sausage, and a bottle of red wine that had already been uncorked. The sausage was offered politely around the compartment and politely refused. With dignity the man began to eat his lunch.

"What time is it?" Barbara asked.

Harold showed her his watch. If only there were porters in the station in Coutances . . . He looked searchingly at the other faces in the compartment. He was in love with them all.

There were no porters in the railway station at Coutances, and the crisis had to be gone through all over again, but nothing is ever as bad the second time. The station platform was not torn up, and he did not wait for somebody to see that they were in difficulty; instead, he turned and asked for help and got it. As he shook hands with one person after another, looking into their intelligent French eyes and thanking them with all his heart, he began to feel as if an unlimited amount of kindness had been deposited somewhere to his account and he had only to draw on it. Coupled with this daring idea was an even more dangerous one: he was becoming convinced by what had happened to them that in France things are different, and people more the way one would like them to be.

At Pontorson he saw a baggage truck and helped himself to it, thinking that this time he had surely gone too far and an indignant station agent would come running out and make a scene. No one paid any attention to him. The bus parked in front of the station said *Le Mont-Saint-Michel* over the windshield but it was empty, and they discovered from a timetable posted on the wall nearby that it did not leave for an hour and a half. He looked at her drawn, white face and then walked out into the middle of the station plaza in search of a taxi. The square was deserted. For a moment he did not know what to do. Then he saw a bus approaching and hailed it. The bus came to a stop in front of him, and he saw the letters *St. Servan–St. Malo* and that there were no passengers.

"Nous cherchons un hôtel," he said when the driver put his head close to the open window. "Nous avons beaucoup de baggages, et il n'y a pas de taxi. . . . Ma femme est malade," he lied, out of desperation, and then corrected it in favor of the truth. "Elle est très fatiguée. Nous désirons—"

The door swung open invitingly and he hopped in. The big bus made a complete turn in the middle of the square and came to a stop in front of the pile of luggage. He jumped out and ran into the station and found Barbara, and they got in the bus, which went racing through the very narrow, curving streets, at what seemed like sixty miles an hour, and stopped in front of a small hotel. The driver refused to take any money, shook hands, and drove on.

Harold took the precaution of looking the hotel up in the Guide Michelin. "Simple mais assez confortable," it said. He stuffed the Michelin back in his raincoat pocket.

The hotel was old and dark and it smelled of roasting coffee beans. The concierge led them up a flight of stairs and around a corner, to a room with windows looking out on the street. The room was vast. So was the double bed. So was the adjoining bathroom. There was no difficulty about hot water. The concierge took their passports and went off down the hall.

"Whenever I close my eyes I see houses without any roofs," he said.

"So do I."

"And church steeples." He loosened his tie and sat down to take off his shoes. "And Cinzano signs."

The automatic images fell on top of one another, as though they were being dealt like playing cards.

"There's something queer about this bed," she said. "Feel it."

"I don't have to. I can see from here. I don't think we'll have any trouble sleeping, though."

"No."

"The way I feel, I could sleep hanging from a hook."

While she was undressing, he went into the bathroom and turned on both faucets. Above the sound of the plunging water, he heard her saying something to him from the adjoining room. What she said was, she was glad they hadn't gone on to Mont-Saint-Michel.

"I am too," he called back. "I don't think I could bear it. If I saw something beautiful right now, I'd burst into tears. The only thing in the world that appeals to me is a hot bath."

The waitress was at the foot of the stairs when they came down, an hour later. "Vous désirez un apéritif, monsieur-dame?"

She hadn't the slightest objection to their sitting at one of the tables outdoors, in front of the hotel, and before they settled down, he raced back upstairs and got the camera and took Barbara's picture. He managed to get in also the furled blue and white striped umbrella, the portable green fence with geraniums and salvia growing in flower boxes along the top and bottom, and the blue morning-glories climbing on strings beside the hotel door.

"Quel apéritif?" demanded the waitress, when the camera had

been put away. Finding that they didn't know, because they had had no experience in the matter, she took it upon herself to begin their education. She returned with two glasses and six bottles on a big painted tin tray, and let them try one apéritif after another, and, when they had made their decision, urged them to have the seven-course dinner rather than the five; the seven-course dinner began with écrevisses.

"Ecrevisses" turned out to be tiny crawfish, fried, with tartar sauce. There were only two other guests in the dining room, a man and a woman who spoke in such low tones and were so absorbed in each other that it was quite clear to anyone who had ever seen a French movie that they were lovers.

As the waitress changed their plates for the fourth time, Barbara said: "Wonderful food!" The color had come back into her face.

"Wonderful wine," Harold said, and asked the waitress what it was that they were drinking. The wine was Algerian and had no name, so he couldn't write it down in his little notebook.

When they went up to their room, the images started coming once more. Their eyelids ached. They felt strung on wires.

The street outside their window was as quiet as a cemetery. They undressed and sank sighing into the enormous bed, so like a mother to them in their need of rest.

After ten o'clock there was no sound in the little hotel, and no traffic in the street. The night trucks passed by a different route.

At midnight it rained. Between three and four in the morning, the sky cleared and there were stars. The wind was off the sea. The air was fresh. A night bird sang.

The sleepers knew nothing whatever about any of this. One minute they were dropping off to sleep and the next they heard shouting and opened their eyes to broad daylight. When they sat up in bed they saw that the street was full of people, walking or riding bicycles. The women all wore shapeless long black cotton dresses. An old woman went by, leading her cow. Chickens and geese. Goats. The shops were all open. A man with a vegetable cart was shouting that his string beans were tender and his melons ripe.

"It's like being in the front row at the theater," she said. "How do you feel?"

"Wonderful."

"So do I. Do you think if I pressed this button anything would happen?"

"You mean like breakfast?"

She nodded.

"Try it," he said with a yawn.

Five minutes later there was a knock at the door and the waitress came in with a breakfast tray. "Bonjour, monsieur-dame."

"Bonjour, mademoiselle," he said.

"Avez-vous bien dormi?"

"Oui, merci. Très bien. Et vous?"

"Moi aussi."

"Little goat, bleat. Little table, appear," Harold said as the door closed after her. "Have some coffee."

After breakfast, they got up and dressed. She packed while he was downstairs paying the bill. The concierge called a taxi for them.

"I hate to leave that little hotel," she said, looking back through the rear window as they drove off.

"I didn't mean for the taxi to come quite so soon," he said. "I was hoping we could explore the village first."

But he was relieved that they were on their way again. Six days on shipboard had made him hungry for movement. They rode through the flat countryside with their faces pressed to the car windows.

I: *Leo and Virgo*

"Just look at that woodpile!"

"Look how the orchard is laid out."

"Never mind the orchard, look at the house!"

"Look at the vegetable garden."

Look, look. . . .

Though they thought they knew what to expect, at their first glimpse of the medieval abbey they both cried out in surprise. Rising above the salt marshes and the sand flats, it hung, dreamlike, mysterious, ethereal. "Le Mont-Saint-Michel," the driver said respectfully. As the taxi brought them nearer, it changed; the various parts dissolved their connection with one another in order to form new connections. The last connection of all was with the twentieth century. There were nine chartered sight-seeing buses outside the medieval walls, and the approach to the abbey was lined on both sides of the street with hotels, restaurants, and souvenir shops.

The concierge of the Hôtel Mère Poulard was not put out with them for arriving a day late. Their room was one flight up, and they tried not to see the curtains, which were a large-patterned design of flowers in the most frightful colors. Without even opening their suitcases, they started up the winding street of stairs. Mermaid voices sang to them from the doorways of the open-fronted shops ("Monsieur-dame . . . monsieur-dame . . .") and it was hard not to stop and look at everything, because everything was for sale. He bought two tickets for the conducted tour of the abbey, and they stood a little to one side, waiting for the tour to begin.

"Did you ask for a guide who speaks English?"

He shook his head.

"Why not?"

"I don't think there are any," he said, arguing by analogy from the fact that there were no porters in the railway stations.

"The other time, we always had a guide who spoke English."

"I know, but that was before the war."

"You could ask them if there is one."

But he was reluctant to ask. Instead, he studied the uniformed guides, trying to make out from their faces if they spoke English. At last he went up to the ticket booth and the ticket seller informed him disapprovingly—rather as if he had asked if the abbey was for sale—that the guides spoke only French.

It was their first conducted tour and they tried very hard to understand what the guide said, but names, dates, and facts ran together, and sometimes they had to fall back on enjoying what their eyes saw as they went from room to room. What they saw—stone carvings, stone pillars, vaulting, and archways—seemed softened, simplified, and eroded not only by time but also by the thousands and thousands of human eyes that had looked at it. But in the end, reality failed them. They felt that some substitution had been effected, and that this was not the real abbey. Or if it was, then something was gone from it, something that made all the difference, and they were looking at the empty shell.

They stood in front of the huge fireplace in the foyer of their hotel and watched the famous omelets being made. With their own omelet they had a green salad and a bottle of white wine, which was half a bottle too much. Half drunk, they staggered upstairs to their room and fell asleep in the room with the frightful curtains, to the sound of the omelet whisk. When they woke, the afternoon was half gone. Lying in one another's arms, dreamy and drained, they heard a strange new sound, and sat up and saw through the open casements the sea come rushing in. Within twenty minutes all the surrounding land but the causeway by which they had come from Pontorson was under water. They waited for that too to be covered, but this wonderful natural effect, so often described by earlier travelers, the tide at Mont-Saint-Michel, had been tampered with. The island was not an island any more; the water did not cover the tops of the sight-seeing buses; it did not even cover their hubcaps.

But another tide rising made them turn away from the window. All afternoon, while they were making love and afterward, whether they were awake or asleep, the omelet whisk kept beating and the human tide came and went under their window: tourists from Belgium, tourists from Denmark and Sweden and Switzerland, tourists from Holland, Breton tourists in embroidered velvet costumes, tourists from all over France.

In the evening, they dressed and went downstairs. The omelet cook was again making omelets in front of the roaring wood fire. Harold found out from the concierge that there was no provision in the timetable of the S.N.C.F. for a quick, easy journey by train from Mont-Saint-Michel to Cap Finisterre. They would have to go to Brest, which they had no desire to see, changing trains a number of times along the way. At Brest they could take a bus or a local train to Concarneau.

They stepped out of the hotel into a surprising silence. The cobblestone street was empty. The chartered buses were all gone.

Turning their back on the street of stairs, they followed the upward-winding dirt paths, and discovered the little gardens, here, there, and everywhere. They stood looking down on the salt marshes and the sandbars. Above them the medieval abbey hung dreamlike and in the sky, and that was where they were also, they realized with surprise. The swallows did not try to sell them anything, and the sea air made them excited. Time had gone off with the sight-seeing buses, and they were free to look to their heart's content. Stone towers, slate roofs, half-timbered houses, cliffs of cut stone, thin Gothic windows and crenelated walls and flying buttresses, the rock cliffs dropping sheer into the sea and the wet sand mirroring the sky, cloud pinnacles that were changing color with the coming on of night, and the beautiful past, that cannot quite bear to go but stands here (as it does everywhere, but here especially) saying *Good-by, good-by. . . .*

SHORTLY BEFORE NOON the next day, they returned to Pontorson by bus, left their luggage at the hotel, where their old room was happily waiting for them, and went off sight-seeing. The bus driver was demonically possessed. Dogs, chickens, old people, and children scattered at the sound of his horn. The people who got on at villages and crossroads kept the bus waiting while they delivered involved messages to the driver or greeted those who were getting off. Bicycles accumulated on the roof of the bus. Passengers stood jammed together in the aisles. On a cool, cloudy, Wednesday afternoon, the whole countryside had left home and was out enjoying the pleasures of travel.

St. Malo was disappointing. Each time they came to a gateway in the ramparts of the old town, they stopped and looked in. The view was always the same: a street of brand-new boxlike, houses that were made of stone and would last forever. They took a motor launch across the harbor to Dinard, which seemed to be made up entirely of hotels and boarding houses, all shabby and in need of paint. The tide was far out, the sky was a leaden gray, the wind was raw. At Concarneau it would be colder still.

They bought postcards to prove to themselves later that they had actually been to Dinard, and tried to keep warm by walking. They soon gave up and took the launch back across the harbor. Something that should have happened had not happened; they had been told that Dinard was charming, and they had not been charmed by it, through no fault of theirs. And St. Malo was completely gone. There was nothing left that anybody would want to see. The excursion had not been a success. And yet, in a way, it had; they'd had a nice day. They'd enjoyed the bus ride and the boat ride and the people. They'd enjoyed just being in France.

They had the seven-course dinner again, and, lying in bed that night, they heard singing in the street below their window. (Who could it be? So sad . . .)

In the morning they explored the village. They read the inscriptions in the little cemetery and, in an atmosphere of extreme cordiality, cashed a traveler's check at the mairie. They stared in shop windows. A fire broke out that was like a fire in a dream. Smoke came pouring out of a building; shopkeepers stood in their doorways watching and made comments about it, but did not try to help the two firemen who came running with a hose cart and began to unreel the hose and attach it to a hydrant in a manhole. Though they couldn't have been quicker or more serious about their work, after twenty minutes the hose was still limp. The whole village could have gone up in flames, and for some strange reason it didn't. The smoke subsided, and the shopkeepers withdrew into their shops. Barbara saw a cowhide purse with a shoulder strap in the window of a leather shop, and when they reappeared a few minutes later, she was wearing the purse and he was writing "purse—1850 fr." in his financial diary.

They went back to the hotel and the waitress drew them into the dining room, where she had arranged on an oak sideboard specimens of woodcarving, the hobby of her brother, who had been wounded in the war and could not do steady work. The rich Americans admired but did not buy his chef-d'œuvre, the art-nouveau book ends. Instead, trying not to see the disappointment in her eyes, they took the miniature sabots (500 fr.), which would do nicely for a present when they got back home and meanwhile take up very little room in their luggage. The concierge inquired about their morning and they told him about the fire. A sliding panel in the wall at the foot of the stairs slid open. The cook and the kitchenmaid were also interested.

Upstairs in their room, he said: "I don't suppose we ought to stay here when there are a thousand places in France that are more interesting."

"I could stay here the rest of my life," Barbara said.

They did nothing about leaving. They squandered the whole rest of the day, walking and looking at things. As for their journey to Brittany, they would do better to go inland, the concierge said; at Rennes, for example, they could get an express train from Paris that would take them straight through to Brest.

The next morning, they closed their suitcases regretfully and paid the bill (surprisingly large) and said good-by to the waitress, the chambermaid, the cook, and the kitchenmaid, all of whom they had grown fond of. Their luggage went by pushcart to the railway station, and they followed on foot, with the concierge. Out of affection and because he was sorry to see them go, the concierge was keeping them company as long as possible, and where else would they find a concierge like him?

When they got off the train in Rennes, the weather had grown colder. There was no train for Brest until the next day, and so they walked half a block to the Hôtel du Guesclin et Terminus. Rennes was an ugly industrial city, and they wished they were in Pontorson. An obliging waiter in the restaurant where they ate dinner gave Barbara the recipe for Palourdes farcies. "Clams, onions, garlic, parsley," Harold wrote in his financial diary. It was raining when they woke the next morning. Their hotel room was small and cramped and a peculiar shape. Only a blind person could have hung those curtains with that wallpaper. They could hardly move for their luggage, which they hated the sight of. What pleasure could they possibly have at the seashore in this weather? They decided to go farther inland, to Le Mans, in the hope that it would be warmer. When they got there, they could decide whether to take the train to Brest or one going in the opposite direction, to Paris. But they had not planned to be in Paris until September, and perhaps they would like Le Mans enough to stay there a week. They had arranged to spend the two weeks after that as paying guests at a château in Touraine.

Late that same afternoon, pale and tired after two train journeys—Le Mans was hideous—they stood in the lobby of the Hôtel Univers in Tours, watching the profile of the concierge, who was telephoning for them and committed heart and soul to their cause. With the door of the phone booth closed, they couldn't hear what he said to the long-distance operator, but they could tell instantly by the way he shed his mask of indif-

for sleeping with one eye open, their sexual promiscuity, their tattooed hearts, flowers, mermaids, anchors, and mottoes, their devout belief that all life is meaningless—all this had not been enough to sustain them in the face of too much history. They were discouraged and ill-fed and worried, like everybody else.

He bought some cotton candy. Barbara took two or three licks and then handed it to him. Pink, oversweet, and hairy, *it* hadn't changed; it was just the way he remembered it from his childhood. Wisps clung to his cheeks. He couldn't finish it. He got out his handkerchief and wiped his chin. "Shall we go?" he asked.

They started walking toward the exit. The whole failing enterprise was as elegiac as a summer resort out of season. They looked around one last time for the little French boy but he had vanished. As they passed the gypsy fortuneteller's tent, Harold felt a slight pressure on his coat sleeve. "All right," he said. "If you want to."

"Just this once," she said apologetically.

He disliked having his fortune told.

The gypsy fortuneteller sat darning her stocking by the light of a kerosene lamp. It turned out that she had lived in Chicago and spoke English. She asked Barbara for the date of her birth and then, nodding, said "Virgo." She looked inquiringly at Harold. "Scorpio," he said.

The gypsy fortuneteller looked in her crystal ball and saw that he was lying. He was Leo. Raising her eyes, she saw that he had kept his hands in his pockets.

She passed her thin brown hand over the crystal ball twice and saw that there was a shadow across their lives but it was not permanent, like the shadows she was used to finding. No blackened chimneys, no years and years of wandering, no loved one vanished forever into a barbed-wire enclosure, no savings stolen, no letters returned unopened and stamped *Whereabouts Un-*

known. Whatever the trouble was, in five or six years it would clear up.

She took Barbara Rhodes's hand and opened the fingers (beautiful hand) and in the lines of the palm discovered a sea voyage, a visitor, popularity and entertainment, malice she didn't expect, and a triumph that was sure to come true.

Chapter 2

THE AMERICANS were last in line at the gate, because of their luggage, and as the line moved forward, he picked up a big suitcase in each hand and wondered which of the half-dozen women in black waiting outside the barrier would turn out to be Mme Viénot. And why was there no car?

The station agent took their tickets gravely from between Harold's teeth, and as he walked through the gate he saw that the street was empty. He went back for the dufflebag and another suitcase. When the luggage was all outside they stood and waited.

The sign on the roof of the tiny two-room station said: *Brenodville-sur-Euphrone*. The station itself had as yet no doors, windows, or clock, and it smelled of damp plaster. The station platform was cluttered with bags of cement and piled yellow bricks. Facing the new station, on the other side of the tracks, was a wooden shelter with a bench and three travel posters: the Côte D'Azur (a sailboat) and Burgundy (a glass of red wine) and Auvergne (a rocky gorge). Back of the shelter a farmyard, with the upper story of the barn full of cordwood and the lower story stuffed with hay, served as a poster for Touraine.

They waited for five minutes by his wrist watch, and then he went back inside and consulted the station agent, who said that the Château Beaumesnil was only two and a half kilometers outside the village and they could easily walk there. But not with the luggage, Harold pointed out. No, the station agent agreed, not with their luggage.

There was no telephone in the station and so, leaving the dufflebag and the suitcases on the sidewalk where they could keep an eye on them, they walked across the cobblestone street to the café. He explained their situation to the four men sitting at a table on the café terrace, and learned that there was no telephone here either. One of the men called out to the proprietress, who appeared from within, and said that if Monsieur would walk in to the village, he would find several shops open, and from one of these he could telephone to the château.

Standing on the sidewalk beside the luggage, Barbara followed Harold with her eyes until the street curved off to the left and he disappeared between two slate-roofed stone houses. He was gone for a long, long time. Just as she was beginning to wonder if she would ever see him again, she heard the rattle of an approaching vehicle—a noisy old truck that wheezed and shook and, to her surprise, turned into the station platform at the last minute and drew to a stop beside her. The cab door swung open and Harold hopped out.

In the driver's seat was a middle-aged man who looked like a farmer and had beautiful blue eyes.

"I was beginning to worry about you," she said.

"This is M. Fleury. What a time I've had!"

Sitting in the back of the truck, on the two largest suitcases, they were driven through the village and out into open country. The grain was turning yellow in the fields, and they saw poppies growing along the roadside. The dirt road was rough and full of potholes, and they had to keep turning their faces away to keep from breathing in the dust.

"This is too far to walk even without the luggage," he said.

"I'll have to wash my hair," she said. "But it's beautiful, isn't it?"

I: *Leo and Virgo*

Before long they had a glimpse of the château, across the fields. The trees hid it from view. Then they turned in, between two gate posts, and drove up a long curving cinder drive, and saw the house again, much closer now. It was of white limestone, with tall French windows and a steep slate roof. Across the front was a raised terrace with a low box hedge and a stone balustrade. To the right of the house there was an enormous Lebanon cedar, whose branches fell like dark-green waves, and a high brick wall with ornamental iron gates. To their eyes, accustomed to foundation planting and wisteria or rose trellises, the façade looked a little bare and new. The truck went through the gate and into a courtyard and stopped. For a moment they were aware of how much racket the engine made, and then M. Fleury turned the ignition off to save gasoline, and after that it was the silence they heard. They sat waiting with their eyes on the house and finally a door burst open and a small, thin, black-haired woman came hurrying out. She stopped a few feet from the truck and nodded bleakly to M. Fleury, who touched his beret but said nothing. We must look very strange sitting in the back of the truck with our luggage crammed in around us, Harold thought. But on the other hand, it was rather strange that there was no one at the station to meet them.

They had no way of knowing who the woman was, but she must know who they were, and so they waited uneasily for her to speak. Her eyes moved from them to the fresh Cunard Line stickers on their suitcases. "Yes?" she said coldly in English. "You wanted something?"

"Mme Viénot?" Barbara asked timidly.

The woman clapped her hand to her forehead. "Mme Rhodes! Do forgive me! I thought— Oh how extraordinary! I thought you were middle-aged!"

This idea fortunately struck all three of them as comical. Harold jumped down from the truck and then turned and helped Barbara down. Mme Viénot shook hands with them and, still amazed, still amused at her extraordinary mistake, said: "I cannot imagine what you must think of me. . . . We were just starting to go to the station to meet you. M. Carrère very kindly offered his car. The Bentley would have been more comfortable, perhaps, but you seem to have managed very well by yourselves." She smiled at the camion.

"We thought of telephoning," Barbara said, "but there was no telephone in the station, and at the Café de la Gare they told us—"

"We can't use the telephone after eleven o'clock on Sundays," Mme Viénot interrupted. "The service is cut off. So even if you had tried to reach us by telephone, you couldn't have." She was still smiling, but they saw that she was taking them in—their faces, their American clothes, the gray dust they were powdered with as a result of their ride in the open truck.

"The stationmaster said we could walk," Barbara said, "but we had the suitcases, so I stayed with them, at the station, and my husband walked into the village and found a store that was open, a fruit and vegetable store. And a very nice woman—"

"Mme Michot. She's a great gossip and takes a keen interest in my guests. I cannot imagine why."

"—told us that M. Fleury had a truck," Barbara finished.

Mme Viénot turned and called out to a servant girl who was watching them from a first-floor window to come and take the suitcases that the two men were lifting from the back of the truck. "So you found M. Fleury and he brought you here. . . . M. Fleury is an old friend of our family. You couldn't have come under better auspices."

Harold tried to prevent the servant girl from carrying the two heaviest suitcases, but she resisted so stubbornly that he let go of the handles and stepped back and with a troubled expression on his face watched her stagger off to the house. They were much too heavy for her, but probably in an old country like France, with its own ideas of chivalry and of the physical strength and usefulness of women, that didn't matter as much as who should and who shouldn't be carrying suitcases.

I: *Leo and Virgo*

"You are tired from your journey?" Mme Viénot asked.

"Oh, no," Barbara said. "It was beautiful all the way."

She looked around at the courtyard and then through the open gateway at the patchwork of small green and yellow fields in the distance. Taking her courage in both hands, she murmured: "Si jolie!"

"You think so?" Mme Viénot murmured politely, but in English. A man might perhaps not have noticed it. Barbara's next remark was in English. When Harold started to pay M. Fleury, Mme Viénot exclaimed: "Oh dear, I'm afraid you don't understand our currency, M. Rhodes. That's much too much. You will embarrass M. Fleury. Here, let me do it." She took the bank notes out of his hands and settled with M. Fleury herself.

M. Fleury shook hands all around, and smiled at the Americans with his gentian-blue eyes as they tried to convey their gratitude. They were reluctant to let him go. In a country where, contrary to what they had been told, no one seemed to speak English, he had understood their French. He had been their friend, for nearly an hour. Instinct told them they were not going to manage half so well without him.

The engine had to be cranked five or six times before it caught, and M. Fleury ran around to the driver's seat and adjusted the spark.

"I never hear the sound of a motor in the courtyard without feeling afraid," Mme Viénot said.

They looked at her inquiringly.

"I think the Germans have come back."

"They were here in this house?" Barbara asked.

"We had them all through the war."

The Americans turned and looked up at the blank windows. The war had left no trace that a stranger could see. The courtyard and the white château were at that moment as peaceful and still as a landscape in a mirror.

"It looks as if it had never been any other way than the way it is now," Harold said.

"The officers were quartered in the house, and the soldiers in the outbuildings. I cannot say that we enjoyed them, but they were correct. 'Kein Barbar,' they kept telling us—'We are not barbarians.' And fancy, they expected my girls to dance with them!"

Mme Viénot waited rather longer than necessary for the irony to be appreciated, and then with a hissing intake of breath she said: "It's exciting to be in the clutches of the tiger . . . and to know that you are quite helpless."

The truck started up with a roar, and shot through the gateway. They stood watching until it disappeared from sight. The silence flooded back into the courtyard.

"So delicious, your arriving with M. Fleury," Mme Viénot said.

He searched through his coat pockets for a pencil and the little notebook, wherein the crises were all recorded: "Rennes départ $7^{h}50$ Le Mans $10^{h}20$, départ $11^{h}02$," etc. Also the money paid out for laundry, hotel rooms, meals in restaurants, and conducted tours. This was a mistake, he thought. We shouldn't have come here. . . . He wrote: "100 fr transportation Brenodville-sur-Euphrone to chateau" and put the pencil and notebook back in his breast pocket.

Mme Viénot was looking at him with her head cocked to one side, frankly amused. "I wonder what it was that made me decide you were middle-aged," she said. "Why, you're *babies!*"

He started to shoulder the dufflebag and she said: "Don't bother with the luggage. Thérèse will see to it." Linking her arm cozily through Barbara's, she led them into the house by the back door and along a passageway to the stairs.

When they reached the second-floor landing, the Americans glanced expectantly down a long hallway that went right through the center of the house, and then saw that Mme Viénot had continued on up the stairs. She threw open the door on the left in the square hall at the head of the stairs and said: "My daughter's room. I think you'll find it comfortable."

I: *Leo and Virgo*

Harold waited for Barbara to exclaim "How lovely!" and instead she drew off her black suede gloves. He went to the window and looked out. Their room was on the front of the château and overlooked the park. The ceiling sloped down on that side, because of the roof. The wallpaper was black and white on a particularly beautiful shade of dark red, and not like any wallpaper he had ever seen.

"Sabine is in Paris now," Mme Viénot said. "She's an artist. She does fashion drawings for the magazine *La Femme Elégante*. You are familiar with it? . . . It's like your *Vogue* and *Harper's Bazaar*, I believe. . . . We dine at one thirty on Sunday. That won't hurry you?"

Barbara shook her head.

"If you want anything, call me," Mme Viénot said, and closed the door behind her.

There was a light knock almost immediately, and thinking that Mme Viénot had come back to tell them something, Barbara called "Come in," but it was not Mme Viénot, it was the blond servant girl with the two heaviest suitcases. As she set them down in the middle of the room, Barbara said "Merci," and the girl smiled at her. She came back three more times, with the rest of the luggage, and the last time, just before she turned away, she allowed her gaze to linger on the two Americans for a second. She seemed to be expecting them to understand something, and to be slightly at a loss when they didn't.

"Should we have tipped her?" Barbara asked, when they were alone again.

"I don't think so. The *service* is probably *compris*," Harold said, partly because he was never willing to believe that the simplest explanation is the right one, and partly because he was confused in his mind about the ethics of tipping and felt that, fundamentally, it was impolite. If he were a servant, he would resent it; and refuse the tip to show that he was not a servant. So he alternated: he didn't tip when he should have and then, worried by this, he overtipped the next time.

"I should have told her that we have some nylon stockings for her," Barbara said.

"Or if it isn't, I'll do something about it when we leave," he said. "It's too bad, though, about M. Fleury. After those robbers in Cherbourg it would have been a pleasure to overtip him—if four hundred francs was overtipping, which I doubt. She was probably worrying about herself, not us." Trying one key after another from Barbara's key ring with the rabbit's foot attached to it, he found the one that opened the big brown suitcase. "What about the others?" he asked, snapping the catches.

"Maybe we'll run into him in the village," Barbara said. "Just that one and the dufflebag." She took the combs out of her hair, which then fell to her shoulders. "The rest can wait."

He carried the dufflebag into the bathroom, and she changed from her suit into a wool dressing gown, and then began transferring the contents of the large brown suitcase, a pile at a time, to the beds, the round table in the center of the room, and the armoire. She was pleased with their room. After the violent curtains and queer shapes of the hotel rooms of the past week, here was a place they could settle down in peacefully and happily. An infallible taste had been at work, and the result was like a wax impression of one of those days when she woke lighthearted, knowing that this was going to be a good day all day long—that whatever she had to do would be done quickly and easily; that the telephone wouldn't ring and ring; that dishes wouldn't slip through her nerveless hands and break; that it wouldn't be necessary to search through the accumulation of unanswered letters for some reassurance that wasn't there, or to ask Harold if he loved her.

Standing in the bathroom door, with his shirt unbuttoned and his necktie trailing from one hand, he surveyed the red room and then said: "It couldn't be handsomer."

"It's cold," she said. "I noticed it downstairs. The whole house is cold."

He glanced at the fireplace. The ornamental brass shield over the opening was held in place with screws and it looked permanent. There was no basket of wood and kindling on the hearth. In her mind the present often extended its sphere of influence until it obscured the past and denied that there was going to be any future. When she was cold, when she was sad, she was convinced that she would always be sad or cold and there was no use doing anything about it; all the sweaters and coats and eiderdown comforters and optimism in the world would not help, and all she wanted him to do was agree that they would not help. Unfortunately, she could not get him to agree. It was a basic difference of opinion. He always tried to do something. His nature required that there be something practical you could do, even though he knew by experience that it took some small act of magic, some demonstration of confidence or proof of love, to make her take heart, to make her feel warm again.

"Why don't you take a hot bath? You've got time if you hurry," he said, and turned to the bookcase. Because there were times when he was too tired, or just couldn't produce any proof of love, or when he felt a deep disinclination to play the magician. At other times, nothing was too much trouble or exhausted his strength and patience.

His finger, in the pursuit of titles, stopped at Shaw and Wells, in English; at Charles Morgan and Elizabeth Goudge, in French, and so inconsistent from the point of view of literary taste with the first two; at *La Mare au Diable*, which he had read in high school and could no longer remember anything about; at *Le Grand Meaulnes*, which he remembered hazily. The letters of Mme de Sevigné (in three small volumes) he had always meant to read some time. The *Fables* of La Fontaine, and the *Contes*, which were said to be indecent. A book of children's songs, with illustrations by Boutet de Monvel. A book of the religious meditations of someone that he, raised a Presbyterian, had never heard of. He said: "Say, whose books *are* these, do you suppose?" and she answered from the bathroom in a shocked voice: "Why, there's no hot water!"

"Let it run," he called back.

"There's no water to let run."

He went into the bathroom and tried both faucets of the immense tub. Nothing came out of them, not even air.

"It's the war," he said.

"I don't see how we can stay here two weeks without a bath," Barbara said.

He moved over to the washstand. There the cold-water faucet worked splendidly but not the faucet marked *chaud*.

"She said in her letter 'a room with a bath.' If this is what she means, I don't think it was at all honest of her."

"Mmmm."

"And I don't see any toilet."

They looked all around the room, slowly and carefully. There was one door they hadn't opened. He opened it confidently, and they found themselves staring into a shallow clothes closet with three wire coat hangers on the metal rod. They both laughed.

"In a house this size there's bound to be a toilet somewhere," he said, by no means convinced that this was true.

They washed simultaneously at the washbowl, and then he put on a clean shirt and went out into the hall. He listened at the head of the stairs. The house was steeped in silence. He put his head close to the paneling of the door directly opposite theirs, heard nothing, and placed his hand on the knob. The door swung open cautiously upon a small lumber room under the eaves. In the dim light he made out discarded furniture, books, boxes, pictures, china, bedclothes, luggage, a rowing machine, a tin bidet, a large steel engraving of the courtyard and Grand Staircase of the château of Blois. He closed the door softly, struck with how little difference there is in the things people all over the world cannot bring themselves to throw away.

The remaining door of the third-floor hall revealed a corridor, two steps down and uncarpeted. The fresh paint and clean wallpaper ended here, and it seemed unlikely that their toilet would be in this wing of the house, which had an air of disuse, of decay, of being a place that outsiders should not wander into. The four dirty bull's-eye windows looked out on the back wing of the château. There were doors all along the corridor, but spaced too far apart to suggest the object of his search, and at the end the corridor branched right and left, with more doors that it might be embarrassing to open at this moment. He opened one of them and saw a brass bed, made up, a painted dresser, a commode, a rag rug on the painted floor, a single straight chair. He had ended up in the servants' quarters.

Retracing his steps, he listened again at the head of the stairs. The house was as still as houses only are on Sunday. When he opened the door of their room, Barbara had changed back into her traveling suit and was standing in front of the low dresser. "I couldn't find it," he said.

"Probably it's on the second floor." She leaned toward the mirror. She was having difficulty with the clasp of her pearls. "But it's funny she didn't tell us."

"She has dyed hair," he said.

"Sh-h-h!"

"What for?"

"There may be someone in the room across the hall."

"I looked. It's full of old junk."

She stared at him in the mirror. "Weren't you afraid there'd be somebody there?"

"Yes," he said. "But how else was I going to find it?"

"I don't believe that she was about to go to the station to meet us."

"Do you think she forgot all about us?"

"I don't know."

He put on a coat and tie and stood waiting for her.

"I'm afraid to go downstairs," she said.

"Why?"

"We'll have to speak French and she'll know right away that Muriel helped me with those letters. She'll think I was trying to deceive her."

"They don't expect Americans to speak idiomatic French," he said. "And besides, she was trying to overcharge us."

"You go down."

"Without you? Don't be silly. The important thing is you got her to figure the price by the week instead of by the day. She probably respects you more for it than she would have if we—"

"Do you think if we asked for some wood for the fireplace—"

"I don't know," he said doubtfully. "Probably there isn't any wood."

"But we're right next door to a forest."

"I know. But if there's no hot water and no toilet— Anyway, we're in France. We're living the way the French do. This is what goes on behind the high garden walls."

"I don't trust her," Barbara said.

"Fortunately, we don't have to trust her. Come on, let's go."

Chapter 3

AS THEY DESCENDED THE STAIRS, they listened for the sound of voices, and heard the birds outside. The second-floor hall was deserted. In the lower hall, at the foot of the stairs, they were confronted with two single and two double curtained French doors. One of the single doors led to the passageway through which Mme Viénot had brought them into the front part of the house. He opened one of the double doors, and they saw a big oval dining table. The table was set, the lights in the crystal chandelier were turned on, the wine and water carafes were filled. "At least we're not late for dinner," he said, and pulled the door to.

The other single door opened into a corner room, a family parlor. Two large portraits in oil of the epoque of Louis XV; a radio; a divan with a row of pillows; a fireplace with a Franklin stove in front of it; a huge, old-fashioned, square, concert-grand piano littered with family photographs. In the center of the room, a round table and four straight chairs. The windows looked out on the courtyard and on the park in front of the château.

He crossed the room to examine the photographs. "Mme Viénot has changed surprisingly little in the last quarter of a century," he said. His eyes lingered for a moment on the photograph of a thin, solemn schoolboy in the clothes of a generation ago. "Dead," he said softly. "The pride of the family finished off at the age of twelve or thirteen."

"How do you know that?" Barbara asked from the doorway.

"There are no pictures of him as a grown man."

As he deferred to her judgment of people, so she deferred to his imagination about them, which was more concrete than hers, but again not infallible. (Maurice Bonenfant died at the age of twenty-seven, by his own hand.)

They went back into the hall and tried again. This time when the door swung open, they heard voices. The doorway was masked by a folding screen, and there was just time as they emerged from behind it to be aware that they were in a long pink and white room. Mme Viénot rose to greet them, and then led them around the circle of chairs.

"My mother, Mme Bonenfant . . ." (a very old woman)

"Mme Carrère . . ." (a woman of fifty)

"M. Carrère . . ." (a tall, stoop-shouldered man, who was slightly older)

"And M. Gagny . . . who is from Canada . . ." (a young man, very handsome, with prematurely gray hair and black eyebrows)

When the introductions had been accomplished, the old woman indicated with a smile and a slight gesture that Barbara was to take the empty chair beside her, and Harold sat down next to Mme Viénot.

Perceiving that their arrival had produced an awkward silence, he leaned forward in his chair and dealt with it himself. He began to tell them about his search through the village for the house of M. Fleury. "Je ne comprends pas les directions que Mme Michot m'a données, et par consequence il me faut demander à tout le monde: 'Où est la maison de M. Fleury—du côté de là, ou du côté de là?' On m'a dirigé encore . . . et encore je ne comprends pas. Alors . . . je demande ma question à un petit garçon, qui me prendre par la main et me conduire chez M. Fleury, tout près de la bureau de poste. . . . Je dis 'merci' et je frappe à la porte. La porte ouvre un très peu. C'est Mme Fleury qui l'ouvre. Je commence à expliquer, et elle ferme la porte dans ma figure."

He saw that the tall middle-aged man was amused, and breathed easier.

"Le garçon frappe à la porte," he continued, "et la porte ouvre un peu. C'est le fils de M. Fleury, cette fois. Il écoute. Il ne ferme pas la porte. . . . Quand j'ai fini, il me dit 'Un instant! Attendez, monsieur! . . . J'attends, naturellement. J'attends et j'attends. . . . La porte ouvre. C'est M. Fleury lui-même, les pieds en bas, pas de souliers. . . . J'explique que madame et les baggages sont à la gare et que nous désirons aller au château. . . . Il entends. Il est très sympathique, M. Fleury, très gentil. Il envoie son fils en avant pour prendre le clef du garage où le camion repose. Le garage est fermé parce que c'est dimanche. . . . Et puis, nous commençons. M. Fleury—" He paused, unable to remember the word for "pump," and realized that he was out in deep water. "—M. Fleury pompe l'air dans les tires, et moi, je lève quelques sacs de grain qui sont dans le derrière du camion. Le camion est plus vieil que le Treaty de Versailles. . . . Plusier années plus vieil. Et le fils de M. Fleury versait un litre de petrol dans le tank, que est empty, et l'eau dans le radiator. . . ."

Out of the corner of his eyes, he saw Mme Viénot nervously unfolding her hands. Was the story going on too long? He tried to hurry it up, and when he couldn't think of the French word he fell back on the English, which he hopefully pronounced as if it were French. Sometimes it was. The camion that antedated the Treaty of Versailles shuddered and shook and came to life, and the company burst out laughing. Harold sat back in his chair. He had pulled it off, and he felt flooded with pleasure.

There was a pause, less awkward than before. Mme Bonenfant confided to Barbara that she was eighty-three and a great-grandmother.

Mme Viénot said to Harold: "M. Gagny has just been telling us why General de Gaulle is not held in greater esteem in London."

"So many noble qualities," M. Carrère said in French, "so many of the elements of true greatness—all tied to that unfortunate personality. My older brother went to school with him, and even then his weaknesses—especially his vanity—were apparent.

The conversation shifted to the Mass they had just come from. It had a special interest in that the priest, who was saying his first Mass, was a boy from the village. Mme Viénot explained parenthetically to the Americans that, since the war, young men of aristocratic family, really quite a number of them, were turning to the priesthood or joining holy orders. It was a new thing, a genuine religious awakening. There had been nothing like it in France for more than two generations.

The Americans were conscious of the fact that the gray-haired young man could have talked to them in English and, instead, continued to speak to the others in French. The rather cool manner in which he acknowledged the introduction implied that he felt no responsibility for or interest in Americans.

Harold looked around at the room. It was a long rectangle, with a fireplace at either end. The curtains and the silk upholstery were a clear silvery pink. The period furniture was light and graceful and painted a flat white, like the molding and the fireplaces, which were identical. So were the two horizontal mirrors over the Adam mantelpieces. In the center of the room, four fluted columns and a sculptured plant stand served as a reminder that in France neo-classicism is not a term of reproach. Along one side of the room, a series of French doors opened onto the terrace and made the drawing room well lighted even on a gray day. The circle of chairs where they were sitting now was in front of one of the fireplaces. At the other end of the room, in front of the other fireplace, there were two small sofas and some chairs that were not arranged for conversation. In its proportions and its use of color and the taste with which it was furnished, it was unlike any drawing room he had ever seen. The more he looked at it, the more strange and beautiful it became.

The sermon had exceeded the expectations of the company, and they continued to talk about it complacently until the servant girl opened the hall doors and removed the folding screen. The women rose and started toward the dining room. M. Carrère had to be helped from his chair, and then, leaning on his cane, he made his way into the hall. Harold, lightheaded with the success of his story, waited for the Canadian to precede him through the doorway. The Canadian stopped too, and when Harold said: "After you," he changed. Right in front of Harold's eyes he stopped being a facsimile of a Frenchman and became exactly like an American. With his hand on Harold's shoulder, he said: "Go on, go on," goodnaturedly, and propelled him through the door ahead of him.

In the dining room Harold found himself seated between Mme Carrère and old Mme Bonenfant. Mme Carrère was served before him, and he watched her out of the corner of his eye, and was relieved to see that there was no difference; table manners were the same here as at home. But his initial attempts to make conversation met with failure. Mme Carrère seemed to be a taciturn woman, and something told him that any attempt to be friendly with her might be regarded as being overfriendly. Mme Bonenfant either did not understand or was simply not interested in his description of the terraced gardens of Mont-Saint-Michel.

George Ireland, the American boy who had spent the previous summer at the château and was indirectly responsible for their being here now had said that it was one of his duties to keep Mme Bonenfant's water glass filled. Harold saw that there was a carafe of water in front of him and that her glass was empty.

Though she allowed him to fill it again and again during dinner, she addressed her remarks to M. Carrère.

As the soup gave way to the fish and the fish in turn to the entree, the talk ranged broadly over national and international politics, life in Paris before the war, travel in Spain and Italy, the volcanic formations of Ischia, the national characteristics of the Swiss. In his effort to follow what was being said around the table, Harold forgot to eat, and this slowed up the service. He left his knife and fork on his plate and, too late, saw them being carried out to the pantry. A clean knife and fork were brought to him with the next course. Mme Viénot interrupted the flow of wit and anecdote to inquire if he understood what was being said.

"I understand part of it," he said eagerly.

A bleak expression crossed her face. Instead of smiling or saying something reassuring to him, she looked down at her plate. He glanced across the table at Barbara and saw, with surprise, that she was her natural self.

After the dessert course, Mme Viénot pushed her chair back and they all rose from the table at once. Mme Carrère, passing the sideboard, lifted the lid of a faïence soup tureen and took out a box of Belgian sugar. The Canadian kept his sugar in a red lacquer cabinet in the drawing room, and Mme Viénot hers and her mother's in the writing desk in the petit salon. Harold excused himself and went upstairs to their room. Strewing the contents of the dufflebag over the bathroom floor, he finally came upon the boxes of cube sugar they had brought with them from America. When he walked into the drawing room, the servant girl had brought the silver coffee service and Mme Viénot was measuring powdered coffee into little white coffee cups.

The Canadian lit a High Life cigarette. Harold, conscious of the fact that their ten cartons had to last them through four months, thought it might be a good idea to wait until he and

Barbara were alone to smoke, but she was looking at him expectantly, and so he took a pack from his coat pocket, ripped the cellophane off, and offered the cigarettes to her and then around the circle. They were refused politely until he came to Mme Viénot, who took one, as if she was not quite sure what it might be for but was always willing to try something new.

"I think the church is in Chartres," Barbara said, and he knew that she had been talking about the little church at the end of the carline. There were two things that she remembered particularly from that earlier trip to France and that she wanted to see again. One was a church, a beautiful little church at the end of a streetcar line, and the other was a white château with a green lawn in front of it. She had no idea where either of them was.

"You don't mean the cathedral?" Mme Viénot asked.

"Oh, no," Barbara said.

Though there were matches on the table beside her, Mme Viénot waited for Harold to return and light her cigarette. Her hand touched his as she bent over the lighted match, and this contact—not accidental, he was sure—startled him. What was it? Was she curious? Was she trying to find out whether his marriage was really pink and happy or blue like most marriages?

"There is no tram line at Chartres," she said, blowing a cloud of smoke through her nostrils. "I ought to know the château, but I'm afraid I don't. There are so many."

And what about M. Viénot, he wondered. Where was he? Was he dead? Why had his name not come up in the conversation before or during dinner?

"It was like a castle in a fairy tale," Barbara said.

"Cheverny has a large lawn in front of it. Have you been there?" Mme Viénot asked. Barbara shook her head.

"I have a brochure with some pictures of châteaux. Perhaps you will recognize the one you are looking for. . . . You are going to be in France how long?"

"Until the beginning of August," Barbara said. "And then we're going to Switzerland and Austria. We're going to Salzburg for the Festival."

"And then to Venice," Harold said, "and down through Italy as far as Florence—"

"You have a great deal in store for you," Mme Viénot said. "Venice is enchanting. You will adore Venice."

"—and back through the Italian and French Rivieras to Paris, and then home."

"It is better not to try to see too much," Mme Viénot said. "The place one stays in for a week or ten days is likely to be the place one remembers. And how long do you have? . . . Ah, I envy you. One of the most disagreeable things about the Occupation was that we were not permitted to travel."

"The luggage is something of a problem," he said.

"What you do not need you can leave here," she said.

Tempting though this was, if they left their luggage at the château they would have to come back for it. "Thank you. I will remember if we . . ." He managed not to commit them to anything.

The Canadian was talking about the Count of Paris, and it occurred to Harold that for the first time in his life he was in the presence of royalists. His defense of democracy was extremely oblique; he said: "Is the Count of Paris an intelligent man?"—having read somewhere that he was not.

"Unfortunately, no," Mme Viénot said, and smiled. "Such an amusing story is going the round. It seems his wife was quite ill, and the doctors said she must have a transfusion—you say 'transfusion' in English?—or she would die. But the Count wouldn't give his consent. He kept them waiting for two whole days while he searched through the Almanach de Gotha."

"It was a question of blue blood?"

She nodded. "He could not find anyone with a sufficient number of royal quarterings in his coat of arms. In the end he had to compromise, I believe, and take what he could get." She took a sip of coffee and then said: "Something similar happened in our family recently. My niece has just had her first child, and two days after it was born, she commenced hemorrhaging. They couldn't find her husband—he was playing golf—so the doctor went ahead and arranged for a transfusion, without his consent—and when Eugène walked in and saw this strange man—he was a very common person—sitting beside his wife's bed, he was most upset."

"The blood from a transfusion only lasts forty-eight hours," Harold said, in his own peculiar way every bit as much of a snob as the Count of Paris.

"My niece's husband did not know that," Mme Viénot said. "And he did not want his children to have this person's blood in their veins. My sister and the doctor had a very difficult time with him."

On the other side of the circle of chairs, M. Carrère said that he didn't like Germans, to Mme Bonenfant, who was not defending them.

Mme Viénot took his empty cup and put it on the tray. Turning back to Harold and Barbara, she said: "France was not ready for the war, and when the Germans came we could do nothing. It was like a nightmare. . . . Now, of course, we are living in another; we are deathly afraid of war between your country and the Union of Soviet Republics. You think it will happen soon? . . . I blame your President Roosevelt. He didn't understand the Russian temperament and so he was taken in by promises that mean nothing. The Slav is not like other Europeans. . . . Some years ago I became acquainted with a Russian woman. She was delightful to be with. She was responsive and intelligent. She had all the qualities one looks for in a friend. And yet, as time went on, I realized that I did not really know her. I was always conscious of something held back."

She was looking directly at Harold's face but he was not sure she even saw him. He studied her, while she took a sip of coffee, trying to see her as her friend the Russian woman saw her—the pale-blue eyes, the too-black hair, the rouged cheeks. She must be somewhere in Proust, he thought.

"Never trust a Slav," she said solemnly.

And what about the variations, he wondered. There must be variations, such as never trust an Englishman; never trust a Swede. And maybe even never trust an American?

"Are French people always kind and helpful to foreigners?" he asked. "Because that has been our experience so far."

"I can't say that they are, always," Mme Viénot said. She put her cup and saucer on the tray. "You have perhaps been fortunate."

She got up and moved away, leaving him with the feeling that he had said something untactful. His own cup was empty, but he continued to hold it, though the table was within reach.

M. Gagny was talking about the British royal family. He knew the Duke of Connaught, he said, and he had danced with the Princess Elizabeth, but he was partial to the Princess Margaret Rose.

Mme Viénot sat down beside her mother, patted her dry mottled hand, and smiled at her and then around at the company, lightly and publicly admitting her fondness.

M. Carrère explained to Barbara that he could speak English, but that it tired him, and he preferred his native tongue. Mme Carrère's English was better than his, but on the other hand he talked and she didn't. Mme Bonenfant did not know English at all, though she spoke German. And the Canadian was so conspicuously bilingual that his presence in the circle of chairs was a reproach rather than a help to the Americans. Harold told himself that it was foolish—that it was senseless, in fact—to make the effort, but nevertheless he couldn't help feeling that he must live up to his success before dinner or he would surrender too much ground. A remark, a question addressed directly to him, he understood sufficiently to answer, but then the conversation became general again and he was lost. He sat balancing the empty cup and saucer in his two hands, looked at whoever was speaking, and tried to catch from the others' faces whether the remark was serious or amusing, so that he could smile at the right time. This tightrope performance and fatigue (they had got up early to catch the train, and it had already been a long day) combined to deprive him of the last hope of understanding what was said.

Watching him, Barbara saw the glazed look she knew so well —the film that came over his eyes whenever he was bored or ill-at-ease. As she got ready to deliver him from his misery, it occurred to her suddenly how odd it was that neither of them had ever stopped to think what it might be like staying with a French family, or that there might be more to it than an opportunity to improve their French.

"COULD YOU UNDERSTAND THEM?" he asked, as soon as they were behind the closed door of their room.

She nodded.

"I couldn't."

"But you talked. I was afraid to open my mouth."

This made him feel better.

"There's a toilet on this floor, at the far end of the attic corridor. I asked Mme Bonenfant."

"Behind one of the doors I was afraid to open," he said, nodding.

"But it's out of order. It's going to be fixed in a day or two. Meanwhile, we're to use the toilet on the second floor.

They undressed and got into their damp beds and talked drowsily for a few minutes—about the house, about the other guests, about the food, which was the best they had had in France—and then fell into a deep sleep. When they woke, the afternoon was gone and it was raining softly. He got into her bed, and she put her head in the hollow of his shoulder.

"I wish this room was all there was," he said, "and we lived in it. I wish it was ours."

"You wouldn't get tired of the red wallpaper?"

"No."

"Neither would I. Or of anything else," she said.

"It's not like any room that I've ever seen."

"It's very French."

"What is?" he asked.

"Everything. . . . Why isn't she here?"

"Who?"

"The French girl. If this was my room, I'd be living in it."

"She's probably having a much better time in Paris," he said, and looked at his wrist watch. "Come on," he said, tossing the cover back. "We're late."

After dinner, Mme Viénot led her guests into the family parlor across the hall. The coffee that Harold was waiting for did not appear. He and Barbara smoked one cigarette, to be sociable, and then wandered outside. It had stopped raining. They walked up and down the gravel terrace, admiring the house and the old trees and the view, which was gilded with the evening light. They were happy to be by themselves, and pleased with the way they had managed things—for they might, at this very moment, have been walking the streets of Le Mans, or freezing to death at the seashore, and instead they were here. They would be able to include this interesting place among the places they had seen and could tell people about when they got home.

From the terrace they went directly to their room, their beautiful red room, whose history they had no way of knowing.

The village of Brenodville was very old and had interesting historical associations. The château did not, if by history you mean kings and queens and their awful favorites, battles and treaties, ruinous entertainments, genius harbored, the rise and fall of ambitious men. Its history was merely the history of the family that had lived in it tenaciously, generation after generation. The old wing, the carriage house, the stables, and the brick courtyard dated from the seventeenth century. Around the year 1900, the property figured in still another last will and testament, duly signed and sealed. Beaumesnil passed from the dead hands of a rich, elderly, unmarried sportsman, who seldom used it, into the living, eager hands of a nephew who had been sufficiently attentive and who, just to make things doubly sure, had been named after him. Almost the first thing M. Jules Bonenfant did with the fortune he had inherited was to build against the old house a new wing, larger and more formal in design. From this time on, instead of facing the carp pond and the forest, the château faced the patchwork of small fields and the River Loire, which was too far away to figure in the view. For a number of years, the third-floor room on the left at the head of the stairs remained empty and unused. Moonlight came and went. Occasionally a freakish draft blew down the chimney, redistributing the dust. A gray squirrel got in, also by way of the chimney, and died here, while mud wasps beat against the windowpanes. The newspapers of 1906 did not penetrate this far and so the wasps never learned that a Captain Alfred Dreyfus had been decorated with the Légion d'Honneur, in public, in the courtyard of the artillery pavilion at St. Cyr. In September of that same year, Mme. Bonenfant stood on the second-floor landing and directed the village paperhanger, with his scissors, paste, steel measuring tape, and trestle, up the final flight of stairs and through the door on the left. When the room was finished, Mlle Toinette was parted from a tearful governess and found herself in possession of a large bedroom that was directly over her mother's and the same size and shape. The only difference was that the ceiling sloped down on one side and there was one window instead of two. With different wallpaper and different furniture, the room was now her younger daughter's. So much for its history. Now what about the two people who are asleep in it? Who are they? What is their history?

Well, where to begin is the question. The summer he spent in bed with rheumatic fever on an upstairs sleeping porch? Or the street he lived on—those big, nondescript, tree-shaded, Middle Western white houses, beautiful in the fall when the leaves turned, or at dusk with the downstairs lights turned on, or in winter when the snow covered up whatever was shabby and ugly? Should we begin with the tree house in the back yard or with the boy he was envious of, who always had money for ice-cream cones because his mother was dead and the middle-aged aunt and uncle he lived with felt they had no other way to make it up to him? Given his last name, Rhodes, and the time and place he grew up in, it was inevitable that when he started to go to school he should be called Dusty. Some jokes never lose their freshness.

It helps, of course, to know what happened when they were choosing up sides and he stood waiting for his name to be called. And about the moment when he emerged into the public eye for the first time, at the age of six, in a surgical-cotton wig, knee britches, buckles on his shoes, and with seven other costumed children danced the minuet in the school auditorium.

The sum total of his memories is who he is, naturally. Also the child his mother went in to cover on her rounds, the last thing at night before she went to bed—the little boy with his own way of sleeping, his arm around some doll or stuffed animal, and his own way of recognizing her presence through layers and layers of sleep. Also the little boy with a new navy-blue suit on Easter Sunday, and a cowlick that would not stay down. Then there is that period when he was having his teeth straightened, when he corresponded with postage-stamp companies. The obedient, sensible, courteous ten-year-old? Or the moody boy in his teens, who ate them out of house and home and had to be sent from the table for talking back to his father? Take your choice, or take both of them. His mother's eyes, the Rhodes nose and mouth and chin; the Rhodes stubbornness, his mother said. This book belongs to Harold Rhodes, Eighth Grade, Room 207, Central School. . . . And whatever became of those boards for stretching muskrat skins on, the skins he was going to sell and make a fortune from? Or his magic lantern and his postcard projector? Or his building blocks, his Boy Scout knife, his school report cards? And that medicine-stained copy of *Mr. Midshipman Easy?* And the Oz books? Somewhere, all these unclaimed shreds of his personality, since matter is never entirely lost but merely changes its form.

As a boy of thirteen he was called up on the stage of the Majestic Theater by a vaudeville magician, and did exactly what the magician told him (under his breath) to do; even though the magician told him out loud not to do it, and so made a monkey of him, and the audience rocked with perfectly kind laughter. Since then he hasn't learned a thing. The same audience would rock with the same laughter if he were called up on the stage of the Majestic Theater tomorrow. Fortunately it has been torn down to make a parking lot.

In college he was responsive, with a light in his eye; he was a pleasure to lecture to; but callow, getting by on enthusiasm because it came more natural to him than thinking, and worried about his grades, and about the future, and because, though he tried and tried, he could not break himself of a shameful habit. If he had taken biology it would have been made clear to him that he too was an animal, but he took botany instead.

But who is he? which animal?

A commuter, standing on the station platform, with now the *Times* and now the *Tribune* under his arm, waiting for the 8:17 express. A liberal Democrat, believing idealistically in the cause of labor but knowing few laborers, and a member in good standing of the money-loving class he was born into, though, as it happens, money slips through his fingers. A spendthrift, with small sums, cautious with large ones. Who is he? Raskolnikov—that's who he is.

Surely not?

Yes. Also Mr. Micawber. And St. Francis. And Savonarola. He's no one person, he's an uncountable committee of people who meet and operate under the handy fiction of his name. The minutes of the last meeting are never read, because it's still going on. The committee arrives at important conclusions which it cannot remember, and makes sensible decisions it cannot possibly keep. For that you need a policeman. The committee members know each other, but not always by their right names. The bachelor who has sat reading in the same white leatherette chair by the same lamp with the same cigarette box within reach on the same round table for so long now that change is no longer possible to him—that Harold Rhodes of course knows the bridegroom with a white carnation in his buttonhole, sipping a glass of champagne, smiling, accepting congratulations, aware of the good wishes of everybody and also of a nagging doubt in the back of his mind. Just as they both know the head of the family, the born father, with the Sunday paper scattered around him on the living-room rug, smiling benignly at no children after three years of marriage. And the child of seven (in some ways the most mature of all these facets of his personality) who is being taken, with his hand in his father's much bigger hand, to see his mother in the hospital on a day that, as it turned out, she was much too sick to see anyone.

What does he—what do all these people do for a living?

Does it matter?

Certainly.

After two false starts he now has a job with a future. He is working for an engraving firm owned by a friend of his father.

What did he do, where was he, during the war?

He wasn't in the war . . . 4F. He has to be away from Barbara, traveling, several times a year, but the rest of the time he can be home, where he wants to be. His hours are long, but he has already had two raises, and now this four months' leave of absence, proof that his work is valued.

And who is she? whom did he marry?

Somebody who matches him, the curves and hollows of her nature fitting into all the curves and hollows of his nature as, in bed, her straight back and soft thighs fit inside the curve of his breast and belly and hips and bent legs. Somebody who looks enough like him that they are mistaken occasionally for brother and sister, and who keeps him warm at night, taking the place of the doll that he used to sleep with his arm around: Barbara Scully. Barbara S. Rhodes, when she writes a check.

And what was her childhood like?

Well, where to begin is again the question. At the seashore? Or should we take up, one after another, the dogs, the nursemaids? Or the time she broke her arm? She was seven when that happened. Or the period when she cared about nothing but horses? Or that brief, heartbreaking, first falling in love? Or the piles of clothes on the bed, on the chairs in her room, all with name tapes sewed on them, and the suitcases waiting to be filled?

Or should we open that old exercise book that by some accident has survived?

"One day our mother gave the children a party.
There were fourteen merry girls and boys at the party.
They played games and raced about the lawn with Rover.
But John fell from a tree and broke his arm.
Mother sent a boy to bring the doctor.
The doctor set the arm and said that it would soon be better.
Was not John a brave boy to bear the pain as he did."

Three times 269 is not 627, of course; and neither does 854 minus 536 equal 316. But it is true that there are seven days in the week, and that all the children must learn their lessons. Also that it is never the raveled sleeve of just one day's care that sleep knits up. She should have been at home nursing her baby, and instead here they both are in Europe. And every month contains doomed days, such sad sighs, the rain that does not rain, and blood that is the color of bitter disappointment when it finally flows. This is the lesson she is now learning.

The shadow that showed up in the crystal ball?

Right. And all the years he was growing up, he would have liked to be somebody else—an athlete, broad-shouldered, blond, unworried, and popular. Even now he avoids his reflection in mirrors and wants to be liked by everybody. Not loved; just liked. On meeting someone who interests him he goes toward that person unhesitatingly, as if this were the one moment they would ever have together, their one chance of knowing each other. He is curious and at the same time he is tactful. He lets the other person know, by the way he listens, by the sympathetic look in his brown eyes, that he wants to know everything; and at the same time the other person has the reassuring suspicion that Harold Rhodes will not ask questions it would be embarrassing to have to answer. He tries to attach people to him, not so that he can use them or so that they will add to his importance but only because he wants them to be a part of his life. The landscape must have figures in it. And it never seems to occur to him that there is a limit to the number of close friendships anyone can decently and faithfully accommodate.

If wherever you go you are always looking for eyes that meet your eyes, hands that do not avoid touching or being touched by you, then you must have more than two eyes and two hands; you must be a kind of monster. If, on meeting someone who interests you, you go toward them unhesitatingly as if this is the only moment you will ever have for knowing each other, then you must learn to deal with second meetings that aren't always successful, and third meetings that are even less satisfactory. If on your desk there are too many unanswered letters, the only thing to do is to write to someone who hasn't written to you lately. And if sometimes, hanging by your knees head down from a swinging trapeze high under the canvas tent, you find too many aerial artists are coming toward you at a given moment and you have to choose one and let the others drop, you can at least try not to see their eyes accusing you of an inhuman betrayal you did not mean and cannot avoid. Harold Rhodes isn't a monster, he doesn't try to escape the second meetings, he answers some of the letters, and he spends a great deal of time, patience, and energy inducing performers with hurt feelings to climb the rope ladder again and fling themselves across the intervening void. Some of them do and some of them don't.

That's all very interesting, but just exactly what are these two people doing in Europe?

They're tourists.

Obviously. But it's too soon after the war. Traveling will be much pleasanter and easier five years from now. The soldiers have not all gone home yet. People are poor and discouraged. Europe isn't ready for tourists. Couldn't they wait?

No, they couldn't. The nail doesn't choose the time or the circumstances in which it is drawn to the magnet.

They would have done better to do a little reading before they came, so they would know what to look for. And they could at least have brushed up on their French.

They could have, but they didn't. They just came. They are the first wave. As Mme Viénot perceived, they are unworldly, and inexperienced. But they are not totally so; there are certain areas where they cannot be fooled or taken advantage of. But there is, in their faces, something immature, reluctant—

You mean they are Americans.

No, I mean all those acts of imagination by which the cupboard is again and again proved to be not bare. And putting so much faith in fortunetelling. Playing cards, colored stones, bamboo sticks, birthday-cracker mottoes, palmistry, the signs of the zodiac, the first star—she trusts them all, but only with a partial trust. Each new prognostication takes precedence over the former ones, and when the cards are not accommodating, she reshuffles them and tells herself a new fortune. Her right hand lies open now, relaxed on the pillow, her palm ready and waiting for a fortuneteller who can walk through locked doors and see in the dark.

Unaccustomed to sleeping in separate beds, they toss and turn and are cold and have tiring dreams that they would not have had if their two bodies were touching. But they won't be here long, or anywhere else. Ten days in Paris after they leave here. A night in Lausanne. Six days in Salzburg. Four days in Venice. Four more days in Florence. Ten days in Rome, a night in Pisa, two days in San Remo . . . No place can hold them.

And it is something that they are turned towards each other in their sleep. It means that day in and day out they are companionable and happy with one another; that they have identical (or almost) tastes and pleasures; and that when they diverge it is likely to be in their attitude toward the world outside their marriage. For example, he thinks he does not believe in God, she thinks she does. If she is more cautious about people than he is, conceivably this is because in some final way she needs them more. He needs only her. Parted from her in a crowd he becomes anxious, and in dreams he wanders through huge houses calling her name.

Chapter 4

WHAT TIME IS BREAKFAST?" he asked, rising up from his bed. She did not know. They had forgotten to ask about breakfast. They saw that it was a dark, rainy Monday morning.

They washed in ice-cold water, dressed, and went downstairs. He peered around the folding screen, half expecting the household to be assembled in the drawing room, waiting for them. The beautiful pink and white room was deserted, and the rugs were rolled up, the chairs pushed together. In the dining room, the table was set for five instead of seven, and their new places were pointed out to them by their napkin rings. Talking in subdued tones, they discovered the china pitcher of coffee under a quilted cozy, and, under a large quilted pad, slices of bread that were hard as a rock and burned black around the edges from being toasted over a gas burner. The dining-room windows offered a prospect of wet gravel, long grass bent over by the weight of the rain, and dripping pine branches. The coffee was tepid.

"I think it would have been better if we hadn't got her to lower the price," he said suddenly.

"Did she say anything about it?"

He shook his head. "The amount she asked was not exorbitant."

"It was high. Muriel said it was high. She lived in France for twenty years. She ought to know."

"That was before the war. In the total expenses of the summer, it wouldn't have made any difference, one way or the other."

"She said it was not right, and that it was a matter of principle."

"Muriel, you mean? I know, but the first two or three days after we got off the boat, I consistently undertipped people, because I didn't know what the right amount was, and I didn't want us to look like rich Americans throwing our money around, and in every case they were so nice about it."

"How do you know you undertipped them?"

"By the way they acted when I gave them more."

"Mme Viénot has a romantic idea of herself," Barbara said. "The way she flirts with you, for instance . . ."

He took the green Michelin guide to the château country from his coat pocket and put it beside his plate. After a week of sight-seeing, any other way of passing the time seemed unnatural.

"You're sure she was flirting with me?"

"Certainly. But it's a game. She's attempting to produce, with your help, the person she sees herself as—the worldly, fascinating adventuress, the heroine of *Gone with the Wind*."

He filled their cups again and offered her the burned bread, which she refused. Then he opened the guidebook and began to turn the pages as he ate. Programmes de voyage . . . Un peu d'histoire . . . wars and maps . . . medieval cooking utensils . . . The fat round towers of Chaumont, and Amboise as it was in the sixteenth century.

"How old do you think Gagny is?" Barbara said.

"I don't know. He varies so. Somewhere between twenty-three and thirty-five."

More maps. Visit rapide . . . Visite du Château . . .

"Why isn't he married?"

"People don't have to get married," he said. "Sometimes they just—"

I: *Leo and Virgo*

Rain blew against the windowpanes, so hard that they both turned and looked.

"Besides, he's in the diplomatic service," Harold said. "He can't just marry any pretty girl he feels like marrying. He needs a countess or somebody like that, and I suppose they won't have him because he isn't rich."

"How do you know he isn't rich?"

"If he were rich he wouldn't *be* here. He'd be somewhere where the sun is shining."

Behind his back a voice said: "Good morning!" and Mme Viénot swept into the dining room, wearing a dark-red housecoat, with her head tied up in a red and green Liberty scarf. She sat down at the head of the table. "You slept well? . . . I'm so glad. You must have been very tired after your journey." She placed her box of sugar directly in front of her, so there could be no possible misunderstanding, and then said: "What a pity it is raining again! M. Gagny is very discouraged about the weather, which I must say is not what we are accustomed to in July."

"Is it bad for the grain?" Harold asked.

Mme Viénot lifted the quilted pad and considered the burned bread with a grimace of disapproval. "Not at this time of year. But my gardener is worried about the hay." She peered into the china pitcher and her eyebrows rose in disbelief. "Perhaps it is only a shower. I hope so." She picked up the plate of toast and pushed her chair back. "The cook, poor dear, forgot to moisten the bread. I don't care for it when it is hard like this. Taking the pitcher also with her, she went out to the kitchen.

"We shouldn't have had a second cup," Barbara whispered.

"I think it was all right," he said.

"But she looked—"

"I know. I saw it. Coffee is rationed, but surely that wasn't coffee. . . . There wasn't enough for the others, in any case."

"You won't forget to speak to her about the beds, will you?" Barbara said. "I wrote her that we wanted a room with a *grand lit*, and if she didn't have anything but twin beds, it was up to her to tell us. And she didn't."

"No," he agreed, shifting in his chair, the uneasy male caught between two females.

"And the bicycles . . . You don't think she overheard what we were saying?"

"It wouldn't matter, unless she was standing out in the hall the whole time."

"She could have been."

They sat in wary silence until the pantry door opened.

"We must plan some excursions for you," Mme Viénot said. "You are in the center of one of the most interesting parts of France. The king used to come here with the court, for the hunting. They each had their own château and it was marvelous."

"We want to see Azay-le-Rideau," he said, "and Chinon, and Chenonceau—"

"Chinon is a ruin," Mme Viénot said disapprovingly. "Unless you have some particular reason for going there—" She surveyed the table and then got up again and pried open the door of the sideboard with her table knife. They heard a faint exclamation and then: "Within twenty-four hours after I open a jar of *confitures* it is half gone.

"Do have some," she said as she sat down again. "It is plum."

They both refused.

"Chenonceau is ravishing," Mme Viénot said, and helped herself sparingly to the jam. "It belonged to Diane de Poitiers. She was the king's mistress. She adored Chenonceau, and Catherine de Médicis took it away from her and gave her Chaumont instead."

He asked the reason for this exchange.

"She was jealous," Mme Viénot explained, with a shrug.

"But couldn't the king stop her?"

"He was killed in a tournament."

"Are the châteaux within walking distance?" Barbara asked.

"Alas, no," Mme Viénot said.

"But we can bicycle to some of them?" he asked.

In one of the two polite letters that arrived before they left New York, Mme Viénot had assured them that bicycles would be waiting for them when they arrived. Now she filled their cups and then her own and said plaintively: "I inquired about bicycles for you in the village, and it appears there aren't any. Perhaps you can arrange to rent them in Blois. Or in Tours. Tours is a dear old city—you know it?"

"We were there overnight," Barbara said.

"You saw the cathedral?"

Barbara shook her head.

"You must see the cathedral," Mme Viénot said. "The old part of the city was badly damaged during the war. Whole blocks went down between the center of town and the river. So shocking, isn't it?"

The servant girl appeared with a plate of fresh toast that had not been burned and the china pitcher, now full of steaming hot coffee. Mme Viénot remarked in French to the surrounding air that someone in the house was extremely fond of *confitures*, and with a sullen look Thérèse withdrew to the kitchen.

"Now, with the rubble cleared away," Mme Viénot said cheerfully: "you can have no idea what it was like. . . . The planes were American."

For a whole minute nobody said anything. Then Harold said: "Riding on the train we saw a great deal of rebuilding. Everywhere, in fact."

"Our own people raised the money for the new bridge at Tours," Mme Viénot said. "Naturally we are very proud of it. They are of stone, the new buildings?"

He nodded. "There's one thing, though, I kept noticing, and that is that the openings—the windows and doors—were all the same size. Do they have to do that? The new buildings look like barracks."

"In Tours all the new buildings are of stone. It would have

been cheaper to use wood, but that would have meant sacrificing the style of the locality, which is very beautiful," Mme Viénot said firmly, and so prevented him from pursuing a subject that, he now perceived, might well be painful to her. Probably it wasn't possible to rebuild, exactly as they were before, houses that had been built hundreds of years ago, and added onto and changed continually ever since.

He said: "Is there a taxi in the village?"

"There is one," Mme Viénot said. "A woman has it, and I'm afraid you will find her expensive. I'm sorry we haven't a car to offer you. We sold our Citroën after the war, thinking we could get a new one immediately, and it was a dreadful mistake. You can take the train, you know."

"From Brenodville?"

She nodded. Rearranging her sleeves so they wouldn't trail across her plate, she said: "I used to go to parties at Chaumont before the war. The Princesse de Broglie owned it then. She married the Infant Louis-Ferdinand, of Spain, and he was not always nice to her." She looked expectantly at them and seemed to be waiting for some response, some comment or anecdote about a royal person they knew who was also inconsiderate. "The Princesse was a very beautiful woman, and immensely rich. She was of the Say family—they manufacture sugar—and she wanted a title. So she married the Prince de Broglie, and he died. And then in her old age she married the Infant, and mothered him, and gave parties to which everyone went, and kept an elephant. The bridge at Chaumont is still down, but there is a ferry, I am told. I must find out for you how often it goes back and forth. . . . The Germans blew up all the bridges across the Loire, and for a while it was most inconvenient."

"How do we get to Chenonceau?" Harold asked.

"You take a train to Amboise, and from there you take a taxi. It's about twelve kilometers."

"And there are lots of trains?"

"There are two," Mme Viénot said. "One in the morning and one at night. I'll get a schedule for you. Before the war, the mayor of Brenodville was a member of the Chamber of Deputies and we had excellent service; all the fast trains between Paris and Nantes stopped here. . . . Amboise is also worth seeing. Léonard de Vinci is buried there. And during the seventeenth century, there was an uprising—it was the time of the Huguenot wars—and a great many men were put to death. They say that Marie Stuart and the young king used to dine out on the battlements at Amboise, in order to watch the hangings."

"What about buses?"

"I don't think you'll find the bus at all convenient," Mme Viénot said. "You have to walk a mile and a half to the highway where it passes, and usually it is quite crowded." Then as the silence in the dining room became prolonged: "I've been meaning to ask you about young George Ireland. We grew very fond of him while he was here, and he was a great favorite in the village. What is he doing now?"

"George is in school," Harold said.

"But now, this summer?"

"He's working. He's selling little dolls. He showed them to us the last time we were at the Irelands' for dinner. A man and a woman this high . . . You wind them up and they dance around and around."

"How amusing," Mme Viénot said. "He sells them on the street corner?"

"To tobacco stores, I believe."

"And is he successful?"

"Very. He's on his way to becoming a millionaire."

Mme Viénot nodded approvingly. "When he arrived, he didn't know a word of French, and it was rather difficult at first. But he spoke fluently by the end of the summer. We also discovered that he was fond of chocolate. He used to ride into the village after dinner and spend untold sums on candy and sweetmeats. And he was rather careless with my bicyclette. I had to have it repaired after he left. But he is a dear, of course. That reminds me—I haven't answered his mother's letter. I must write her today, and thank her for sending me two such charming clients.

It was most kind of her. I gather that she knows France well?"

Harold nodded.

"Such an amusing thing happened—I must tell you. My younger daughter became engaged last summer, and before she had quite made up her mind, George came to me and said that Sabine must wait until he could marry her. Fancy his thinking she would have him? I thought it was very fresh—a fifteen-year-old boy!"

"He speaks of you all—and of the place—with great affection," Harold said.

"It was a responsibility," Mme Viénot said. There are so many kinds of trouble a boy of that age can get into. You're quite sure you won't have anything more? Some bread, perhaps? Some more coffee?" She rolled her napkin and thrust it through the silver ring in front of her, and pushed her chair back from the table. "When George left, he kissed me and said: 'You have been like a mother to me!' I thought it sweet of him—to say that. And I really did feel like his mother."

As they were moving toward the door, he said hurriedly: "We've been meaning to ask you— Is there some way we could have hot water?"

"In your room? But of course! Thérèse will bring it to you. When would you like it? In the evening, perhaps?"

"At seven o'clock," Barbara said.

"I could come and get it myself," he said. "Or would that upset them?"

"Oh, dear no!" Mme Viénot exclaimed. "I'm afraid that wouldn't do. They'd never understand in the kitchen. You must tell Maman about the *poupées*. She will be enchanted."

"PORC-ÉPIC is French for porcupine," he announced. He was stretched out on the chaise longue, in the darkest corner of their room, reading the green Michelin guide to the château country. "The porcupine with a crown above it is the attribute—emblem, I guess it means—of Louis XII. The emblem of François premier is the salamander. The swan with an arrow sticking through its breast is the emblem of Louise of Savoy, mother of François premier. And it's also the emblem of Claude de France, his wife. Did you know we have a coat of arms in our family?"

"No," Barbara said. "You never told me." She had covered the towel racks in the bathroom with damp stockings and lingerie, and was now sitting at the kidney-shaped desk, with her fur coat over her shoulders and the windows wide open because it was no colder outside than it was in, writing notes to people who had sent presents to the boat. There were letters and postcards he should have been writing but fortunately there was only one pen.

"The ermine is Anne of Brittany and Claude de France," he said, turning back to the guidebook.

"Why does she have two emblems?"

"Who?"

"Claude de France. You said—"

"So she does . . . Ummm. It doesn't say. But it gives the genealogy of the Valois kings, the Valois-Orléans, the Valois-Angoulême, and the Bourbons through Louis XIV. . . . Charles V, 1364–1380, married Jeanne de Bourbon. Charles VI, 1380–1422, married Isabeau de Bavière. Charles VII—"

"Couldn't you just read it to yourself and tell me about it afterward?"

"All right," he said. "But it's very interesting. Charles VIII and Louis XII both married Anne of Brittany."

"The salamander?"

"No, the ermine. I promise not to bother you any more." But he did, almost immediately. "Listen to this, I just want to read you the beginning paragraph. It's practically a prose poem."

"Is it long?"

" 'Between Gien and Angers, the banks of the Loire and the

affluent valleys of the great river present an incomparable ensemble of magnificent monuments.' That's very good, don't you think? Don't you think it has sweep to it? 'The châteaux, by their number, their importance, and their interest appear in the foreground. Crammed with art and history, they occupy the choicest sites in a region that has a privileged light—' "

"It looks like just any gray day to me," she said, glancing out at the sky.

"Maybe the light is privileged and maybe it isn't. The point is you'd never find an expression like that in an American guidebook. . . . 'The landscapes of the Loire, in lines simple and calm'—that's very French—' owe their seductiveness to the light that bathes them, wide sky of a light blue, long perspectives of a current that is sometimes sluggish, tranquil streams with delicate reflections, sunny hillsides with promising vineyards, fresh valleys, laughing flower-filled villages, peaceful visions. A landscape that is measured, that charms by its sweetness and its distinction—' "

He yawned. The guidebook slipped through his fingers and joined the pocket dictionary on the rug. After a minute or two, he got up and stood at the window. The heavy shutters opened in, and the black-out paper was crinkled and torn and beginning to come loose. Three years after the liberation of France, it was still there. No one in a burst of happiness and confidence in the future had ripped it off. Germans, he thought, standing where he stood now, with their elbows on the sill. Looking off toward the river that was there but could not be seen. Lathering their cheeks in front of the shaving stand . . . Did Mme Bonenfant and Mme Viénot eat with their unwelcome guests, or in the kitchen, or where?

It had stopped raining but the air was saturated with moisture and the trees dripped. In the park in front of the château, the gardener and his wife and boy were pulling the haystacks apart with their forks and spreading the hay around them on the wet ground. He was tempted to go down and offer his services. But if they wouldn't understand in the kitchen, no doubt they wouldn't understand outdoors either.

"What time is it?" Barbara asked.

"Quarter of eleven. How time flies, doesn't it. Are you warm enough?"

"Mmmm."

"It's like living at the bottom of the sea."

He left the window and stood behind her, reading as she wrote. She had started a letter to her mother and father. The quick familiar handwriting moved across the page, listing the places they had been to, describing the château and the countryside and the terribly interesting French family they were now staying with. The letter seemed to him slightly stepped up, the pleasures exaggerated, as if she were trying to conceal from them (or possibly from herself) the fact that they were not as happy in their present surroundings as they had been in the Hôtel Ouest et Montgomery in Pontorson.

He moved on to the big round table in the center of the room. Among the litter of postcards, postage stamps, and souvenirs, a book caught his eye. Mme Viénot had come upon him in the drawing room after breakfast, and had made a face at the book he was looking at—corrections, additions, and objections to the recently issued grammar of the French Academy—and had said, with a smile: "I don't really think you are ready for that kind of hair-splitting." Taking the book out of his hands, she had given him this one instead. It was a history of the château of Blois. He opened it in the middle, read a paragraph, and then retired to the chaise longue.

Barbara finished her letter, folded it, and brought it to him to read. "Is it all right?"

"Mmmm," he said.

"Should I do it over?"

"No," he said. "It's a very nice letter. Why should you do it over? It will make them very happy."

"You don't like it."

"Yes, I do. It's a fine letter." The insincerity in his voice was so marked that he even heard it himself.

"There isn't a thing wrong with that letter," he said, earnestly this time. "There's no point in writing it over." But she had already torn it in half, and she went on tearing it in smaller pieces, which she dropped in the wastebasket.

"I didn't mean for you to do that!" he exclaimed. "Really, I didn't!" And a voice in his head that sounded suspiciously like the voice of Truth asked if that wasn't exactly what he had wanted her to do. . . . But why, he wondered. What difference did it make to him what she wrote to her father and mother? . . . No difference. It was just that they were shut up together in a cold house, and it was raining.

She sat down at the desk and took a blank sheet of paper and began over again. Ashamed of his petty interfering, he watched her a moment and then retrieved the pocket dictionary from the rug and placed it on the chaise longue beside his knees. While he was trying to untangle the personal and political differences of Henri III and the Duc de Guise, he raised his eyes from the print and observed Barbara's face, bent over her letter. Her face, on every troubled occasion, was his compass, his Pole Star, the white pebbles shining in the moonlight by which Hop-O'-My-Thumb found his way home. When she was happy she was beautiful, but the beauty came and went; it was at the mercy of her feelings. When she was unhappy she could be so plain it was frightening.

After a short while—hardly five minutes—she pushed the letter aside and said, quite cheerfully: "It's stopped raining. Should we go for a walk?"

They went downstairs and through the drawing room and outdoors without seeing anyone. Something kept them from quite liking the front of the house, which was asymmetrical and bare to the point of harshness. They looked into the courtyard at the carriage house, the stables, the high brick wall, and windows they had now looked out of. They followed the cinder drive around the other end of the house. Climbing roses and English ivy struggled for possession of the back wing, which had a much less steeply sloping roof and low dormers instead of bull's-eyes.

The drive took them on up a slope, between two rain-stained statues, and past a pond that had been drained, and finally to another iron gate. Peering through the bars, they saw that there was no trace of a road on the other side. Nothing but the forest. They tried the gate; it was locked. They turned and looked back, and had an uncomfortable feeling that eyes were watching them from the house.

On the way down again, they stopped and looked at the statues. They looked again at the clock that straddled the roof tree of the back wing. It had stopped at quarter of twelve. But quarter of twelve how long ago? And why was there no water in the pond? Seen from the rear, the whole place cried out that there had once been money and the money was gone, frittered away.

They noticed a gap in the hedge, and, walking through it, found themselves in a huge garden where fruit trees, rose trees, flowers, and vegetables were mingled in a way that surprised and delighted them. So did the scarecrow, which was dressed in striped morning trousers and a blue cotton smock. Under the straw hat the stuffed head had sly features painted on it. They saw old Mme Bonenfant at the far end of the garden, and walked slowly toward her. By the time they arrived at the sweet-pea trench her basket was full. She laid her garden shears across the long green stems and took the Americans on a tour of the garden, pointing out the espaliered fruit trees and telling them the French names of flowers. She did not understand their schoolroom French. They felt shy with her. But the tour did not last very long, and they understood that she was being kind, that she wanted them to feel at home. Leading them to some big fat bushes that were swathed in burlap against the birds, she told them to help themselves to the currants and gooseberries, and then she went on down the garden path to the house.

A few minutes later they left the garden themselves and followed the cinder drive down to the public road, where they turned left, in the opposite direction from the village. The road led them past fields on one side and the forest on the other. They came to a farmhouse and an excitable dog, detecting an odor that was not French, barked furiously at them; then to an opening in the forest, where a wagon track wound in through tall oak trees and out of sight. They left the road and followed the wagon track. The tree trunks were green with moss and there was no underbrush, which made the forest look unreal. The ground under their feet was covered with delicate ferns. Barbara kept stooping to gather acorns. These had a high polish and a beautiful shape and were smaller than the acorns she was accustomed to. Her pockets were soon full of them.

"We don't have to stay," she said, turning and looking at him.

"No," he agreed doubtfully. He was relieved, now she had given voice to his own uneasiness. But at the same time, how could they leave? "Of course we don't," he said. "Not if we don't want to."

"But we said we'd stay two weeks. What if she's counting on that, and has turned other people away?"

"I know."

"So in a way, we're bound to do what we said we'd do."

"We could tell her, I guess," he said. "The trouble is, we'll never have anywhere else as good a chance to learn to speak French."

"That's true."

"And later we may be glad we stuck it out. We may find when we get to Paris that it is possible to talk to people in a way that we haven't been able to, so far."

"So let's stay," she said.

"We'll try it for a few days, and then if it doesn't work, we can leave."

There seemed to be no end to the forest. After a short while they turned back, not because they were afraid of getting lost—there was only one road—but the way swimmers confronted with the immensity of the ocean swim out a little way and then, though they could easily swim farther, give way to a nameless fear and turn and head for the shore.

As they came back up the cinder drive, they saw the Canadian pacing the terrace in front of the château and staring up at the sky. The clouds had coalesced for the first time in several days, and the sun was trying to break through.

Away from the French, he seemed perfectly friendly, and willing to acknowledge the fact that Canada is right next to the United States.

"I congratulate you," he said, smiling.

"On what?" Harold asked.

"On the way you made your escape last night, after dinner. The evenings are very long."

"Then we ought to have stayed?" Barbara said.

"You have established a precedent. From now on, they expect you to be independent."

"But we didn't mean to," Harold said, "and if it was really impolite—"

"Oh, yes," Gagny said, smiling. "I quite understood, and the others did too. There was no comment."

"Are *you* expected to remain with them after dinner?" Harold persisted.

"As Americans you are in an enviable position," Gagny said, ignoring the question. Still smiling, he held the door open for them to pass into the drawing room, where Mme Carrère, with tortoise-shell glasses on, sat reading a letter. In her lap were half a dozen more. Mme Viénot was also reading a letter. Mme Bonenfant was reading *Le Figaro,* without glasses.

"Sabine has seen the King of Persia," Mme Viénot announced. And then, turning the page: "There is to be an illumination on Bastille Day. . . . I inquired about ration stamps for you in the village, M. Rhodes, and it seems you must go to Blois and apply for the stamps in person. I'm going there tomorrow afternoon. I could take you to the ration bureau."

"Oh, fine," he said.

"I'm sorry to put you to this trouble, but I do need the stamps."

On the way upstairs, Barbara said: "Do you think we ought to write to the Guaranty Trust Company and have our mail forwarded here?"

"I don't know," he said. "I can't decide."

The first thing they saw when they walked into their room was the big bouquet of pink and white sweet peas on their table. "Aren't they lovely!" Barbara exclaimed, and as she put her face down to smell the flowers, he said: "Let's wait. We've only been gone ten days, and that way there'll be more when we do get it."

"Think of her climbing all the way up here to bring them to us," Barbara said, and then, as she began to brush her hair: "I'm glad we decided to stay."

M. Carrère had breakfast in his room and came downstairs for the first time shortly before lunch. He walked with a cane, and Mme Carrère had to help him into his chair, but once seated he ignored his physical infirmity and so compelled the others to ignore it also. Mme Viénot explained privately to the Americans that he was recovering from a very serious operation. His convalescence was fulfilling the doctors' best hopes. He had gained weight, his appetite was improved, each day he seemed a little stronger. In her voice there was a note of wonder. So many quiet country places he could have gone to, she seemed to be saying, and he had come to her, instead.

He was not like anybody they had ever seen before. Though he seemed a kind man, there was an authority in his manner that kind men do not usually have. His face was long and equine. His eyes were set deep in his head. His hands were extraordinary. You could imagine him playing the cello or praying in the desert. When he smiled he looked like an expert old circus clown. He did not appear to want the attention of everybody when he spoke, and yet he invariably had it, Harold noticed. If he was aware of the dreary fact that there are few people who are not ready to take advantage of natural kindness in the eminent and the well-to-do, it did not bother him. The overlapping folds of his eyelids made his expression permanently humorous, and his judicious statements issued from a wide, sensual, shocking red mouth.

M. Carrère's great-grandfather, Mme Viénot said, had financed the building of the first French railway. M. Carrère himself was of an order of men that was becoming extremely rare in France today. His influence was felt, his taste and opinions were deferred to everywhere, and yet he was so simple, so sincere. To know him informally like this, to have the benefit of his conversation, was a great privilege.

She did not say—she did not have to say—that it was a privilege they were ill-equipped to enjoy.

Mme Carrère, quiet in her dress and in her manner, with black eyes and a Spanish complexion and neat gray hair parted in the middle, looked as if she were now ready for the hard, sharp pencil of Ingres—to whom, it turned out, her great-grandparents had sat for their portrait. She sat in a small armchair, erect but not stiff or uneasy, and for the most part she listened, but occasionally she added a remark when she was amused or interested by something. To Harold Rhodes' eyes, she had the look of a woman who did not need to like or be liked by other people. She was neither friendly nor unfriendly, and when her eyes came to rest on him for a second, what he read in them was that chance had brought them all together at the château, and if she ever met up with him elsewhere or even heard his name mentioned, it would again be the work of chance.

Unable to say the things he wanted to say, because he did not know how to say them in French, able to understand only a minute part of what the others said, deprived of the view from the train window and the conducted tour of the remnants of history, he sat and watched how the humorous expression around M. Carrère's eyes deepened and became genuine amusement when Mme Bonenfant brought forth a *mot*, or observed Mme Carrère's cordiality to Mme Viénot and her mother, not with the loving eye of a tourist but the glazed eye of a fish out of water.

He thought of poor George Ireland, stranded in this very room and only fifteen years old. If I could lie down on the floor I'd probably understand every word they're saying, he thought. Or if I could take off my shoes.

M. Carrère made a point of conversing with the Americans at the lunch table. They were delighted with his explanation of the phrase "entre la poire et le fromage" and so was Mme Viénot, who said: "I hope you will remember what M. Carrère has just said, because it is the very perfection of French prose style. It should be written down and preserved for posterity."

M. Carrère had recently paid a visit to his son, who was living in New York. He had seen the skyscrapers, and also Chicago and the Grand Canyon, on his way to the West Coast. "I could converse with people vis-à-vis but not when the conversation became general, and so I missed a great deal that would have been of interest to me. I found America fascinating," he added, looking at Harold and Barbara as if it had all been the work of their hands. "I particularly liked the 'ut doaks that are served everywhere in your country." They looked blank and he repeated the word, and then repeated it again impatiently: " 'ut doaks, 'ut doaks—le saucisson entre les deux pièces de pain."

"Oh, you mean hot dogs!" Barbara said, and laughed.

M. Carrère was not accustomed to being laughed at. The resemblance to a clown was accidental. " 'ut doaks," he said defensively, and subsided. The others sat silent, the luncheon table under a momentary pall. Then the conversation was resumed in M. Carrère's native tongue.

Chapter 5

THE BENTLEY was waiting in front of the house when they got up from the table and went across the hall for their coffee. As the last empty cup was returned to the silver tray, Mme Carrère rose. Ignoring the state of the weather, which they could all see through the drawing-room windows, she helped M. Carrère on with his coat, placed a lilac-colored shawl about his shoulders, and handed him his hat, his pigskin gloves. Outside, the Alsatian chauffeur held the car door open for them, and then arranged a fur robe about M. Carrère's long, thin legs. With a wistful look on their faces, the Americans watched the car go down the drive.

As they turned away from the window, Mme Viénot said: "I have an errand to do this afternoon, in the next village. It would make a pleasant walk if you care to come."

Off they went immediately, with the Canadian. Mme Viénot led them through the gap in the hedge and down the long straight path that bisected the potager. Over their heads storm clouds were racing across the sky, threatening to release a fresh downpour at any moment. She stopped to give instructions to the gardener, who was on his hands and knees among the cabbages, and the walk was suspended a second time when they encountered a white hen that had got through the high wire netting that enclosed the chicken yard. It darted this way and that when they tried to capture it. With his arms spread wide, Gagny ran at the silly creature. "Like the Foreign Office, she can't bear to commit herself," he said. "Steady . . . steady, now . . . Oh, blast!"

When the hen had been put back in the chicken yard, where she wouldn't offer a temptation to foxes, they resumed their walk. The path led past an empty potting shed with several broken panes of glass, past the gardener's hideous stucco villa, and then, skirting a dry fountain, they arrived at a gate in the fence that marked the boundary of Mme Bonenfant's property. On the other side, the path joined a rough wagon road that led them through a farm, and the farm provoked Mme Viénot to open envy. "It is better kept than my garden!" she exclaimed mournfully.

"In Normandy," Harold said, "in the fields that we saw from the train window, there were often poppies growing. It was so beautiful!"

"They are a pest," Mme Viénot said. "We have them here, too. They are a sign of improper cultivation. You do not have them in the fields in America? . . . I am amazed. I thought they were everywhere."

He decided that this was the right moment to bring up the subject of the double bed in their room.

"We never dreamed that it would take so long to recover from the Occupation," she said, as if she knew exactly what he was on the point of saying, and intended to forestall him. "It is not at all the way it was after the Guerre de Quatorze. But this summer, for the first time, we are more hopeful. Things that haven't been in the shops for years one can now buy. There is more food. And the farmers, who are not given to exaggeration, say that our wheat crop is remarkable."

"Does that mean there will be white bread?" he asked.

"I presume that it does," Mme Viénot said. "You dislike our dark bread? Coming from a country where you have everything in such abundance, you no doubt find it unpalatable."

Ashamed of the abundance when his natural preference was to be neither better nor worse off than other people, he said untruthfully: "No, I like it. We both do. But it seemed a pity to be in France and not be able to have croissants and brioches."

They had come to a fork in the road. Taking the road that led off to the right, she continued: "Of course, your government has been most generous," and let him agree to this by his silence before she went on to say, in a very different tone of voice: "You knew that in order to get wheat from America, we have had to promise to buy your wheat for the next ten years—even though we normally produce more wheat than we need? One doesn't expect to get something for nothing. That isn't the way the world is run. But I must say you drive a hard bargain."

And at that moment Hector Gagny, walking a few feet behind them, with Barbara, said: "We're terribly restricted, you know. Thirty-five pounds is all we can take out of England for travel in a whole year, and the exchange is less advantageous than it is with your dollars."

What it is like, Harold thought, is being so stinking rich that there is no hope of having any friends.

Walking along the country road in silence, he wondered uneasily about all the people they had encountered during their first week in France. So courteous, so civilized, so pleasant; so pleased that he liked their country, that he liked talking to them. But what would it have been like if they'd come earlier—say, after the last excitement of the liberation of Paris had died down, and before the Marshall Plan had been announced? Would France have been as pleasant a place to travel in? Would the French have smiled at them on the street and in train corridors and in shops and restaurants and everywhere? And would they have been as helpful about handing the suitcases down to him out of train windows? In his need, he summoned the driver of the empty St. Malo–St. Servan bus who was so kind to them, the waitress in the hotel in Pontorson, the laborer who had offered to share his bottle of wine in the train compartment, the nice woman with the little boy, the little boy in the carnival, M. Fleury and his son—and they stood by him. One and all they assured Harold Rhodes solemnly in their clear, beautiful, French voices that he was not mistaken, that he had not been taken in, that the kindness he had met with everywhere was genuine, that he had a right to his vision.

"Americans love your country," he said, turning to look directly at the Frenchwoman who was walking beside him. "They always have."

"I am happy to hear it," Mme Viénot said.

"The wheat is paid for by taxation. *I* am taxed for it. And everybody assumes that it comes to you as a gift. But there are certain extremely powerful lobbying interests that operate through Congress, and the State Department does things that Americans in general sometimes do not approve of or even know about. With Argentina, and also with Franco—"

"Entendu!" Mme Viénot exclaimed. "It is the same with us. The same everywhere. Only in politics is there no progress. Not the slightest. Whatever we do as individuals, the government undoes. If France had no government at all, it would do much better. No one has faith in the government any more."

"There is nothing that can be done about it?"

"Nothing," she said firmly. "It has been this way since 1870."

As they walked along side by side, his rancor—for he had felt personally attacked—gradually faded away, and they became once more two people, not two nationalities, out walking. Everything he saw when he raised his eyes from the dirt road pleased him. The poppy-infested fields through which they were now passing were by Renoir, and the distant blue hills by Cézanne. That the landscape of France had produced its painters seemed less likely than that the painters were somehow responsible for the landscape.

The road brought them to a village of ten or twelve houses, built of stone, with slate roofs, and in the manner of the early Gauguin. He asked if the village had a name.

"Coulanges," Mme Viénot said. "It is very old. The priest at Coulanges has supernatural powers. He is able to find water with a forked stick."

"A peach wand?"

"How did you know?" Mme Viénot asked.

He explained that in America there were people who could find water that way, though he had never actually seen anyone do it.

"It is extraordinary to watch," she said. "One sees the point of the stick bending. I cannot do it myself. They say that the priest at Coulanges is also able to find other things—but that is perhaps an exaggeration."

A mile beyond the village, they left the wagon road and followed a path that cut diagonally through a meadow, bringing them to a narrow footbridge across a little stream. On the other side was an old mill, very picturesque and half covered with climbing blush roses. The sky that was reflected in the millpond was a gun-metal gray. A screen of tall poplars completed the picturesque effect, which suggested no special painter but rather the anonymous style of department-store lithographs and colored etchings.

"It's charming, isn't it?" Mme Viénot said.

"Is it still used as a mill?" Harold asked.

"Indeed yes. The miller kept us in flour all through the war. He has a kind of laying mash that is excellent for my hens. I have to come and speak to him myself, though. Otherwise, he isn't interested."

When she left them, they stood watching some white ducks swimming on the surface of the millpond.

The Canadian said, after quite some time: "Why did you come here?" It was not an accusation, though it sounded like one, but the preface to a complaint.

"We wanted to see the châteaux," Barbara said. "And also—"

"Mmmm," Gagny interrupted. "I'd heard about this place, and I thought it would be nice to come here, but I might as well have stayed in London. There hasn't been one hour of hot sunshine in the last five days."

"We were hoping to rent bicycles," Barbara said. "She wrote

us that it had been arranged, and then this morning at breakfast she—"

"There are no bicycles for rent," Gagny said indignantly.

"I know there aren't any in the village," Barbara said. "But in Blois?"

He shook his head.

"Then I guess we'll have to go by train," she said.

"It's no use trying to get around by train. It will take you all day to visit one château."

"But she said—"

"If you want to see the châteaux, you need a car," he said, looking much more cheerful now that his discouragement was shared.

They saw Mme Viénot beckoning to them from the door of the mill.

"If this weather keeps up," Gagny said as they started toward her, "I'm going to pack my things and run up to Paris. I've told her that I might. I have friends in Paris that I can stay with, and Wednesday is Bastille Day. It ought to be rather lively."

"I've just had a triumph," Mme Viénot said. "The miller has agreed to let me have two sacks of white flour." The Americans looked at her in surprise, and she said innocently: "I'm not sure that it is legal for him to sell it to me, but he is very attached to our family. I'm to send my gardener around for it early tomorrow morning, before anyone is on the road."

Instead of turning back the way they had come, she led them across another footbridge and they found themselves on a public road. Walking four abreast, they reached the crest of a long ridge and had a superb view of the valley of the Loire.

Turning to Barbara, Mme Viénot said: "When did you come out?"

"Come out?" Barbara repeated blankly.

"Perhaps I am using the wrong expression," Mme Viénot said. "I am quite out of the habit of thinking in English. Here, when a young girl reaches a certain age and is ready to be introduced to society—"

"We use the same expression. I just didn't understand what you meant. . . . I didn't come out."

"It is not necessary in America, then?"

"Not in the West. It depends on the place, and the circumstances. I went to college, and then I worked for two years, and then I got married."

"And you liked working? So does Sabine. I must show you some of her drawings. She's quite talented, I think. When you go to Paris, you must call on her at *La Femme Elégante*. She will be very pleased to meet two of my guests, and you can ask her about things to see and do in Paris. There is a little bistro that she goes to for lunch—no doubt she will take you there. The clientele is not very distinguished, but the food is excellent, and most reasonable, and you will not always want to be dining at Maxim's."

Harold opened his mouth to speak and then closed it; Mme Viénot's smile made it clear that her remark was intended as a pleasantry.

"I think I told you that my daughter became engaged last summer? After some months, she asked to be released from her engagement. She and her fiancé had known each other since they were children, but she decided that she could not be happy with him. It has left her rather melancholy. All her friends are married now and beginning to have families. Also, it seems her job with *La Femme Elégante* will terminate the first of August. The daughter of one of the editors of the American *Vogue* is coming over to learn the milieu, and a place has to be made for her."

"But that doesn't seem fair!" Barbara exclaimed.

Mme Viénot shrugged. "Perhaps they will find something else for her to do. I hope so."

The road led them away from the river, through fields and

vineyards and then along a high wall, to an ornamental iron gate, where the Bentley was waiting. The gatehouse was just inside, and Mme Viénot roused the gatekeeper, who came out with her. His beret was pulled down so as to completely cover his thick gray hair, and he carried himself like a soldier, but his face was pinched and anxious, and he obviously did not want to admit them. Mme Viénot was pleasant but firm. As they talked she indicated now the lane, grown over with grass, that led past the gatehouse and into the estate, now the car that must be allowed to drive up the lane. In the end her insistence prevailed. He went into the gatehouse and came out again with his bunch of heavy keys and opened the gates for the Bentley to drive through.

The party on foot walked in front of the car, which proceeded at a funeral pace. Ahead of them, against the sky, was the blackened shell of a big country house with the chimneys still standing.

It looks like a poster urging people to buy war bonds, Harold thought, and wondered if the planes were American. It turned out that the house had been destroyed in the twenties by a fire of unknown origin. At the edge of what had once been an English garden, the chauffeur stopped the car, and M. and Mme Carrère got out and proceeded with the others along a path that led to a small family chapel. Inside, the light came through stained-glass windows that looked as if they had been taken from a Methodist church in Wisconsin or Indiana. The chapel contained four tombs, each supporting a stone effigy.

With a hissing intake of breath Mme Viénot said: "Ravissant!"

"Ravissant!" said M. and Mme Carrère and Hector Gagny, after her.

Harold was looking at a vase of crepe-paper flowers in a niche and said nothing. The chapel is surely nineteenth-century Gothic, he thought. How can they pretend to like it?

The effigies were genuine. Guarded by little stone dogs and

gentle lap lions, they maintained, even with their hands folded in prayer, a lifelike self-assertiveness. Looking down at one of them—at the low forehead, the blunt nose, the broad, brutal face—he said: "These were very different people."

"They were Normans," Mme Viénot said. "They fought their way up the rivers and burned the towns and villages and then settled down and became French. He's very beautiful, isn't he? But not very intelligent. He was a crusader."

There was no plaque telling which of the seven great waves of religious hysteria and tourism had picked the blunt-nosed man up and carried him all the way across Europe and set him down in Asia Minor, under the walls of Antioch or Jerusalem. But his dust was here, not in the desert of Lebanon; he had survived, in any case; the tourist had got home.

"What I brought you here to see," Mme Viénot said, "is the *prieuré* on the other side of the garden. I don't know the word in English."

"Priory," Barbara said.

"The same word. How interesting!"

While they were in the chapel, it had commenced to sprinkle. They hurried along a garden path. The garden still had a few flowers in it, self-sown, among the weeds and grass. Except for the vaulting of the porch roof, the priory looked from the outside like an ordinary farm building. The entrance was in the rear, down a flight of stone steps that M. Carrère did not attempt. He stood under the shelter of the porch, leaning on his cane, looking ill and gray. When they were around the corner of the building, Harold asked Mme Carrère if the expedition had been too much for him and she said curtly that it had not. Her manner made it as clear as words would have that, though he had the privilege of listening to M. Carrère's conversation, he did not know him, and Mme Carrère did see that he had, therefore, any reason to be interested in the state of her husband's health. He colored.

The key that Mme Viénot had obtained from the gatekeeper they did not need after all. The padlock was hanging open. The two young men put their weight against the door and it gave way. When their eyes grew accustomed to the feeble light, they could make out a dirt floor, simple carving on the capitals of the thick stone pillars, and cross-vaulting.

Barbara was enchanted.

"It is considered a jewel of eleventh-century architecture," Mme Viénot said. "There is a story— It seems that one of the dukes was ill and afraid he would die, and he made a vow that if he recovered from his sickness he would build a prieuré in honor of the Virgin. And he did recover. But he forgot all about the prieuré and thought of nothing but his hawks and his hounds and hunting, until the Virgin appeared in a dream to someone in the neighborhood and reminded him, and then he had to keep his promise."

The interior of the building was all one room, and not very large, and empty except for an object that Harold took for a medieval battering ram until Mme Viénot explained that it was a wine press.

"In America," he said, "this building would have been taken apart stone by stone and shipped to Detroit, for Henry Ford's museum."

"Yes?" Mme Viénot said. "Over here, we have so many old buildings. The museums are crammed. And so things are left where they happen to be."

He examined the stone capitals and walked all around the wine press. "What became of the nuns?" he asked suddenly.

"They went away," Mme Viénot said. "The building hasn't been lived in since the time of the Revolution."

What the nuns didn't take away with them other hands had. *If you are interested in those poor dead women*, the dirt floor of the priory said—*in their tapestries, tables, chairs, lectuaries, cooking utensils, altar images, authenticated and unauthenticated visions, their needlework, feuds, and forbidden pets, go to the public library and read about them. There's nothing here, and hasn't been, for a hundred and fifty years.*

ON THE WAY HOME the walking party was caught in a heavy shower and drenched to the skin.

Dressing hurriedly for dinner, Barbara said: "It's so like her: 'Thérèse will bring you a can—what time would you like it?' and then when seven o'clock comes, there isn't a sign of hot water."

"Do you want me to go down and see about it?"

"No, you'd better not."

"Maybe she does it on purpose," he said.

"No, she's just terribly vague, I've decided. She only half listens to what people are saying. I wouldn't mind if we were on a camping trip, but to be expected to dress for dinner, to have everything so formal, and not even be able to take a bath! Do you want to button me up in back? . . . I've never seen anyone look as vague as she does sometimes. As if her whole life had been passed in a dream. Her eyelids come down over her eyes and she looks at us as if she couldn't imagine who we were or what we were doing here."

"M. Carrère likes Americans, but Mme Carrère doesn't. I don't think she likes much of anybody."

"She likes the Canadian."

"Does she?"

"She laughs at his jokes."

"I don't think Gagny's French is as good as he thinks it is. It's an exaggeration of the way the others speak. Almost a parody."

"M. Carrère speaks beautiful French."

"He speaks French the way an American speaks English. It

just comes out of him easily and naturally. Gagny shrugs his shoulders and draws down the corners of his mouth and says 'mais oui' all the time, and it's as if he had picked up the mannerisms of half a dozen different people—which I guess you can't help doing if the language isn't your own. At least, I find myself beginning to do it."

"But it *is* his language. He's bilingual."

"French-Canadian isn't the same as French." He pulled his tie through and drew the knot snugly against his collar. "While you are trying to make the proper sounds and remember which nouns are masculine and which feminine, the imitation somehow unconsciously— M. Carrère's *English* is something else again. His pronunciation is so wide of the mark that sometimes I can't figure out what on earth he's talking about. " 'ut doaks, 'ut doaks!" And so impatient with us for not understanding."

"I shouldn't have laughed at him," Barbara said sadly. "I was sorry afterward. Because our pronunciation must sound just as comic to the French, and they never laugh at us."

At dinner, Mme Viénot's navy-blue silk dress was held together at the throat by a diamond pin, which M. Carrère admired. He had a passion for the jewelry of the Second Empire, he said. And Mme Carrère remarked dryly that there was only one thing she would do differently if she had her life to live over again. She let her husband explain. In the spring of 1940, as they were preparing to escape from Paris by car, she had entrusted her jewel case to a friend, and the friend had handed it over to the Nazis. The few pieces that she had now were in no way comparable to what had been lost forever. Even so, Barbara had to make an effort to keep from looking at the emerald solitaire that Mme Carrère wore next to her plain gold wedding ring, and she was sorry that she had listened to Harold when he suggested that she leave everything but a string of cultured pearls in the bank at home.

Having established a precedent, the Americans were concerned to live it down. They remained in the petit salon with the others, after dinner. The company sat, the women with sweaters and coats thrown over their shoulders, facing the empty Franklin stove. Observing that Gagny smoked one cigarette and then no more, the Americans, not wanting to be responsible for filling the room with smoke, denied the impulse each time it recurred, and sometimes found to their surprise that they had a lighted cigarette in their hand.

While Hector Gagny and M. Carrère were solemnly discussing the underlying causes of the defeat of 1940, the present weakened condition of France, and the dangers that a reawakened Germany would present to Europe and the rest of the world, a quite different conversation was taking place in the mirror over the mantelpiece. Harold Rhodes's reflection, leaning forward in his chair, said to Mme Viénot's reflection: "I am not accustomed to bargaining. It makes me uneasy. But we have a friend who lived in France for years, and she said—"

"Where in France?" Mme Viénot's reflection interrupted.

"In Paris. They had an apartment overlooking the Parc Monceau."

"The Monceau quarter is charming. Gounod lived there. And Chopin."

"She said it was a matter of principle, and that in traveling we must keep our eyes open and not be above bargaining or people would take advantage of us . . . of our inexperience. It was she who told us to ask you to figure the price by the week instead of by the day, but if I had it to do over again, I wouldn't listen to her. I'd just pay you what you asked for, and let it go at that."

Instead of giving him the reassurance he wanted, Mme Viénot's reflection leaned back among the sofa pillows, with her hand to her cheek. It would have been better, he realized, not to have brought the matter up at all. It was not necessary to bring it up. It had been settled before they ever left America. In his embarrassment he turned for help to the photograph of the schoolboy on the piano. "What I am trying to say, I guess, is that it's one thing to live up to your principles, and quite another thing to live up to somebody else's idea of what those principles should be."

"My likeness is here among the others," the boy in the photograph said, "but in their minds I am dead. They have let me die."

"The house is cold and damp and depressing," Barbara Rhodes's reflection said to the reflection of M. Carrère. "Why must we all sit with sweaters and coats over our shoulders? Why isn't there a fire in that stove? I don't see why we all don't get pneumonia."

"People born to great wealth—"

All the other reflections stopped talking in order to hear what M. Carrère's reflection was about to say.

"—are also born to a certain kind of human deprivation, and soon learn to accept it. For example, those letters that arrive daily, even in this remote country house—letters from my lawyer, from my financial advisors, from bankers and brokers and churchmen and politicians and the heads of charitable organizations, all read and acknowledged by Mme Carrère, lest they tire me (which indeed they would). The expressions of personal attachment, of concern for my health, are judged according to their sincerity, in most instances not great, and a few are read aloud to me, lest I think that no one cares. I am accustomed to the fact that in every letter, sooner of later, self-interest shows through. I do not really mind, any more. Music is my delight. When I want companionship, I go to the Musée des Arts Décoratifs and look at the porcelains and the period furniture."

"I used to have a friend—" Mme Bonenfant's reflection said. "She has been dead for twenty years: Mme Noë—"

"Mme Noë?" M. Carrère interrupted. "I knew her also. That is, I was taken to see her as a young man."

"Mme Noë was fond of saying, and of writing in letters and on the flyleaf of books: 'Life is something more than we believe it to be.' "

"Since my illness," M. Carrère said, "I have become aware for the first time of innumerable—reconciliations, I suppose one would call them, that go on around us all the time without our noticing it. Again and again, Mme Carrère hands me something just as I am on the point of asking for it. And in her dreams she is sometimes a party to financial transactions that I am positive I have not told her about. . . . But it is strange that you should speak of Mme Noë. I was thinking about her this very afternoon as I stood looking at that grass-choked garden and that house gutted by fire. She was quite old when I was taken to see her. And she asked me all sorts of questions about myself that no one had ever asked me before, and that I went on answering for days afterward."

"She had that effect on everyone," Mme Bonenfant said.

"I remember that she led me to a vase of flowers and we talked."

"And what did you say?" Barbara Rhodes asked.

"I said something that pleased her," M. Carrère said, "but what it was I can no longer remember. All I know is that it was not at all like the sort of thing I usually said. And when she left me to speak to someone else, I did not have the feeling that I was being abandoned. Or that she would ever confuse me afterward with anyone else. . . . She is an important figure in the memoirs of a dozen great men, and reading about her the same question always occurs to me. What manner of woman she was really, if you made no claim on her, if you asked for nothing (as she asked for nothing) but merely sat, silent, content merely to be there beside her, and let her talk or not talk, as she felt like doing, all through a summer afternoon, none of them seem to know."

"She was frail," Mme Bonenfant said. "She was worn out by ill-health, by the demands, the endless claims upon her time and energy—"

"Which she must have encouraged," M. Carrère said.

"No doubt," Mme Bonenfant said. "By temperament she was

not merely kind, she was angelic, but there was also irony. Once or twice, toward the end of her life, she talked to me about herself. It seems she suffered always from the fear that, wanting only to help people, she nevertheless unwittingly brought serious harm to them. This may have been true but I do not know a single instance of it. For my own part, I am quite content to believe that life is nothing more than our vision of it—of what we believe it to be. Tacitus says that the phoenix appears from time to time in Egypt, that it is a fact well verified. Herodotus tells the same story, but skeptically."

"At the Council of Nicaea," M. Carrère said, "three hundred and eighteen bishops took their places on their thrones. But when they rose as their names were called, it appeared that they were three hundred and nineteen. They were never able to make the number come out right; whenever they approached the last one, he immediately turned into the likeness of his neighbor."

"Before Harold and I were married," Barbara said, "a woman in a nightclub read our palms, and she said Leo and Virgo should never marry. Their horoscopes are in conflict. If they love each other and are happy it is a mistake. . . . That's why he doesn't like fortunetellers. I don't think our marriage is a mistake, but on the other hand, sometimes I lie awake between three and four in the morning, planning dinner parties and solving riddles and worrying about curtains that don't hang straight in the dark, and about my clothes and my hair, and about whether I have been unintentionally the cause of hurt feelings. And about Harold, sound asleep beside me and sharing not only the same bed but some of my worst faults. . . . Does anybody know the answer to the riddle that begins: 'If three people are in a room and two of them have a white mark on their forehead—' "

"The answer to the riddle of why I am not married," Hector Gagny said, "is that I am. And my wife hates me."

"So did the woman I gave my jewel case to," Mme Carrère said. "But I didn't know it."

I: *Leo and Virgo*

"She has all but ruined my career," Gagny said. "She is beautiful and willful and perverse, and in her own way quite wonderful. But she makes no concessions to the company she finds herself in, and I sit frozen with fear of what may come out of her mouth."

"Do not despair," Mme Bonenfant said. "Be patient. Your wife, M. Gagny, may only be acting the way she does out of the fear that you do not love her."

"In the beginning we seemed to be happy, and only after a while did it become apparent that there were things that were not right. And that they were not ever going to be right. I began to see that behind the fascination of her mind, her temperament, there was some force at work that was not on my side, and bent on destroying both of us. But what is it? Why is she like that?"

"Though there was only two years difference in our ages," Mme Viénot said, "my mother held me responsible for my brother's safety when we were children. I used to have nightmares in which something happened to him or was about to happen to him. When we played together, I never let go of his hand."

"Maurice was delicate," Mme Bonenfant said.

"He cried easily," Mme Viénot said. "He was always getting his feelings hurt. My daughter Sabine is very like him in appearance. I only hope that her life is not as unhappy as his."

"I see that you haven't forgiven me," the boy in the photograph said. "I failed to distinguish myself in my studies but I made three friendships that were a credit to me, and I died bravely. It took me almost an hour to kill myself. . . . Now I am an effect of memory. When you have completely forgotten me, I assume that I will pass on to other places."

"They say that people who talk about committing suicide never actually do it," Mme Viénot said. "Maurice was the exception. When his body was brought home for burial we were warned that it would be better not to open the coffin."

"It was an accident," Mme Bonenfant said.

"And M. Viénot?" Harold Rhodes asked the boy in the photograph. "Why does nobody speak of him? His name is never mentioned."

"Do not interrupt," the boy in the photograph said. "They are speaking of me—of what happened to me."

At quarter of eleven, when the Americans went upstairs, they found a large copper can in their bathroom. The temperature of the water in the can was just barely warm to the touch.

Lying awake in the dark, she heard the other bed creak.

"Are you awake?" she whispered, when he turned again.

He was awake.

"We don't have to stay," she said, in a small, sad voice.

"If it's no good I think we could tell her that we're not happy and just leave." He sat up and rearranged the too-fat pillows and then said: "It's funny how it comes and goes. I have periods of clarity and then absolute blankness. And my mind gets so tired I don't care any more what they're saying." The bed creaked as he turned over again. He tried to go to sleep but he had talked himself wide awake. "Good night. I love you," he said. But it didn't work. This declaration, which on innumerable occasions had put his mind at rest, had no effect because she was not in his arms.

"It isn't simply the language," he said, after several minutes of absolute silence. "Though that's part of it. There's a kind of constraint over the conversation, over everything. I think they all feel it. I think it's the house."

"I know it's the house," she said. "Go to sleep."

Five minutes later, the bed creaked one last time. "Do I imagine it," he asked, "or is it true that when they speak of the Nazis—downstairs, I mean—the very next sentence is invariably some quite disconnected remark about Americans?"

Chapter 6

THE VILLAGE OF BRENODVILLE was too small and unremarkable to be mentioned in guidebooks, and derived its identity from the fact that it was not some other village—not Onzain or Chouzy or Chailles or Chaumont. It had two principal streets, the Grande Rue and the avenue Gambetta, and they formed the letter T. The avenue Gambetta went from the Place de l'Eglise to the railway station. The post office, the church, the mairie, and the cemetery were all on the Grande Rue. So was the house of M. Fleury. It ought to have given some sign of recognition, but it didn't; it was as silent, blank, secretive, and closed to strangers as every other house up and down the village street. While they stood looking at it, Mme Viénot came out of the post office and caught them red-handed.

"You are about to pay a call on M. Fleury?"

"We weren't even sure this was where he lived," Harold said, blushing. "The houses are all alike."

"That is the house of M. Fleury. You didn't make a mistake," Mme Viénot said. "I think it is unlikely that you will find him at home at this hour, but you can try."

After an awkward moment, during which they did not explain why they wanted to pay a call on M. Fleury, she got on her bicycle and pedaled off down the street. Watching the figure on the bicycle get smaller and smaller, he said: "She's going to be soaked on the way home. Look at the sky."

"A hundred francs was probably enough," Barbara said. "In a place as small as this."

"It would reflect on her, in any case," he said.

"And if he isn't there, we'd have to explain to his wife."

"Let's skip it."

They bought stamps at the post office, and wondered, too late, if the postmistress could read the postcards they had just mailed to America. The woman who sold them a sack of plums to eat in their room may have been, as Mme Viénot said, a great gossip, but she did not gossip with them. They tried unsuccessfully to see through, over, or around several garden gates. With the houses that were directly on the street, shutters or lace curtains discouraged curiosity. They stood in the vestibule of the little church and peered in. Here there was no barrier but their own Protestant ignorance.

The Grande Rue was stopped by a little river that was a yard wide. Wild flags grew along the water's edge. A footbridge connected an old house on this side with its orchard on the other. They decided that the wooden shelter on the river bank was where the women brought their linen to be washed in running water.

"I don't suppose you could have a washing machine if you wanted to," he said.

"No, but you'd have other things," she said. "You'd live in a different way. You wouldn't want a washing machine."

The sky had turned a greenish black while they were standing there, and now a wind sprang up. Out over the meadows a great abstract drama was taking place. In the direction of Pontlevoy and Montrichard and Aignan, the bodies and souls of the unsaved fell under the sway of the powers of darkness, the portions of light in them were lost, and the world became that much poorer. In the direction of Herbault and St. Amand and Selommes, all glorious spirits assembled, the God of Light himself appeared, accompanied by the aeons and the perfected just ones. The angels supporting the world let go of their burden and everything fell in ruins. A tremendous conflagration consumed meadows and orchard, and on the very brink of the little river, a perfect separation of the powers of light and darkness took place. The kingdom of light was brought into a condition of completeness, all the grass bent the same way. Darkness should, from this time on, have been powerless.

"We'd better start home," Barbara said.

On the outskirts of the village they had to take shelter in a doorway. The rain came down in front of their faces like a curtain. At times they couldn't even see through it. Then the sky began to grow lighter and the rain slackened.

"If we had a car," he said, "it would be entirely different. We wouldn't feel cooped up. The house is damp and cold. The books accumulate on the table in our room and I read a few sentences and my mind gets tired of translating and having to look up words and begins to wander."

"A lot of it's our fault," she said, "for not speaking French."

"And part of it isn't our fault. It wasn't like this anywhere else. With time hanging heavy on our hands, we always seem to be hurrying, always about to be late to lunch or dinner. We ask for a double bed and nothing is done about it, and she says nothing *can* be done about it because of the lamp. What actually has the lamp got to do with it? We didn't ask for a lamp. Nothing is done about anything we ask for in the way of comfort or convenience. And neither is it refused. The hot water arrives while we're at dinner. The cook's bicycle is too frail for us to borrow, and we can't borrow hers because it has just been repaired. The buses and trains run at the wrong time, the taxi is expensive. George Ireland showed me a snapshot of the horse hitched up to a dog cart, but that was last summer. Now the horse is old and needed in the garden. When I try to find her to ask her about some arrangement, she's never anywhere. I don't even know where her room is."

"Did you hear her say 'I like your American custom of not shaking hands in the morning'?"

"They shake hands at *breakfast?*"

"Apparently."

"The cozy atmosphere of the breakfast table is a fabrication that we are supposed to accept and even contribute to," he went on, "as the other guests politely accept and support the fiction that Mme Viénot and her mother are the very cream of French society and lost nothing of importance when they lost their money."

"Perhaps they *are* the cream of French society," Barbara said.

"From the way Mme Viénot kowtows to Mme Carrère, I would say no. Mme Viénot is a social climber and a snob. And that's another thing. Yesterday evening before dinner, Mme Carrère asked the Canadian to call on them. In Paris."

"And did he accept?"

"He behaved like a spaniel that has just been petted on the head."

"Probably if you were French the Carrères would be very useful people to know."

"I found myself wondering whether—before they go on Monday—they would invite *us* to call on them," he said.

"Do you want to see the Carrères in Paris?"

"I don't care one way or the other."

"Our French isn't good enough," she said. "Besides, I don't think they do that sort of thing over here. It isn't reasonable to expect it of them."

"Who said anything about being reasonable? He gave Gagny his card, and I want him to do the same thing to us. And it isn't enough that he should invite us to call on him at his office. I want us to be invited to their home."

"We have nothing to say to them here. What point is there in carrying it any farther?"

"No point," he said. "There's no excuse for our ever seeing them again, except curiosity."

They saw that they were being stared at by a little boy in the open doorway of the house across the street.

"If they did ask us, would you go?"

"No," he said.

"It would be interesting to see their apartment," she said, and so, incriminating herself, sharing in his dubious desires, made him feel better about having them.

"They give me the creeps," he said. "Mme Carrère especially."

"What did she say that hurt your feelings?"

"Nothing."

"It isn't raining so hard," Barbara said.

He stepped out of the shelter of the doorway with his palm extended to the rain.

"We might as well be starting back or we'll be late again," he said.

He took off his coat and put it around her shoulders. As they went off down the street, she tried not to listen to what he was saying. In the mood he was in, he exaggerated, and his exaggerations gave rise to further exaggerations, and helplessly, without wanting to, analyzing and explaining and comparing one thing with another that had no relation to it, he got farther and farther from the truth.

They stopped to look at a pink oleander in a huge tub. The blossoms smelled like sugar and water.

"As soon as we're outside," he said, "in the garden or stopping to pick wildflowers along the road or like now—the moment we're off somewhere by ourselves, everything opens up like a fan. And as soon as we're indoors with them, it closes."

"We could go to Paris," she said.

"With the Canadian?"

"If you like."

"And be there for Bastille Day? That's a wonderful idea. We could run up to Paris and come back after two or three days."

"Or not come back," she said.

AT LUNCH Mme Viénot said: "We should leave the house by two o'clock."

But when two o'clock came, they were on the terrace, leaning against the stone balustrade, and she had not appeared.

"I'd go look for her," he said, "if it weren't so much like looking for a needle in a haystack."

"Don't talk so loud," Barbara said, glancing up at an open window directly above them.

"I'm not talking loud. I'm practically whispering."

"Your voice carries."

He noticed that she was wearing a cotton dress and said: "Are you going to be warm enough?"

"I meant to bring a sweater."

He jumped down and started across the terrace, and she called after him: "The cardigan."

He pushed the door open and saw a small elderly woman standing in an attitude of dramatic indecision beside the white columns that divided the drawing room in half. She was wearing a tailored suit with a high-necked silk blouse. A lorgnette hung by a black ribbon from her collar. Her hair was mouse-colored. Like the old ladies of his childhood she wore no rouge or lipstick. She saw him at the same moment that he saw her, and advanced to meet him, as if his sudden appearance had resolved the question that was troubling her.

"Straus-Muguet," she said.

He put out his hand and she took it. To his surprise, she knew his name. She had heard that he was staying in the house, and she had been hoping to meet him. "J'adore la jeunesse," she said.

He was not all that young; he was thirty-four; but there was no one else in the room that this remark could apply to, and so he was forced to conclude that she meant him. He looked into her eyes and found himself in another climate, the one he had been searching for, where the sun shines the whole day long, the prevailing wind is from the South, and the natives are friendly.

She was not from the village, he decided on the way upstairs. She was a lady, but a lady whose life had been lived in the country; a character out of Chekhov or Turgenev. Probably she belonged in one of the big country houses in the neighborhood and was a family friend—a lifelong friend of old Mme Bonenfant, who had come to call, to spend the afternoon in quiet reminiscences over their embroidery or their knitting, with tea and cake at the proper time, and, at parting, the brief exchange of confidences, the words of reassurance and continuing affection that would make it seem worth while, for both of them, to go on a little longer.

When he came back with the sweater, the drawing room was empty and Mme Viénot and the Canadian were standing on the terrace with Barbara. Walking at a good pace they covered the two kilometers to the concrete highway that followed the river all the way into Blois. The bus came almost immediately and was crammed with people.

"I'm afraid we won't get seats," Mme Viénot said. "But it's only a ten-minute ride."

There was hardly room to breathe inside the bus, and all the windows were closed. Harold stood with his arm around Barbara's waist, and craned his neck. His efforts to see out were defeated everywhere by heads, necks, and shoulders. It took him some time to determine which of the passengers was responsible for the suffocating animal odor that filled the whole bus. It was twenty-five minutes before they saw the outskirts of Blois.

Threading her way boldly between cyclists, Mme Viénot led them down the rue Denis Papin (inventor of the principle of the steam engine), through the Place Victor Hugo, up a long ramp, and then through a stone archway into the courtyard of the château, the glory of Blois. They saw the octagonal staircase, the chapel, and a splendid view, all without having to purchase tickets of admission. Then they followed her back down the ramp, through the crowded narrow streets, to a charcuterie, where she bought blood sausage, and then into the bicycle shop next door, where they saw a number of bicycles, none of which were for rent. They saw the courtyard of the ancient Hôtel d'Alluye, built by the treasurer of François premier, but did not quite manage to escape out onto the sidewalk before the concierge appeared. While Harold stood wondering if they should be there at all and if the concierge would be as unpleasant as she looked, Hector Gagny extracted fifty francs from his wallet and the threat was disposed of. Climbing a street of stairs, they saw the cathedral. There they separated. Gagny went off in search of a parfumerie, and Mme Viénot took the Americans to the door of the ration bureau and then departed herself to do some more shopping. They stood in line under a sign—*Personnes Isolées*—that had for them a poignancy it didn't have for those who were more at home in the French language. They could not get ration coupons because Harold had not thought to bring their passports.

When they emerged from the building, they saw that it was at one end of a long terrace planted in flower beds, with a view over the lower part of the city. Leaning against a stone balustrade, with his guidebook open in front of him, he started to read about the terrace where they now were.

"What's that?" Barbara asked.

He looked up. At the far end of the terrace a crowd had gathered. The singing came from that direction. They listened intently. It sounded like children's voices.

"It's probably something to do with Bastille Day," he said, and stuffed the guidebook in his raincoat pocket, and they hurried off down the gravel paths.

For tourists who fall in love with the country they are traveling in, charms of great potency are always at work. If there is a gala performance at the Opéra, they get the last two tickets. Someone runs calling and gesturing the whole length of the train to find them and return the purse that was left on a bench on the station platform. And again and again they are drawn, as if by wires, to the scene that they will never be able to forget as long as they live.

At first the Americans stood politely on the outskirts of the crowd, thinking that they had no right to be here. But then they worked their way in gradually, until at last they were clear inside.

The children, dressed all in white, had no leader, and did not need one. They had been preparing for this occasion for years. Their voices were very high, pure, on pitch, thoroughly drilled, and happy. Music heard in the open air is not like music in a concert hall. It was as if the singing came from one's own heart.

Remember what the lark sounds like, said the stones of the Bishop's Palace. *Try for perfection. . . .*

Try for joy, said the moss-stained fountain.

Do not be afraid to mark the contrasts if it is necessary, said the faded tricolor. *But do not let one voice dominate. . . . Remember that you are French. Remember that in no other country in the world do children have songs that are as beautiful and gay and unfading as these. . . .*

The exact sound of joy is what you must aim for. . . .

. . . of a pure conscience . . .

. . . of an enthusiastic heart . . .

"Oh, oh, oh," Harold exclaimed under his breath, as if he had just received a fatal wound.

Full of delight but still exact and careful and like one proud voice the children sang: "Qui n'avait jam-jam-jamais naviGUÉ!"

He looked at Barbara. They shook their heads in wonder.

"They must be very old songs," he whispered.

Turning, he studied the adults, dressed in somber colors and shabby suits, but attentive, critical, some of them probably with ears only for the singing of a particular child. They appeared to take the songs for granted. This is what it means to be French, he thought. It belongs with the red-white-and-blue flags and the careful enunciation and the look of intelligence in every eye and the red poppies growing in the wheat. These songs are their birthright, instead of "London Bridge Is Falling Down. . . ."

The children finished singing and marched off two by two, and the crowd parted to let in some little boys, who performed a ferocious staff dance in which nobody got hurt; and then six miniature couples, who marched into the open space and formed a circle. The boys had on straw hats, blue smocks, and trousers that were too large for them. The little girls wore white caps and skirts that dragged the ground and in some instances had to be held up with a safety pin. At a signal from an emaciated man with a violin, the gavotte began. In the patterns of movement, and quite apart from the grave self-conscious children who danced, there was a gallantry that was explicitly sexual, an invitation now mocked, now welcomed openly. But because they were only eight-year-olds, the invitation to love was like a melody transposed from its original key and only half recognizable. Suddenly he turned and worked his way blindly toward the outer edge of the crowd. Barbara followed him out into the open, where a group of fifteen-year-old girls in diaphanous costumes waited to go on. If the sight of a foreigner wiping his eyes with his handkerchief interested them, they did not show it. They stretched and bent over, practicing, or examined the blackened soles of their feet, or walked about in twos and threes. He saw that Barbara was looking at him anxiously and tried to explain and found he could not speak. Again he had to take his handkerchief out.

"There's Mme Viénot," Barbara said.

Turning, he saw her hurrying toward them between the flower beds. Ignoring his condition, she said: "M. and Mme Carrère are waiting in the pâtisserie," and hurried them off down the gravel path.

The pastry shop was down below, in the rue de Commerce, and it was crowded and noisy. Cutting her way through clots of people, squeezing between tables, frustrating waitresses with trays, Mme Viénot arrived at the large round table in the rear of the establishment where M. and Mme Carrère and Mme Bonenfant were waiting, their serenity in marked contrast to the general noise and confusion. Mme Carrère invited Harold and Barbara to sit down, and then she allowed her eyes to roam over the room, as if something were about to happen of so important a nature that talk was not necessary. Mme Bonenfant asked if they had found Blois a beautiful city and was pleased when he said that they preferred Brenodville. The village was charming, she agreed; very old, and just the way a village should be; she herself had great affection for it. Mme Viénot went off in search of M. Gagny, and for the next ten minutes M. Carrère devoted himself to the task of capturing a busboy and ordering a carafe of "fresh" water. Human chatter hung in the air like mist over a pond.

They saw that Mme Viénot had returned, with the Canadian. She stopped to confer with the proprietress and he came straight back to their table. He had found the parfumerie, he explained as he sat down, but it did not have the kind of perfume his mother had asked him to get for her. The proprietress of the pâtisserie nodded, shrugged, and seemed in no way concerned about what Mme Viénot was saying to her. Arriving at the table in the rear, Mme Viénot said: "She's going to send someone to take our order." She sat down, glanced at her watch nervously, and said: "The Brenodville bus leaves at seven minutes to six and it is now after five," and then explained to the Americans that the pâtisserie was well known.

The water arrived, was tested, was found to be both cool and fresh. They sat sipping it until a waitress came to find out what they wanted. This required a good five minutes of animated conversation to decide. The names meant nothing to Barbara and Harold, and since they could not decide for themselves, Mme Carrère acted for them; Mme Rhodes should have *demi-chocolat* et *demi-vanille* and M. Rhodes chocolat-praliné. The ices arrived, and with them a plate of pâtisseries—cream puffs in the shape of a cornucopia, strawberry tarts, little cakes that were rectangular, diamond-shaped, or in layers, with a soft filling of chocolate, or with almond paste or whipped cream. The enthusiasm of the Americans was gratifying to the French, who agreed among themselves that the pâtisseries, though naturally not what they had been before the war, were acceptable. "If you consider that they have not been made with white flour," M. Carrère said, "and that the ices have to be flavored with saccharine . . ."

Harold was conscious of a genuine cordiality in the faces around the table. They were being taken in, it seemed; he and Barbara were being initiated into the true religion of France.

The *addition*, on a plate, was placed in front of M. Carrère, who motioned to Harold to put his wallet away. In America, he said, he had been treated everywhere with such extraordinary kindness. He was grateful for this opportunity of paying it back.

There was a crowd waiting in the rue Denis Papin for the bus, but they managed to get seats. Six o'clock came and nothing happened; the driver was outside stowing bicycles away on the roof. More people kept boarding the bus until the aisle was blocked. Sitting beside Barbara, with his hand in hers, Harold saw Gagny get up and give his seat to a colored nun, but it did not occur to him to follow this example, and he was hardly aware of when the bus started at last. The children's voices, high, clear, and only half human, took him far outside his ordinary self. He felt as if he were floating on the end of a long kite string, the other end of which was held by the hand that was, in actuality, touching his hand. He did not remember anything of the ride home.

WHEN THE HOUSEHOLD ASSEMBLED before dinner, Harold saw that the elderly woman who had introduced herself to him earlier in the afternoon was still here, and he was pleased for her sake that she had been asked to stay and eat with them. In that first glimpse of her, standing beside the white columns in the drawing room, she had seemed uneasy and as if she was not sure of her welcome. He sat down beside her now, ready to take up where they had left off. She leaned toward him and confessed that it was the regret of her life that she had never learned English. She had a nephew—or a godson, he couldn't make out which—living in America, she said, and she longed to go there. Harold began to talk to her about New York City, in French, and after a minute or two she shook her head. He smiled and sat back in his chair. Her answering smile said that though they were prevented from conversing, they needn't let that stand in the way of their being friends. He turned his head and listened to what Mme Bonenfant was saying to M. Carrère.

" . . . To them the entry into Paris was a perfectly agreeable occasion, and they insisted on showing us snapshots. They could see no reason why we shouldn't enjoy looking at them."

"The attitude is characteristic," M. Carrère said. "And extraordinary, if you think how often their own country has been invaded. . . . I had an experience . . ."

In his mind Harold still heard the children's voices. Mme Viénot addressed a remark to him, which had to be repeated before he could answer it. He noticed that Mme Straus-Muguet was wearing a little heart encrusted with tiny diamonds, on a fine gold chain. So appropriate for her.

M. Carrère's experience was that a Nazi colonel had sent for him, knowing that he was ill and would have to get up out of bed to come, and had then kept him waiting for over an hour in his presence while he engaged in chit-chat with another officer. But then he committed an error; he remarked on the general lack of cultivation of the French people and the fact that so few of them knew German. With one sentence, in the very best *hoch Deutsch*, M. Carrère had reduced him to confusion.

"I have a friend," Mme Viénot said, "who had a little dog she was very fond of. And the German officers who were quartered in her house were correct in every way, and most courteous to her, until the day they left, when one of them picked the little dog up right in front of her eyes and hurled it against the marble floor, killing it instantly."

It's their subject, Harold thought. This is what they are talking about, everywhere. This is what I would be talking about if I were a Frenchman.

Mme Straus-Muguet described how, standing at the window of her apartment overlooking the Etoile, peering through the slits of the iron shutter, with the tears running down her face, she had watched the parade that she thought would never end. "Quelle horreur!" she exclaimed with a shiver, and Harold checked off the first of a whole series of mistaken ideas about her. She was not a character out of Turgenev or Chekhov. Her life had not been passed in isolation in the country but at the center of things, in Paris. She had been present, she said—General Weygand had invited her to accompany him to the ceremony at the Invalides, when the bronze sarcophagus of Napoléon II, which the Nazis had taken from its crypt in Vienna, was placed beside the red porphyry tomb of his father, Napoléon Ier.

The room was silent, the faces reflecting each in its own way the harsh wisdom of history.

Since she was a friend of General Weygand, it was not likely that she was socially unsure in the present company, Harold said to himself. He must have been mistaken. He turned to Mme Viénot and explained that they were thinking of going up to Paris with M. Gagny in the morning, and would probably return on Friday. To his surprise, this plan met with her enthusiastic approval. He asked if they should pack their clothes, books, and whatever they were not taking with them, so that the suitcases could be removed from their room during the three days they would be gone.

"That won't be necessary," Mme Viénot said, and he took this to mean that they would not be charged during their absence, and was relieved that this delicate matter had been settled without his having to go into it. For the first time, he found himself liking her.

She offered to telephone the hotel where they were planning to stay, and make a reservation for them. As she went toward the hall, M. Carrère called out the telephone number. The hotel was around the corner from their old house, he said, and he knew it well. During the war it had been occupied by German officers.

Mme Bonenfant reminded Barbara that there was to be an illumination on the night of July 14, and Harold took out his financial notebook and wrote down the route that Mme Carrère advised them to follow: if they began with the Place de la Concorde and the Madeleine, and then went on to the Place de l'Opéra, and then to the Place du Théâtre Français and the Comédie Française, with its lovely lamps, and then to the Louvre, and finally Notre Dame reflected in the river, they would see all the great monuments, the city at its most ravishing.

They got up and went in to dinner, and something that Mme Straus-Muguet said during the first course made Harold realize at last that she was not a caller but a paying guest like them. He looked across the table at her, at the winking reflections of the little diamond-encrusted heart, and thought what a pity it was that she should have come to stay at the château just as they were leaving.

When the company left the dining room, Mme Straus-Muguet excused herself and went upstairs and brought back down with her a box of *diamonoes*. She asked Harold if he knew this delightful game and he shook his head.

"I take it with me everywhere I go," she said.

Mme Bonenfant removed the cover from the little round table in the center of the petit salon, and the ivory counters were dumped onto the green felt center. While Mme Straus-Muguet was explaining the rules of the game to Barbara, Mme Viénot captured M. Carrère and then indicated the place beside her on the sofa where Harold was to sit.

The Canadian, Mme Carrère, Mme Bonenfant, Barbara, and Mme Straus-Muguet sat down at the table and commenced playing. The game, a marriage of dominoes and anagrams, was agreeable and rather noisy. M. Carrère excused himself and went upstairs to read in bed.

Mme Viénot, reclining against the sofa cushions with her hand to her temple, defended the art of conversation. "The young people of today are very different from my generation," she said, setting Harold a theme to develop, a subject to embroider, as inclination or experience prompted. "They are serious-minded and idealistic, and concerned about the future. My daughter's husband works until eleven or twelve every night at his office in the Ministry and Suzanne sits at home and knits for the children. At their age, my life was made up entirely of parties and balls. Nobody thought about the future. We were having too good a time."

She sat up and rearranged the pillows. Her face was now disturbingly close to his. He shifted his position.

"My nephew maintains that we were a perverted generation," Mme Viénot said cheerfully, "and I dare say he is right. All we cared about was excitement. . . ."

Though he was prevented from going toward the gaiety in the center of the room, he was aware that Mme Carrère had come out of her shell at last and, pleased with the extent of Barbara's vocabulary, was coaching her.

"I'm no good at anything that has to do with words," the Canadian said mournfully. "When something funny happens to me, I never can put it in a letter. I have to save it all up until I go home."

Mme Bonenfant was slower still, and kept the others waiting, and had to be shown where her pieces would fit into the meandering diagram. Mme Straus-Muguet was quick as lightning, and when Barbara completed a word, she complimented her, seized her hand, called her "chérie," taught her an idiom to go with the word, and put down a counter of her own—all in thirty seconds.

"MME CARRÈRE loves words," Barbara said later as she was transferring four white shirts from the armoire to an open suitcase. "Any kind of abstraction. Anything sufficiently intellectual that she can apply her mind to it. When we started to play that game she became a different person."

"I saw that she was. Gagny asked us to have lunch with him on Thursday at a bistro he goes to. He said it was quite near our hotel."

"Did you say we would?"

He shook his head. "I left it up in the air. I wasn't sure that was what we'd most want to be doing."

"Did you enjoy your conversation with Mme Viénot?"

"It was interesting. I had a different feeling about the house tonight. And the people. I'm glad we decided not to leave."

"So am I."

"All in all, it's been a nice day."

"Very."

He pulled the covers back and jumped into bed.

"They seemed very pleased with us when I said we were thinking of going up to Paris. . . . As if we were precocious children who had suddenly grasped an idea that they would have supposed was too old for us."

"I expect they'd all like to be going up to Paris in the morning," Barbara said.

"Or as if we had found the answer to a riddle. Or managed to bring a long-drawn-out parlor game to an end."

Chapter 7

The Canadian did not appear at breakfast, and Mme Viénot did not offer any explanation of why he was not coming, but neither did she appear to be surprised, so he must have spoken to her. Either his threats had been idle and he had no friends in Paris who were waiting for him with open arms, or else he was avoiding a long train journey in their company. If he was, they did not really care. They were too lighthearted, as they sipped at their peculiar coffee and concealed the taste of the bread with marmalade, to care about anything but their own plans. They were starting on a train journey across an entirely new part of France. They were going to have to speak French with all kinds of strangers, some of whom might temporarily become their friends. They were going to change trains in Orléans, and at the end of their journey was Paris on Bastille Day. They could hardly believe their good fortune.

The taxi was old, and the woman who sat behind the wheel looked like a man disguised as a woman. Mme Viénot stood in the open doorway and waved to them until they were out of sight around the corner of the house. As the taxi turned into the public road, they looked back but they could not see the house from here. He felt the bulge in his inside coat pocket: passports, wallet, traveler's checks. He covered Barbara's gloved hand with his bare hand, and leaned back in the seat. "This is more like it," he said.

"JUST WHERE is the Hôtel Vouillemont?" Harold said when they were out in the street in front of the Gare d'Austerlitz.

Barbara didn't know.

He managed to keep from saying: "How can you not know where it is when you spent two whole weeks there?" by saying instead: "I should have asked Mme Viénot." But she was aware of his suppressed impatience with her, and sorry that she couldn't produce this one piece of helpful information for him when he, who had never been to Europe before, had got them in and out of so many hotels and railroad stations. Actually she could have found it all by herself, simply by retracing her steps. It was the only way she ever found her way back to some place she didn't know the location of. Back through three years of being married to him, and two years of working in New York, to the day she graduated from college, and from there back to the day she sat watching her mother and Mrs. Evans sewing name tapes on the piles of new clothes that were going off with her to boarding school, and then back to the time when the walls of her room were covered with pictures of horses, and so finally to the moment when they were leaving the Hôtel Vouillemont to go to the boat train—which was, after all, only what other people do, she thought; only they do it in their minds, in large jumps, and she had to do it literally.

She tried, anyway. She thought very carefully and then said: "I think it's not far from the Louvre."

They went into the Métro station, and there he found an electrified map and began to study it.

Also, she thought, when she was here before, it was with her father, who had an acutely developed sense of geography and never got lost in strange cities, any more than in the woods. Instead of trying to figure out for themselves where they were, they always stood and waited for him to make up his mind which was north, south, east, and west. As soon as he had arrived at the points of the compass, he started off and they followed, talking among themselves and embroidering on old jokes and keeping an eye on him without difficulty even in crowds because he was half a head taller than anybody else.

Harold pushed a button, lights flashed, and he announced: "We change trains at Bastille."

With a sense that they were journeying through history, they climbed the steps to the platform. They were delighted with the beautiful little toy train, all windows and bright colors and so different from the subway in New York. They changed at Bastille and got off at Louvre and came up out onto the sidewalk. The big forbidding gray building on their left was the Louvre, Barbara was positive, but there was no dancing in the street in front of it. A short distance away, they saw another building with a sign *Louvre* on it, but that turned out to be a department store. It was closed. All the shops were closed. Paris was as empty and quiet as New York on a Sunday morning. They listened. No sound of distant music came from the side streets. Neither did a taxi. Their suitcases grew heavier with each block, and at the first sidewalk café they sat down to rest. A waiter appeared, and Harold ordered two glasses of red wine. When he had drunk his, he got up and went inside. The interior of the café was gloomy and ill-lit, and he was glad he had left Barbara outside. It was clearly a tough joint. He asked if he could see the telephone directory and discovered that there was more than one, and that they were compiled according to principles he didn't understand, and in that poor light the Hôtel Vouillemont did not seem to be listed in any of them. So he appealed to the kindness of Madame la Patronne, who left the bar untended and came over to the shelf of telephone books and looked with him.

"The Hôtel Vouillemont?" she called out, to the three men who were standing at the bar.

"In the rue Boissy d'Anglas," Harold said.

"The rue Boissy d'Anglas . . ."

"The rue Boissy d'Anglas?"

"The rue Boissy d'Anglas."

One of them remembered suddenly; it was in the sixteenth arrondissement.

"No, you are thinking of the rue Boissière," the waiter said. "I used to help my cousin deliver packages for a shop in the sixteenth arrondissement, and I know the quarter well. There is no Hôtel Vouillemont."

The three men left their drinks and came over and started thumbing through the telephone directories. The waiter joined them. "Ah!" he exclaimed. "Here it is. The Hôtel Vouillemont . . . It's in the rue Boissy d'Anglas."

"And where is that?" Harold asked.

The waiter peered at the directory and said: "The eighth arrondissement. You got off too soon. You should have descended at Concorde."

"Is that far from here?"

They all five assured him that he could walk there.

"But with suitcases?"

"In that case," Madame said, "you would do well to return to the Métro station."

He shook hands all around, hesitated, and then took a chance. It didn't work; they thanked him politely but declined the invitation to have a glass of wine with him. So his instinct must have been wrong.

"Is there any way that one can call a taxi?" he asked.

The waiter went to the door with him and showed him which direction they must go to find a taxi stand. Harold shook hands with him again, and then turned to Barbara. "We should have descended at Concorde," he said, and picked up the suitcases. "It's miles from here."

I: *Leo and Virgo*

The taxi driver knew exactly where the Hôtel Vouillemont was, and so they could sit back and not worry. They peered through the dirty windows at Paris. The unfamiliar streets had familiar names—the rue Jean-Jacques Rousseau; the rue Marengo. They caught a glimpse down a long avenue of the familiar façade of the Opéra. The arcades of the rue de Rivoli were deserted, and so were the public gardens on the other side of the street. So was the Place de la Concorde. The sky over the fountains and the Egyptian obelisk was cold and gray. The driver pointed out the American Embassy to them, and then they were in a dark, narrow street. The taxi stopped.

"He's made a mistake," Barbara said. "This isn't it."

"It says 'Hôtel Vouillemont' on the brass plate," Harold said, reaching for his wallet. And then, though he disliked arguments, he got into one with the taxi driver. Mme Viénot had said he must refuse to pay more than the amount on the meter. The driver showed him a chart and explained that it was the amount on the chart he must pay, not the amount on the meter. Harold suggested that they go inside and settle the matter there. The driver got out and followed him into the hotel, but declined to help with the suitcases. To Harold's surprise, the concierge sided with the driver, against Mme Viénot.

Still not sure they hadn't cheated him, he paid the driver what it said on the chart and turned back to the concierge's desk. If it turned out that the concierge was dishonest, he was not going to like staying at the Hôtel Vouillemont. He studied the man's face, and the face declined to say whether the person it belonged to was honest or dishonest.

While he was registering, Barbara stood looking around her at the lobby. She could not even say, as people so often do of some place they knew as a child, that it was much smaller than she remembered, because she didn't remember a thing she saw. She wondered if, all these years, she could have misremembered the name of the hotel they stayed in. It was not until they were in the elevator, with their suitcases, that she knew suddenly that they were in the right hotel after all. She remembered the glass elevator. No other hotel in the world had one like it. It was right out in the center of the lobby, and it had a red plush sofa you could sit down on. As they rose through the ceiling, the past was for a moment superimposed on the present, and she had a wonderful feeling of lightness—as if she were rising through water up to the surface and sunshine and air.

Their room was warm, and when they turned on the faucets in the bathroom, hot water came gushing out of the faucet marked *chaud*. They filled the tub to the brim and had a bath, and dressed, and went off down the street to have lunch at a restaurant that Barbara remembered the name of: Tante Louise. Like the glass elevator, the restaurant hadn't changed. After lunch they strolled. Harold stopped at a kiosk and bought a map-book of Paris by arrondissements, so that he wouldn't ever again be caught not knowing where he was and how to get to where he wanted to go. They looked in the windows of the shops in the rue St. Honoré, full of beautiful gloves and scarves, and purses that probably cost a fortune.

They were in Paris at last, and aware that they should have been happy, but there was no indication anywhere that Paris was happy. No dancing in the streets, no singing, no decorations, no flags, even. They discovered the Madeleine and the American Express and Maxim's, none of which gave off any effervescence of gaiety, and finally, toward the end of the afternoon, they gave up searching for Paris on Bastille Day, since it appeared to be only an idea in their minds, and went back to their hotel.

That evening, before it was quite dark, they set off to see the illuminations. They were encouraged when they saw that the streets had begun to fill up with people. They went first to the Place de la Concorde, and admired the light-soaked fountains and the flood-lighted twin buildings. With lights trained on it, the Madeleine, at the end of the rue Royale, no longer looked quite so gloomy and Roman. They were about to start off on the route that Mme Carrère had recommended, when a skyrocket exploded and long yellow ribbons of light fell down the sky. So, instead, they joined the throngs of people hurrying toward the river. For half an hour they stood in the middle of the Pont de la Concorde, looking now at the fireworks and now at the upraised, expectant French faces all around them. Bouquet after bouquet of colored lights exploded in the sky and in the black water. They decided that, rather than retrace their steps, they would reverse the directions Mme Carrère had given them. This turned out to be a mistake. They rushed here and there, got lost, doubled back on their route, and wasted a good deal of time changing trains in the Métro. And they never did see the lighted lamps of the Comédie Française.

At one o'clock, exhaustion claimed them. They were lost again, and a long way from home. They asked directions of a gendarme, who hurried them into a Métro station just in time to catch the last train back to Concorde.

THE ADDRESS of the editorial officers of *La Femme Elégante* turned out to be a courtyard, and the entrance was up a short flight of steps. They gave the receptionist their name and, as they waited for Sabine Viénot to appear, Harold's eyes roamed around the small foyer, trying to make out something, anything, from the little he saw—nobly proportioned doors with heavy molding painted dove gray, nondescript lighting fixtures, and dove-gray carpet. When Mme Viénot spoke of her daughter's career, her tone of voice suggested that she was at the forefront of her profession. But then she had showed them some of her daughter's work—thumbnail sketches of dress patterns buried in the back of the magazine. The girl who came through the doorway and shook hands with them was very slight and pale and young, with observant blue eyes and brown hair and a high, domed forehead, like the French queens in the *Petit Larousse*.

Harold started to explain who they were and she said that she knew; her mother had written to her about them. "You can speak English if you prefer," she said. "I speak it badly but— They are all well in the country?"

Barbara nodded.

"I'm afraid you haven't had very nice weather. It has been cold and rainy here, also. You arrived in Paris when?"

"Yesterday," Barbara said.

"But we didn't see any dancing in the streets," Harold said. "Last night at midnight we saw a crowd of people singing and marching in the square in front of Notre Dame, but they were Communists, I think. Anyway, there was no dancing.

"In Montmartre you would have seen it, perhaps," the French girl said. "Or the Place Pigalle."

They couldn't think what to say next.

"Mother has written how much she enjoyed having you with her," the French girl said.

"We are returning to Brenodville tomorrow," Harold said, "and your mother asked us to let you know the train we are taking. She thought you might also be intending to—"

"I may be going down to the country tomorrow," the French girl said thoughtfully. "I don't know yet."

"We're taking the four o'clock train," he said. "Your mother suggested that we might all three take one taxi from Blois."

"That is very kind of you. Perhaps I could telephone you tomorrow morning. You are staying where?"

"It's quite near here, actually." He tore a leaf out of his financial diary, wrote down the name of their hotel, and held it out to her. She glanced at the slip of paper but did not take it from him. They shook hands, and then she was gone.

Standing on the sidewalk, waiting for the flow of traffic to stop so they could cross over, he said: "I thought at first she was like her mother—like what Mme Viénot was at that age. But she isn't."

"Not at all," Barbara said.

"Her voice made me realize that she wasn't."

"She has a lovely voice—so light. And silvery."

"She has a charming voice. Something of the French intonation carries over into her English, of course. But it's more than that, I think. It's an amused voice. It has a slight suggestion of humor, at no one's expense. As if she had learned to see things with a clarity that—that was often in excess of whatever need there was for seeing things clearly. And the residue had turned into something like amusement."

"But she didn't ask us to lunch."

"I know."

They went to the Guaranty Trust Company and were directed to the little upstairs room where their mail was handed to them.

"So what do we do now?" Barbara asked when they were outside again.

He looked at his watch. They had spent a considerable part of their first twenty-four hours in Paris walking the streets. He was dog-tired, his feet hurt, and Notre Dame in daylight faced the wrong way. For the moment, they were satiated with looking, and ready to be with someone they knew, it didn't matter how slightly, so long as they could talk about what they had seen, ask questions, and feel that they were a part of the intense sociability that they were aware of everywhere around them. Paris on the day after Bastille Day was not a deserted city. Also the sun was shining, and it was warm; it was like summer, and that lifted their spirits.

He said: "What about having lunch with Gagny at that bistro he told us about?"

"But we don't know where it is."

"Rue de Castellane." He consulted the plan of Paris by arrondissements. "It's somewhere behind the Madeleine . . . L17." He turned the pages. "Here it is. See?"

She pretended to look at the place he pointed out to her on the map, and then said: "If you're sure it's not too far."

The rue de Castellane proved to be farther than it appeared to be on the map, and when they got there, they found two, possibly three, eating places that answered to Gagny's description. Also, they were not very clear in their minds about the distinction between a bistro and a restaurant. They walked back and forth, peering at the curtained windows and trying to decide. They took a chance on one, the smallest. Gagny had said that it was a hangout of doubtful characters, and that there was sometimes brawling. The bistro was very quiet, and it looked respectable. They were shown to the last free table. Harold ordered an apéritif, and they settled down to read their mail from home, unaware that they were attracting a certain amount of attention from the men who were standing at the bar. Thugs and thieves do not, of course, wear funny hats or emblems in their buttonholes, like Lions and Elks, and some types of human behavior have to be explained before they are at all noticeable. The bistro was what Hector Gagny had said it was. In her letter about him, the cousin of the Canadian Ambassador failed to inform Mme Viénot of something that she happened to know, and that he didn't know she knew. It was in his folder in the Embassy files: he had a taste for low company. He enjoyed watching heated arguments, stage after stage of intricate insult, so stylized and at the same time so personal, all leading up to the point where the angry arguers could have exchanged blows—and never did. He also enjoyed being the unengaged spectator to situations in which the active participants must feel one another out. His eyes darting back and forth between their eyes, he measured accurately the risk taken, and then calculated enviously the chance of success.

In places the police knew about, Gagny never disguised his

education, or pretended to be anything but an observer. He sat, well dressed, well bred, quiet, and conspicuous, with his glass of wine in front of him, until the *type* who had been eying him for some time disengaged himself from the others and wandered over and was invited to sit down at his table.

"We're terribly restricted, you know," Gagny would tell the character with franc notes to be converted into dollars or, if worst came to worst, pounds sterling. "I mean to say, thirty-five pounds is all we're allowed to take out of England." Or, as he handed the pornographic postcards back to their owner: "Why do the men all have their shoes and socks on?" The *type*, a cigarette hanging from his lips and sometimes a question hanging in his eyes, would begin to talk. After a moment or two, Gagny would interrupt him politely in order to signal to the waiter to bring another glass.

In exchange for the glimpses of high life that he offered casually, not too much or too many at a time, he himself was permitted glimpses into the long corridor leading down, where crimes are committed for not very much money, or out of boredom, or because the line between feeling and action has become blurred; where the gendarme is the common enemy, and nobody knows the answer to a simple question, and danger is ever-present, the oxygen in the wine-smelling, smoke-filled air.

Only in France did Gagny allow himself this sort of diversion. In London it was not safe. He might be followed. His name was in the telephone directory. And he might have the bad luck to run into some acquaintance who also had a taste for low company.

Also, it was a matter of the Latin sensibility as compared with Anglo-Saxon. Oftener than not in Paris the *type* proved to be gentle, amiable, confused and more than willing (though the occasion for this had never presented itself) to pass over into the world of commonplace respectability. His education may have been sordid, pragmatic, and one-sided, but at least it had taught him how to stay alive, and he had a story to tell, invariably. Gagny had a story to tell, too, but he refrained from telling it. The *types* understood this. They were responsive, they understood many things—states of feeling, human needs, gradations of pleasure, complexities of motive—that people of good breeding unfortunately do not.

The sense of unreality—the dreadful recognition that he belonged not to the white race but to the pink or gray—that often came over him at official functions, among people of the highest importance and social distinction, he never experienced in any place where there was sawdust on the floor. He enjoyed the tribute that was paid to his social superiority (sometimes it only lasted a second, but it was there, nevertheless—a flicker of incredulity that he should be talking to them) and also their moment of vanity, encouraged by his lack of condescension. Though their fingernails were dirty and their clothes had been bought and worn by somebody else, they thought well of themselves; they were not apologetic. As a rule they understood perfectly what he wanted of them, and when he had checked the *addition* and put the change in his pocket notebook, they clapped him on the shoulder, smiling at his way of doing business, and went back to theirs. Now and then, misunderstanding, they offered him their friendship—were ready to throw in their lot, such as it was, with his, whatever that might prove to be. And when this offer was not accepted, they became surly or abusive, and it was a problem to get rid of them.

The Americans passed their letters back and forth, and when they were all read, Harold glanced at his watch again and said: "It looks as if he isn't coming."

Before he could catch the eye of the waitress, they saw Gagny, and saw that he had already seen them, but it was a very different Gagny from the one they had known in the country—erect and handsome and as wildly happy as if he had just succeeded in extricating himself from a long-standing love affair with a woman ten years older than he, and very demanding, given to emotional scenes, threats, tears, accusations that could only be answered in bed. He was delighted that they had kept their engagement with him. He had checked in at his hotel, he said, and come straight here, hoping to find them. They had been missed, he told them cheerfully. Mme Viénot and Mme Carrère had agreed that the house was not the same without the Americans. Then, seeing the look of surprise on their faces, he said: "You can believe me. I never make anything up." He surveyed the bar, in one fleeting glance, and for this afternoon renounced its interesting possibilities.

The waitress came and stood beside the table.

"Let me order for you," Gagny said, "since I know the place. And this is *my* lunch."

"Oh no it's not!" Harold cried.

"Oh yes it is!"

By the time the pâté arrived, they were all three talking at once, exchanging confidences, asking questions, being funny. The Americans found it a great relief to confide to someone their feelings about staying at the château, and who was in a better position to understand what they meant than someone who had seen them floundering? But if they had only known what he was really like . . .

He kept saying "Well exactly!" and they kept saying "I know. I know." They talked steadily through course after course. They finished the carafe of red wine and Gagny ordered a second, and cognac after that. The bistro was empty when they finally pushed their chairs back from the table. In spite of the adverse exchange, Gagny seized the check and would not hear of any other arrangement.

The sun was shining in the street outside. Gagny had an errand to do in the rue St. Honoré, and they walked with him as far as the rue Boissy d'Anglas. He was their favorite friend, and they felt sure that he was just as fond of them, but when the moment came for exchanging addresses, they were all three silent.

Standing on the street corner, Gagny smiled at the blue sky and then at them, and said: "You don't happen to know where Guerlain is, by any chance?"

"Just one moment," Harold said, "I'll look it up." He brought out his plan of Paris and began thumbing the pages. " 'Théâtres et spectacles . . . cabarets artistiques . . . cinémas . . .' "

"You won't find it in there," Gagny said.

" 'Cultes,' " Harold read. " 'Eglises Catholiques . . . Chapelles Catholiques Etrangères . . . Rite Melchite Grec' . . . Certainly it's in here. 'Eglises Luthériennes . . . Eglises réformées de France . . . Eglises protestantes étrangères . . . Science Chrétienne . . . Eglise Adventiste . . . Eglises Baptistes . . . Eglises Orthodoxes . . . Culte Israélite, Synagogues . . . Culte Mahométan, Mosquée . . . Facultés, Ecoles Supérieures . . .' "

Barbara put a restraining hand on his arm, and he looked up and saw that Gagny was ten feet away, in lively conversation with an English couple—friends, obviously—who had just arrived in Paris, by car, they said, from the south of France. They were very brown.

After a few minutes they said good-by and went off down the street. Gagny rejoined Harold and Barbara and said with a note of pure wonder in his voice: "They had beautiful weather the whole time they were on the Riviera."

"We came up out of the Métro," Harold said earnestly, all that wine having caught up with him at last, "and there it was right in front of us, with searchlights trained on the flying buttresses, and it was facing the *opposite* direction from Cleopatra's Needle and the Place de la Concorde."

"You're sure about that?" Gagny said, looking at him affectionately.

"Positive," Harold said.

"Well, old chap, all I can say is, there's something wrong somewhere."

"*Terribly* wrong," Harold said.

"I'd love to help you straighten it out," Gagny said. "But not this afternoon. I've got to buy perfume for my mother. Cheerio."

THEY SPENT all Friday morning at the Louvre and had lunch sitting on the sidewalk looking at the Comédie Française, but it was broad daylight and the lamps were not lighted; it was impossible to imagine what they were like at night. By not doing what they were told to do they had missed their one chance of having this beautiful experience. There was not going to be another illumination the whole rest of the summer.

They went back to the Louvre, and barely left time to check out of their hotel and get to the station. Sabine Viénot had not called, and they did not see her on the station platform. On the train they amused themselves by filling two pages of the financial diary with a list of things they would like to steal from the Louvre. Harold began with a Romanesque statue of the Queen of Sheba, and then took *The Lacemaker* by Vermeer, and *Lot and His Daughters* by Lucas van Leyden, and some panels by Giotto. Barbara took a fragment of a Greek statue—the lower half of a woman's body—and a section of the frieze of the Parthenon, and a Bronzino portrait. He took a Velasquez, a Goya, a Murillo, some Fra Angelico panels, La Belle Ferronière, and a fragment of a horse's head. She took two Rembrandts, a Goya, an El Greco crucifixion, and a Bruegel winter scene. . . . And so on and so on, as the shadows outside the train window grew longer and longer. When the compartment began to seem oppressive, they stood in the crowded corridor for a while. They saw a church spire that was like the little church in Brenodville, and here and there on the line of hills a big country house half hidden by trees, and sometimes they saw the sky reflected in a river. When they grew tired of standing, they ground out their cigarettes and went back into their compartment and read. From time to time they raised their eyes to observe the other passengers or the sunset.

Mme Viénot had said that she was expecting some relatives on Friday, and would Harold look around for them when he got off the train? But there was no one in the railway station in Blois who appeared uncertain about where he was going or to be looking for two Americans. The taxi brought them by a back road through the forest instead of by the highway along the river, and this reminded Harold of something. "We thought they would come from the direction of the highway," Mme. Bonenfant had said, "and they came through the forest instead." He turned and looked back. There were no Germans in the forest now, but would it ever be free of them? Was that why the gate was kept locked?

It was just getting dark when they turned into the drive and saw the lights of the house. Leaving their suitcases in the hall, they walked past the screen and into the drawing room. Mme Viénot and her mother and M. and Mme Carrère and Mme Straus-Muguet were all sitting around the little table in front of the fireplace. Seeing their faces light up with pleasure and expectancy, Harold thought: Why, it's almost as if we had come home. . . .

"We've been waiting dinner for you," Mme Viénot said as she shook hands with them. "How did you like Paris?"

"Did anyone ever not like Paris?" Harold said.

"And you were comfortable at the Vouillemont?"

He laughed. "Once we found it, we were comfortable," he said.

"And the weather?"

"The weather was beautiful."

"Sabine telephoned this evening," Mme Viénot said, on the way into the dining room. "She tried to reach you, it seems, after you had gone. I'm afraid she does not have a very exact idea of time."

"But she wasn't on the train with us? We looked for her—"

"She is coming next week end instead," Mme Viénot said as he drew her chair out for her. "I hope you didn't give yourself any anxiety on her account?"

He shook his head.

"She enjoyed meeting you," Mme Viénot said.

"We enjoyed meeting her," he said, and then, since she seemed to be waiting for something more: "She's charming."

Mme Viénot smiled and unfolded her napkin.

He noticed that there were two people handing the soup plates around the table—Thérèse and a boy of seventeen or eighteen, in a white coat, with thick glasses and slicked-down hair. His large hands were very clean but looked like raw meat. He served unskillfully, in an agony of shyness, and Harold wondered if Mme Viénot had added a farm boy to her staff.

As always, he could speak better when he was sure he had an audience. ". . . There we were in the Métro," he said, "with no idea of what station to get off at, or what arrondissement our hotel was in."

"I should have told you," Mme Viénot said. "I'm so sorry. And this time you didn't have M. Fleury to take you there."

"Barbara thought it was somewhere near the Louvre—"

"Oh dear no! You should have descended at Concorde."

"So we discovered. But we got off at the Louvre, instead, and walked two or three blocks until we came to a sidewalk café, and the waiter showed me where the telephone books were, but there were so many and I couldn't make head nor tail of them, so he and the proprietress and everybody there dropped what they were doing and thumbed through telephone directories and finally the waiter found it."

"I should have thought anyone could have told you where it is," M. Carrère said. "It is very well known."

"*They* didn't know about it. . . . I tried to buy them all a drink before I left—they had been so kind—and they refused. Was that wrong? In America it would not have been wrong."

"Not at all," Mme Viénot said. "Another time just say: 'I insist that you have a glass of wine with me,' and the offer will be accepted. But it wasn't at all necessary."

"I wish I'd known that."

"They were no doubt happy to have been of assistance to you. And you found your hotel?"

"We took a taxi," he said. "And the fares have gone up. They have a chart they show you. I remembered that you had said not to pay more than the amount on the meter, and when the driver got angry I made him come into the hotel with me and the concierge straightened it out. After that, whenever we took a taxi I was careful to ask the driver if I had given him enough."

"But they will cheat you!" Mme Viénot exclaimed.

"They didn't. I knew from the chart what it *should* be, and added the tip, and they none of them asked for more."

"Perhaps they found you sympathetic," Mme Bonenfant said.

"It was pleasanter than arguing."

He saw that Mme Straus-Muguet was looking at him and he said to her with his eyes: *I was afraid you wouldn't be here when we got back. . . .*

Mme Viénot lifted her spoon to her lips and then exclaimed. Turning to Barbara, she said: "My cook gave notice while you were gone. The new cook, poor dear, is very nervous. Last night there was too much salt in everything, so I spoke to her about it, and tonight there is no salt whatever in the soup. Do I dare speak to her again?" She turned to M. Carrère, who said, his clown's eyes crinkling: "In your place I don't think I should. It might bring on something worse."

"I hope you will be patient with her," Mme Viénot said. "She has a sister living in the village, whom she wanted to be near. The boy is her son. He has had no experience but she begged me to take him on so that he can learn the métier and they can hire themselves out as a couple. . . . Tell us what happened to you in Paris."

"We spent all our time walking the streets," Barbara said, "and looking in shop windows."

"They are extraordinary, aren't they?" Mme Carrère agreed. "Quite like the way they were before the war."

"And we had lunch with M. Gagny," Harold said.

"Yes? You saw M. Gagny?" Mme Viénot said, and Mme Carrère asked if they had followed her directions on the night of the illumination. Harold hesitated, and then, not wanting to spoil her pleasure, said that they had. He had a feeling that she knew he was not telling the truth. She did not attempt to catch him out, but the interest went out of her face.

As he and Barbara were undressing for bed, they remarked upon a curious fact. They had hoped before they came here that a stay at the château would make them better able to deal with what they found in Paris, and instead a stay of three days in Paris had made them able, really for the first time, to deal with life in the château. Neither of them mentioned their reluctance to leave Paris, that afternoon, or the fact that their room, after the comforts of the hotel, seemed cold and cheerless. Thérèse had again forgotten to bring them a can of hot water; the fan of experience was already beginning to close, and in Paris it had opened all the way.

Chapter 8

THEY SPENT Saturday morning in their room. Barbara filled the washbasin with cold water and while she washed and rinsed and washed again, Harold sat on the edge of the tub and told her about the murder of the Duc de Guise, in the château of Blois, in the year 1588.

"He got in, and then he found he couldn't get out. . . . He was warned on the Grand Staircase, but by that time it was too late; there were guards posted everywhere. He asked for the Queen, who could have saved him, and she didn't come. He sent his servant for a handkerchief, as a test, and the servant didn't come back. . . . Are you listening to me?" he demanded above the sound of the soapy water being sucked down the drain.

"Yes, but I've got to change the water in the sink."

"You don't have to make so much noise. . . . Everywhere he looked, people avoided meeting his eyes. He had just come from the bed of one of the Queen's ladies-in-waiting."

"Which queen was this?"

"Not Queen Victoria. Catherine de Médicis, I think. Anyway, it was two days before Christmas. And he was cold and hungry. He stood in front of the fireplace, warming himself and eating some dried prunes, I guess it was. It's hard to make out, from that little dictionary. The council of state convened, and they told him the King had sent for him. So he left the room—"

At this point Barbara left the bathroom and went to the armoire. Harold followed her. "The eight hired assassins in the next room bowed to him," he said, helping himself to a piece of candy from the box on the table. "I suppose it comes from living in the same house with *her*, but somebody's been at the chocolates while we were away."

"Oh, I don't think so," Barbara said, and closed the doors of the armoire and went back to the bathroom with a nightgown and a slip, which she added to the laundry in the washbasin.

"Want to bet?"

"It doesn't matter if they did."

"I know it doesn't. But I don't think it was Thérèse, even so."

"Who else could have?"

"Somebody that likes chocolate. . . . He got as far as the door to the King's dressing room, and saw that there were more of them, at the end of the narrow passageway, waiting for him with drawn swords in their hands."

"Poor man!"

"Mmm. Poor man, indeed—he was responsible for the Massacre of St. Bartholomew. It took forty men to do him in. He was huge and very powerful. And when it was all over, the King bent down cautiously and slapped his face."

"After he was *dead?*"

"Yes. Then he went and told his mother. What people!"

"If you knew what it is like to wash silk in cold water!" Barbara said indignantly.

"Why do you do it, then? I could go down and ask them for a can of hot water?"

There was no answer.

He wandered back into the bedroom, and stood looking around the room, seeing it with the eyes of the person who took the chocolates. Not Mme Bonenfant. The flowers hadn't been changed. And anyway, she wouldn't. Not the houseboy, in all probability. He was new, and he had no reason to be in this part of the house. Mme Viénot? Who else? If they were curious about her, why shouldn't she be curious about them?

She had stood in the doorway waving to them until the taxi disappeared around the corner of the house. And then what happened? Was she relieved? Was she happy to see them go? He put himself in her shoes and decided that he would have been relieved for a minute or two, and then he would have begun to worry. He would have been afraid that they would find in Paris what they were looking for—they were tourists, after all—and not come back. He had offered to have the luggage packed so that it could be removed from their room, and if she remembered that, she would surely think they had planned not to come back, and that in a day or so she would get a letter saying they'd changed their plans again, and would she send their luggage, which was all packed and ready, to the Hôtel Vouillemont. . . . Only the luggage was not packed, of course. And what she must have seen when she threw open the door of the room was that they had left everything—clothes, books, all their possessions, scattered over the room. There was a half-finished letter on the desk, and the box of Swiss chocolates open on the table. The room must have looked as if they had left it to go for a walk.

He stood reading the letter, which had lain on the pad of the writing desk since last Tuesday. It was to Edith Ireland, of all people. Barbara was thanking her for the book and the bottle of champagne she had sent to the boat. Barbara's handwriting was very dashing, and not very legible, because of a tendency to abbreviate and leave off parts of letters, but if you were patient you could get the hang of it, and no doubt Mme Viénot had.

On the table, beside a pile of guidebooks, were three pages—also in Barbara's handwriting—of a diary she was keeping. The entries covered the period from July 11, when they came to the château from Tours, through July 13, the day before they went up to Paris. He turned away from the table, relieved and grinning.

I: *Leo and Virgo*

She had a façade that she retired behind when she was with strangers—the image of an unworldly, well-bred, charming-looking, gentle young woman. The image was not even false to her character; it merely left out half of it. Who could possibly have any reason to say anything rude or unkind to anyone so shy and unsure of herself? Nobody ever did.

It was the façade that was keeping the diary.

WHEN THEY WENT down to lunch they learned that Mme Viénot's relatives had arrived sometime during the morning. The dining-room table was larger by two leaves to accommodate them and there were three empty chairs. Two of them were soon filled, by a middle-aged woman and a young man. The cook's son brought two more soup plates, and Mme Viénot said: "How do you find Maman? Doesn't she look well?"

"She is more beautiful than ever," the young man said, his face totally without expression, as if it had been carved out of a piece of wood and could not change.

"The weather has been most discouraging here," Mme Viénot said.

"In Paris it is the same. Rain day after day," the young man said. "One hears everywhere that it is the atomic bomb that is responsible. I myself think it is by analogy with the political climate, which is damp, cold, unhopeful. . . . Alix said to tell you that she is giving Annette her bottle. She will be down presently."

"Perhaps she can manage some slight adjustment of the baby's schedule which will permit her to come to meals at the usual time," Mme Viénot said. "It is not merely the empty chair. It upsets the service. . . . Your father and mother are well?"

"My father is having trouble with his eyes. It is not cataracts, though it seems that the difficulty may be progressive. It is a question of the arteries not carrying enough food to the optic nerve. Maman is well—at least, well enough to go to weddings. There has been a succession of them. My cousin Suzanne, in Brittany. And Philippe Soulès. You remember that de Cléry girl everyone thought was a mental defective? She has turned out to be the clever one of the family. They are going to live with his parents, it seems. And my Uncle Eugène, for the third time. Or is it the fourth? And Simone Valéry. Maman has been thinking of taking a job. She has been approached by Jacques Fath. She has just about decided to say no. It is rather an amusing idea, and if she could come and go as she pleased—but it seems they would expect her to keep regular hours, and she is quite incapable of that. Besides, she has set her heart on a trip to Venice. In August."

"The Biennale?"

"No, another wedding. I have not seen Jean-Claude. I read about him in *Figaro*. And Georges Dunois had lunch with him last Wednesday in London. Georges asked me to pay you his devoted respects. He said Jean-Claude has aged."

"The responsibility is, of course, very great," Mme Viénot said modestly, and then turning to Barbara: "We are discussing my son-in-law, who is in the government."

"He now looks twenty-two or three, Georges said."

"Suzanne writes that he is being sent to Oran, on an important mission, the details of which she is not free to disclose."

"Naturally."

"She is expecting another child in November."

"She is my favorite of the entire family, and I am not sure I would recognize her if I saw her. I never see her, not even at those functions where one would have supposed her husband's career might be affected by her absence. Proving that the Ministry is helpless without him."

"She is absorbed in her family duties," Mme Viénot said.

"So one is told. As for Jean-Claude, one hears everywhere

that he is immensely valued, successful, happy, and— Ah, there you are."

The young woman who sat down in the chair next to Barbara was very fair, and her blue eyes had a look of childlike sweetness and innocence. She acknowledged the introductions in the most charming French accent Harold had ever heard, and then said: "I did not expect to be down for another quarter of an hour, but she went right off to sleep. She was exhausted by the trip, and so many new sensations."

Harold decided that he liked her, and that he didn't like the man, who seemed to have a whole repertoire of manners—one (serious, intellectual) for M. Carrère; another (simpering, mock-gallant) for Mme Viénot; another (devoted, simple, respectful) for Mme Bonenfant; and still another for Barbara, whose hand he had raised to his lips. Harold was put off by the hand-kissing (though Barbara was not; she did not, in fact, turn a hair; where had she learned that?) and by the limp handshake when he and the young Frenchman were introduced and the look of complete indifference now when their eyes met across the table.

AT TWO O'CLOCK, when they came downstairs from their room, Mme Straus-Muguet was waiting for them in the second-floor hall at the turn of the stairs. Speaking slowly and distinctly, the way people do when they are trying to impress careful instructions on the wandering minds of children, she asked if they would do an errand for her. She had overheard them telling Mme Viénot that they were going to Blois this afternoon. On a scrap of paper she had written the name of a confiserie and she wanted them to get some candy for her, a particular kind, a delicious bonbon that was made only at this shop in Blois. She gave Barbara the colored tinsel wrapper it came in, to show the confiseur, and a hundred-franc note. They were to get eight pieces of candy—six for her and two for themselves.

This time the bus was not crowded. They found seats together and all the way into town sat looking out of the window at scenery that was simple and calm, as Harold's guidebook said —long perspectives of the river, with here and there a hill, some sheep, a house, two trees, women and children wading, and then the same hill (or so it seemed), the same sheep, the same house, the same two trees, like a repeating motif in wallpaper. It was a landscape, one would have said, in which no human being had ever raised his voice. They went straight to the ration bureau and stood in line at the high counter, with their green passports ready, and were quite unprepared for the unpleasant scene that took place there. A grim-faced, gray-haired woman took their passports, examined them efficiently, and then returned them to Harold with ration stamps for bread, sugar, etc. She also said something to him in very rapid French that he did not understand. Speaking as good French as he knew how to speak, he asked her if she would please repeat what she had said, and she shrieked furiously at him in English: "They're for ten days only!"

They stood staring at each other, her face livid with anger and his very pale. Then he said mildly: "If you ever come to America, you will find that you are sometimes obliged to ask the same question two or three times." And because this remark was so mild, or perhaps because it was so illogical (the woman behind the counter had no intention ever of setting foot out of France, and if by any stretch of the imagination she did, it would not be to go to a country that so threatened the peace of the world), there was no more shouting. He went on looking directly into her eyes until she looked away.

Outside, standing on the steps of the building, he said: "Was it because we are taking food out of the mouths of starving Frenchmen?"

"Possibly," Barbara said.

"But we haven't seen anybody who looked starving. And they *want* American tourists. The French government is anxious to have them come."

"I know. But she isn't the French government."

"Maybe she hates men." His voice was unsteady and he felt weak in the knees. "Or it could be, I suppose, that her whole life has been dreadful. But the way she spoke to us was so—"

"It's something that happens to women sometimes," Barbara said. "An anger that comes over them suddenly, and that they feel no part in."

"But why?"

She had no answer.

If it is true that nothing exists without its opposite, then the thing they had just been exposed to was merely the opposite of the amiability and kindness they had encountered everywhere in France. Also, the gypsy fortuneteller had promised Barbara malice she didn't expect.

Facing the ration bureau was a small open-air market, and they wandered through it slowly, looking at straw hats, cotton dresses, tennis sneakers, and cheap cooking utensils. They were unable to get the incident out of their minds, though they stopped talking about it. The day was blighted.

From the market they made their way down into the lower part of the city, and found Mme Straus's candy shop. They also spent some time in the shop next door, where they bought an intermediate French grammar, two books on gardening, and postcards. Then they walked along the street, dividing their attention between the people on the sidewalk and the contents of shop windows, until they arrived at the ramp that led up to the château.

They stood in the courtyard, looking at the octagonal staircase and comparing what the Michelin said with the actuality in front of them. Because it was getting late and they weren't sure they wanted to join a conducted tour—they were, in fact, rather tired of conducted tours—they walked in the opposite direction from the sign that said *guide du château*, and toward the wing of Gaston d'Orléans. Harold put his hand out and tried a doorknob. It turned and the door swung open. They walked in and up a flight of marble stairs, admiring the balustrades and the ceiling, and at the head of the stairs they came upon two large tapestries dealing with the Battle of Dunkerque—a previous battle, in the seventeenth century, judging by the costumes and theatrical-looking implements of war. The doors leading out of this room were all locked, and so they made their way down the stairs again, trying other doors, until they were out in the courtyard once more. They were just in time to see two busloads of tourists from the American Express stream out of the wing of Louis XII and crowd into the tiny blue and gold chapel. The tourists were with a guide and the guide was speaking English.

Standing under an arcade, surrounded by their countrymen, Barbara and Harold learned about the strange life of Charles d'Orléans, who was a poet and at fifteen married his cousin, the daughter of Charles VI. She had already been married to Richard II of England, when she was seven years old. The new marriage did not last long. She died in childbirth, and the poet remarried, lost the battle of Agincourt, and was imprisoned for twenty-five years, after which, a widower of fifty, he again married—this time a girl of fourteen—and surrounded himself with a little court of artists and writers, and at seventy-one had at last, by his third wife, the son he had waited more than fifty years for.

"I see what you mean about having a guide who speaks English," Harold said as they followed the crowd back across the courtyard and up a flight of steps to the Hall of State. They were waiting to learn about that, too, when the guide came over to them and asked Harold to step outside for a moment, with Madame.

He was about thirty years old, with large dark intelligent eyes, regular features, a narrow face cleanly cut, and dark skin.

I: *Leo and Virgo*

An aristocratic survival from the time of François premier, Harold thought as they followed the guide across the big room, with the other tourists looking at them with more interest than they had shown toward the Hall of State. He did not know precisely what to expect, or why the guide had singled them out, but whatever he wanted or wanted to know, Harold was ready to oblige him with, since the guide was not only a gentleman but obviously a far from ordinary man.

Though the guide made his living taking American tourists through historical monuments, he did not understand Americans the way he understood history. If you are as openhanded as they mostly are, you cannot help rejoicing in small accidental economies, being pleased when the bus conductor fails to collect your fare, etc., and it doesn't at all mean that you are trying to take advantage of anybody. The guide asked them if they were members of his party, and Harold said no, and the guide said would they leave the château immediately by that little door right down there?

The whole conversation took place in English, and so Harold had no trouble understanding what the guide said, but for a few seconds he went right on looking at the Frenchman's face. The expression in the gray eyes was contempt.

Blushing and angry, with the guide and with himself (for he had had in his wallet the means of erasing this embarrassment as completely as if it had never happened), he made his way down the ramp with Barbara, past the château gift shop, and into the street.

It was too soon for the bus, and so they turned in at the pâtisserie, and ordered tea and cakes, and found that they had no appetite for them when they came. They got up and left, and a few minutes later had a third contretemps. The bus driver, misunderstanding Harold's "deux" for "douze," gave him the wrong change and would not rectify his mistake or let them get on the bus until everybody else had got on. So they had to stand, after being first in line at the bus stop.

"So far," he said, peering through the window at the river, "we've had very few experiences like what happened this afternoon, and they were really the result of growing confidence. We were attempting to behave as if we were at home."

Out of consideration for his feelings, Barbara did not point out that this was only partly true; at home he was neither as friendly nor as trusting as he was here, and he did not expect strangers to be that way with him. She herself did not mind what had happened half as much as she minded having to come down to dinner in a dress that she had already worn three times.

Mme Straus-Muguet was waiting for them on the stairs. She praised them for carrying out her errand so successfully, in a city they did not know well, and invited them to take an apéritif with her before lunch on Sunday morning. She seemed subdued, and as if during their absence in Paris she had suffered a setback of some kind—a letter containing bad news that her mind kept returning to, or unkindness where she least expected it.

Feeling tired and bruised by their own series of setbacks, they hurried on up the stairs, conscious that the house was cold and there would not be any hot water to wash in and they would have to spend still another evening trying to understand people who could speak English but preferred to speak French.

From the conversation at the lunch table, Harold had pieced together certain facts about Mme Viénot's relatives. The blonde young woman with the charming low voice and the beautiful accent was Mme Viénot's niece, and the young man was her husband. Listening and waiting, he eventually found out their names: M. and Mme de Boisgaillard. And they had brought with them not only their own three-months-old baby but Mme de Boisgaillard's sister's two children, who were too young to come to the table, and a nursemaid. But when they sat down to dinner he still did not know who the middle-aged woman directly across from him was. There was something that separated her from everybody else at the table. Studying her, he saw that she wore no jewelry of any kind, and her blue dress was so plain and inexpensive-looking that he wasn't absolutely sure that it wasn't a uniform—in which case, she was the children's nurse. Or perhaps M. de Boisgaillard's mother, he decided; a woman alone in the world, and except for her claim on her son, without resources. Now that he was married, the claim was, of course, much slighter, and so she was obliged to be grateful that she was here at all. No one spoke to her. Thinking that it might ease her shyness, her feeling of being (as he was) excluded from the conversation, he smiled directly at her. The response was polite and impersonal, and he decided that, as so often was the case with him, she was past rescuing.

He listened to the pitch, the intonations, of Mme de Boisgaillard's voice as if he were hearing a new kind of music, and decided that there were as many different ways of speaking French as there were French people. Because of her voice he would have trusted absolutely anything she said. But he trusted her anyway, because of the naturalness and simplicity of her manner. Looking at her, he felt he knew her very well, without knowing anything at all about her. It was as if they had played together as children. Her husband's voice was rather high, thin, and reedy. It was also the voice of someone who knows exactly what to respect and what to be contemptuous of. So strange that two such different people should have married . . .

Mme de Boisgaillard spoke English fluently. In an undertone, with a delicate smile, she supplied Barbara, who sat next to her, with the word or phrase that would limit the context of an otherwise puzzling statement or explain the point of an amusing remark. Harold clutched at these straws eagerly. When Mme Viénot translated for them, it was usually some word that he knew already, and so she was never the slightest help. He watched M. de Boisgaillard until their eyes met across the table.

The young Frenchman immediately looked away, and Harold was careful not to look at him again.

Mme Viénot was eager to learn whether her nephew thought the Schumann cabinet would jump during September. The young man and M. Carrère both thought it would—not because of a crisis, easy though it was to find one, but because of political squabbles that were of no importance except to the people directly involved.

"Why would they wait until September?" Harold asked. "Why not in August?"

"Because August is the month when Parliament takes its annual vacation," Mme Viénot said. "No government has ever been known to jump at this time of year. They always wait until September."

The joke was thoroughly enjoyed, and Mme Straus-Muguet nodded approvingly at Harold for having made it possible.

After the dessert course, napkins were folded in such a way as to conceal week-old wine stains and then inserted in their identifying rings.

Barbara saw that Mme Straus was aware that she had been looking at her, and said: "I have been admiring your little diamond heart."

"You like it?" Mme Straus said. From her tone of voice one would almost have supposed that she was about to undo the clasp of the fine gold chain and present the little heart, chain and all, to the young woman at the far end of the table. However, her hands remained in her lap, and she said: "It was given to me by a friend, long long ago," leaving them to decide for themselves whether the fiery little object was the souvenir of a romantic attachment. Mme Viénot gave her a glance of frank disbelief and pushed her chair back from the table.

The ladies left the dining room in the order of their age. Harold started to follow M. Carrère out of the room and to his surprise felt a hand on his sleeve, detaining him. M. de Boisgaillard drew him over to the other side of the room and asked him, in French, how he liked it at the château. Harold started to answer tactfully and saw that the face now looking down into his expected a truthful answer, was really interested, and would know if he was not candid; so he was, and the Frenchman laughed and suggested that they walk outside in the garden.

He opened one of the dining-room windows and stepped out, and Harold followed him around the corner of the house and through the gap in the hedge and into the potager. With a light rain—it was hardly more than a mist—falling on their shoulders, they walked up and down the gravel paths. The Frenchman asked how rich the ordinary man in America was. How many cars were there in the whole country? Did American women really rule the roost? And did they love their husbands or just love what they could get out of them? Was it true that everybody had running water and electricity? But not true that everybody owned their own house and every house had a dishwasher and a washing machine? Did Harold have any explanation to offer of how, in a country made up of such different racial strains, every man should be so passionately interested in machinery? Was it the culture or was it something that stemmed from the early days of the country—from its colonial period? How was America going to solve the Negro problem? Was it true that all Negroes were innately musical? And were they friendly with the white people who exploited them or did they hate them one and all? And how did the white people feel about Negroes? What did Americans think of Einstein? of Freud? of Stalin? of Churchill? of de Gaulle? Did they feel any guilt on account of Hiroshima? Did they like or dislike the French? Had he read the Kinsey Report, and was it true that virtually every American male had had some homosexual experience? And so on and so on.

The less equipped you are to answer such questions, the more flattering it is to be asked them, but to answer even superficially in a foreign language you need more than a tourist's vocabulary.

"You don't speak German?"

Harold shook his head. They stood looking at each other helplessly.

"You don't speak *any* English?" Harold said.

"Pas un mot."

A few minutes later, as they were walking and talking again, the Frenchman forgot and shifted to German anyway, and Harold stopped him, and they went on trying to talk to each other in French. Very often Harold's answer did not get put into the right words or else in his excitement he did not pronounce them well enough for them to be understood, the approximation being some other word entirely, and the two men stopped and stared at each other. Then they tried once more, and impasses that seemed hopeless were bridged after all; or if this didn't happen, the subject was abandoned in favor of a new subject.

It began to rain in earnest, and they turned up their coat collars and went on walking and talking.

"Shall we go in?" the Frenchman asked, a moment later.

As they went back through the gap in the hedge, Harold said to himself that it was a different house they were returning to. By the addition of a man of the family it had changed; it had stopped being matriarchal and formal and cold, and become solid and hospitable and human, like other houses.

At the door of the petit salon, they separated. Harold took in the room at a glance. M. Carrère sat looking quite forlorn, the one man among so many women. And did he imagine it or was Mme Viénot put out with them? There was an empty chair beside Mme de Boisgaillard and he sat down in it and tried once more to follow the conversation. He learned that the woman he had taken for the children's nurse or possibly M. de Boisgaillard's mother was Mme de Boisgaillard's mother instead; which meant that she was Mme Viénot's sister and had a perfect right to be here. What he had failed to perceive, like the six blind men and the elephant, was that she was deaf and so could not take part in general conversation. During dinner she did not even try, but now if someone spoke directly to her she adjusted the pointer of the little black box that she held to her ear as if it were a miniature radio, and seemed to understand.

When the others retired to their rooms at eleven o'clock, Eugène de Boisgaillard swept the Americans ahead of him, through a doorway and down a second-floor hall they had not been in before, and they found themselves in a bedroom with a dressing room off it. They stood looking down at the baby, who was fast asleep on her stomach but escaped entirely from the covers, at right angles to the crib, with her knees tucked under her, her feet crossed like hands, her rump in the air.

Her mother straightened her around and covered her, and then they tiptoed back into the larger room and began to talk. Mme de Boisgaillard translated and summarized quickly and accurately, leaving them free to go on to the next thing they wanted to say.

Unlike M. Carrère, Eugène de Boisgaillard did not hate all Germans. His political views were Liberal and democratic. He was also as curious as a cat. He wanted to know how long Harold and Barbara had been married, and how they had met one another, and what part of America they grew up in. He asked their first names and then what their friends called them. He asked them to call him by his first name. And then the questions began again, as if the first thing in the morning he and they were starting out for the opposite ends of the earth and there was only tonight for them to get to know each other. Once, when a question was so personal that Harold thought he must have misunderstood, he turned to Mme de Boisgaillard and she smiled and shook her head ruefully and said: "I hope you do not mind. That is the way he is. When I think he cannot possibly have said what I think I have heard him say, I know that is just what he did say."

At her husband's suggestion, she left them and went downstairs to see what there was in the larder, and they were surprised to discover that without her they couldn't talk to each other.

They waited awkwardly until she came into the room carrying a tray with a big bowl of sour cream and four smaller bowls, a sugar bowl, and spoons.

Eugène de Boisgaillard pointed to the empty fireplace and said: "No andirons. Does the one in your room work?"

Harold explained that it had a shield over it.

"During the Occupation the Germans let the forests be depleted—intentionally—and so one is allowed to cut only so much wood," Mme de Boisgaillard said, "and if they used it now there would not be enough for the winter. Poor Tante! She drives herself so hard. . . . The thing I always forget is what a beautiful smell this house has. It may be the box hedge, though Mummy says it is the furniture polish, but it doesn't smell like any other house in the world."

"Have your shoes begun to mildew?" Eugène de Boisgaillard said.

Barbara shook her head.

"They will," he said.

"You will drive them away," Mme de Boisgaillard said, "and then we won't have anyone our age to talk to."

"We will go after them," Eugéne de Boisgaillard said, "talking every step of the way. The baby's sugar ration," he said, saluting the sugar bowl.

Sweetened with sugar, the half-solidified sour cream was delicious.

"Have you enjoyed knowing M. Carrère?" Eugène asked.

Harold said that M. Carrère seemed to be a very kind man.

"He's also very rich," Eugène said. "Everything he touches turns into more money, more gilt-edged stock certificates. He is a problem to the Bank of France. Toinette has a special tone of voice in speaking of him—have you noticed? Where does she place him, I wonder? On some secondary level. Not with Périclès, or Beethoven. Not with Louis XIV. With Saint-Simon, perhaps . . . In the past year I have learned how to interpret the public face. It has been very useful. The public face is much more ponderous and explicit than the private face and it asks only one question: 'What is it you want?' And whatever you want is unfortunately just the thing it isn't convenient for you to be given. . . . Do you get on well with your parents, Harold?"

He listened attentively to Alix's translation of the answer to this question and then said: "My father is very conservative. He has never in his whole life gone to the polls and voted."

"Why not?" Barbara asked.

"His not voting is an act of protest against the Revolution."

"You don't mean the Revolution of 1789?"

"Yes. He does not approve of it."

Tears of amusement ran down Harold's cheeks and he reached for his handkerchief and wiped them away.

"What does your father do?" Barbara asked.

"He collects porcelain. That's all he has done his whole life."

In a moment Harold had to get his handkerchief out again as Eugène launched forth on the official and unofficial behavior of his superior, the Minister of Planning and External Affairs.

At one o'clock the Americans stood up to go, and, still talking, Eugène and Alix accompanied them down the upstairs hall until they were in their own part of the house. Whispering and tittering like naughty children, they said good night. Was Mme Viénot awake, Harold wondered. Could she hear them? Did she disapprove of such goings on?

Eugène said that he had one last question to ask.

"Don't," Alix whispered.

"Why not? Why shouldn't I ask them? . . . Is there a double bed in your room?"

Harold shook his head.

"I knew it!" Eugène said. "I told Alix that there wouldn't be. Don't you find it strange—don't you think it is *extraordinary* that all the double beds in the house are occupied by single women?"

They said good night all over again, and the Americans crept up the stairs, which, even so, creaked frightfully. When Barbara fell asleep, Harold wrapped the covers around her snugly and moved over into his own damp bed and lay awake for some time, thinking. What had happened this evening was so different from anything else that had happened to them so far on their trip, and he felt that a part of him that had been left behind in America, without his realizing it, had now caught up with him. He thought with wonder how far off he could be about people. For Eugène was totally unlike what he had seemed at first to be. He was not cold and insincere but amusing and unpredictable, and masculine, and direct, and intelligent, and like a wonderful older brother. Knowing him was reason enough for them to come back time after time, through the years, to France. . . .

Chapter 9

At breakfast the next morning, Mme Viénot's manner with the Americans did not convey approval or disapproval. She urged on them a specialty of the countryside—bread with meat drippings poured over it—and then, folding her napkin, excused herself to go and dress for church. Harold asked if they could go to church also, and she said: "Certainly."

At ten thirty the dog cart appeared in front of the house, with the gardener in the driver's seat and his white plow horse hitched to the traces. It had been arranged that Barbara should go to church in the cart with Mme Straus-Muguet and Alix and Eugène; that Mme Bonenfant should ride in the Bentley with M. and Mme Carrère; that Harold and Mme Viénot should bicycle. She rode her own, he was given the cook's, which got out of his control, in spite of Mme Viénot's repeated warnings. Unaccustomed to bicycles without brakes, he came sailing into the village a good two minutes ahead of her.

They were in plenty of time for Mass, but instead of going directly to the little church she went to Mme Michot's, where she stood gazing at the fruit and vegetables, her expression a mixture of disdain and disbelief, as if Mme Michot were trying to introduce her to persons whose social status was not at all what they pretended. Madame Michot's tomatoes were inferior and her plums were too dear. In the end she bought two lemons, half a pound of dried figs, and some white raisins that were unaccountably cheap.

As they came out of the little shop, she explained that she had one more errand; her seamstress was making her a green silk dress that was to have the New Look, and it had been promised for today.

At the seamstress's house, Mme Viénot knocked and waited. She knocked again. She stood in the street and called. She stopped and questioned a little girl, who told her reluctantly where the seamstress had said she could be found. Mme Viénot looked at her wrist watch. "I really don't see why she couldn't have been home!" she exclaimed. "We are already quite late for church, and it means going clear to the other side of the village."

Once more they got on their bicycles. As they were riding side by side over the bumpy cobblestones, she remarked that the village was older than it looked. "There is a legend—whether it is true I cannot say—that Jeanne d'Arc, traveling toward Chinon with her escort of three or four soldiers, arrived at Brenodville at nightfall and was denied a lodging by the monks."

"Why?"

"Because of her sex, no doubt."

"Where did she go?" Harold asked.

"She slept in a farmhouse, I believe."

He looked around for Gothic stonework and found, here and there, high up out of harm's way, a small gargoyle at the end of a waterspout, a weathered stone pinnacle, a carved lintel, or some other piece of medieval decoration, proving that the story was at least possible. The houses themselves—sour, secretive, commonplace-looking—said that if Jeanne d'Arc were to come again in the middle of the twentieth century, she would get the same inhospitable reception, and not merely from the monks but from everybody.

The house where the little girl had said the seamstress said she could be found was locked and shuttered, and no one came to the door. At five minutes of twelve, they arrived at the vestibule of the church. Mme Viénot genuflected in the aisle outside the family pew and then moved in and knelt beside her mother. Harold followed her. Half kneeling and half sitting, he tried not to look so much like a Protestant. The drama on the altar was reaching its climax. A little silver bell tinkled. The congregation spoke. (Was it Latin? Was it French?) Mme Viénot struck her flat chest three times and seemed to be asking for something from the depths of her heart, but though he listened intently, he could not hear what it was; it was lost in the asking of other low voices all around them. The bell tinkled again and again, insistently. There was a moment of hushed expectation and then the congregation rose from their knees with a roaring sound that nobody paid any attention to, filled the aisle, streamed out of the chill of the little church into the more surprising chill of a cold gray July day, and, pleased that an essential act was done, broke out into smiles and conversation.

Harold waited beside the two bicycles while Mme Viénot went into the stationer's for her mother's *Figaro*. He looked around for Mme Straus-Muguet, not sure whether she had meant them to meet her here in the village after church or where. And if he saw her beckoning to him, how would he escape from Mme Viénot? Mme Straus was nowhere in sight now, and he had made two trips downstairs after breakfast without encountering her.

When Mme Viénot took a long, thin, empty wine bottle out of her saddlebag and went into still another shop, he followed her out of curiosity and was introduced to M. Canourgue, whose stock was entirely out of sight, under a wooden counter or in the adjoining room. She counted out more ration coupons, and explained that Harold was American and a friend of M. Georges who was so fond of chocolates. The wine bottle went into the back room and came back full of olive oil. Mme Viénot bought sardines, and this and that. When they were outside in the street again, Harold saw that the canvas saddlebag of her bicycle was crammed, and so he took the bottle from her and placed it carefully on its side in his saddle bag, which was empty.

As they rode home, he asked where she had learned English and she said: "From my governess . . . And in England."

Her education had been rounded off with a year in London, during which she had lived with a private family. She admired the British, she said, but did not particularly like them. "They dress so badly, in those ill-fitting suits," she said. He waited, hoping that she would say that she liked Americans, but she didn't.

They dismounted in the courtyard and wheeled their bicycles into the kitchen entry, where Mme Viénot let out a cry of distress. He saw that she was looking at his saddlebag, and said: "What's the matter?" She pointed to the wine bottle lying on its side. "The cork has come out," she said, in the voice of doom.

He started to apologize, and then realized that she wasn't paying any attention to what he said. She had picked up the bottle and was examining the outside, turning it around slowly. It was dry. They examined the saddlebag. Not a drop of oil had been spilled! He learned a new French phrase—"une espèce de miracle"—and used it frequently in conversation from that time on.

Mme Straus-Muguet was in the drawing room, with M. and Mme Carrère and Mme Bonenfant and Barbara and Alix and Eugène. They had all been invited to take an apéritif with her on Sunday morning. An unopened bottle of Martinique rum stood on the little round table. Thérèse brought liqueur glasses and the corkscrew. The rum loosened tongues, smoothed away differences of background, of age, of temperament, of nationality. The conversation became animated; their eyes grew bright. Thérèse removed the screen, and they all rose and, still talking, floated on a wave of intense cordiality through the hall and into the dining room, where the long-promised poulet awaited them. As Harold unfolded his clean napkin, he decided that life in the country was not so bad, after all.

I: *Leo and Virgo*

The gaiety did not quite last out the meal. The nine people around the table sank back, one after another, into their ordinary selves. There had been no real, or at least no lasting, change but merely a sleight-of-hand demonstration. As some people know how to make three balls appear and disappear and a whole flock of doves fly out of an opera hat, Mme Straus-Muguet knew how to lift a dead social weight. Out of the most unpromising elements she had just now constructed an edifice of gaiety, an atmosphere of concert pitch. Shreds of her triumph lasted until teatime, when Mme Viénot surrendered the silver teapot to her, and she presided—modestly, but also as if she were accustomed to having this compliment paid her.

Sitting with the others, in the circle of chairs at one end of the drawing room, Barbara listened to what Alix and Eugène were saying to each other. His train left at six, and there were last-minute instructions and reminders, of a kind that she was familiar with, and that made her feel she knew them intimately merely because the French girl was saying just what she herself might have said in these circumstances.

"You know where the bread coupons are?"

"You put them in the desk, didn't you?"

"Yes. You'll have to go and get new ones when they expire. Do you think you will remember to?"

"If I don't, my stomach will remind me."

"I have arranged with Mme Emile to buy ice for you, and butter once a week. And if you want to ask someone to dinner, Françoise will come and cook it for you. She will be there Fridays, to clean the apartment and change the linen on your bed. Can you remember to leave a note for the laundress? I meant to do it and forgot. She is to wash your dressing gown. Is it late?"

"There is plenty of time," Eugène said, glancing at his wrist watch.

"If it should turn hot, leave the awning down at our window and close the shutters, and it will be cool when you come home at night. It might be better to leave all the shutters closed—but then it will be gloomy. Whatever you think best. And if you are too tired after work to write to me, it will be all right. I will write to you every day. . . ."

A few minutes more passed, and then he stood up and started around the circle, shaking hands and saying good-by. His manner with M. and Mme Carrère was simply that of a man of breeding. And yet beneath the confident surface there was something a little queer, Harold thought, watching them. Was Eugène trying to convey to them that his father would not have permitted them to be introduced to him?

When he arrived at Harold and Barbara, he smiled, and Harold said as they shook hands: "We'll see you on Friday."

Eugène nodded, turned away, and then turned back to them and said: "You are coming up to Paris—"

"Next Sunday."

"Good. We will all be taking the train together. That is what I had hoped. And where will you stay?"

Harold told him.

"Why do you spend money for a hotel," Eugène said, "when there is room in my mother-in-law's apartment?"

Harold hesitated, and Eugène went on: "I won't be able to spend as much time with you as I'd like, but it will be a pleasure for me, having you and Barbara there when I come home at night."

"But it will make trouble for you."

"It will be no trouble to anyone."

Harold looked at Barbara inquiringly, and misinterpreted her answering look.

"In that case—" he began, and before he could finish his sentence she said: "Can we let you know later?"

"When I come down next week end," Eugène said, and bent down to kiss Mme Bonenfant's frail hand.

Harold thought a slight shadow had passed over his face when they did not accept his invitation, and then he decided that this was not so. The relations between them were such that there was no possibility of hurt feelings or any misunderstanding.

Later, Barbara said that she would have been delighted to accept the invitation except for one thing: it should have come from Alix's mother. "Or at least he should have made it clear that Mme Cestre had been consulted before he invited us. And also, perhaps we ought to be a little more cautious; we ought to know a little more what we're getting into."

"EUGÈNE ENJOYED TALKING to you so much," Alix said, in the petit salon after dinner. "It was a great pleasure to him to find you here. He learned many things about America which interested him."

"The things he wanted to know about, most of the time I couldn't tell him," Harold said. "Partly because nobody knows the answer to some of his questions, and partly because I didn't know the right words to explain in French the way things are. Also, there are lots of things I should know that I don't. Sometimes we couldn't understand each other at all, and when I was ready to give up he would insist that I go on. And eventually, out of my floundering, he seemed to understand what it was I was trying to say. I've never had an experience quite like it."

"Eugène is very intuitive. . . . I have been telling him that he ought to learn English, and until now he hasn't cared to take the trouble. But it distressed him that I could speak to you in your language, badly though I do it, and he—"

"Your English is excellent."

"I am out of the habit. I make mistakes in grammar. Eugène has decided to go to the Berlitz School and learn English, so that when you come back to France he will be able to talk to you. So you see, you have accomplished something which I try to do and couldn't."

She turned away in order to repeat to her mother a remark of M. Carrère's that had pleased the company. Mme Cestre's face lit up. She was reminded of an observation of her husband's that in turn pleased M. Carrère. Alix waited until she saw that this conversation was proceeding without her help and then she turned back to Harold. "Eugène was so excited to learn that you have been married three years. We thought you were on your wedding journey."

"How long have you been married?"

"A little over a year. Eugène thought that in marriage, after a while, people changed. He thought they grew less fond of one another, and that there was no way of avoiding it. When he saw you and your wife together, the way you are with each other, it made him more hopeful."

"Where did you meet?" Harold said, to change the subject. He was perfectly willing to discuss most subjects but not this, because of a superstitious fear that his words would come back to him under ironical circumstances.

"When the Germans came," she said, "my father was in the South, and we were separated from him for some time. We were here with my grandmother. But as soon as we were able, we joined my father in Aix-en-Provence, and it was there that I met Eugène. He was different from the boys I knew. I thought he was very handsome and intelligent, and I enjoyed talking to him. At that time he was thinking of taking holy orders. I felt I could say anything to him—that he was like my brother."

"That's what he seems like to me," Harold said. "Like a wonderful older brother, though actually he is younger than I am."

"Do you have any brothers and sisters?"

"One brother," he said. "When we were growing up, we couldn't be left together in the back seat of the car, because we always ended up fighting. But now we get along all right."

"It never occurred to me that Eugène would want me to love him," she said. "When he asked me to marry him, I was surprised. I was not sure I would marry. I don't know why, exactly. It just didn't seem like something that would happen to me. . . . As a child I always played by myself."

"So did I," Harold said.

"I lived in a world of my own imagination. . . . When I grew older I began to notice the people around me. I saw that there were two kinds—the bright and the stupid—and I decided that I would choose the bright ones for my friends. Later on, I was disappointed in them. Clever people are not always kind. Sometimes they are quite cruel. And the stupid ones very often are kind."

"Then what did you do?"

"I had to choose my friends all over again. . . . I have a sister. The two small children we brought with us are hers. She is two years younger than I, and for a long time I was hardly aware of her. One day she asked me who is my best friend, and I named some girl, and she began to cry. She said: '*You* are *my* best friend.' I felt very bad. After that we became very close to each other."

Mme Viénot addressed a question to her, and Alix turned her head to answer. If I only had a tape recording of the way she says "father," "brother," and "other," Harold thought, smiling to himself. When she turned back to him, he said: "It must have been very difficult—the Occupation, I mean."

"We lived on turnips for weeks at a time. I cannot endure the sight of one now."

She saw that her grandmother was watching them and said in French: "I have been telling Harold how we lived on turnips during the Occupation." It was the first time she had used his Christian name, and he was pleased.

Mme Bonenfant had an interesting observation to make: perpetual hunger makes the middle-aged and the elderly grow thinner, as one would expect, but the young become quite plump. Was that why she thought she would never marry, he wondered.

"The greatest hardship was not being allowed to write letters," Alix said.

"The Germans didn't allow it?"

"Only postcards. Printed postcards with blanks that you filled in. Five or six sentences. You could say that so-and-so had died, or was sick. That kind of thing. We used to make up names of people that didn't exist, and we managed to convey all sorts of information that the Germans didn't recognize, just by filling in the blanks."

"Did my niece tell you that during the Occupation she and my sister hid a girl in their apartment in Paris?" Mme Viénot said. "The Gestapo was looking for her."

"She was a school friend," Alix explained. "I knew she was in the Résistance, and one day she telephoned me and asked if she could spend the night with me. I told her that it wasn't convenient—that I had asked another girl to stay with me that night. And after she had hung up, I realized what she was trying to tell me."

"How did you manage to reach her again?"

"I sent word, through a little boy in the house where she lived. She came the next night, and stayed four months with us."

"I was in and out of the apartment all the time," Mme Viénot said, "and never suspected anything. I saw the girl occasionally and thought she had come to see Alix."

"We didn't dare tell anyone," Alix said, "for her sake."

"After the war was over, my sister told me what had been going on right under my nose," Mme Viénot said. "But it was very dangerous for them, you know. It might have cost them their lives."

Mme Cestre raised her hearing aid to her ear, and Alix leaned toward her mother and explained what they were talking about.

"She was rather imprudent," Mme Cestre said mildly.

"She went out at night sometimes," Alix said. "And she told several people where she was hiding. She enjoyed the danger of their knowing."

"Were many people you know involved in the Résistance?" Harold asked.

"In almost every French family something like that was going on," Mme Viénot said.

A silence fell over the room. When the conversation was resumed, Harold said: "There is something I have been wanting to ask you: when people do something kind, what do you say to them?"

" 'Merci,' " Alix said.

"I know, but I don't mean that. I mean when you are really grateful."

" 'Merci beaucoup.' Or 'Merci bien.' "

"But if it is something really kind, and you want them to know that you—"

"It is the same."

"There are no other words?"

"No."

"In English there are different ways of saying that you are deeply grateful."

"In French we use the same words."

"How do people know, then, that you appreciate what they have done for you?"

"By the way you say it—by your expression, the intonation of your voice."

"But that makes it so much more difficult!" he exclaimed.

"It is a question of sincerity," she said, smiling at him as if she had just offered him the passkey to all those gates he kept trying to see over.

Chapter 10

On Monday morning the Bentley appeared in front of the château for the last time. The chauffeur carried the luggage out, and then a huge bouquet of delphiniums wrapped in damp newspaper, which he placed on the floor of the back seat. Mme Viénot, Mme Bonenfant, Harold, Barbara, and Alix accompanied M. and Mme Carrère out to the car. Harold watched carefully while Mme Carrère was thanking Mme Viénot for the flowers and the quart of country cream she held in her hand. They did not embrace each other, but then Mme Carrère was not given to effusiveness. The fact that she didn't speak of seeing Mme Viénot again in Paris might mean merely that it wasn't necessary to speak of it. One thing he felt sure of—there was not one stalk of delphinium left in the garden.

The necessary handshaking was accomplished, and Mme Carrère got into the back seat of the car. M. Carrère put his hand in his pocket and drew out his card, which he handed Harold. It was a business card, but on the back he had written the address and telephone number of the apartment in the rue du faubourg St. Honoré. As Harold tucked the card in his wallet, he felt stripped and exposed, a small boy in the presence of his benign, all-knowing father. If they found themselves in any kind of difficulty, M. Carrère said, they were to feel free to call on him for help. What he seemed to be saying (so kind was the expression in the expert old clown's eyes, so comprehending and tolerant his smile) was that human thought is by no means as private as it seems, and all you need in order to read somebody else's mind is the willingness to read your own. With his legend intact and his lilac-colored shawl around his shoulders, he leaned forward one last time and waved, through the car window.

Waving, Harold said: "I hope the drive isn't too much for him."

"They are going to stop somewhere for lunch and a rest," Mme Viénot said. Already, though the car had not yet turned into the public road, she seemed different, less conventional, lighter, happier. "They are both very dear people," she said, but he could not see that she was sorry to have them go.

"We are thinking of going to Chaumont this afternoon," he said.

"And you'd like me to arrange about the taxi? Good. I'll tell her to come at two."

"Alix is coming with us," he went on, and then, spurred by his polite upbringing: "We hope you will come too." He did not at all want her to come; it would be much pleasanter with just the three of them. But in the world of his childhood nobody had ever said that pleasure takes precedence over not hurting people's feelings, even when there is a very good chance that they don't have any feelings. "If the idea appeals to you," he said, hoping to hear that it didn't. "Perhaps it would only be boring, since you have seen the château so many times."

"I would enjoy going," Mme Viénot said. "And perhaps the taxi could bring us home by way of Onzain? I have an errand there, and it is not far out of the way."

But if Mme Viénot was coming to Chaumont with them, what about poor Mme Straus-Muguet? Wouldn't she feel left out?

"And will you please invite Mme Straus-Muguet for us," he said.

"Oh, that won't be necessary," Mme Viénot exclaimed. "It is

very nice of you to think of it, but I'm sure she doesn't expect to be asked, and it will make five in the taxi."

When he insisted, she agreed reluctantly to convey the invitation, and a few minutes later, meeting him on the stairs, she reported that it had been accepted.

The taxi came promptly at two, and all five of them crowded into it, and still apologizing cheerfully to one another for taking up too much space they arrived at a point directly across the river from Chaumont, which was as far as they could go by car. The ferry was loading on the opposite shore, and Alix and Mme Viénot did not agree about where it would land. After they had scrambled down the steep sandbank to the water's edge, they saw some hikers and cyclists waiting a hundred yards upstream, at the exact spot where Mme Viénot had said the ferry would come. She and Harold began to help Mme Straus-Muguet up the bank again. The two girls took off their shoes and waded into the water. The sound of their voices and their laughter made him turn and look back. Alix tucked the hem of her skirt under her belt. Then the two girls waded in deeper and deeper, with their dresses pulled up and their white thighs showing.

There are certain scenes that (far more than artifacts dug up out of the ground or prehistoric cave paintings, which have a confusing freshness and newness) serve to remind us of how old the human race is, and of the beautiful, touching sameness of most human occasions. Anything that is not anonymous is all a dream. And who we are, and whether our parents embraced life or were disappointed by it, and what will become of our children couldn't be less important. Nobody asks the name of the athlete tying his sandal on the curved side of the Greek vase or whether the lonely traveler on the Chinese scroll arrived at the inn before dark.

He realized with a pang that he had lost Barbara. He was up here on the bank helping an old woman to keep her balance instead of down there with his shoes and stockings off, and so he had lost her. She had turned into a French girl, a stranger to him.

The girls' way was blocked by a clump of cattails. They stopped and considered what to do. Then, taking each other by the hand, they started slowly out into still deeper water. . . . The water was too deep. They could not get around the cattails without swimming, and so they turned back and went the rest of the way on dry land.

The ferryboat coming toward them from the opposite shore was long and narrow, and the gunwales were low in the water. When it was about fifty yards from the bank, the ferryman turned off the outboard motor, which was on the end of a long pole, and lifted it out of the water. The boat drifted in slowly. Harold did not see how it could possibly hold all the people who were now waiting to cross over—hollow-cheeked, pale, undernourished hikers and cyclists, dressed for *le sport*, in shorts and open-collared shirts, with their sleeves rolled up. The slightest wind would have blown them away like dandelion fluff.

They pulled the prow of the boat up onto the mud bank and took the bicycles carefully from the hands of the ferryman. When the passengers had jumped ashore, the hikers and cyclists stood aside politely while the party from the château went on board. Mme Viénot and Mme Straus-Muguet sat in the stern, in the only seat there was. Barbara and Alix perched on the side of the boat, next to them. Harold stood among the other passengers. Under the ferryman's direction a dozen bicycles were placed in precarious balance. The boat settled lower and lower as more people, more bicycles with loaded saddle bags came on board. There were no oars, and the ferryman, on whom all their lives depended, was a sixteen-year-old boy with patches on his pants. He pushed his way excitedly past wire wheels and bare legs, shouting directions. When everybody was on board, he shoved the boat away from the shore with his foot, all but fell in, ran to the stern, making the boat rock wildly, and lowered the outboard motor. The motor caught, and they turned around slowly and headed for the other shore.

"This boat is not safe!" Mme Viénot told the ferryman, and when he didn't pay any attention to her she said to Barbara: "I shall complain to the mayor of Brenodville about it. . . . The current is very treacherous in the middle of the river."

Mme Straus-Muguet took Barbara's hand and confessed that she could not swim.

"Harold is a very good swimmer," Barbara said.

"M. Rhodes will swim to Mme Straus and support her if the boat capsizes," Mme Viénot decided.

"Très bien," Mme Straus-Muguet said, and called their attention to the scenery.

Harold's mind ran off an unpleasant two-second movie in which he saw himself in the water, supporting an aged woman whose life was nearly finished, while Barbara, encumbered by her clothes, with no one to help her, drowned before his eyes.

Out in the middle of the river there was a wind, and the gray clouds directly over their heads looked threatening. Mme Straus-Muguet was reminded of the big painting in the Louvre of Dante and Virgil crossing the River Styx. She was so gallant and humorous, in circumstances a woman of her age could hardly have expected to find herself in and few would have agreed to, that she became a kind of heroine in the eyes of everyone. The cyclists turned and watched her, admiring her courage.

The shore they had left receded farther and farther. They were in the main current of the river for what seemed a long long time, and then slowly the opposite shore began to draw nearer. They could pick out details of houses and see the people on the bank. As Harold stepped onto the sand he felt the triumph and elation of a survivor. The ferryboat had not sunk after all, and he and everybody in it were braver than they had supposed.

The climb from the water's edge up the cliff was clearly too much for a woman in the neighborhood of seventy. Mme Straus-Muguet took Harold's arm and clung to it. With now Alix and now Barbara on her other side supporting her, she pressed on, through sand, up steep paths and uneven stone stairways, stopping again and again to exclaim to herself how difficult it was, to catch her breath, to rest. Her face grew flushed and then it became gray, but she would not hear of their turning back. When they were on level ground at last and saw the towers and drawbridge of the château, she stopped once more and exclaimed, but this time it was pleasure that moved her. "You do not need to worry any more about me," she said. "I am quite recovered."

While they were waiting for the guide, she bought and presented to Harold and Barbara a set of miniature postcards of the rooms they were about to see. She called Barbara's attention to the tapestries in the Salon du Concert before the guide had a chance to speak of them. Confronted with a glass case containing portrait medallions by the celebrated Italian artist Nini, she said that she had a passion for bas-relief and could happily spend the rest of her life studying this collection. They were shown the dressing table of Catherine de Médicis, and Mme Straus insisted on climbing the steep stone staircase to the tower where the Queen had learned from her astrologer the somber fate in store for her three sons who would sit on the throne of France: one dead of a fever, within a year of his coronation, one the victim of melancholy, and one of the assassin's dagger. As Mme Straus listened to this story, her sensitive face reflected the surprise and then the consternation of Catherine de Médicis, whose feelings she, a mother, could well appreciate, though they were separated by four centuries. Mme Viénot congratulated the guide on his diction and his knowledge of history, and Mme Straus-Muguet congratulated him on the view up and down the river. She was reluctant to leave the stables where the elephant had been housed, but perfectly willing to return to the river bank and for the second time in one day risk death by drowning.

The taxi was where they had left it. It had waited all afternoon for them, time in Brenodville being far less dear than gasoline. Mme Viénot's errand took them a considerable distance out of their way but gave them an opportunity to see the villages of

Chouzy and Onzain. The grain merchant at Onzain was away, and his wife refused to let Mme Viénot have the laying mash she had come for. They rode home with two large sacks of inferior horse feed tied across the front and back of the taxi.

That evening before dinner, Harold heard a knock and went to the door. Mme Straus entered breathing harshly from the stairs. "What a charming room!" she exclaimed.

She was leaving tomorrow morning, to go and stay with friends at Chaumont, and she wanted to give them her address and telephone number in Paris. "When you come," she said, squeezing Barbara's hand, "we will have lunch together, and afterward take a drive through the city. It will be my great pleasure to show it to you."

She had brought with her two books—two thin volumes of poetry, which they were to read and return to her when they met again—and also some letters. They lay mysteriously in her lap while she told them about the convent in Auteuil where she now lived. She was most fortunate that the sisters had taken her in; the waiting list was long. And the serenity was so good for her.

She looked down at the letters in her lap. They were from Mme Marguerite Mailly, of the Comédie Française, whose Phèdre and Andromaque were among the great performances of the French theater. Mme Straus considered these letters her most priceless possession, and took them with her wherever she went. Mme Mailly's son, such a gifted and handsome boy, so intelligent, was only eighteen when his plane was shot down at the very beginning of the war.

"I too lost a son in this way," Mme Straus said.

"Your son was killed in the war?" Harold asked.

"He died in an airplane accident in the thirties," Mme Straus-Muguet said. The look in her eyes as she told them this was not tragic but speculative, and he saw that she was considering their chaise longue. Because she knew only too well the dangers of giving way to immoderate grief, she had been able, she said, to lead her friend gently and gradually to an attitude of acceptance. She opened her lorgnette and, peering through it, read excerpts from the actress's letters, in which Mme Mailly thanked her dear friend for pointing out to her the one true source of consolation.

Harold read the inscription on the flyleaf of one of the books (the handwriting was bold and enormous) and then several of the poems. They seemed to be love poems—incestuous love sonnets to the actress's dead son, whose somewhat girlish countenance served as a frontispiece. But when would he ever have time to read them?

"I'm afraid something might happen to them while they're in our possession," he said. "I really don't think we ought to keep them."

But Mme Straus was insistent. They were to keep the two volumes of poetry until they saw her again.

The next morning, standing in the foyer, with her suitcases around her on the black and white marble floor, she kept the taxi waiting while she thanked Mme Viénot elaborately for her hospitality. When she turned and put out her hand, Harold bent down and kissed her on the cheek. Her response was pure pleasure. She dropped her little black traveling bag, raised her veil, said: "You have made it possible for me to do what I have been longing to do," and with her hands on both his shoulders kissed him first on one cheek and then on the other.

"Voilà l'amour," Mme Viénot said, smiling wickedly. The remark was ignored.

Mme Straus kissed Barbara and then, looking into their eyes affectionately, said: "Thank you, my dear children, for not allowing the barrier of age to come between us!"

Then she got into the taxi and drove off to stay with her friends at Chaumont. In order that her friends here should not be totally without resource during her absence, she was leaving behind the box of *diamonoes*.

THAT AFTERNOON, Barbara and Harold and Alix took the bus into Blois. The Americans were paying still another visit to the château; Harold wanted to see with his own eyes the rooms through which the Duc de Guise had moved on the way to his death. They suggested that Alix come with them, but she had errands to do, and she wanted to pay a visit to the nuns at the nursery school where she had worked during the early part of the war. They would gladly have given up the château for the nursery school if she had asked them to go with her, but she didn't ask them, and she refused gently to meet them for tea at the pâtisserie. They did not see her again until they met at the end of the afternoon. She was pushing a second-hand baby carriage along the sidewalk and they saw that she was radiantly happy.

"It is a very good carriage," she said, "and it was cheap. Eugène will be very pleased with me."

The baby carriage was hoisted on top of the bus, and they took turns pushing it home from the highway. Alix pointed out the house of Thérèse's family, and in a field Harold saw a horse-drawn reaper. "Why, I haven't seen one of those since I was a child!" he said excitedly, and then proceeded to describe to Alix the elaborate machine that had taken its place.

It was a nice evening, and they were enjoying the walk. "I hope you will decide to stay in our apartment," Alix said suddenly. "It would be so pleasant for Eugène. It would mean company for him."

They did not have to answer because at that moment they were passing a farmhouse and she saw a little boy by the woodshed and spoke to him. He was learning to ride a bicycle that was too big for him. She left the baby carriage in the middle of the road and went over to give him some pointers.

When they got home, the Americans went straight to their room, intending to rest before dinner. Harold had just got into bed and pulled the covers up when they heard a knock. Barbara slipped on her dressing gown, and before she got to the door it opened. Though one says the nail is drawn to the magnet, if you look very closely you see that the magnet is also drawn to the nail. Mme Viénot had come to tell them about her visit to the mayor of Brenodville.

". . . I said that the ferry at Chaumont was extremely dangerous, and that some day, unless something was done about it, a number of people would lose their lives. . . . You won't believe what he said. The whole history of modern France is in this one remark. He said"—her eyes shone with amusement—"he said: 'I know but it's at Chaumont.' . . . How was your afternoon?"

She sat down on the edge of Harold's bed, keeping him a prisoner there; he was stark naked under the covers.

Since she did not seem concerned by the fact that his shoulders and arms were bare, he did his best to forget this, and she went on talking cozily and cheerfully, as if their intimacy were long established and a source of mutual pleasure. He realized that, with reservations and at arm's length, he really did like her. She was intelligent and amusing, and her pale-blue eyes saw either everything or nothing. Her day was full of small but nevertheless remarkable triumphs. In spite of rationing and shortages of almost everything you could think of, the food was always interesting. Though the house was cold, it was also immaculately clean. And there were never any awkward pauses in the conversations that took place in front of the empty Franklin stove or around the dining-room table.

She told them how she had searched for and finally found the wallpaper for this room; and about the picturesque fishing villages and fiords of Ile d'Yeu, where, in happier circumstances, the family always went in August, for the sea air and the bathing; and about the year that Eugène and Alix had spent in Marseilles. Rather than be a fonctionnaire in Paris, Eugène chose to work as a day laborer, carrying mortar and rubble, in Marseilles. They lived in the slums, and their evenings were spent among working people, whom he hoped to educate so that France would have a future and not, like Italy, merely a past. He was not the only young man of aristocratic family to dedicate himself to the poor in this way; there were others; there was, in fact, a movement, which was now losing its impetus because the church had not encouraged it. Eugène should perhaps have taken holy orders, as he once thought seriously of doing. It was in his temperament to go the whole way, to go to extremes, to become a saint. Shortly before the baby was born, they came back to Paris. Alix did not want their child to grow up in such sordid surroundings. He was not very happy in his job at the Ministry of Planning and External Affairs, and Mme Viénot could not help thinking that both of them were less happy than they had been before, but the decision was, of course, the only right one. And after all, if one applied oneself, and had the temperament for it, one could do very well in the government. Her son-in-law, for instance— "I hope you didn't repeat to M. Carrère what I said about his being talked about as the future Minister of Finance?"

Harold shook his head.

"I'm afraid it was not very discreet of me," she said. "Jean-Claude is quite different from the rest of his family, who are charming but hors de siècle."

"Does that mean 'old-fashioned'?"

"They are gypsies."

"Real gypsies? The kind that travel around in wagons?"

"Oh mercy no, they are perfectly respectable, and of a very old family, but— How shall I put it? They are unconventional. They come to meals when they feel like it, wear strange clothes, stay up all night practicing the flute, and say whatever comes into their minds. . . . Is there a word for that in English?"

"Bohemian," Barbara said.

"Yes," Mme Viénot said, nodding. "But not from the country of Bohemia. His mother is so amusing, so unlike anyone else. Sometimes she will eat nothing but cucumbers for weeks at a time. And Jean-Claude's father blames every evil under the sun on the first Duke of Marlborough—with perhaps some justice but not a great deal. There are too many villains of our own époque, alas. . . . I am keeping you from resting?"

Reassured, she stayed so long that they were all three late for dinner. The box of *diamonoes* remained unopened on Mme Viénot's desk in the petit salon, and the evening was given over, as before, to the game of conversation.

ON WEDNESDAY MORNING the cook prepared a picnic lunch and the Americans took the train to Amboise. There was a new bridge across the river at Amboise, and so they did not have to risk their lives. After they had seen the château they went and peered into the little chapel where Leonardo da Vinci either was or was not buried.

Down below in the village, Harold saw a row of ancient taxis near the Hôtel Lion d'Or, and arranged with the driver of the newest one to take them to Chenonceau, twelve kilometers away. After they had eaten their lunch on the river bank, they went back to where the row of taxis had been and, mysteriously, there was only one and it was not their taxi, but the man Harold had talked to was sitting in the driver's seat and seemed to be waiting for them. It was a wood-burning taxi, and for the first few blocks they kept looking out of the back window at the trail of black smoke they were leaving in their wake.

Crossing a bridge on the narrow dirt road to Chenonceau, they passed a hiker with a heavy rucksack on his back. The driver informed them that the hiker was a compatriot of theirs, and Harold told him to stop until the hiker had caught up with them. He was Danish, not American, but on finding out that he was going to the château, Harold invited him into the car anyway. He spoke English well and French about the way they did.

The taxi let them out at an ornamental iron gate some distance from the château itself. They stayed together as far as the drawbridge, and then suddenly the Dane was no longer with them or in fact anywhere. Half an hour later, when they emerged from the château with a dozen other sight-seers, they saw him standing under a tree that was far enough away from the path so that they did not have to join him if they did not care to. The three of them studied the château from all sides and found the place where they could get the best view of the inverted castle in the river. The formal gardens of Catherine de Médicis and Diane de Poitiers were both planted in potatoes. A small bronze sign said that the gardens had been ruined by the inundation of May 1940, and since the river flowing under the château at that moment was only a few inches deep, they took this to be a reference to the Germans, though as a matter of fact it was not. They rode back to Amboise in the wood-burning taxi and, sitting on the bank of the Loire, Harold and Barbara shared what was left of their lunch and a bottle of red wine with the Dane, who produced some tomatoes for them out of his rucksack and told them the story of his life. His name was Nils Jensen, he was nineteen years old, and he had cut himself off from his inheritance. It had been expected that he would go into the family business in Copenhagen and instead he was studying medicine. He wanted to become a psychiatrist. He could only bring a small amount of money out of Denmark, and so he was hiking through France. Harold saw in his eyes that there was something he wanted them to know about him that he could not say—that he was well bred and a gentleman. He did not need to say it, but he was a gentleman who had been living largely on tomatoes and he badly needed a bath and clean clothes.

He had not yet decided where he was going to spend the night; he might stay here; but if he went on to Blois he would be taking the same train they were taking. He had not yet seen the château of Amboise, and so they said good-by, provisionally. The Americans went halfway across the bridge and down a flight of stairs to a little island in the middle of the river, and there they walked up and down in a leafy glade, searching for just some small trace of the Visigoths and the Franks who, around the year 500 A.D., met here and celebrated a peace treaty, the terms of which neither army found it convenient to honor.

At the railroad station, Harold and Barbara looked around for Nils Jensen, and Harold considered buying third-class tickets, in case he turned up later, but in the end decided that he was not coming and they might as well be comfortable. When the train drew in, there he was. He appeared right out of the ground, with a second-class ticket in his hand—bought, it was clear, so that he could ride with them.

The god of love could be better represented than by a little boy blindfolded and with a bow and arrow. Why not a member of the Actors' Equity, with his shirt cuffs turned back, an impressive diamond ring on one finger, his long black hair heavily pomaded, his magic made possible by a trunkful of accessories and a stooge somewhere in the audience. Think of a card—any card. There is no card you can think of that the foxy vaudeville magician doesn't have up his sleeve or in a false pocket of his long coattails.

The train carried them past Monteux, past Chaumont on the other side of the river. There was so much that had to be said in this short time, and so much that their middle-class upbringing prevented them from saying or even knowing they felt. The Americans did not even tell Nils Jensen—except with their eyes, their smiles—how much they liked being with him and everything about him. Nils Jensen did not say: "Oh I don't know which of you I'm in love with—I love you both! And I've looked everywhere, I've looked so long for somebody I could be happy with. . . ." Nevertheless, they all three used every minute that they had together. The train, which could not be stopped, could not be made to go slower, carried them past Onzain and Chouzy. At Brenodville they shook hands, and Angle A and Angle B got out and then stood on the brick platform waving until the train took Angle C (as talented and idealistic and tactful and congenial a friend as they were ever likely to have) away from them, with nothing to complete this triangle ever again but an address in Copenhagen that must have been incorrectly copied, since a letter sent there was never replied to.

Walking through the village, with the shadows stretching clear across the road in front of them, they saw windows and doors that were wide open, they heard voices, they met people who smiled and spoke to them. They thought for a moment that the man returning from the fields with his horse and his dog was one of the men who were sitting on the café terrace the day they arrived, and then decided that he wasn't. Coming to an open gate, they stopped and looked in. There was no one around and so they stood there studying the courtyard with its well, its neat woodpile, its bicycle, its two-wheeled cart, its tin-roofed porch, its clematis and roses growing in tubs, its dog and cat and chickens and patient old farm horse, its feeding trough and watering trough, so like an illustration in a beginning French grammar: *A* is for *Auge*, *B* is for *Bicyclette*, *C* is for *Cheval*, etc.

When they were on the outskirts of the village, they saw Mme Viénot's gardener coming toward them in the cart and assumed he had business in the village. He stopped when he was abreast of them, and waited. They stood looking up at him and he told them to get in. Mme Viénot had sent him, thinking that they would be tired after their long day's excursion. They *were* tired, and grateful that she had thought of them.

In the beautiful calm evening light, driving so slowly between fields that had just been cut, they learned that the white horse was named Pompon, and that he was thirty years old. The gardener explained that it was his little boy who had taken Harold by the hand and led him to the house of M. Fleury. They found it easy to talk to him. He was simple and direct, and so were the words he used, and so was the look in his eyes. They felt he liked them, and they wished they could know him better.

On the table in their room, propped against the vase of flowers, was a letter from Mme Straus-Muguet. The handwriting was so eccentric and the syntax so full of flourishes that Harold took it downstairs and asked Alix to translate it for them. Mme Straus was inviting them to take tea with her at the house of her friends, who would be happy to meet two such charming Americans.

He watched Alix's face as she read the protestations of affection at the close of the letter.

"Why do you smile?"

She refused to explain. "You would only think me uncharitable," she said. "As in fact I am."

He was quite sure that she wasn't uncharitable, so there must be something about Mme Straus that gave rise to that doubtful smile. But what? Though he again urged her to tell him, she would not. The most she would say was that Mme Straus was "roulante."

He went back upstairs and consulted the dictionary. "Roulante" meant "rolling." It also meant a "side-splitting, killing (sight, joke)."

Reluctantly, he admitted to himself, for the first time, that there was something theatrical and exaggerated about Mme Straus's manner and conversation. But there was still a great gap between that and "side-splitting." Did Alix see something he didn't see? Probably she felt that as Americans they had a right to their own feelings about people, and did not want to spoil their friendship with Mme Straus. But in a way she *had* spoiled it, since it is always upsetting to discover that people you like do not think very much of each other.

When he showed Barbara the page of the dictionary, it turned out that she too had reservations about Mme Straus. "The thing is, she might become something of a burden if she attached herself to us while we're in Paris. We'll only be there for ten days. And I wouldn't like to hurt her feelings."

Though they did not speak of it, they themselves were suffering from hurt feelings; they did not understand why Alix would not spend more time with them. For reasons they could not make out, she was simply inaccessible. They knew that she slept late, and she was, of course, occupied with the baby, and perhaps with her sister's children. But on the other hand, she had brought a nursemaid with her, so perhaps it wasn't the children who were keeping her from them. Perhaps she didn't want to see any more of them. . . . But if that were true, they would have felt it in her manner. When they met at mealtime, she was always pleased to see them, always acted as if their friendship was real and permanent, and she made the lunch and dinner table conversation much more enjoyable by the care she took of them. But why didn't she want to go anywhere with them? Why did she never seek out their company at odd times of the day?

She was uneasy about Eugène—that much she did share with them. She had hoped that he would write and there had been no letter. Harold suggested that he might be too busy to write, since the government had jumped after all, without waiting this time for the August vacation to be over. He asked if the crisis would affect Eugène's position, and she said that, actually, Eugène had two positions in the Ministry of Planning and External Affairs, neither of which would suffer any change under a different cabinet, since they were not that important.

The dining-room table was now the smallest the Americans had seen it and, raising her hearing aid to her ear, Mme Cestre took part in the conversation.

Alix explained that her mother's health was delicate; she was a prey to mysterious diseases that the doctors could neither cure nor account for. There would be an outbreak of blisters on the ends of her fingers, and then it would go away as suddenly as it had come. She had attacks of dizziness, when the floor seemed to come up and strike her foot. She could not stand to be in the sun for more than a few minutes. Alix herself thought sometimes that it was because her mother was so good and kind—really much kinder than anybody else. Beggars, old women selling limp, tarnished roses, old men with a handful of pencils had only to look at her and she would open her purse. She could not bear the sight of human misery.

Leaning toward her mother, Alix said: "I have been telling Barbara and Harold how selfish you are."

Mme Cestre raised the hearing aid to her ear and adjusted the little pointer. The jovial remark was repeated and she smiled benignly at her daughter.

When she entered the conversation, it was always abruptly, on a new note, since she had no idea what they were talking about. She broke in upon Mme Bonenfant's observation that there was no one in Rome in August—that it was quite deserted, that the season there had always been from November through Lent—with the observation that cats are indifferent to their own reflection in a mirror.

"Dogs often fail to recognize themselves," she said, as they all stared at her in surprise. "Children are pleased. The wicked see what other people see . . . and the mirror sees nothing at all."

Or when Alix was talking about the end of the war, and how she and Sabine suddenly decided that they wanted to be in Paris for the Liberation and so got on their bicycles and rode there, only to be sent back to the country because there wasn't enough food, Mme Cestre remarked to Barbara: "My husband used to do the packing always. I did it once when we were first married, but he had been a bachelor too long, and no one could fold coatsleeves properly but him. . . . It is quite true that when I did it they were wrinkled."

It was hard not to feel that this note of irrelevance must be part of her character, but once she was oriented in the conversation, Mme Cestre's remarks were always pertinent to it, and interesting. Her English was better than Alix's or than Mme Viénot's, and without any trace of a French accent.

Sometimes she would sit with her hearing aid on her lap, content with her own thoughts and the perpetual silence that her deafness created around her. But then she would raise the hearing aid to her ear and prepare to re-enter the conversation.

"Did Alix tell you that I am writing a book?" she said to her sister as they were waiting for Thérèse and the boy to clear the table for the next course.

"I didn't know you were, Maman," Alix said.

"I thought I had told you. It is in the form of a diary, and it consists largely of aphorisms."

"You are taking La Rochefoucauld as your model," Mme Bonenfant said approvingly.

"Yes and no," Mme Cestre said. "I have a title for it: 'How to Be a Successful Mother-in-Law.' . . . The relationship is never an easy one, and a treatise on the subject would be useful, and perhaps sell thousands of copies. I shall ask Eugène to criticize it when I am finished, and perhaps do a short preface, if he has the time. I find I have a good deal to say. . . ."

"My sister also has a talent for drawing," Mme Viénot said. "She does faces that are really quite good likenesses, and at the same time there is an element of caricature that is rather cruel. I do not understand it. It is utterly at variance with her nature. Once she showed me a drawing she had done of me and I burst into tears."

THURSDAY WAS A NICE DAY. The sun shone, it was warm, and Harold and Barbara spent the entire afternoon on the bank of the river, in their bathing suits. When they got home they found a scene out of *Anna Karenina*. Mme Bonenfant, Mme Viénot, Mme Cestre, and Thérèse were sitting under the Lebanon cedar, to the right of the terrace, with their chairs facing an enormous burlap bag, which they kept reaching into. They were shelling peas for canning.

Alix was in the courtyard, making some repairs on her bicycle. She had had a letter from Eugène. "He sends affectionate greetings to you both," she said. "He is coming down to the country tomorrow night. And Mummy asked me to tell you, for her, that it would give her great pleasure if you would stay in the apartment while you are in Paris."

This time the invitation was accepted.

After dinner, Mme Viénot opened the desk in the petit salon and took out a packet of letters, written to her mother at the château. She translated passages from them and read other passages in French, with the pride of a conscientious historian. Most of the letters were about the last week before the liberation of the city. The inhabitants of Paris, forbidden to leave their houses, had kept in active communication with one another by telephone.

"But couldn't the Germans prevent it?" Harold asked.

"Not without shutting off the service entirely, which they didn't dare to do. We knew everything that was happening," Mme Viénot said. "When the American forces reached the southwestern limits of the city, the church bells began to toll, one after another, on the Left Bank, as each section of the city was delivered from the Germans, and finally the deep bell of Notre Dame. In the midst of the street fighting I left the apartment, to perform an errand, and found myself stranded in a doorway of a house, with bullets whistling through the air around me." In the letter describing this, she neither minimized the danger nor pretended that she had been involved in an act of heroism. The errand was a visit, quite essential, to her dressmaker in the rue du Mont-Thabor.

On Friday afternoon, Mme Viénot rode with Harold and Barbara in their taxi to Blois, where they parted. She went off down the street with an armful of clothes for the cleaner's, and they got on a sight-seeing bus. They chose the tour that consisted of Chambord, Cheverny, and Chaumont instead of the tour of Azay-le-Rideau, Ussé, and Chinon, because Barbara, looking through the prospectus, thought she recognized in Cheverny the white château with the green lawn in front of it. Cheverny did have a green lawn in front of it but it was not at all like a fairy-tale castle, and Chambord was too big. It reminded them of Grand Central Station. Since they had already seen Chaumont, they got the driver to let them out at the castle gates, and stood looking around for a taxi that would take them to the house of Mme Straus-Muguet's friends. It turned out that there were no taxis. The proprietor of the restaurant across the road did not know where the house was, and it was rather late to be having tea, so instead they sat for a whole hour on the river bank, feeling as if they had broken through into some other existence. They watched the sun's red reflection on the water, the bathers, the children building sand castles, the goats cropping and straying, and the next two trips of the ferryboat; and then it was time for them to cross over, themselves, and take the train home.

Though they were very late, dinner was later still. They sat in the drawing room waiting for Eugène and Sabine to arrive.

When they met again at the château, Harold's manner with Mme Viénot's daughter was cautious. He was not at all sure she liked him. He and Eugène shook hands, and there was a flicker of recognition in the Frenchman's eyes that had in it also a slight suggestion of apology: at the end of a long day and a long journey, Harold must not expect too much of him. Tomorrow they would talk.

As Sabine started toward the stairs with her light suitcase, Mme Viénot said: "The Allégrets are giving a large dinner party tomorrow night. I accepted for you." Then, turning to Harold and Barbara: "My daughter is very popular. Whenever she is expected, the telephone rings incessantly. . . . You are included in the invitation, but you don't have to go if you don't want to."

"Are Alix and Eugène going?" he asked.

"Yes."

He and Barbara looked at each other, and then Barbara said: "Are you sure it is all right for us to go?"

"Quite sure," Mme Viénot said. "The Allégrets are a very old family. They are half Scottish. They are descended from the Duke of Berwick, who was a natural son of the English King James II, and followed him into exile, and became a marshal of France under Louis XIV."

During dinner, Eugène entertained them with a full account of the fall of the Schumann government. Day after day the party leaders met behind closed doors, and afterward they posed for the photographers on the steps of the Palais Bourbon, knowing that the photographers knew there was nothing of the slightest importance in the brief cases they held so importantly. What made this crisis different from the preceding ones was that no party was willing to accept the portfolios of Finance and Economics, and so it was quite impossible to form a government.

"But won't they have to do something?" Harold asked.

"Eventually," Mme Vienot said, "but not right away. For a while, the administrative branches of the government can and will go right on functioning."

"In my office," Eugène said, "letters are opened and read, and copies of the letters are circulated, but the letters are not answered, because an answer would involve a decision, and all decisions, even those of no consequence, are postponed, or better still, referred to the proper authority, who, unfortunately, has no authority. I have been working until ten or eleven o'clock every night on a report that will never be looked at, since the man who ordered it is now out of office."

At that moment, as if the house wanted to point out that there is no crisis that cannot give way to an even worse situation, the lights went off. They sat in total darkness until the pantry door opened and Thérèse's sullen peasant face appeared, lighted from below by two candles, which she placed on the dining-room table. She then lit the candles in the wall sconces and in a moment the room was ablaze with soft light. Looking at one face after another, Harold thought: This is the way it must have been in the old days, when Mme Viénot and Mme Cestre were still young, and they gave dinner parties, and the money wasn't gone, and the pond had water in it, and everybody agreed that France had the strongest army in Europe. . . . In the light of the still candle flames, everyone was beautiful, even Mme Viénot. As her upper eyelids descended, he saw that that characteristic blind look was almost (though not quite) the look of someone who is looking into the face of love.

At the end of dinner she pushed her chair back and, with a silver candlestick in her hand, she led them across the hall and into the petit salon, where they went on talking about the Occupation. It was the one subject they never came to the end of. They only put it aside temporarily at eleven o'clock, when, each person having been provided with his own candle, they went up the stairs, throwing long shadows before and behind them.

Chapter 11

"AVEZ-VOUS BIEN DORMI?" Harold asked, and Eugene held up his hand as if, right there at the breakfast table, with his hair uncombed and his eyes puffy with sleep, he intended to perform a parlor trick for them. Looking at Barbara, he said: "You don't lahv your hus-band, do you?" and to Harold's astonishment she said: "No."

He blushed.

"I mean yes, I do love him," Barbara said." I didn't understand your question. Why, you're speaking *English!*"

Delighted with the success of his firecracker, Eugène sat down and began to eat his breakfast. He had enrolled at the Berlitz. He had had five lessons. His teacher was pleased with his progress. Still in a good humor, he went upstairs to shave and dress.

Thérèse brought the two heaviest of the Americans' suitcases down from the third floor, and then the dufflebag, and put them in the dog cart. Mme Viénot had pointed out that the trip up to Paris would be less strenuous if they checked some of their luggage instead of taking it all in the compartment with them. Harold and the gardener waited until Eugène came out of the house and climbed up on the seat beside them. Then the gardener spoke to his horse gently, in a coaxing voice, as if to a child, and they drove off to the village. At the station, Eugène took care of the forms that had to be filled out, and bought the railroad tickets with the money Harold handed him, but he was withdrawn and silent. Either his mood had changed since breakfast or he did not feel like talking in front of the gardener. When they got back to the château, Harold went upstairs first, and then, finding that Barbara was washing out stockings in the bathroom and didn't need him for anything, he went back downstairs and settled himself in the drawing room with a book. No one ever used the front door—they always came and went by the doors that opened onto the terrace—and so he would see anybody who passed through the downstairs. When Eugène did not reappear, Harold concluded that he was with Alix and the baby in the back wing of the house, where it did not seem proper to go in search of him, since he had been separated from his family for five days.

It was not a very pleasant day and there was some perverse influence at work. The village electrician could not find the short circuit, which must be somewhere inside the walls, and he said that the whole house needed rewiring. And Alix, who was never angry at anyone, was angry at her aunt. She wanted to have a picnic with Sabine and the Americans on the bank of the river, and Mme Viénot said that it wasn't convenient, that it would make extra work in the kitchen. This was clearly not true. They ate lunch in the dining room as usual, and at two thirty they set out on their bicycles, with their bathing suits and towels and four big, thick ham sandwiches that they did not want and that Mme Viénot had made, herself.

The sunshine was pale and watery and without warmth. They hid the bicycles in a little grove between the highway and the river, and then withdrew farther into the trees and changed into their bathing suits. When Barbara and Harold came out, they saw Alix and Sabine down by the water. Eugène was standing some distance away from them, fully dressed, and looking as if he were not part of this expedition.

"Aren't you going in?" Harold called, and, getting no answer, he turned to Alix and said: "Isn't he going in swimming with us?"

She shook her head. "He doesn't feel like swimming."

"Why not?"

"He says the water is dirty."

Then why did he bring his bathing suit if he didn't feel like swimming in dirty water, Harold wondered. Didn't he know the river would be dirty?

The water was also lukewarm and the current sluggish. And instead of the sandy bottom that Harold expected, they walked in soft oozing mud halfway up to their knees, and had to wade quite far out before they could swim. Alix had a rubber ball, and they stood far apart in the shallow water and threw it back and forth. Harold was self-conscious with Sabine. They had not spoken a word to each other since she arrived. The ball passed between the four of them now. They did not smile. It felt like a scene from the Odyssey. When the rubber ball came to him, sometimes, aware of what a personal act it was, he threw it to Sabine. Sometimes she sent it spinning across the water to him. But more often she threw it to one of the two girls. He didn't dislike or distrust her but he couldn't imagine what she was really like, and her gray wool bathing suit troubled him. It was the cut and the color of the bathing suits that are handed out with a locker key and a towel in public bathhouses, and he wondered if she was comparing it with Barbara's, and her life with what she imagined Barbara's life to be like.

From down river, behind a grove of trees, they heard some boys splashing and shouting. On the other bank, sheep appeared over the brow of the green hill, cropping as they came. Farther down the river, out of sight, was Chaumont, with its towers and its drawbridge. Then Amboise, and back from the river, on a river of its own, Chenonceau. Much farther still were those other châteaux that he knew only by their pictures in the guidebook—Villandry and Luynes and Langeais and Azay-le-Rideau and Ussé and Chinon. And no more time left to see them.

They stopped throwing the ball, and he waded in deeper and started swimming. The current in the channel was swifter but it did not seem very strong, even so, and he wanted to swim to the other bank, but he heard voices calling—"Come back!" (Barbara's voice) and "Come back, it's dangerous!" (Alix's voice) and so, reluctantly, rather than cause a fuss, he turned around. "People have drowned near here," Alix said as he stood up, dripping, and walked toward them. "And there is quicksand on the other bank."

They wiped their feet on the grass and then, using their towels, managed to get the mud off. Near the highway, two girls with bicycles and knapsacks were putting up a small tent for the night. Eugène stood watching them. The bathers went into the grove to dress and came out and sat on the ground and dutifully, without appetite, ate the thick ham sandwiches. Alix called to Eugène to come and join them and he replied that he was not hungry.

"Why is Eugène moody?" Sabine asked.

"He is upset because he has to wear a tweed coat to the Allégrets' party," Alix said.

"But so do I!" Harold exclaimed.

"No one expects you to have a dinner coat," she said gently. "It is quite all right. If Eugène had known, he could have brought his dinner coat down with him. That is why he is angry. He thinks I shouldn't have accepted without consulting him. Also, he is angry that there aren't enough bicycles."

"Aren't there?" Sabine asked.

"There are now," Alix said. "Eugène went and borrowed two from the gardener. But it annoys him that he should have to do that—that there aren't bicycles enough to go round."

She herself had long since reverted to her usual cheerful, sweet-tempered self.

Harold went into the trees and brought out the bicycles and they started home, the three girls pedaling side by side, since the highway was empty. After a quarter of a mile, Harold slowed down until Eugène drew abreast of him, and they rode along in what he tried to feel was a comfortable silence. The afternoon had been a disappointment to him, and not at all what he expected, but perhaps, now that they were alone, Eugène would open up—would tell him why he was in such an unsociable mood. For it couldn't be the coat or the bicycles. Something more serious must have happened. Something about his job, perhaps.

Eugène began to sing quietly, under his breath, and Harold rode a little closer to the other bicycle, listening. It was not an old song, judging by the words, but in the tune there was a slight echo of the thing that had moved him so, that day in Blois. When Eugène finished, Harold said: "What's the name of that song you were singing?"

"It's just a song," Eugène said, with his eyes on the road, and pure, glittering, personal dislike emanating from him like an aura.

The painful discovery that someone you like very much does not like you is one of the innumerable tricks the vaudeville magician has up his sleeve. Think of a card, any card: now you see it, now you don't . . . .

Struggling with the downward drag of hurt feelings, as old and familiar to him as the knowledge of his name, Harold kept even with the other bicycle for a short distance, as if nothing had happened, and then, looking straight ahead of him, he pedaled faster and moved ahead slowly until he was riding beside the three girls.

THE BICYCLES WERE BROUGHT out of the kitchen entry at six o'clock, and just as they were starting off, Mme Viénot appeared with three roses from the garden. Alix pinned her rose to the shoulder of her dress, and so did Sabine, but Barbara fastened hers in her hair.

"How pretty you look!" Mme Viénot said, her satisfied glance taking in all three of them.

With Eugène leading and Harold bringing up the rear, and the girls being careful that their skirts did not brush against the greasy chain or the wire wheels, they filed out of the courtyard and then plunged directly into the woods behind it. There were a number of paths, and Eugène chose one. The others followed him, still pushing their bicycles because the path was too sandy to ride on. After a quarter of a mile they emerged from the premature twilight of the woods into the open country and full daylight. Eugène took off his sport coat, folded it, and put it in the handlebar basket. Then he got on his bicycle and rode off down a dirt road that was not directly accessible to the château. Harold disposed of his coat in the same way. At first they rode single file, because of the deep ruts in the road, but before long they came to a concrete highway, and the three girls fanned out so that they could ride together. The two men continued to ride apart. Sometimes they all had to get off and push their bicycles uphill as the road led them up over the top of a long arc. At the crest, the land fell away in a panorama—terraced vineyards, the river valley, more hills, and little roads winding off into he wondered where—and they mounted their bicycles and went sailing downhill with the wind rushing past their ears.

"Isn't this a lovely way to go to a party?" Barbara said as Harold overtook her. "It's so unlike anything we're used to, I feel as if I'm dreaming it."

"Are you getting tired?" Alix called to them, over her shoulder.

"Oh no!" Barbara said.

"How far is it?" Harold asked.

"About five miles," Alix said.

"Such a beautiful evening," he said.

"Coming home there will be a moon," Alix said.

Just when the ride was beginning to seem rather long, they left the highway and took a narrow lane that was again loose sand and that forced them to dismount for a few yards. Pushing their bicycles, they crossed a small footbridge and started up a steep hill. When they got to the top, they had arrived. The Americans saw a big country house of gray stone with castellated trimming and lancet windows and a sweep of lawn in front of it. The guests—girls in long dresses, young men in dinner jackets—were standing about in clusters near a flight of stone steps that led up to the open front door.

The party from the château left their bicycles under a grape arbor at the side of the house. The two men put on their coats, and felt their ties. The girls straightened their short skirts, tucked in stray wisps of hair, looked at their faces in pocket mirrors and exclaimed, powdered their noses, put on white gloves. In front of the house, Alix and Eugène and Sabine were surrounded by people they knew, and Harold and Barbara were left stranded. It was a party of the very young, they perceived; most of the guests were not more than eighteen or nineteen. How *could* Mme Viénot have let them in for such an evening!

"I foresee one of the longest evenings of my entire life," Harold said out of the corner of his mouth.

Just when he was sure that Alix had abandoned them permanently, she came back and led them from group to group. The boys, thin and coltlike, raised Barbara's hand two thirds of the way to their lips, without enthusiasm or gallantry. The gesture was not at all like hand-kissing in the movies, but was, instead, abrupt, mechanical: they *pretended* to kiss her hand.

Alix was called away, and the Americans found themselves stranded again but inside the party this time, not outside. They struck up a conversation in French with a dark-haired girl who was studying music; then another conversation, in English, with a girl who said that she wanted to visit America. They talked about America, about New York. Alix returned, bringing a blond young man who was very tall and thin. An old and very dear friend of hers and Eugène's, she said. He bowed, started to say something, and was called away to answer a question, and didn't return. Then Alix too left them.

Barbara began to talk to another young man. Harold turned and gave his attention to the view—an immense sweep of marsh-land, the valley of the Cher, now autumn-colored with the setting sun. He looked back at the house, which was Victorian Gothic, and nothing like as handsome as Beaumesnil. It was, in fact, a perfectly awful house. And he was the oldest person he could see anywhere.

Once when he was a small child, he had had an experience like this. He must have been about six years old, and he was visiting his Aunt Mildred, who took him with her on a hay-ride party. But that time he was the youngest; he was the only child in a party of grownups; and so he opened his mouth and cried. But it didn't change anything. The hay-ride party went on and on and on, and his aunt was provoked at him for crying in front of everybody.

There was a sudden movement into the house, and he looked around for Alix and Sabine, without being able to find them. And then he saw Barbara coming toward him, against the flow of people up the stone steps to the front door. With her was a young man whom he liked on sight.

"I am Jean Allégret," the young man said as they shook hands. "Your wife tells me you are going to Salzburg for the Festival. I was stationed there at the end of the war. It is a beautiful city, but sad. It was a Nazi headquarters. Don't be surprised if— You are to sit with me at dinner." Taking Harold by the arm, he led him toward the stone steps.

As they passed into the house, Harold looked around for Barbara, who had already disappeared in the crowd. He caught a glimpse of rooms opening one out of another; of large and small paintings on the walls, in heavy gilt frames; of brocade armchairs, thick rugs, and little tables loaded with *objets*. The house had a rather stiff formality that he did not care for. In the dining room, the guests were reading the place cards at a huge oval table set for thirty places. Jean Allégret led him to a small table in an alcove, and then left him and returned a moment later, bringing a tall pretty blonde girl in a white tulle evening dress. She looks like a Persian kitten, Harold thought as he acknowledged the introduction. The girl also spoke English. Jean Allégret held her chair out for her and they sat down.

"In America," Harold said as he unfolded his napkin, "this would be called 'the children's table.' "

"I saw a great deal of the Americans during the war," Jean Allégret said. "Your humor is different from ours. It is three-quarters fantasy. Our fantasy is nearly always serious. I understand Americans very well. . . ."

Harold was searching for Barbara at the big table. When he found her, he saw that she was listening attentively, with her head slightly bowed, to the very handsome young man on her right. He felt a twinge of jealousy.

"—but children," Jean Allégret was saying. "I never once found an American who knew or cared what they were fighting about. And yet they fought very well. . . . What you are doing in Germany now is all wrong, you know. You make friends with them. And you will bring another war down on us, just as Woodrow Wilson did."

"Where did you get that idea?" Harold asked, smiling at him.

"It is not an idea, it is a fact. He is responsible for all the mischief that followed the Treaty of Versailles."

"That is in your history books?"

"Certainly."

"In our history books," Harold said cheerfully, "Clemenceau and Lloyd George are the villains, and Wilson foresaw everything." He began to eat his soup.

"He was a very vicious man," Jean Allégret said.

"Wilson? Oh, get along with you."

"Well, perhaps not vicious, but he didn't understand European politics, and he was thoroughly wrong in his attitude toward the German people. My family has a house in the north of France, near St. Amand-les-Eaux. It was destroyed in 1870, and rebuilt exactly the way it was before. My grandfather devoted his life to restoring it. In 1914 it was destroyed again, burned to the ground, and my father rebuilt it so that it was more beautiful than before. Thanks to the Americans, I am now living in a farmhouse nearby, because there is no roof on the house my father built. I manage the farms, and when it is again possible, I will rebuild the house for the third time. My life will be an exact repetition of my father's and my grandfather's."

"Does it have to be?" Harold asked, raising his spoon to his lips.

"What do you mean?"

"Why not try something else? Let the house go."

"You are joking."

"No. Everyone has dozens of lives to choose from. Pick another."

"I am the eldest son. And if the house is destroyed a fourth time, I will expect my son to rebuild it. But if the Americans were not such children, it wouldn't have to be rebuilt."

"We didn't take part in the war of 1870," Harold said mildly. "And we didn't start either of the last two wars."

The Frenchman pounced: "But you came in too late. And you ruined the peace by your softness—by your idealism. And now, as the result of your quarrel with the Russians, you are going to turn France into a battlefield once more. Which is very convenient for you but hard on us."

Harold studied the blue eyes that were looking so intently into his. Their expression was simple and cordial. In America, he thought, such an argument was always quite different. By this time, heat would have crept into it. The accusations would have become personal.

"What would you have us do?" he asked, leaning forward. "Stay out of it next time?"

"I would have you take a realistic attitude, and recognize that harshness is the only thing the German people understand."

"And hunger."

"No. They will go right back and do it over again."

Harold glanced at the girl who was sitting between them, to see whose side she was on. Her face did not reveal what she was thinking. She took a sip of wine and looked at the two men as if they were part of the table decorations.

Caught between the disparity of his own feelings—for he felt a liking for Jean Allégret as a man and anger at his ideas—Harold was silent. No matter what I say, he thought, it will sound priggish. And if I don't say anything, I will seem to be agreeing.

"It is true," he said at last, "it is true that we understand machinery better than we understand European politics. And I do not love what I know of the German mentality. But I have to assume that they are human—that the Germans are human to this extent that they sleep with their wives"—was this going too far?—"and love their children, and want to work, at such times as they are not trying to conquer the world, and are sometimes discouraged, and don't like growing old, and are afraid of dying. I assume that the Japanese sleep with their wives, the Russians love their children and the taste of life, and are sometimes discouraged, don't like growing old, and are afraid of—"

"You don't think that your niggers are human," Jean Allégret said triumphantly.

"Why not? Why do you say that?"

"Because of the way you treat them. I have seen it, in Normandy. You manage them very well."

"We do not manage them at all. They manage us. They are a wonderful people. They have the virtues—the sensibility, the patience, the emotional richness—we lack. And if the distinction between the two races becomes blurred, as it has in Martinique, and they become one race, then America will be saved."

"They are animals," the Frenchman said. "And you treat them like animals."

The girl stirred, as if she were about to say something. Both men turned toward her expectantly.

"I prefer a nigger to a Jew," she said.

AT THE END OF THE MEAL, the guests at the large table pushed their chairs back. Barbara Rhodes, turning away from the young man who had bored her so with his handsome empty face, his shallow eyes that did not have the thing she looked for in people's eyes but only vanity, glanced toward the little table in the alcove. She saw Harold rise, still talking (what could they have found to talk about so animatedly all through dinner?) and draw the little table toward him so that the girl could get up. . . . *Oh no!* she cried as the table started to tilt alarmingly. She saw the Frenchman with a quick movement try to stop it but he was on the wrong side of the table and it was too late. There was an appalling crash.

"Une table pliante," a voice said coolly beside her.

Unable to go on looking, she turned away, but not before she had seen the red stain, like blood, on the beautiful Aubusson carpet, and Harold, pale as death, standing with his hands at his side, looking at what he had done.

"THESE IDEAS OF YOURS are foolish and will not work," Jean Allegret said an hour later.

"Perhaps not," Harold said.

They were sitting on a bench on the lawn, facing the lighted windows but in the dark. On another bench, directly in front of them, Barbara and Sabine and another girl whose name Harold didn't know were sitting and talking quietly. There were five or six more people here and there, on the steps, in chairs, or on other benches, talking and watching the moon rise. The others were inside, in the library, dancing to the music of a portable record player.

"Perhaps they *are* foolish," he said, "but I prefer them, for my own sake. If it is foolish to think that all men are brothers, it is at least more civilized—and more agreeable—than thinking that all men—you and I, for instance—are enemies, waiting for a chance to run a bayonet through each other's back."

The wine had made him garrulous and extravagant in speech; also, he had done much less than the usual amount of talking since they had landed in France, and it gave him the feeling of being in arrears, of having a great deal backed up that he urgently needed to say.

"If it is really a question of that," he went on, "then I will get up and turn around and—since I like you too much to put a bayonet in your back—offer you my back instead. Hoping that you won't call my bluff, you understand. Or that something will distract your attention long enough for me to—"

"Very dear, your theories. Very gentle and sweet and impossible to put into practice. Nevertheless, you interest me. You are not the American type. I didn't know there were Americans like that."

"But that's what I keep telling you. Exactly what I am *is* the American type."

"You have got everything all wrong, but your ideas interest me."

"They are not my ideas. I have not said one original thing all evening."

"I like you," Jean Allégret said. "And if it were possible, if there was the slightest chance of changing human nature for the better, I would be on your side. But it does not change. Force is what counts. Idealism cannot survive a firing squad. . . . But in another way, another world, maybe, what you say is true. And in spite of all I have said, I believe it too. I am an artist. I paint."

"Seriously?"

"Excuse me," the Frenchman said. "I neglect my duties as a host. I will be back in a moment." He got up and went across the lawn and into the house.

The moon was above the marshes now, round and yellow and enormous. The whole sky was gilded by it. The house was no longer ugly. By this light you could see what the Victorian architect had had in mind. Harold stood behind Barbara, with his hand on her shoulder, listening to the girls' conversation. Then, drawn by curiosity, he went up the steps and into the house, as far as the drawing-room door. The fruitwood furniture was of a kind he had little taste for, but around the room were portraits and ivory miniatures he would have liked to look at. But would it (since the French were said to be so reluctant to ask people into their homes) be considered an act of rudeness for him to go around looking at things all by himself?

He turned back toward the front door and met Jean Allégret in the hall. "Oh there you are," the Frenchman said. "I was looking for you."

They went and sat down where they had been before, but turned the bench around so that they could watch the moon rising through the night sky.

"I do not like the painting of our time," Jean Allégret said. "It is sterile and it has nothing to do with life. What I paint is action. I stand and watch a man cutting a tree down, a farmer in the field, and I love the way he swings the ax blade, I see every motion, and it's that motion that interests me—not color or design. It's life I want to paint."

"You are painting now?"

"I have not painted since the war. I am rebuilding what was destroyed, you understand. I cannot do that and also paint. The painting is my personal life, which has to give way to the responsibilities I have inherited."

"You are not married?"

The Frenchman shook his head. "When the house is rebuilt and the farms are under cultivation again, then I will find a wife who understands what I expect of her, and there will be children."

"And she must expect nothing of you? There can be no alteration of your ideas to fit hers?"

"None whatever. I do not approve of American ideas of how to treat women. They are gallant only on the surface. You lose control over your women. And you have no authority over your children or your home. You continually divorce and remarry and make a further mess of it."

"Modern marriage is very complicated."

"It need not be."

Harold saw Eugène stop in front of Barbara and say something. After a moment he walked away. He did not appear to be having a good time. The tweed coat, Harold thought.

Turning to Jean Allégret, he said: "You do not know my name, do you?"

The Frenchman shook his head.

"Very good," Harold said. "I have a suggestion to make. Suppose I do not tell you my name. Some day you may find that you cannot go on carrying the burden of family responsibilities, or that you were wrong in laying aside your personal life. And you may have to drop everything and start searching for what you once had. Or for something. Everybody at one time or another has to go on a search, and if I do not tell you my name, or where I live, then you will have an object to search for, an excuse. America is a large country, it may take years and years to find me, but while you are searching you will be discovering all sorts of things, you will be talking to people, having experiences, and even if you never find me— You don't like my idea?"

"It's completely impractical. Romantic and charming and impractical—a thoroughly American idea."

"I suppose it is," Harold said. He took his financial diary out of his pocket and wrote his name and forwarding address in Paris and their address in America. Then he tore the page out and handed it to the Frenchman, and went over to the bench where the three girls were sitting. They looked up as he approached.

"Do you want to come and join us?" he asked.

"Are you having a pleasant conversation?" Barbara asked.

"Very."

"Then I think I'll stay here. We're talking about America."

"When you come back to Paris in September," Jean Allégret said as Harold sat down, "I'd like very much to have you come and stay with me in the country. At my own place, I mean. This is my uncle's house, you understand."

Harold noticed that he had said "you," not "you and your wife."

"We'd like to very much," he said.

"We could have some shooting. It's very primitive, you understand. Not like this. But I think you will find it interesting. Actually," Jean Allégret said, his voice changing to accommodate a note of insincerity, "I am young to have taken on so large a responsibility. I'm only twenty-seven, you know." Behind the insincerity was the perfectly sincere image that he projected on the screen of his self-approval—of the man who lays aside his youth prematurely.

Like those people who, weeping at the grave of a friend, have no choice but to dramatize the occasion, Harold thought, and search around in their mind for a living friend to write to, describing how they stood at the grave, weeping, etc. The grief is no less real for requiring an audience. What the person doubts and seeks confirmation of is his own reality.

"There are six farms to manage," the Frenchman went on, "and I am—in spite of my lack of experience—in the position of a father to the village. They wanted to make me mayor. They bring all their problems to me, even their marital problems. I am also working with the boys. . . . The whole life of the community was destroyed, and slowly, a little at a time, I am helping them rebuild it. But it means that I have very little time to myself, and no time for painting. If the Communists take over, I will be the first to be shot, in our village."

"Are there many?"

"Five or six."

"And you know who they are?"

"Certainly. They have nothing against me personally, but if I am successful I will defeat their plans, and so I will be the first person taken out and shot. But you must come and see my village. . . . I want to give you my address, before I forget it."

Harold produced the financial diary again and while the Frenchman was writing, he sat looking at the dancers framed by the lighted windows. He still felt amazed and numb when he thought of what happened in the dining room, but most of the time he didn't think about it. A curtain had come down over his embarrassment. After a startled glance at the wreckage of the children's table, the guests had politely turned away and filed from the room as if nothing had happened. Jean Allégret went to the kitchen and came back with a damp cloth and scrubbed at the wine stain in the rug. Harold started to pick up the broken glass and found himself gently pushed out of the dining room. The sliding doors closed behind him. In a few minutes, Jean Allégret reappeared and brushed his apology aside—it was nothing, it was all the fault of the table pliante—and took him by the arm and led him outdoors and they went on talking.

Now, when the financial diary and the pencil had been returned to him, Harold said: "Would you take me inside and show me the house? I didn't want to walk around by myself looking at things. Just the two rooms they're dancing in."

To his surprise, the Frenchman stood up and said stiffly: "I will speak to my uncle."

"If it means that, never mind. I don't want to bother anyone. I just thought you could take me around and tell me about the portraits, but it isn't in the least important."

"I will speak to my uncle. It is his house."

Twice in one evening, Harold thought with despair. For it was perfectly clear from the gravity with which his request had been received that it was not the light thing he had thought it was.

Jean Allégret conducted him up the steps and into the hall and said: "Wait here." Then he turned and went back down the steps. Watching through the open doorway, Harold saw him approach a tall elderly man who was standing with a group of people in the moonlight. He bent his head down attentively while Jean Allégret spoke to him. Then, instead of turning and coming toward the house, they left the group and walked up and down, talking earnestly. A minute passed, and then another, and another. Harold began to feel more and more conspicuous, standing in the lighted hall as on a stage, in plain sight of everyone on the terrace. He had already been *in* those two rooms. The others were dancing there now. And he could have looked at the pictures, the tapestries, the marble statuary, by himself, if he hadn't been afraid that it would be bad-mannered. And in America people were always pleased when you asked to see their house.

Uncle and nephew made one more complete turn around the terrace, still talking, and apparently arrived at a decision, for they turned suddenly and came toward the house. Jean Allégret introduced Harold to his uncle and then left them together. M. Allégret spoke no English. He was about sixty, taller than Harold, dignified, and soft-spoken. For a minute or two he went on making polite conversation. Then he said abruptly, as if in reply to something Harold had just said: "Vous prenez un intérêt aux maisons?"

"Je prends un intérêt dans cette maison. Mais—"

"Alors." Turning, M. Allégret led him over to a lithograph

hanging on the wall beside the door into the salon. "Voici un tableau d'une chasse à courre qui a eu lieu ici en mille neuf cent sept," he said. "La clef indique l'identité des personnes. Voici le Kaiser, et auprès de lui est le Prince Philippe zu Eulenberg . . . le Prince Frédéric-Guillaume . . . la Princesse Sophie de Württemberg, portant l'amazone noire, et le roi d'Angleterre . . . Mon père et ma mère . . . le Prince Charles de Saxe . . . avec leurs chasseurs et leurs laquais. Le tableau a été peint de mémoire, naturellement. Ces bois de cerf que vous voyez le long du mur. . . ."

AT ELEVEN O'CLOCK Alix came toward the circle in the library, where Harold and four or five young men were talking about French school life, and said: "Eugène thinks it is time we went home."

Harold shook hands around the circle and then sought out Jean Allégret.

"We have to go," he said, "and I wanted to be sure I said good night to all your cousins. Would you take me around to them? I am not sure which—"

This request presented no difficulties. Barbara and Harold said good night to Mme Allégret, to various rather plain young girls, and to M. Allégret, who came out of the house with them. The others were waiting with the bicycles, under the grape arbor. Jean Allégret and his uncle conducted the party from the château along the driveway as far as the place where it dropped steeply downhill, and there they said good night. Harold and Jean Allégret shook hands warmly, one last time. Calling good night, good night, they coasted down the hill, through the dark tunnel of branches, with the dim carbide bicycle lamps barely showing the curves in the road, and emerged suddenly into bright moonlight. Dismounting at a sandy patch before the bridge, Harold risked saying to Eugène: "Did you have a pleasant evening?"

"No. They were too young. There was no one there who was very interesting." His voice in the moonlight was not unfriendly, but neither was it encouraging.

Out on the main road, Harold pedaled beside Barbara, whose lamp was brighter than his. "Wasn't it awful about the folding table?" he said.

"It wasn't your fault."

"I felt terrible about it, but they were so kind. They just closed the doors on it, and it was exactly as if it had never happened. But I keep thinking about the broken china and glasses that can never be replaced probably. And that stain on the carpet."

"What were you talking about?"

"I don't remember. Why?"

"I just wondered."

"They attacked poor dead Woodrow Wilson. And then they started on the Jews and Negroes. I thought France was the one country where Negroes were accepted socially. They sounded just like Southerners. What was it like at dinner?"

"All right. I didn't like the boy I sat next to."

"He was very handsome."

"He is coming to America on business, and he thought we could be useful to him. I didn't like him at all."

"And Alix's friend, who sat on the other side of you?"

"He was nice, but he was talking to Alix."

"I had a lovely time. And I saw the house. Jean Allégret's uncle showed me all through the downstairs, as far as the kitchen, and then he took me upstairs, through all the bedrooms, which were wonderful. It was like a museum. And in a dressing room I saw the family tree, painted on wood. It was interminable. It must have gone back at least to Charlemagne. And then we went outside and saw the family chapel. Jean Allégret wants us to come and stay with him up near the Belgian border. . . . Did you have a nice evening? Afterward, I mean?"

"All except for one thing. I think I hurt Eugène's feelings. He came and asked me to dance with him and I refused. I was interested in what Sabine was saying, and I didn't feel like dancing at the moment, and I'm afraid he was offended."

"He probably understood. . . . They don't use the chapel as a chapel any more. They keep wine in it."

"And I don't think Sabine had a very good time," Barbara said. "She sat with Alix or me all evening, and the boys didn't ask her to dance. I don't understand it. She's very pretty, and Mme Viénot said that she was so popular and had so many invitations."

"The money," he said.

"What money?"

They were overtaking Alix, and so he did not answer. The winding road was almost white, the distant hills were silver, and they could see as well as in daylight. They rode now in single file, now all together.

"Think of going five miles to a party on bicycles," Barbara said to Harold, "and coming home in the moonlight!"

In a high, thin, eerie voice, Sabine began to sing: "Au clair de la lune, mon ami Pierrot, prête-moi ta plume pour écrire un mot . . ." The tune was not the one the Americans knew, and they drew as near to her as their bicycles permitted. After that she sang "Cadet Rouselle a trois maisons qui n'ont ni poutres ni chevrons . . ." and they were so taken with the three houses that had no rafters, the three suits, the three hats, the three big dogs, the three beautiful cats, that they begged her to sing it again. Instead she told them a ghost story.

In a village near here, she said, but a long time ago, there was a schoolmaster who drove himself into a frenzy trying to teach reading and writing and the catechism to boys who wanted to be out working in the fields with their fathers. He had a birch cane, which he used frequently, and an expression which he used still more. Whenever any boy didn't know his lesson, the schoolmaster would say: "One dies as one is born. There is never any improvement." Then he'd reach for his birch rod.

One rainy autumn evening when he got home, he discovered that he had left his examination books at the school. And though he could have waited until next day to correct them, he was so anxious to find what mistakes his pupils had made that he went back that night, after his supper. A waning moon sailed through black clouds, and the wind whipped his cloak up into the air, and the familiar landscape looked different, as everything does on a windy autumn night. And when he opened the door of the schoolhouse, he saw that one of the pupils was still there, sitting on his bench. "Don't you even know enough to go home?" he shouted. "One dies as one is born." And the boy said, in a voice that chilled the schoolmaster's blood: "I was never born, and therefore I cannot die." With that he vanished.

Now I know what she's like, Harold thought. This is her element—telling ghost stories. And this filtered moonlight. All this silveriness.

The supernatural shouldn't be understood too well; it should have gaps in it for you to think about afterward. . . . What he missed because he didn't know the words or because their bicycles swerved, drawing them apart for a moment, merely added to the effect.

The next day, the schoolmaster was very nervous when he came to teach the class. He looked at each face carefully, and saw with relief only the usual ones. But one thing was not usual. André, who had never in his life recited, knew his whole day's lesson without a fault. Growing suspicious, the schoolmaster stopped calling on him. Even then the hand waved in the air, so anxious was he to recite. That evening, the schoolmaster walked home the long way round, and stopped at André's house, and learned that he was sick in bed. So then he knew.

After that, somebody always knew his lesson, and it wasn't long before the boys caught on. One at a time they played hookey, knowing that whatever it was—a ghost, a fairy, an uneasy spirit—would come to school that day looking exactly like them, and recite and recite. The schoolmaster grew thin. He began to make mistakes in arithmetic and to misspell words. He would start to say: "One dies as one is—" and then be afraid to finish. Finally, unable to stand the strain any more, he went to the curé one morning before school and told him his troubles. The curé reached for his hat and coat, and filled a small bottle with holy water from the font. "There is only one way that a person can be born," he said, "and that is in Jésus-Christ. When the possessed boy—because it can only be a case of possession—stands up to recite, I will baptize him." And that's what happened. The schoolmaster called on one boy who didn't know his lesson after another, until he came to Joseph, who was a great doltish boy with arms as long as an ape's. And when Joseph began to name the kings of France without a single mistake, the curé said: "In nomine patris et filii et spiritus sanctus," and uncorked the vial of holy water and flung it all in his face. The boy looked surprised and went on reciting. When he had finished, he sat down. There was no change in his appearance. The schoolmaster and the curé rushed off to Joseph's house and it was as they feared: Joseph was not there. "Isn't he at school?" his mother asked, in alarm.

"Yes, yes," the curé said, "he's at school," and they left without explaining.

As they were going through the wood, the curé said: "There is only one thing you can do. You must adopt this orphaned spirit, give him your name, and make him your legal heir." When they came out of the wood they went to the mairie and began to fill out the necessary adoption papers, which took all the rest of the day. When they finished, the maire took them, looked at them blankly, and handed them back. There was no writing on the documents they had spent so much time filling out.

So when the class opened the next day, the boys saw to their surprise that the schoolteacher was not at his desk in the front of the room but sitting on the bench that was always reserved for dunces. They were afraid to titter because of his birch rod, and when he saw their eyes go to it he got up and broke the rod over his knee. Then they sat there and waited. Finally one of the boys summoned enough courage to ask: "What are we waiting for?" "For the schoolmaster," the man said. "I have tried very hard to teach you, but I had a harsh unloving father and I never learned how to be a father to anybody else, and so you boys learn nothing from me. But I have learned something from the spirit that takes your place on the days when you are absent, and I know that he should be teaching you, and I am waiting now in the hope that he will come and teach us all."

After a time, Joseph left his seat and went to the desk and in a voice of the utmost sweetness began to conduct the lesson.

"Are you the spirit?" the boys asked.

"No, I am Joseph," he said.

"Then how is it you know the lesson?"

"I learned it last night. It took me a long time and it was very hard, but now I know it."

The next day, the same thing happened, only it was André who went to the front of the class. And right straight through the room, they took turns, each day a different boy, until it was the schoolmaster's turn. Looking very pale, he stood in front of them once more, and they waited, expecting him to say: "One dies as one is born." Instead, he began to hear the lesson, which they all knew. "But are you really the schoolmaster, or are you the spirit that takes our place?" they asked. "I am the schoolmaster," the man said sadly. "One dies as one is born, and I was born a man. But through the grace of Heaven, one is—one can hope to be of the company of spirits." That was the last time they ever heard him utter this familiar expression, though he stayed at his desk and taught them patiently, in a voice of the utmost gentleness and reasonableness, from that time on.

If the ride to the party seemed long, the ride home was too brief. Harold found himself pushing his bicycle into the darkness of the woods behind Beaumesnil long before he expected to. The courtyard, like everywhere else, was flooded with moonlight. There was a lighted kerosene lamp on the kitchen table. All the rest of the château was either white in the moonlight or in total shadow.

They piled their bicycles in a heap in the kitchen entry. Alix lit the other lamps that had been left for them. In a procession, they went through the pantry and the dining room to the stairs and parted in the second-floor hallway. They were relaxed and sleepy and easy with each other; even Eugène. It was as if they had come home from any number of parties in just this way ("Good night") and were all one family ("Good night, Barbara") and knew each other's secrets ("Good night, good night") and took for granted the affection that could be heard in their voices. ("It was lovely, wasn't it? . . . I hope you sleep well. . . . Good night. . . .")

Chapter 12

On Sunday morning, Harold sat tense and ready, his week-old, wine-stained, really horrible-looking napkin rolled and inserted in its ivory ring. He refused another cup of coffee and pretended to be following the history of the Allégret family that Mme Viénot was telling with so much pleasure. He was waiting for her to leave the table. When she pushed her chair back, he got up also and followed her out into the hall.

"If it would be convenient," he began, "if there is time before church, that is, could we—"

"Yes, of course," Mme Viénot said, as if she were grateful to him for reminding her of something she should have thought of, herself. She led the way through the pink and white drawing room to a room beyond it, a study, which Harold had not been in before. Composed and businesslike, she indicated a chair for him and sat down at the flat-topped mahogany desk in the center of the room. To be embarrassed by a situation one has deliberately contrived to bring about in one's own interests is not realistic; is not intelligent; in short, is not French. As Mme Viénot opened a drawer and drew out a blank sheet of paper, she saw that his eyes were focused on the wall directly behind her and said: "That is a picture of Beaumesnil as it was when my father inherited it. As you see, it was a small country house. I find it rather charming. Even though the artist was not very talented. As a painting it is rather sentimental. . . . I spoke to my cook about the pommes de terre frites."

He looked blank.

"You remember that Mme Rhodes asked for the recipe—and it was as I suspected. She is unwilling to divulge her secret. They are so peculiar in this respect."

"It doesn't matter," he said.

"I'm sorry. I would have liked to have got it for her. You came here on the eleventh—"

He nodded.

"—and today is Sunday the twenty-fifth. That makes two full weeks—"

His eyes opened wide. So they were being charged, after all, for the three days they were in Paris.

"—and one day," Mme Viénot concluded.

They had arrived at one o'clock; they would be leaving for the train at three thirty this afternoon. The extra day was two and a half hours long.

A moment later, Mme Viénot interrupted her writing to say: "I did not think it proper to allow M. Carrère to pay for the ices and the pâtisseries that afternoon in Blois. Your share of the *addition* came to a hundred and eighty francs." The amount was written down, while he tried to reconcile M. Carrère's pleasant gesture toward America with the fact that he had afterward allowed the cost of the gesture to be deducted from his bill and added onto theirs. Only in dreams are such contradictions reconciled; in real life, fortunately, it isn't necessary. Nothing was deducted for the ten or eleven meals they had not taken at the château, or for the taxi ride to Blois that Mme Viénot had shared with them. The taxi to and from the ferry, the day they went to Chaumont, was six hundred francs. He had not intended that Mme Viénot, Mme Straus-Muguet, and Alix should have to pay a share of this amount; he would not have allowed it. Apparently it was, as Alix said, a question of sincerity. But *had* M. Carrère allowed her to deduct their ices and pastry from his bill? It did not seem at all like him. And had Mme Straus-Muguet been charged for her share of the taxi to and from the ferry at Chaumont?

The sense of outrage, clotted in his breast, moved him to fight back, and the form his attack took was characteristic. In one of her letters she had written them that the *service* was included. He offered her now a chance to go the whole hog.

"What about the cook and Thérèse and Albert?"

"I shall give them something," Mme Viénot said.

But will she, he wondered.

The sheet of paper that she handed across the desk read:

Note de Semaine de M. Harold Rhodes

2 semaines	
+ 1 jour	32,100 f
5 téléphones	100 f
Goûter à Blois	180 f
Laundry	125 f

payé le 24 Juillet 48

Château Beaumesnil
Brenodville s/Euphrone

With the pen that she offered to him he wrote the date and his signature on four American Express traveler's checks—a fifty, two twenty-fives, and a ten—and handed them to her as he wrote.

"Will you also give me a statement that you have cashed these four checks?"

"Is that necessary?" Mme Viénot asked.

"For the customs," he said. "The amount we brought in is declared in our passports, and the checks have to be accounted for when we leave."

"I have been advised not to put down the money I receive from my clients, when I make out my tax statement," Mme Viénot said. "If they do not ask to see the statement when you go through customs, I would appreciate your not showing it."

He agreed to this arrangement.

She opened a little metal box and produced four hundred-franc notes, a fifty, a twenty-five, and two tens, and gave them to him. He folded the huge paper currency and put it in his coat pocket. With the traveler's checks neatly arranged in front of her, she said: "It has been a great pleasure having you. . . . I hope that when you come again it will be as friends."

He said nothing. He had paid the full amount, which was perhaps reasonable, since he had not asked outright if they would be charged for the three days they were in Paris. If she had really felt kindly toward them, or had the slightest impulse toward generosity or fairness, she could have made some slight adjustment. She hadn't, and he was therefore not obliged to pretend now.

His eyes met hers in a direct glance and she looked away. She picked up the checks and put them down again, and then said: "There is something I have wanted to tell you, something I would like to explain. But perhaps you guessed— We have not always lived like this."

"I understand that."

"There has been a *drame* in our family. Two years ago, my husband—"

She stopped talking. Her eyes were filled with tears. He leaned forward in his chair, saw that it was too late for him to say anything, and then sat back and waited for the storm of weeping to pass. He could not any more help being moved, as he watched her, than if she had proved in a thousand ways that she was their friend. Whatever the trouble was, it had been real.

FIVE MINUTES LATER he closed the door of their third-floor room and said: "I almost solved the mystery."

"What mystery?" Barbara asked.

"I almost found out about M. Viénot. She started to tell me, when I finished paying her—"

"Did she charge us for the full two weeks?"

"How did you know that? And then she started to tell me about *him*."

"What happened to him?"

"I don't know," he said. "I didn't let her tell me."

"But *why*, if she wanted to tell you?"

"She broke down. She cried."

"Mme Viénot?"

He heard the sound of wheels and went to the window. The dog cart had come to a stop in front of the château, and the gardener was helping Mme Bonenfant up into the seat beside him. She sat, dressed for church, with her prayerbook in her hand.

Harold turned away from the window and said: "I could feel something. She changed, suddenly. She started searching for her handkerchief. And from the way she looked at me, I had a feeling she was asking me to deliver her from the situation she had got herself into. So I told her she didn't need to tell me about it. I said I was interested in people, that I observed them, but that I never asked questions."

"But are you sure she changed her mind about telling you?"

"Not at all sure. She may have been play-acting. I may have given her the wrong cue, for all I know. But she didn't cry on purpose. That much I'm sure of."

Leaning on his elbows, he looked out at the park. The hay stacks were gone, and the place had taken on a certain formality. He saw how noble the old trees were that lined the drive all the way out to the road. The horse restlessly moved forward a few paces and had to be checked by the gardener, who sat holding the reins. Mme Bonenfant arranged her skirt and then, looking up at the house, she called impatiently.

From somewhere a voice—light, unhurried, affectionate,

silvery—answered: "Oui, Grand'maman. A l'instant. Je viens, je viens . . ."

"What an idiotic thing to do," Barbara said. "Now we'll never know what happened to him."

"Yes we will," he said. "Somebody will tell us. Sooner or later somebody always does."

On Sunday afternoon, an hour before it was time to start for the train, Mme Viénot said to her American guests: "Would you like to see the house?"

Alix and Mme Bonenfant went with them. The tour began on the second floor at the head of the stairs, with Mme Bonenfant's bedroom, which was directly under theirs. The counterpane on the huge bed was of Persian embroidery on a white background. The chair covers were of the same rich material. They were reminded of the bedchamber of Henri IV at Cheverny. The bedroom at Beaumesnil smelled of camphor and old age, and the walls were covered with family photographs. As they were leaving the room, Harold glanced over at the bedside table and saw that the schoolboy whose photograph was on the piano in the petit salon had not been finished off at the age of twelve; here he was, in the uniform of the French army.

They saw the two rooms that had been occupied by M. and Mme Carrère and that would have been theirs, Mme Viénot said, if they had come when they originally planned. And at the end of the hall, they were shown into Mme Cestre's room, on which her contradictory character had failed to leave any impression whatever. The curtains, the bedspread were green and white chintz that had some distant connection with water lilies.

Mme Viénot's room, directly across the hall from her mother's but around a corner, where they had never thought to search for her, was much smaller, and furnished simply and apparently without much thought. It was dominated not by the bed but by the writing desk.

Mme Viénot opened a desk drawer and took out some postcards. "I think you have no picture of Beaumesnil," she said.

"We took some pictures with our camera," Barbara said, "but they may not turn out. We're not very good at taking pictures."

"You may choose the one you like best," Mme Viénot said.

They looked through the cards and took one and handed the others to Mme Viénot, who gave them to her mother as they were going along the second-floor passageway that connected the two parts of the house. Mme Bonenfant gave the cards back to Barbara, saying: "Keep them. Keep all of them."

Alix did not speak of the fact that they had already seen her room. It almost seemed that the room itself, as they stood in the doorway looking in, was denying that that illicit evening had ever taken place. They passed on to the bare, badly furnished room that had been Mme Straus-Muguet's. It was so much less comfortable than their own third-floor room or than any of the rooms they had just seen that Harold wondered if a deliberate slight had been involved. As Mme Viénot closed the door she said dryly: "It seems Mme Straus saw your room and she has asked for it when she comes back in August. I do not think I can see my way clear to letting her have it."

But why did Mme Viénot not want her to have their room, he wondered. Unless Mme Straus was unwilling to pay what they had paid, or perhaps was unable to pay that much. And if that was so, should they allow her to entertain them in Paris?

In this back wing of the house there was a box-stair leading up to a loft that had once been used as a granary. It still smelled of the dust of grain that had been stored there, though it was empty now, except for a few old-fashioned dolls (whose dolls, he wondered; how long ago had their place been usurped by children?) and, in the center of the high dim room, the wooden works of the outdoor clock.

They were quite beyond repair, Mme Viénot said, but the

wooden cogwheels had turned, the clock had kept time, as recently as her girlhood. The pineapple-shaped weights were huge, and a hole had had to be cut in the floor for them to rise and descend through. Standing in this loft, Harold had the feeling that they had penetrated into the secret center of the house, and that there were no more mysteries to uncover.

As ALWAYS at the end of a visit, there was first too much time and then suddenly there was not enough and they were obliged to hurry. Alix and Eugène had already started out for the village on foot. The gardener's bicycles having been returned to him, again there weren't enough to go round. The Americans took one last survey of the red room, free of litter now, the armoire and the closet empty, the postcards, guidebooks, and souvenirs all packed, the history of the château of Blois and the illustrated pamphlet returned to their place downstairs. The dying sweet peas in their square vase on the table in the center of the room said: *It is time to go. . . .*

"Where will we find another room like this?" he said, and closed the door gently on that freakish collection of books, on the tarnished mirrors, the fireplace that could not be used, the bathtub into which water did not flow, the map of Ile d'Yeu, the miniatures, the red and black and white wallpaper, the now familiar view, through that always open window, of the bottom of the sea. As he started down, he thought: *We will never come here again. . . .*

Mme Viénot was waiting for them at the foot of the stairs, and they followed her along the back passageway by which they had first entered the house, around a corner, and then another corner. A door opened silently, on the right, and Harold found himself face to face with a maniacal old woman, who clawed at his coat pocket and for a second scared him out of his wits. It was the cook. He was seeing the cook at last, and she had put something in his pocket. Too astonished to speak, he pressed a five-hundred-franc note into her hand, and she withdrew behind the door. He glanced ahead of him and saw Mme Viénot's skirt disappearing around the next corner. He was more than half convinced that she had seen—that she had eyes in the back of her head. She must, in any case, have sensed that something strange was going on. But when he caught up with her in the courtyard, she made no reference to what had happened in the corridor and, blushing from the sense of complicity in a deception he did not understand, he also avoided any mention of it.

Mme Bonenfant and Mme Cestre were waiting outside with the two children, whom the Americans had scarcely laid eyes on, and Alix's baby in her stroller. The Americans shook hands with their hostess, with Mme Bonenfant, with Mme Cestre. They disposed of the dressing case and the two small suitcases among the three of them. Sabine kissed her mother and grandmother, and then, mounting their bicycles, waving and calling good-by, they rode out of the courtyard, past the Lebanon cedar that was two hundred years old, and down the cinder drive.

Harold did not dare look at the piece of paper until they had turned into the road and there was no possibility of his being seen from the house. He let Barbara and Sabine draw ahead and then, balancing a suitcase with one hand, he put his other into his pocket. By all the rules of narration it should have been a communication from M. Viénot, a prisoner somewhere in the attic, crying out for help through his only friend, the cook. It was, instead, a recipe for French-fried potatoes, and with it, on another piece of paper three inches square, a note:

> Si, par hasard, M. et Mme Rhodes connaissaient quelqu'un desirant du personnel français mon fils et moi partirions très volontiers à l'Etranger. Voici mon addresse Mme Foëcy à St. Claude de Diray Indre-et-Loire. . . .

So he was not so far off, after all. It was the cook who wanted them to rescue her, from Mme Viénot and the unhappy country of France.

In all the fields between the château and the village, the grain had been cut and stacked. The scythe and the blades of the reaper had spared only those poppies that grew along the road, among the weeds and the wildflowers. The *bluets* had just come into flower.

"My sister was married at Beaumesnil," Sabine said, "and because of the Occupation we couldn't have the kind of flowers that are usual at weddings, so, half an hour before the ceremony, the bridesmaids went out and picked their own bouquets, at the side of the road."

"It sounds charming," Barbara said.

"It was." Sabine swerved to avoid a rut. "There were some people from the village present, and they thought that if my sister had field flowers for her wedding it must be the fashion. Since that time, whenever there is a wedding in Brenodville the bride carries such a bouquet."

The note of condescension he heard in her voice was unconscious, Harold decided, and had nothing to do with the fact that she belonged to one social class and the village to another but was simply the smiling condescension of the adult for the child. He kept turning to look back at the château, so white against the dark woods. Since he couldn't do what he would have liked to do, which was to fold it up and stuff it in the suitcase and take it away with him, he tried to commit it to memory.

Then they were at the outskirts of Brenodville, and it looked as if the whole village had come out to meet them and escort them to their train. Actually, as he instantly realized, it was simply that it was Sunday afternoon. The people they met spoke to Sabine and sometimes nodded to the Americans. They cannot not know who we are, he thought, and at that moment someone spoke to him—a middle-aged man in a dark-blue Sunday suit, with his two children walking in front of him and his wife at his side. Surprised and pleased, Harold answered: "Bonjour, monsieur!" and when they were past, he turned to Sabine and asked: "Who is that?"

"That was M. Fleury."

He looked back over his shoulder to see if their old friend had stopped and was waiting for him to ride back, but M. Fleury had kept on walking.

"Have I got time to ride back and speak to him?" he said.

"You did speak to him," Barbara said.

"But I didn't recognize him. He looked so different."

The girls were talking and didn't hear him.

Riding past the cemetery, he took one last look at the monuments, which were surely made of papier-mâché, and at the graves decorated with a garish mixture of real and everlasting wreaths and flowers. As for the village itself, in two weeks' time they had come to know every doorway, every courtyard, every purple clematis, climbing rose, and blue morning-glory vine between here and the little river.

In the cobblestone square in front of the mairie they turned left, into a street that led them downhill in the direction of the railway station, and soon overtook Eugène, striding along by himself, with his coat on one arm and in the other hand his light suitcase. Alix was not with him. Harold looked around for her and saw that she wasn't anywhere. He slowed down, ready to ride beside Eugène. Receiving no encouragement, he rode on.

"What do we do with the bicycles?" he asked, when the two girls caught up with him.

"Someone will call for them," Sabine said.

On the station platform, he saw their two big suitcases and the dufflebag, checked through to Paris. The smaller suitcases they could manage easily with Eugène's help, even though they had to change trains at Blois. Traveling with French people, there would be no problems. He wouldn't have to ask the same question four different times so that he would have four answers to compare.

Eugène arrived, and drew Sabine aside, and stood talking to her farther down the platform, where they were out of earshot. Harold turned to Barbara and said in a low voice: "Where is Alix?"

"I don't know," she answered.

"Something must have happened."

"Sh-h-h."

"It's very queer," he said. "She didn't say good-by. There is only one direct way home—the way we came—and we didn't meet her, so she must have wanted to avoid us."

"Possibly."

"Do you think they quarreled?"

"Something has happened."

"Do you think it has anything to do with us?"

"What could it have to do with us?"

"I don't know," he said.

When Sabine came and joined them on the station platform, he thought: Now she will explain, and everything will be all right again. . . . But her explanation—"Alix has gone home. She said to say good-by to you"—only deepened his sense of something being held back.

The station was surrounded by vacant land, and the old station still existed, but in the form of a low mound covered with weeds. Harold kept looking off in the direction of the château, thinking that he might see Alix; that she might suddenly appear in the space between two buildings. She didn't appear. Eugène remained standing where he was. The bell started to ring, though there was no train as far as the eye could see down the perfectly straight tracks in the direction of Blois, Orléans, and Paris or in the direction of Tours, Angers, and Nantes. The ringing filled the air with intimations of crisis. The four men seated on the terrace of the Café de la Gare paid no attention to it, which meant that they were either stone deaf or long accustomed to this frightful sound.

After five minutes the station agent appeared. He walked the length of the brick platform and, cranking solemnly, looking neither at the avenue Gambetta on his right nor at the bed of blue pansies on his left, let down the striped gates and closed the street to traffic.

A black poodle leaning out of the window of the house next to the café waited hopefully for something to happen, with its paws crossed in an attitude that was half human. The woolly head turned, betraying a French love of excitement, and the poodle watched the street that led toward the river. The bell went on ringing but with less and less conviction, like a man giving perfectly good advice that he knows from past experience will not be followed. Just when it seemed that nothing was ever going to happen, there was a falsetto cry and the four men on the terrace turned their heads in time to see the train from Tours rush past the café and come to a sudden stop between the railway station and the travel posters. Carriage doors flew open and passengers started descending. They reached up for suitcases that were handed down to them by strangers. They shouted messages to relatives who were going on to Blois, remembered a parcel left on the overhead rack, were alarmed, were reassured (the parcel was on the platform), held small children up to say good-by, or hurried to be first in line at the gate.

Eugène found a third-class compartment that was empty, and they got in, and he pulled the door to from the inside. Harold let the glass down and kept his head out, with all the other heads, until the train had carried them past the place where they had waited for the bus. Having seen the last of the country he wanted especially to remember, he sat down. Barbara and Sabine were talking about their schools. He waited to see what Eugène would do. Eugène had a book in his coat pocket, and he took it out and read until the train drew into the station at Blois.

Eugène made his way along the crowded cement platform, and Harold followed at his heels, and the two girls tagged along after him, as relaxed as if they were shopping. Suddenly they came upon a group of ten or twelve of the guests at the Allégrets' party. Their youth, their good looks, their expensive clothes and new English luggage made them very noticeable in the drab crowd. Harold would have stopped but Eugène kept on going. Several of them nodded or smiled at Harold, whose eyes, as he spoke to them, were searching for Jean Allégret. He was there too, a little apart from the others. Harold started to put the suitcase down and shake hands with him, and then realized that he had just that second received all that was coming to him from Jean Allégret—a quick, cold nod.

Fortunately, the suitcases were still in his hands and he could keep on walking. He remembered but did not resort to a trick he had learned in high school: when you made the mistake of waving to somebody you did not know or, as it sometimes happened, somebody you knew all right but who for some unknown reason didn't seem to know you, the gesture, caught in time, could be diverted; the direction of the hand could be changed so that what began as a friendly greeting ended as smoothing the hair on the side of your head. Bewildered, he took his stand beside Eugène, a hundred feet further along the platform.

In giving him the money to buy Sabine's ticket, Mme Viénot had explained that third class was just as comfortable as second and only half as expensive. The second part of this statement was true, the first was not. He didn't look forward to a four-hour ride, on a hot July night, on wooden slats.

Just before the train drew in, the announcer's voice, coming over the loud-speaker system, filled the station with the sound of rising panic, as if he were announcing not the arrival of the Paris express, stopping at Orléans, etc., etc., but something cataclysmic—the fall of France, the immanent collision of the earth and a neighboring planet. When the train drew to a stop, they were looking into an empty compartment. Again Eugène closed the door from the inside, to discourage other passengers from crowding in. Just before the train started, the door was wrenched open and a thin, pale young man—Eugène and Alix's friend—looked in. Behind him, milling about in confusion, was the house party. Surely *they're* not traveling third class, Harold thought.

Eugène told them there was room for four in the compartment. After a hurried consultation, they decided that they did not want to be separated. Leaning out of the window, Harold saw them mount the step of a third-class carriage farther along the train. Were they all as poor as church mice, he wondered. The question could not be asked, and so he would never know the answer.

As the train carried them north through the evening light, Sabine and Barbara and Harold whiled away a few miles of the journey by writing down the names of their favorite books. *A Passage to India*, he wrote on the back of the envelope that Sabine handed to him. Barbara took the envelope and wrote *Fear and Trembling*. He gave Sabine the financial diary and on a blank page she wrote *Le Silence de la Mer*, while he looked over her shoulder. "Vercors," she wrote. And then, "un petit livre poétique." Barbara wrote *Journey to the End of the Night* on the back of the envelope. He took it and wrote *To the Lighthouse*. He glanced carefully at Eugène, who was sitting directly across from him. Eugène looked away. *A Sportsman's Notebook*, he wrote, and turned the envelope around so that Sabine could read it.

Shortly after that, Eugène got up and went out into the corridor and stood by an open window. After Orléans, Barbara and Sabine went out into the corridor also and stood by another window, and when Barbara came back into the compartment she said in a low voice: "I asked Sabine if she knew what was the matter with Eugène, and she said he was moody and not like other French boys." Though, during the entire journey, Eugène had nothing whatever to say to the three people he was traveling with, he had a long, pleasant, animated conversation with a man in the corridor.

In the train shed in Paris, they met up with the house party again, and this time Jean Allégret acknowledged the acquaintance with a smile and a wave of his hand, as if not he but his double had had doubts in the station at Blois about the wisdom of accepting an American as a friend.

Harold put his two suitcases down and searched through his pockets for the luggage stubs. After four hours of ignoring the fact that he was being ignored, it was difficult to turn casually as if nothing had happened and ask where he should go to see about the two big suitcases and the dufflebag. Eugène shrugged, looked impatient, looked annoyed, looked as if he found Harold's French so inaccurately pronounced and so ungrammatical that there was no point in trying to understand it, and Harold felt that his education had advanced another half-semester. (Though there is only one way of saying "Thank you" in French, there are many ways of being rude, and you don't have to stop and ask yourself if the rudeness is sincere. The rudeness is intentional, and harsh, and straight from the closed heart.)

Too angry to speak, he turned on his heel and started off to find the baggage office by himself. He had only gone a short distance when he heard light footsteps coming after him. Sabine found the right window, took the stubs from him, gave them to the agent, and in her calm, soft, silvery voice dictated the address of her aunt's apartment.

The four of them took the Métro, changed at Bastille, and stepped into a crowded train going in the direction of the Porte de Neuilly. More and more people got on. Farther along the aisle a man and a woman, neither of them young, stood with their arms around each other, swaying as the train swayed, and looking into each other's eyes. The man's moist mouth closed on the woman's mouth in a long, indecent kiss, after which he looked around with a cold stare at the people who were deliberately not watching him.

Harold and Barbara found themselves separated from Sabine and Eugène. Barbara whispered something that Harold could not hear, because of the train noise. He put his head down.

"I said 'I think we'd better go to the Vouillemont.' "

"So do I. But I'm a little worried. It's after eleven o'clock, and we have no reservations."

"If there's no room at the Vouillemont, we can go to some other hotel," she said. "I'd rather spend the night on a park bench than put up with this any longer."

"But why did he ask us?"

"Something is wrong. He's changed his mind. Or perhaps he enjoys this sort of thing."

"The son of a bitch. You saw what happened when I asked him where to go about the big suitcases? . . . The only reason I hesitate at all is Alix and Mme Cestre. I hate to have them know we were—"

"He may not tell them what happened."

"But Sabine will."

The train rushed into the next station. They peered through the window and saw the word *Concorde*. Over the intervening heads, Eugène signaled that they were to get off.

Harold set the suitcases down and extended his hand. "We'll leave you here," he said stiffly. "Good night."

"But why?" Eugène demanded, astonished.

"The hotel is near this station, and we don't want to put you to any further trouble. Thank you very much."

"For what?"

"For taking care of us on the way up to Paris," Harold said. But then he spoiled the effect by blushing.

There was a brief silence during which both of them struggled with embarrassment.

I: *Leo and Virgo*

"I am extremely sorry," Eugène said, "if I have given you any reason to think—"

"It seemed to us that you are a trifle distrait," Harold said, "and we'd rather not put you to any further trouble."

"I am not distrait," Eugène said. "And you are not putting me to any trouble whatever. The apartment is not being used. There is no need for you to go to a hotel."

A train drew in, at that moment, and Harold had the feeling afterward that that was what decided the issue, though trains don't, of course, decide anything. All decisions are the result of earlier decisions; cause, as anyone who has ever studied Beginning Philosophy knows, is another way of looking at effect. They got on the train, and then got off several stations farther along the line, at the Place Pierre-Joseph Redouté. A huge block of granite in the center of the square and dark triangular buildings, with the streets between them leading off in six directions like the rays of a star, were registered on Harold's mind as landmarks he would need to know if they suddenly decided to retrace their steps.

Sabine took her suitcase from Eugène. Then she shook hands with Barbara and Harold. "I am leaving you here," she said, and walked off down a dark, deserted avenue.

The other three turned into a narrow side street, and the Americans stopped when Eugène stopped, in front of the huge door of an apartment house. The door was locked. He rang the bell and waited. There was a clicking noise and the door gave under the pressure of his hand and they passed through a dimly lighted foyer to the elevator. Eugène put the suit cases into it, indicated that Harold and Barbara were to get in also, pressed the button for the sixth floor, and stepped out. "It only holds three," he said. "And with the suitcases it would not rise."

He shut the elevator door, and as they went up slowly, they saw him ascending the stairs, flight after flight. He was there in time to open the elevator door for them. He let them into the dark apartment with his key and then proceeded down the hall, turning on lights as he went, to the bedroom they were to occupy. "It is our room when Alix is here," he explained.

"But we don't want to put you out of your room," Harold protested.

"During the summer I prefer to sleep in the study," Eugène said.

He showed them the toilet, in a separate little room off the hall, and the bathroom they were to use. The gas hot-water heater was in the other bathroom, and he led them there and showed them how to turn the heater on and off when they wanted a bath.

They went back to the room that was to be theirs, and Eugène opened the window and unlatched the metal shutters and pushed them outward, letting in the soft night air. They saw that the room opened onto an iron balcony. Eugène removed the pillows from a big studio couch, and then he drew the Kelly-green bedspread off and folded it and put it over the back of a chair. They watched him solemnly, as if he were demonstrating the French way to fold a bedspread. He showed them how to unhook the pillow covers and where the extra blankets were, and then he said good night. During all this, everybody was extremely polite, as if they had tried everything else and found that nothing works but politeness and patience.

Chapter 13

IN THE FIRST LUMINOUS QUARTER-HOUR of daylight, the Place Pierre-Joseph Redouté in the 16th arrondissement of Paris was given over to philosophical and mathematical speculation. The swallows skimming the wet rooftops said: *What are numbers?*

The sky, growing paler, said: *What is being when being becomes morning?*

What is "five," asked the birds, *apart from "five" swallows?*

The French painter and lithographer who belonged in the center of the Place and who from his tireless study of natural forms might have been able to answer those questions was unfortunately not there any more; he had been melted down and made into bullets by the Germans. The huge block of rough granite that was substituting for him said: *Matter is energy not in motion*, and the swallows said: *Very well, try this, then, why don't you . . . and this . . . and this . . .*

Though proof was easy and the argument had long ago grown tiresome, the granite refrained. But it could not resist some slight demonstration, and so it gave off concentric circles of green grass, scarlet salvia, curbing, and cobblestone.

The wide, wet, empty streets that led away from the Place Redouté like the rays of a star or the spokes of a wheel also at the very same time returned to it—returned from the Etoile, the Place d'Iéna, the Place Victor Hugo, the Trocadéro, and the Bois de Boulogne. The sky went on turning lighter. The pissoir, ill-smelling, with its names, dates, engagements, and obscene diagrams, said: *Everything that happens, in spite of the best efforts of the police, is determined by the space co-ordinates x, y, and z, and the time co-ordinate t.*

God is love, said the leaves on the chestnut trees, and the iron church bell filled the air with a frightful clangor.

Across an attic window in the rue Malène a workshirt hanging on a clothesline to dry grew a darker blue as it absorbed the almost invisible rain.

On the other side of the street, at the same sixth-floor level, a pair of metal shutters folded back gave away the location of a bedroom. The sleepers, both in one bed, were turned toward each other. She moved in her sleep, and he put his hand under her silken knees and gathered them to his loins and went on sleeping. Shortly afterward they turned away from each other, as if to demonstrate that in marriage there is no real resting place. Now love is gathered like great long-stemmed summer flowers, now the lovers withdraw from one another to nourish secretly a secret life. He pulls the blanket and sheet closer, shutting off the air at the back of his neck. She has not committed the murder, the police are not looking for her, and there is just time, between the coming and going of the man in the camel's-hair coat and the footsteps outside the door, to hide the papers. But where? If she puts them inside a book, they will be found, even though there are so many books. She will explain and they will not listen. They will not believe her. And he is asleep, dreaming. She has no one to stand by her when they come. She goes to the closet and finds there the camel's-hair coat worn by the murderer, who knew she was innocent and good, and slipped in and out of the apartment without being seen, and so who will believe her? . . . *Help! Help!* takes the form of a whimper.

Across the room a long-deferred, often-imagined reconciliation is taking place on the wall, behind glass. The Prodigal Son, wearing a robe of stone, kneels on one knee before the Prodigal Father. One arm reaches out and touches the old man's side. One arm, upraised, touches his face. The old man sits, bearded, with a domed forehead, a large stone mouth, blunt nose, and eyes nearly closed with emotion. He has placed one hand against the young man's head, supporting it, but not looking (why is that?) at the face that is looking up at his with such sorrow and love.

The iron balcony, polished by the rain, turns darker, shines, collects puddles. Water dripping from the eaves is caught in the first fold of the awnings.

The sleepers' breath is shallow. His efforts to take her in his arms meet with no response. He cannot blame her for this because she is asleep. The sky goes on turning lighter and whiter. It has stopped raining. A man (out of whose dream?) comes up the rue Malène and, noiseless as a cat, his vibrations sinister, crosses the Place Redouté and disappears down the same street that Sabine Viénot took. But that was last night and now it is morning.

Crowded to the extreme edge of the bed by his half-waking and half-sleeping lust, she turns.

"Are you awake?" he says softly.

"Yes."

"We're back in Paris."

"So I see."

Beside the door to the hall a bookshelf, too far away to read the titles. Then an armchair, with her dress and slip draped over the back and on the seat her bra, panties, and stockings in a soft heap. Her black wedge-soled shoes. Back of the chair a photograph—a detail of sculpture from a medieval church.

"Why the Prodigal Son?"

There is no answer from the other side of the bed.

He continues his investigation of the room. A low round table, elaborately inlaid, with two more period chairs. The radiator, and then the French windows. The room is high up, above the treetops, and there are windows directly across the way, an attic floor above that, and a portion of blue sky. Love in a garret. A door leading into the next room. A little glass table with knick-knacks on it. Another chair. On this chair, his clothes. Beside it his huge shoes—careless, scuffed, wide open, needing to be shined. Then the fireplace, with a mirror over it. Then an arm-chair, with the green spread and pillow covers and bolster piled on it. And over the bed an oil painting, a nude lying on a bed, plump, soft-fleshed, blonde. Alix—but not really. It is eighteenth century. He turns over.

"She was living for his return," he said. "That's all she talked about. And then when he came, they quarreled."

"Perhaps they didn't quarrel. Perhaps they just said good-by and she went back to the château."

"Then why was she avoiding us? It doesn't make sense. She must not have gone home by the road that goes past the cemetery. She probably didn't want us to see that she had been crying. All week long she kept waiting for a letter and there wasn't any letter."

"He called."

"That's true. I forgot that he called on Thursday. But all week end he wasn't himself. He wouldn't go swimming. And he didn't have a good time at the party. Did she?"

"Apparently."

"And the rest of the time, they were off somewhere by themselves. In the back part of the house . . . You don't think it has something to do with us?"

"No."

"I feel that it must have something to do with us. . . . She may not have wanted us here, sleeping in their bed and all."

"She said she was very glad."

"Then it must be all right. She wouldn't lie about it, just to be polite. If they quarreled, I can understand his not wanting to talk afterward. But in that case, why the long cheerful conversation with the man in the corridor?"

I: *Leo and Virgo*

She turned over on her back and looked at the ceiling. "It's an effort for them. They have to choose their words carefully in order to make us understand."

"It's an effort for us too."

"They may not always feel like making the effort."

"Nothing was too much effort at first. . . . Did Sabine say 'Eugène is not like other French boys'? That may be what she meant—that he was friendly one minute and not the next. Or maybe when his curiosity is satisfied, he simply isn't interested any more. . . . I suppose the streets of Paris are safe, but I felt very queer watching her go off alone at that time of night. You think she got home all right?"

"Oh yes."

"I would have offered to take her home myself, but I didn't see how I could leave you, at that point. . . . How can she go on being nice to him?"

"She knows him better than we do."

He turned back again and, finding that she was curled up in a ball and he couldn't get at her, he put his hand between her knees. He felt her drifting back into sleep, away from him.

"What time is it?"

He drew his bare arm out from under the covers and looked at his wrist watch. "Five minutes of eight. Why?"

"Breakfast," she said. "In a strange kitchen."

He sat up in bed. "Do you wish we'd gone to a hotel?"

"We're here. We'll see how it works out."

"I could call the Vouillemont. . . . I didn't know what to do last night. He seemed genuinely apologetic. . . . If we never had to see him again, it would be simpler. But the suitcases are coming here."

She pushed the covers aside and started to get up, and then, suddenly aware of the open window and the building across the street, she said: "They can see us in bed."

"That can't be of much interest to anybody. Not in Paris," he said, and, naked as he was, he went to the curtained windows and closed them. In the dim underwater light they dressed and straightened up the room, and then they went across the hall to the kitchen. She was intimidated by the stove. He found the pilot light and turned on one of the burners for her. The gas flamed up two inches high. They found the teakettle and put water on to boil and then searched through the icebox. Several sections of a loaf of dark bread; butter; jam; a tiny cake of ice. In their search for what turned out to be the right breakfast china but the wrong table silver, they opened every cupboard door in the kitchen and pantry. While she was settling the teacart, he went back across the hall to their bedroom, opened one of the suitcases, and took out powdered coffee and sugar. She appeared with the teacart and he opened the windows.

"Do you want to call Eugène?"

He didn't, but it was not really a question, and so he left the room, walked down the hall to the front of the apartment, hesitated, and then knocked lightly on the closed door of the study. A sleepy voice answered.

"Le petit déjeuner," Harold said, in an accent that did credit to Miss Sloan, his high-school French teacher. At the same time, his voice betrayed uncertainty about their being here, and conveyed an appeal to whatever is reasonable, peace-loving, and dependable in everybody.

Since ordinary breakfast-table conversation was impossible, it was at least something that they were able to offer Eugène the sugar bowl with their sugar in it, and the plate of bread and butter, and that Eugène could return the pitcher of hot milk to them handle first. Eugène put a spoonful of powdered coffee into his cup and then filled it with hot water. Stirring, he said: "I am sorry that my work prevents me from doing anything with you today."

They assured him that they did not expect or need to be entertained.

Harold put a teaspoonful of powdered coffee in his cup and

filled it with hot water, and then, stirring, he sat back in his chair. The chair creaked. Every time he moved or said something, the chair creaked again.

Eugène was not entirely silent, or openly rude—unless asking Harold to move to another chair and placing himself in the fauteuil that creaked so alarmingly was an act of rudeness. It went right on creaking under his own considerable weight, and all it needed, Harold thought, was for somebody to fling himself back in a fit of laughter and that would be the end of it.

Through the open window they heard sounds below in the street: cartwheels, a tired horse's plodding step, voices. Harold indicated the photograph on the wall and asked what church the stone sculpture was in. Eugène told him and he promptly forgot. They passed the marmalade, the bread, the black-market butter, back and forth. Nothing was said about hotels or train journeys.

Eugène offered Harold his car, to use at any time he cared to, and when this offer was not accepted, the armchair creaked. They all three had another cup of coffee. Eugène was in his pajamas and dressing gown, and on his large feet he wore yellow Turkish slippers that turned up at the toes.

"Ex-cuse me," he said in Berlitz English, and got up and left them, to bathe and dress.

The first shrill ring of the telephone brought Harold out into the hall. He realized that he had no idea where the telephone was. At that moment the bathroom door flew open and Eugène came out, with his face lathered for shaving, and strode down the hall, tying the sash of his dressing gown as he went. The telephone was in the study but the ringing came from the hall. Between the telephone and the wall plug there was sixty feet of cord, and when the conversation came to an end, Eugène carried the instrument with him the whole length of the apartment, to his bathroom, where it rang three more times while he was shaving and in the tub. Before he left the apartment he knocked on their door and asked if there was anything he could do for them. Harold shook his head.

"Sabine called a few minutes ago," Eugène said. "She wants you and Barbara to have dinner with her tomorrow night."

He handed Harold a key to the front door, and cautioned him against leaving it unlocked while they were out of the apartment.

When enough time had elapsed so that there was little likelihood of his returning for something he had forgotten, Harold went out into the hall and stood looking into one room after another. In the room next to theirs was a huge cradle, of mahogany, ornately carved and decorated with gold leaf. It was the most important-looking cradle he had ever seen. Then came their bathroom, and then a bedroom that, judging by the photographs on the walls, must belong to Mme Cestre. A young woman who looked like Alix, with her two children. Alix and Eugène on their wedding day. Matching photographs in oval frames of Mme Bonenfant and an elderly man who must be Alix's grandfather. Mme Viénot, considerably younger and very different. The schoolboy. And a gray-haired man whose glance—direct, lifelike, and mildly accusing—was contradicted by the gilt and black frame. It was the kind of frame that is only put around the photograph of a dead person. Professor Cestre, could it be?

With the metal shutters closed, the dining room was so dark that it seemed still night in there. One of the drawing-room shutters was partly open and he made out the shapes of chairs and sofas, which seemed to be upholstered in brown or russet velvet. The curtains were of the same material, and there were some big oil paintings—portraits in the style of Lancret and Boucher.

Though, taken individually, the big rooms were, or seemed to be, square, the apartment as a whole formed a triangle. The apex, the study where Eugène slept, was light and bright and airy and cheerful. The window looked out on the Place Redouté

—it was the only window of the apartment that did. Looking around slowly, he saw a marble fireplace, a desk, a low bookcase of mahogany with criss-crossed brass wire instead of glass panes in the doors. The daybed Eugène had slept in, made up now with its dark-brown velours cover and pillows. The portable record player with a pile of classical records beside it. Beethoven's Fifth was the one on top. Da-da-da-dum . . . Music could not be Eugène's passion. Besides, the records were dusty. He tried the doors of the bookcase. Locked. The titles he could read easily through the criss-crossed wires: works on theology, astral physics, history, biology, political science. No poetry. No novels. He moved over to the desk and stood looking at the papers on it but not touching anything. The clock on the mantel piece was scandalized and ticked so loudly that he glanced at it over his shoulder and then quickly left the room.

THE CONCIERGE CALLED OUT to them as they were passing through the foyer. Her quarters were on the right as you walked into the building, and her small front room was clogged with heavy furniture—a big, round, oak dining table and chairs, a buffet, with a row of unclaimed letters inserted between the mirror and its frame. The suitcases had come while they were out, and had been put in their room, the concierge said.

He waited until they were inside the elevator and then said: "Now what do we do?"

"Call the Vouillemont, I guess."

"I guess."

Rather than sit around waiting for the suitcases to be delivered, they had gone sight-seeing. They went to the Flea Market, expecting to find the treasures of Europe, and found instead a duplication of that long double row of booths in Tours. Cheap clothing and junk of every sort, as far as the eye could see. They looked, even so. Looked at everything. Barbara bought some cotton aprons, and Harold bought shoestrings. They had lunch at a sidewalk café overlooking the intersection of two broad, busy, unpicturesque streets, and coming home they got lost in the Métro; it took them over an hour to get back to the station where they should have changed, in order to take the line that went to the Place Redouté. It was the end of the afternoon when he took the huge key out of his pocket and inserted it into the keyhole. When he opened the door, there stood Eugène, on his way out of the apartment. He was wearing sneakers and shorts and an open-collared shirt, and in his hand he carried a little black bag. He did not explain where he was going, and they did not ask. Instead, they went on down the hall to their room.

"Do you think he could be having an affair?" Barbara asked, as they heard the front door close.

"Oh no," Harold said, shocked.

"Well, this is France, after all."

"I know, but there must be some other explanation. He's probably spending the evening with friends."

"And for that he needs a little bag?"

They went shopping in the neighborhood, and bought two loaves of bread with the ration coupons they had been given in Blois, and some cheese, and a dozen eggs, and a bag of oranges from a peddler in the Place Redouté—the first oranges they had seen since they landed. They had Vermouth, sitting in front of a café. When they got home Harold was grateful for the stillness in the apartment, and thought how, under different circumstances, they might have stayed on here, in these old-fashioned, high-ceilinged rooms that reminded him of the Irelands' apartment in the East Eighties. They could have been perfectly happy here for ten whole days.

He went down the hall to Eugène's bathroom, to turn on the hot-water heater, and on the side of the tub he saw a pair of blue wool swimming trunks. He felt them. They were damp. He reached out and felt the bath towel hanging on the towel rack over the tub. Damp also. He looked around the room and then called out: "Come here, quick!"

"What is it?" Barbara asked, standing in the doorway.

"I've solved the mystery of the little bag. There it is . . . and there is what was in it. But where do people go swimming in Paris? That boat in the river, maybe."

"What boat?"

"There's a big boat anchored near the Place de la Concorde, with a swimming pool in it—didn't you notice it? But if he has time to go swimming, he had time to be with us."

She looked at him in surprise.

"I know," he said, reading her mind.

"I don't know what I'm going to do with you."

"It's because we are in France," he said, "and know so few people. So something like this matters more than it would at home. Also, he was so nice when he *was* nice."

"All because I didn't feel like dancing."

"I don't think it was that, really."

"Then what was it?"

"I don't know. I wish I did. The tweed coat, maybe. The thing about Eugène is that he's very proud."

And the thing about hurt feelings, the wet bathing suit pointed out, is that the person who has them is not quite the innocent party he believes himself to be. For instance—what about all those people Harold Rhodes went toward unhesitatingly, as if this were the one moment they would ever have together, their one chance of knowing each other?

Fortunately, the embarrassing questions raised by objects do not need to be answered, or we would all have to go sleep in the open fields. And in any case, answers may clarify but they do not change anything. Ten days ago, high up under the canvas roof of the Greatest Show on Earth, thinking *Now* . . . Harold threw himself on the empty air, confidently expecting that when he finished turning he would find the outstretched arms, the taped wrists, the steel hands that would catch and hold him. And it wasn't that the hands had had to catch some other flying trapeze artist, instead; they just simply weren't there.

He lit the hot-water heater, went back to their room, threw open the shutters, and stepped out on the balcony. He could see the Place Redouté, down below and to the left, and in the other direction the green edge of the Bois de Boulogne. The street was quiet. There were trees. And there was a whole upper landscape of chimney pots and skylights and trapdoors leading out onto the roof tops. He saw that within the sameness of the buildings there was infinite variety. When Barbara joined him on the balcony, he said: "This is a very different neighborhood from the Place de la Concorde."

"Do you want to stay?" she asked.

"Do you?"

"I don't know."

"I do and I don't want to stay," he said. "I love living in this apartment instead of a hotel. And being in this part of Paris."

"I don't really think we ought to stay here, feeling the way we do about Eugène."

"I know."

"If we are going to leave," she said, "right now is the time."

"But I keep remembering that we wanted to leave the château also."

"Mmm."

"And that we were rewarded for sticking it out. And probably would be here. But I really hate him."

"I don't think we'd be seeing very much of him. The thing I regret, and the only thing, is leaving that kitchen. It isn't like any kitchen I ever cooked in. Everything about it is just right."

"Yes?" he said, and turned, having heard in her voice a sound that he was accustomed to pay attention to.

"If we could only take our being here as casually as *he* does," she said.

He leaned far out over the balcony, trying to see a little more of the granite monument. "Let's not call the hotel just yet," he said. "The truth is, I don't want to leave either."

THEY HAD DINNER in a restaurant down the street and went to a movie, which turned out to be too bad to sit through. They walked home, with the acid green street lights showing the undersides of the leaves and giving their faces a melancholy pallor. Since it was still early, they sat down at a table in front of the café in the Place Redouté and ordered mineral water.

"In Paris nobody is ever alone," Barbara said.

He surveyed the tables all around them, and then looked at the people passing by. It was quite true. Every man had a woman, whom he was obviously sleeping with. Every woman had her arm through some man's arm. "But how do you account for it?" he asked.

"I don't."

"The Earthly Paradise," he said, smiling up into the chestnut trees.

They sat looking at people and speculating about them until suddenly he yawned. "It's quarter of eleven," he said. "Shall we go?"

He paid the check and they got up and went around the corner, into the rue Malène. Just as he put out his hand to ring the bell, a man stepped out of a small car that was parked in front of their door. They saw, with surprise, that it was Eugène. He made them get into the car with him, and after a fashion—after a very peculiar fashion—they saw Paris by night. It was presumably for their pleasure, but he drove as if he were racing somebody, and they had no idea where they were and they were not given time to look at anything. "Jeanne d'Arc, Barbara!" Eugène cackled, as the car swung around a gilded monument on two wheels. Now they were in a perfectly ordinary street, now they were looking at neon-lighted night clubs. "La Place Pigalle," Eugène said, but they had no idea why he was pointing it out to them. Politely they peered at a big windmill without knowing what that was either.

The tour ended in Montmartre. Eugène managed to park the car in a street crowded with Chryslers and Cadillacs. Then he stood on the sidewalk, allowing them to draw their own conclusions from the spectacle provided by their countrymen and by the bearded and sandaled types (actors, could they be, dressed up to look like Greenwich Village artists of the 1920's?) who circulated in the interests of local color. He showed them the lights of Paris from the steps of the Sacré-Coeur, and then all his gaiety, which they could only feel as an intricate form of insult, suddenly vanished. They got in the car and drove home, through dark streets, at a normal rate of speed, without talking. And perhaps because he had relieved his feelings, or because, from their point of view, he had done something for them that (even though it was tinged with ill-will) common politeness required that he do for them, or because they were all three tired and ready for bed, or because the city itself had had an effect on them, the silence in the car was almost friendly.

Chapter 14

THE RINGING OF AN ELECTRIC BELL in the hour just before daylight Harold heard in his sleep and identified: it was the ting-a-ling of the Good Humor Man. He wanted to go right on dreaming, but someone was shaking him. He opened his eyes. The hand that was shaking him so insistently was Barbara's. The dark all around the bed he did not recognize. Then that, too, came to him: they were in Paris.

"There's someone at the door!" Barbara whispered.

He raised himself on his elbows and listened. The bell rang twice more. "Maybe it's the telephone," he said. He could feel his heart racing as it did at home when the telephone woke them—not with its commonplace daytime sound but with its shrill night alarm, so suggestive of unspecified death in the family, of disaster that cannot wait until morning to make itself known. If it was the telephone they didn't have to do anything about it. The telephone was in the study.

"No, it's the door."

"I don't see how you can tell," he said, and, drunk with sleep, he got up out of bed and stumbled out into the pitch-dark hallway, where the ringing was much louder. He had no idea where the light switches were. Groping his way from door to door, encountering a big chair and then an armoire, he arrived at a jog in the hallway, and then at the foyer. After a struggle with the French lock, he succeeded in opening the front door and peered out at the sixth-floor landing and the stairs, dimly lighted by a big window. Confused at seeing no one there, he shut the door, and had just about convinced himself that it was a mistake, that he had dreamed he heard a bell ringing somewhere in the apartment, when the matter was settled once and for all by a repetition of the same silvery sound. So it *was* the telephone after all. . . .

He started across the foyer, intending to wake Eugène, who must be sleeping the sleep of the dead. Before he reached the door of the study a new sound stopped him in his tracks: someone was beating with both fists on a door. Feeling like the blindfolded person who is "it" in a guessing game, he retraced his steps down the dark hallway, as far as the door into the kitchen. The pounding seemed to come from somewhere quite near. He crossed the threshold and to his surprise and horror found that he was walking barefoot in water. The kitchen floor was awash, and there was another sound besides the voices and the pounding—a sound that was like water cascading from a great height. He found the back door and couldn't unlock it. Angry excited voices shouted at him through the door, and try as he might, turning the huge key back and forth and pulling at the spring lever that should have released the lock, he couldn't get the door open. He gave up finally and ran back into the hallway, shouting "Eugène!"

Even so, Eugène did not waken. He had to open the study door and go in and, bending over the bed, shake him into sensibility.

"Il y a un catastrophe!" Harold said loudly.

There was a silence, and then Eugène said, without moving: "Une catastrophe?"

The pounding was resumed, the bell started ringing again, and Eugène sat up and reached for his dressing gown. Harold turned and ran back to the kitchen. Awake at last, he managed to get the door open. The concierge and a boy of fifteen burst in upon him. They were both angry and excited, and he had no idea what they were saying to him. The single word "inondation" was all he understood. The concierge turned the kitchen light on. Harold listened to the cascade. A considerable quantity of water must be flowing over the red-tiled floor and out the door and down six flights of the winding metal stair that led down into the courtyard, presumably. And maybe from there the water was flowing into the concierge's quarters. In any case, it was clear that she blamed him, a stranger in the apartment, for everything.

Eugène appeared, with his brocade dressing gown over his pajamas, and his massive face as calm and contained as if he were about to sit down to breakfast. Without bothering to remove the Turkish slippers, he waded over to the sink and stood examining the faucets. He and the concierge and the boy carried on a three-way conversation that excluded foreigners by its rapidity, volubility, and passion. They turned the faucets on and off. With their eyes, with their searching hands, they followed the exposed water pipes around the walls of the kitchen, and, passing over the electric hot-water heater, arrived eventually at a small iron stove—for coal, apparently, and not a cooking stove. (There were three of those in the kitchen.) It was cylindrical, five feet high, and two feet in diameter, with an asbestos-covered stove pipe rising from the top and disappearing into a flue in the wall. The concierge bent down and opened the door of the ash chamber. From this unlikely source a further quantity of water flowed out over the floor and down the back stairs. For a moment, as if he had received the gift of tongues, Harold understood what Eugène and the concierge and the boy were saying. Eugène inquired about the apartment directly below. The people who lived there were away, the concierge said, and she had no key; so there was no way of knowing whether that apartment also was being flooded. A plumber? Not at this hour, she said, and looked at Harold balefully. Then she turned her attention to the pipes in the pantry, and Eugène stood in front of the electric hot-water heater, which was over the sink. Yesterday morning he had put the plug into the wall socket and explained that the heater took care of the hot water for the dishes. He said nothing about removing the plug when they were finished, and so, remembering how the light in the elevator and the light on the sixth-floor landing both extinguished themselves, barely leaving time to reach the door of the apartment before you were in total darkness, they had left the heater in charge of its own current. Foolishly, Harold now saw, because it must be the heater. Unless by some mischance he had forgotten to turn the gas off after Barbara's bath, last night. He distinctly remembered turning the gas off, and even so the thought was enough to make him have to sit down in a chair until the strength came back into his knees. Once more he inquired if the flood was something that he and Barbara had done. Eugène glanced around thoughtfully, but instead of answering, he joined the search party in the pantry. Cupboard doors were opened and shut. Pipes were examined. Hearing the word "chauffage" again and again from the pantry, Harold withdrew to the bathroom at the end of the hall, expecting to discover the worst—the gas heater left burning all night, a burst pipe, and water everywhere. The heater was cold and the bathroom floor was dry. He was on the point of absolving himself of all responsibility for the inundation when a thought crossed his mind—a quite hideous thought, judging by the expression that accompanied it. He went down the hall past the kitchen and opened the door of the little room that contained the toilet.

As a piece of plumbing, the toilet was done for. It only operated at all out of good will. Last night, while they were getting ready for bed, he had heard it flushing, and then flushing again, and again; and thinking to avoid just such a situation as had now happened, he got the kitchen stepladder, climbed up on it, reached into the water chamber, and closed the valve, intending to open it when they got up in the morning. By so doing, he now realized, he had upset the entire system. It could only be that; they hadn't been near the iron boiler in the kitchen from which water so freely flowed. And it was only a question of time before the search, now confined to the pantry, would lead Eugène, the concierge, and the boy to the real source of the trouble. Nevertheless, like Adam denying the apple, he climbed up on the stepladder and opened the valve. The water chamber filled slowly and then the pipes grew still.

As he reached the kitchen door, the search party brushed past him and went into Eugène's bathroom. Harold turned and went back to their bedroom. Barbara had got up out of bed and was sitting at the window, with her dressing gown wrapped around her, smoking a cigarette.

"Look up the word 'chauffage,' " he said. "The dictionary is in the pocket of my brown coat," and he went on down the hall. Ignoring the gas heater, Eugène searched for and found a valve behind the tub. As soon as the valve was closed, the bathtub began to fill with rusty red water gurgling up out of the drainpipe. He hurriedly opened the valve, and the water receded, leaving a guilty stain.

" 'Chauffage' means heating or a heating system," Barbara said, as Harold came into the bedroom. He closed the door behind him.

"Did he say it was our fault?" she asked.

"I asked him five times and just now he finally said 'Heureusement oui.' "

"That doesn't make any sense, 'heureusement oui.' "

"I know it doesn't, but that's what he said. It *must* be our fault. We ought never to have come here."

The voices and the heavy footsteps passed their door, returning to the kitchen, and wearily he went in pursuit of them. They still had not found the valve that controlled the water pipes, and the cascade down the back stairs was unabated. The landing and the stair well were included in the area under investigation. Locating a new valve, Eugène left his sodden Turkish slippers inside the kitchen door and went into the front of the apartment;

opened the door of the huge sculptured armoire and took out a cigar box; opened the cigar box and took out a pair of pliers.

"There is something I have to tell you," Harold said. "I'm awfully sorry but last night the toilet didn't work properly and so I got the kitchen stepladder and . . ."

Eugène listened abstractedly to this confession and when it was finished he asked where Harold had put the stepladder. Then he went into the little room where the toilet was, picked up the stepladder, and carried it out to the back landing. With the pliers, standing on the stepladder, he closed a valve in the pipeline out there. He and the concierge and the boy listened. Their faces conveyed uncertainty, and then hope, and then triumph, as the sound of falling water began to diminish. It took some time and further discussion, a gradual letting down of tension and a round of congratulations, before the concierge and the boy left. Eugène put away the stepladder and picked up the mop. As he started mopping up the red tiles, Harold said: "Barbara and I will clean the kitchen up."

Eugène stopped and stared at him, and then said: "The floor will be dirty unless it is mopped." They stood looking at each other helplessly. He must think we don't understand anything at all, Harold thought.

"I'm very sorry that your sleep has been disturbed," Eugène said.

Harold studied his face carefully, thinking that he must be speaking sarcastically. He was not. The apology was sincere. Once more, with very little hope of a sensible answer, Harold asked if they had caused the trouble.

"This sort of thing happens since the war," Eugène said. The building is old and needs new plumbing. Now that the water is turned off, there is nothing more that we can do until the plumber comes and fixes the leak."

"Was it caused by turning the water off in the toilet?"

Eugène turned and indicated the little iron stove, inside which a pipe had burst, for no reason.

I: *Leo and Virgo*

"Then it wasn't our fault?"

For a few seconds Eugène seemed to be considering not what Harold had just said but Harold himself. He looked at him the way cats look at people, and did something that cats are too polite ever to do: he laughed. Then he turned and resumed his mopping.

Standing on the balcony outside their room, Harold lit a cigarette. Barbara was in bed and he couldn't tell whether she was asleep or not. The swallows were darting over the roof tops. Directly below him, so straight down that it made him dizzy to look, an old man was silently searching through the garbage cans. On the blue pavement he had placed four squares of blue cloth, and when he found something of value he put it on one or the other of them.

The stoplights at the intersection at the foot of the hill changed from red to green, from green to red. The moon, in its last quarter, was white in a pearly pink sky. The discovery that it was not their fault had come too late. They had had so much time to feel they were to blame that they might just as well have been. Too tired to care any longer, he left the balcony and got into bed. A moment later, he got up and took his wallet out of his coat and found a five-hundred-franc note and then returned to the balcony. When the old man looked up he would make signals at him. Though he waited patiently, the old man did not look up. Instead, he tied his four pieces of cloth at the corners and went off down the street, which by now had admitted it was morning.

Awakened out of a deep sleep by a silvery sound, Harold sat up in bed. It was broad daylight outside. The telephone? he thought wildly. The front door? Or the back? Whatever it was, Barbara was sleeping right through it.

He got up and followed his own wet footprints down the gray carpeting until he came to the foyer. This time when he opened the front door someone was there—the concierge, smiling and cordial, with three blond young men. One of them had a brief case, and they didn't look at all like plumbers. The concierge asked for M. de Boisgaillard, and Harold knocked on the study door and fled.

Ten minutes later, he heard a faint tap on their door.

"Yes?"

As he sat up in bed, the door opened and Eugène came in. Keeping his voice low because Barbara was still asleep, he said: "The people you let in— They just arrived in Paris this morning, from Berlin." He hesitated.

Harold perceived that Eugène was telling him this because there was something they could do for him. Eugène was not in the habit of asking for favors, and it was painful for him to have to now. What he was going to say would alter somewhat the situation between them and him, but he was going to say it anyway.

"They have no money, and they haven't had any breakfast."

"You'd like Barbara to make breakfast for them?" Harold asked, and found himself face to face with his lost friend, Eugène the way he used to be before that picnic on the banks of the Loire.

Bread, oranges, marmalade, eggs, honey—all bought the afternoon before, and with their money. Nescafe in the big suitcase, sugar cubes in the small one. All the wealth of America to feed the hungry of Europe.

"There is plenty of everything," he said.

"Plenty?" Eugène repeated, unconvinced.

"Plenty," Harold said, nodding.

"Good."

The image of a true friend was dimmer; was fading like a rainbow or any other transitory natural phenomenon, but it was still visible. When Eugène left, Harold woke Barbara, and as he was hurriedly getting into his clothes he began to whistle. It was their turn to do something for Eugène. And if they cared to, they could be both preoccupied and moody as they went about it.

When Barbara wheeled the teacart into Mme Cestre's drawing room, the four heads were raised. The four men rose, and the Germans clicked their heels politely as Eugène presented them to her and then to Harold, who had come in after her. All three were pale, thin, and nervous. One had pink-tinted rimless glasses, and one had ears that stuck straight out from his head, and one was tall and blond (the pure Nordic abstraction, the race that never was) with wide, bony shoulders, concave chest, hollow stomach, and the trousers of a much heavier man hanging from his hip bones.

"Do sit down," Barbara said.

Herr von Rothenberg, the Nordic type, spoke French and English fluently, and the two others told him what they wanted to say and he translated for them. They had traveled as far as the French border by plane, and from there by train. They had arrived in Paris at daybreak.

"We were very surprised," Herr von Rothenberg said to the Americans. "We did not expect to find Paris intact. We had understood that it was largely ruins, like London and Berlin."

He was not entirely happy that Paris had been spared. It offended his sense of what is fair. But he did not say this; it only came out in his voice, his troubled expression.

The Germans politely took the cups that Eugène handed them, but allowed their coffee to grow cold. Barbara had to urge it on them, and point again and again to the bread and butter on their plates, before they could bring themselves to eat. Their extreme delicacy in the presence of food seemed to say: *It was most kind of M. de Boisgaillard to offer us these cigarettes, and surely something is to be gained from a discussion of the kind we are having, between the people who have lost a war and those who, for reasons history will eventually make clear, have won it. But as for eating—we do not care to impose on anyone, we are accustomed to being faint with hunger, we have much more often than not, the last few years, gone without breakfast. We would prefer to continue with what M. de Boisgaillard was saying about the establishment of a central bureau that would have control over credit and . . .*

In the end, though, the bread was eaten, the coffee was drunk, and on two of the plates there was a pile of orange peelings. The third orange remained untouched. Barbara looked inquiringly from it to the young man whose ears stuck out, and whose orange it was. He smiled at her timidly and then looked at Eugène, who was telephoning and ignored his appeal. Pointing to the orange, the young man whose ears stuck out said, in halting English: "The first in twelve years." He hesitated and then, since Eugène was still talking into the telephone and Barbara was still waiting and the orange had not been snatched from him, said: "I have a wife. And ten days ago a baby is born. . . . Could I take this orange with me, to give to her?"

Barbara explained that there were more oranges, and that he could eat this one. He put it in his pocket, instead.

Eugène was trying to find a place for the Germans to stay. They listened to the one-sided telephone conversations with a sympathetic interest, as if it were the welfare of three other young men he was devoting himself to with such persistence.

Finally, as the morning dragged on, the Americans excused themselves and left the drawing room, taking the teacart with them.

"Terrible," Harold said.

"Terrible," she agreed.

"I didn't know there were Germans like that."

"Did you hear what he said about the orange?"

"Yes, I heard. We must remember to send some back with them."

"But what will become of them?"

"God knows."

"Do you think they were Nazis?"

"No, of course not. How could they have been? Probably they never even heard of Hitler."

At noon, Barbara wheeled the teacart out of the kitchen again, and down the hall to Mme Cestre's drawing room, which was now murky with cigarette smoke. The men sprang to their feet and waited for her to sit down, but she shook her head and left them. She and Harold ate in the kitchen, sitting on stools. They had just finished cleaning up when Eugène appeared in the doorway.

"I am much obligated to you, Barbara," he said. "It is a very great kindness that you do for me."

"It was nothing," she said. "Did you find a place for them to stay?"

He shook his head. "I have told them that they can stay here. But you will not have to do this any more. I have made other arrangements. The person who comes in by the day when we are all here will cook for them. Her name is Françoise. She is a very nice woman. If you want anything, just tell her and she will do it for you. I did not like to ask her because her son was in a concentration camp and she does not like Germans."

"But what are they doing in Paris?" Harold asked.

"They are trying to get to Rome," Eugène said. "They want to attend an international conference there. Arrangements had been made for them to go by way of Switzerland, but they decided to go by way of Paris, instead. They used up their money on train fare. And unfortunately in all of Paris no one knows of a fund that provides for an emergency of this kind or a place that will take them in. Herr von Rothenberg I met at an official reception in Berlin, last year. He is of a very good family. The other two I did not know before. . . . You have Sabine's address? She is expecting you at eight."

THE ADDRESS that Eugène gave them turned out to be a modern apartment building on a little square that was named after a poet whose works Harold had read in college but could no longer remember; they had joined with the works of three other romantic poets, as drops of water on a window pane join and become one larger drop. A sign by the elevator shaft said that the elevator was out of order. They rang Sabine's bell and started climbing. Craning his neck, he saw that she was waiting for them, six floors up. She called down over the banister: "I'm sorry you have such a long climb," and he called up: "Are you as happy to see us as we are to see you?"

She had on a little starched white apron, over her blouse and skirt. She shook hands with them, took the flowers that Barbara held out to her, and, looking into the paper cone, exclaimed: "Marguerites! They are my favorite. And a book?"

"*A Passage to India*," Harold said. "We saw it in the window of a bookstore."

"I will be most interested to read it," she said. "This is my uncle's apartment—did Eugène tell you? The family is away now. I am here alone. My uncle collects paintings and objets d'art. There is a Sargent in the next room. . . . I must put these beautiful flowers in water. You will not mind if I am a little distracted? I am not used to cooking."

She and Barbara went off to the kitchen together, and Harold stood at the window and peered down at the little square. Then he started around the room, looking at Chinese carvings and porcelains and at the paintings on the walls. When the two girls came back with a bottle of Cinzano and glasses, he was standing in front of a small Renoir.

"It's charming, isn't it?" Sabine said.

"Very," he said.

"In my aunt's apartment there is a bookcase with art books in it— Have you found it yet?"

"In the front hall," he said. "By the study door. But it's locked."

"I know where the key is kept," she said, but before she had a chance to tell him, the doorbell rang. "Are you comfortable in the rue Malène?" she asked as she started toward the hall.

Harold and Barbara looked at each other.

"Something has happened since I saw you?" Sabine asked.

"A great deal has happened," he said. "It's a very long story. We'll tell you later."

The young man she introduced to them was in his middle twenties, small, compact, and alert-looking, with hair as black as an Indian's and dark skin. For the first few minutes, he was self-conscious with the Americans, and kept apologizing for his faulty English. They liked him immediately, encouraged him when he groped for a word, assured him that his English was fine, and in every way possible took him under their wing, enjoying all his comments and telling him that they felt as if they already knew him. The four-sided conversation moved like a piece of music. It was as if they had all agreed beforehand to say only what came into their heads and to say it instantly, without fear or hesitation. In her pleasure at discovering that Sabine had such a handsome and agreeable young man on a string, Barbara was more talkative than usual. She was witty. She made them all laugh. Sabine was astonished to learn of the presence of three Berliners in her aunt's apartment, and said doubtfully: "I do not think that my aunt would like it, if she knew."

"But if you saw them!" Harold exclaimed. "So pale, so thin. And as sensitive as sea horses." Then he began to tell the story of the burst water pipe.

They sat down to dinner at a gateleg table in the drawing-room alcove. The Americans dug out of the young Frenchman that he was in the government. From his description of his job, Harold concluded that it was to read all the newspaper articles and summarize them for his superior, who based his statements to the press on them. This explanation the Frenchman rejected indignantly; it was he who prepared the statements for the press. Looking at him, Harold thought that if he had had to draw up a set of requirements for a husband for Sabine, they would have added up to the young man across the table. Though he must be extremely intelligent to hold down a position of responsibility at his age, there was nothing pompous in his manner or his conversation. He was simply young and quick-witted and unsuspicious. They felt free to tease him, and he defended himself without attacking them or being anything but more agreeable. The evening flew by, and when they left at eleven, they tried to do it in such a way that he wouldn't feel he had to leave too. But he left with them, and as they were passing under a street lamp in the avenue Victor Hugo, they learned that he was not the person they thought he was; he was Sabine's brother-in-law, Jean-Claude Lahovary.

"Mme Viénot told us about you," Barbara said.

"Yes?"

"She told us about your family," Barbara said.

Oh no, Harold begged her silently. *Don't say it. . . .*

But Barbara was a little high from the wine, and on those rare occasions when she did put her trust in strangers, she was incautious and wholehearted. As if no remark of hers could possibly be misunderstood by him, she said: "She said your mother was hors de siècle."

The Frenchman looked bewildered. Harold changed the subject. Exactly how offensive the phrase was, he didn't know, and he hadn't been able to tell from Mme Viénot's tone of voice because her voice was always edged with one kind of cheerful malice or another. Trying to cover up Barbara's mistake he made another.

"Do you know what you remind me of?" he asked, though an inner voice begged him not to say it. (He too had had too much wine.)

"What?" the Frenchman asked politely.

"An acrobat."

The Frenchman was not pleased. He did not consider it a compliment to be told that he was like an acrobat. The tiresome inner voice had been right, as usual. Though table manners are the same in France, other manners are not. We shouldn't have gone so far with him, the first time, Harold thought. Or been quite so personal.

The conversation lost its naturalness. There were silences as they walked along together. They quickly became strangers. As they crossed one of the streets that went out from the Place Redouté, they were accosted by a beggar, the first Harold had seen in Paris. Always an easy touch at home, he waited, not knowing if beggars were regarded cynically by the French, and also not wanting to appear to be throwing his American money around. The future minister of finance reached in his pocket quickly and brought out a hundred-franc note and gave it to the beggar, and so widened the misunderstanding: the French have compassion for the poor, Americans do not, was the only possible conclusion.

They shook hands at the entrance of the Métro and said good night. Still hoping that something would happen at the last minute, that he would give them a chance to repair the damage they had done to the evening, they stood and watched him start down the steps, turn right, and disappear without looking back. Though they might read his name years from now in the foreign-news dispatches, this was the last they would ever see of Mme Viénot's brilliant son-in-law.

As they were walking home, past shuttered store fronts, Barbara said: "I shouldn't have said that about his mother, should I?"

"People are very touchy about their families."

"But I meant it as a compliment."

"I know."

"Why didn't he realize I meant it as a compliment?"

"I don't know."

"I liked him."

"So did I."

"It's very sad."

"It doesn't matter," he said, meaning something quite different—meaning that there was nothing either of them could do about it now.

He called out who they were as they passed through the foyer of the apartment building. They went up in the elevator, and the hall light went out just as he thrust his key at the keyhole. He stepped into the dark apartment and felt around until he found the light switch. The study door was closed and so was the door of Mme Cestre's bedroom.

Lying in bed in the dark, looking through the open window at the one lighted room in the building across the street, he said: "What it amounts to is that you cannot be friends with somebody, no matter how much you like them, if it turns out that you don't really understand one another."

"Also—" he began, five minutes later, and was stopped by the sound of Barbara's soft, regular breathing. He turned over and as he lay staring at the lighted room he felt a sudden first wave of homesickness come over him.

Chapter 15

THE FIRST DAYLIGHT, whitening the sky and making the windows shine, revealed that the three Berliners had spent the night in Mme Cestre's bedroom. Their threadbare, unpressed, spotty coats and trousers, neatly folded, were on three chairs. Also, their shirts and socks and underwear, which had been washed without soap. Two of them slept in the narrow bed, with their mouths open like dead people and their breathing so quiet they might have been dead. The third slept on the floor, with a rug under him, his head on the leather brief case, his pink-tinted glasses beside him, and Mme Cestre's spare comforter keeping him from catching pneumonia. So pale they were, in the gray light. So unaggressive, so intellectual, so polite even in their sleep. *Oh heartbreaking—what happens to children,* said the fruitwood armoire, vast and maternal, bound in brass, with brass handles on the drawers, brass knobs on the two carved doors. The dressing table, modern, with its triple way of viewing things, said: *It is their own doing and redoing and undoing.*

"BONJOUR, monsieur-dame," said the tall, full-bosomed woman with carrot-colored hair and a beautiful carriage. She raised the front wheels of the teacart and then the back, so that they did not touch the telephone cord. When she had gone back to the kitchen, Harold said: "There are plates and cups for three, which can only mean that he is having breakfast with us."

"You think?" Barbara said.

"By his own choice," Harold said, "since there is now someone to bring him a tray in his room."

They sat and waited. In due time, Eugène appeared and drew the armchair up to the teacart.

It was a beautiful day. The window was wide open and the sunlight was streaming in from the balcony. Eugène inquired about their evening with Sabine, and the telephone, like a spoiled child that cannot endure the conversation of the grownups, started ringing. Eugène left the room. When he came back, he said: "It is possible that I may be going down to the country on Friday. A cousin of Alix is marrying. And if I do go—as I should, since it is a family affair—it will be early in the morning, before you are up. And I may stay down for the week end."

They tried not to look pleased.

He accepted a second cup of coffee and then asked what they had done about getting gasoline coupons. "But we don't need them," Harold said, and so, innocently, obliged Eugène to admit that he did. "I seldom enjoy the use of my car," he said plaintively, "and it would be pleasant to have the gasoline for short trips into the country now and then."

He reached into his bathrobe pocket and brought out a slip of paper on which he had written the address of the place they were to go to for gasoline coupons.

"How can we ask for gasoline coupons if we don't have a car?" Harold said.

"As Americans traveling in France you are entitled to the coupons whether you use them or not," Eugène said. "And the amount of gasoline that tourists are allowed is quite considerable."

Harold put the slip of paper on the teacart and said: "Could you tell us— But there is no reason you should know, I guess. We have to get a United States Army visa to enter Austria."

"I will call a friend who works at the American Embassy," Eugène said, rising. "He will know."

Five minutes later, he was back with the information Harold had asked for.

Walking past the open door of the dressing room, Harold saw the Germans for the first time that morning. They were crowded around Eugène, and pressing on him their latest thoughts about their predicament. He avoided looking at whoever was speaking to him, and his attention seemed to be entirely on the arrangement of his shirt tails inside his trousers.

Later he stopped to complain about them, standing in the center of the Americans' room, with the door open, so that there was a good chance that he might be overheard. It was already too late for the Germans to get to the conference in Rome in time to present their credentials, he said. Their places would be taken by alternates.

"What will they do?" Harold asked. "Turn around and go home?"

"There are other conferences scheduled for other Italian cities," Eugène said, "and they hope to be allowed to attend one of these. Unfortunately, there isn't the slightest chance of their getting the visas they need to cross the Italian border. The whole thing is a nuisance—the kind of silliness only Germans are capable of."

Though Eugène was bored with the Germans' dilemma and despised them personally for having got themselves into it, they had thrown themselves on his kindness, and it appeared that he had no choice but to go on trying to help them.

The Americans spent the morning getting to know parts of Paris that are not mentioned in guidebooks. The address on Eugène's slip of paper turned out to be incorrect; there was no such number. Harold was relieved; he had dreaded exposure. The information about where to go to get the Austrian visa was also wrong. They talked to the concierge of the building, who gave them new and explicit directions, and in a few minutes they found themselves peering through locked doors at the marble foyer of an unused public building. Eventually, by asking a gendarme, they arrived at the Military Permit Office. There they stood in line in a large room crowded with people whom no country wanted and whom France could not think what to do with. When Harold produced their American passports, the man next to him turned and looked at him reproachfully. All around them, people were arguing tirelessly with clerks who pretended (sometimes humorously) not to understand what they wanted, not to speak German or Italian, not to know that right there on the counter in front of them was the rubber stamp that would make further argument unnecessary. As Harold and Barbara went from clerk to clerk, from the large room on the first floor to a smaller office on the third floor, and finally outdoors with a new address to find, they began to feel less and less different from the homeless people around them, even though they had a perfectly good home and were only trying to get to a music festival. At the right place at last, they were told that they had to leave their passports with the application for their visas, which would be ready the next day.

After lunch, they walked through the looking glass, leaving the homeless on the other side, and spent the afternoon sightseeing. They took the Métro to the Place du Trocadéro, descended the monumental stairs of the Palais de Chaillot, went through the aquarium, and then strolled across the Pont d'Iéna in the sunshine.

At the top of the Tour Eiffel there was a strong wind and they could not bear to look straight down. All that they remembered afterward of what they saw was the colored awnings all over Paris. They took a taxi home, and as they went down the hall to their own room they could hear the Germans talking to each other, behind the closed door of theirs.

Meeting Herr Rothenberg in the hall, they learned that he and his friends had spent the day going the rounds of the embassies and consulates.

"But you ought to be seeing Paris," Harold said. "It's so beautiful."

"We will come back and see the museums another time," Herr Rothenberg said, smiling and quite pleased with the Paris they had seen.

Shortly afterward, he appeared at their door and said that Françoise had gone home and could they please have some bread and butter and coffee?

Harold followed Barbara into the kitchen and as she was putting the kettle on he said: "Do you suppose they don't realize that all those things are rationed?"

"I don't know," she said, "but let's not tell them."

"All right. I wasn't going to. It just occurred to me that maybe the national characteristics were asserting themselves."

"I'm so in love with this kitchen," Barbara said. "If it were up to me, I'd never leave."

The two Americans and the three Germans had coffee together in Mme Cestre's drawing room, with the shutters open and the light pouring in. The Germans showed Barbara snapshots of their wives, and Harold wrote their names and addresses in his financial diary, and then they all went out on the balcony so that Barbara could take the Berliners' pictures. They stood in a row before her, three pale scarecrows stiffly composed in attitudes that would be acceptable to posterity.

Still in a glow from the success of the tea party, Harold went down into the Place Redouté and found the orange peddler and bought a bag of oranges from him, which he then presented to Herr Rothenberg at the door of their room, with a carefully prepared little speech and three thousand-franc notes, in case the Germans found themselves in need of money on the next lap of their journey. The effect of this act of generosity was partly spoiled because, out of a kind of Anglo-Saxon politeness they were unfamiliar with, he didn't give them a chance to finish their speeches of gratitude. But at all events the money got from his wallet into theirs, where it very much needed to be.

At twenty-five minutes after six, he walked into the study with a calling card in his hand and stood by Eugène's desk, waiting until his wrist watch and the clock on the mantelpiece agreed that it was half-past six. On the back of the card Mme Straus-Muguet had scrawled the telephone number of the convent in Auteuil, and "coup de fil a 6h½." During the three and a half weeks that they had been in France he had managed, through the kindness of one person and another, not to have to talk over the telephone. He would just as soon not have done it now.

A woman's voice answered. He asked to speak to Mme Straus-Muguet and the voice implored him not to hang up. He started to say that he had no intention of hanging up, and then realized by the silence that if he did speak no one would hear him. It was a long, long discouraging silence that extended itself until he wondered why he continued to hold the telephone to his ear. At last a familiar voice said his name and he was enveloped in affectionate inquiries and elaborate arrangements. Mme Straus's voice came through strong and clear and he had no trouble understanding her. They were to meet her on Saturday evening at eight thirty sharp, she said, on the corner of the rue de Berry and the avenue des Champs Elysées. They would dine at the restaurant of her goddaughter and afterward go to the theater to see Mme Marguerite Mailly.

"At the Comédie Française?" he asked. They had not yet crossed that off their list.

Mme. Mailly had had a disagreement with the Comédie Française, Mme Straus said, and had left it to act in a modern comedy. The play had had an enormous success, and tickets were impossible to obtain, but knowing that they were arriving in Paris this week, she had written to her friend, and three places for the Saturday performance would be waiting at the box office.

"I don't know that we should do that," Barbara said doubtfully, when he told her about the arrangements. "It sounds so expensive, and she may not be able to afford it."

"I don't know that I'm up to dissuading her," he said. "Tactfully, I mean, over the telephone, and in French. Besides, it is no longer 6h½, and if I called her back I probably wouldn't reach her. Do *you* want to call her?"

"No, I don't."

"Maybe she'll let us pay for the dinner," he said.

At breakfast the next morning, Eugène surprised them by saying, as he passed his coffee cup across the tray to Barbara: "I am having a little dinner party this evening. You are free? . . . Good. I have asked Edouard Doria. He is Alix's favorite cousin. I think you will like him."

From the way he spoke, they realized that he was giving the dinner party for them. But why? Had Alix asked him to? And were the Berliners invited?

Meeting them in the hall, a few minutes later, Harold stepped aside to let them pass. They greeted him cheerfully, and when he inquired about their situation, they assured him that progress was being made, in the only way that it could be made; their story was being heard, their reasons considered. What they wanted was in no way unreasonable, and so in time some action, positive or negative, surely must result from their efforts. Meanwhile, there were several embassies they did not get to yesterday and that they planned to go to today. . . .

Harold stood outside the dining-room door and listened while Eugène consulted with Françoise about the linen, the china, the menu. They reached an agreement on the fish and the vegetable.

There would be oysters, then soup. He left the soup to her discretion. For dessert there would be an ice, which he would pick up himself on the way home.

The Americans left the apartment in the middle of the morning, and crossed over to the Left Bank. They walked along the river as far as Notre Dame, and had lunch under an awning, in the rain. In the window of a shop on the Quai de la Mégisserie they saw a big glass bird cage, but how to get it home was the question. Also, it was expensive, and the little financial diary kept pointing out that, even though they had no hotel bill to pay, they were spending quite a lot of money on taxis, flowers, books, movies, and food.

As they came through the Place Redouté, they picked up the kodak films they had left to be developed. They were as surprised by what came out as if they had had no hand in it. Some of the pictures were taken on shipboard, and some in Pontorson and Mont-Saint-Michel. But there was nothing after that until the one of Beaumesnil, with the old trees rising twice as high as the roofs, and a cloud castle in the sky above the real one. The best snapshot of all was a family picture, taken on the lawn, their last morning at the château. This picture was mysterious in that, though the focus was sharp enough, there was so much that you couldn't see. Alix's shadow fell across Mme Bonenfant's face. There was only her beautiful white hair, and her hand stretched out to steady herself against the fall all old people live in dread of. Alix's hair blacked out the lower part of Harold's face, and what you could see of him looked more like his brother. Barbara had taken the picture and so she wasn't in it at all. A shadow from a branch overhead fell across the upper part of Mme Cestre's face, leaving only her smile in bright sunlight and the rest in doubt. The two small children they had hardly set eyes on were nevertheless in the picture, and Mme Viénot was wearing the green silk dress with the New Look. Beside her was a broad expanse of white that could have been a castle wall but was actually Eugène's shirt, with his massive face above it looking strangely like Ludwig van Beethoven's. And Sabine, on the extreme right, standing in a diagonal shaft of light that didn't come from the sun but from an inadvertent exposure as the film was being taken from the camera.

"I don't see how we could not have taken more than one roll in all this time," Barbara said.

"We were too busy looking."

"We have no picture of Nils Jensen. Or of Mme Straus-Muguet."

"With or without a picture, I will never forget either of them."

"That's not the point. You think you remember and you don't."

When they got home, she made him go straight out on the balcony where, even though it was late in the afternoon and the light was poor, she took a picture of him in his seersucker suit and scuffed white shoes, peering down into the rue Malène, and he took one of her in her favorite dress of black and lavender-blue, with the buildings on the far side of the Place Redouté showing in the distance and in the foreground a sharply receding perspective of iron railing and rolled-up awnings.

There were no sounds from behind the closed door of Mme Cestre's room. Nothing but a kind of anxious silence. Were they gone? Had somebody at last reached for a rubber stamp?

The Germans were not at the dinner party, and Eugène did not mention them all evening. The dinner party was not a success. The food was very good and so was the wine, and Alix's cousin was young and likable, but when he spoke to the Americans in English, Eugène fidgeted. Barbara never came out from behind the shy, well-bred young woman whom nobody could ever have any reason to say anything unkind to, and Harold did not want to repeat the mistake they had made with Jean-Claude Lahovary, and so he did not proceed as if this was the one moment he and Edouard Doria would ever have for knowing each other (though as a matter of fact it was). He did not ask personal questions; he tried to speak grammatically when he spoke French; he waited to see what course the evening would take. In short, he was not himself. Edouard Doria sat smiling pleasantly and replied to the remarks that were addressed to him. Eugène did not explain to his three guests why he had thought they would like one another, and neither did he take the conversation into his own hands and make tears of amusement run down their cheeks with the outrageous things he said. As the evening wore on, the conversation was more and more in French, between the two Frenchmen.

IN THE MORNING, the study door was open and the room itself neat and empty. All through breakfast the Americans breathed the agreeable air of Eugène's absence from the apartment, and they kept assuring each other that he would not possibly return that night; it was a long hard journey even one way.

When Harold took the mail from Mme Emile there were several letters for M. Soulès de Boisgaillard, which he put on the table in the front hall, by the study door, and one for M. et Mme Harold Rhodes. It was from Alix, and when Barbara drew it out of the envelope, they saw that she had put a four-leaf clover in it.

" '. . . I was so sad not to say good-by to you at the station on Sunday. But I love writing to you now. It was delightful to know you both, and I wish you to go on in life loving more and more, being happier and happier, and making all those you meet feel happy themselves, as you did here—' "

"Oh God!" Harold exclaimed.

Barbara stopped reading and looked at him.

"Read on," he said.

" 'We miss you a lot. Do write and give some of your impressions of Paris or Italy. And I hope we shall see one another very often in September. I should like to be in Paris with you and Eugène now. I hope you have at least nice breakfasts. I suppose you are a little too warm—but I will know all that on Friday as Mummy and I will join Eugène in the train for Tours. Good-by, dear you two, and my most friendly thoughts. Alix.' "

He put the four-leaf clover in his financial diary, and then said: "It's a nice letter, isn't it? So affectionate. It makes me feel better about our staying here. At least her part wasn't something we dreamed."

"If she were here, it would be entirely different," Barbara said.

"Do you think he will tell her how he has acted?"

"No, do you? . . . On the other hand, she may not need to be told. That may be the reason she waited so long to speak about our staying here."

"But the letter doesn't read as if she had any idea."

"I don't think she has."

They went and stood in the kitchen door, talking to Françoise, who was delighted with the nylon stockings that Barbara presented to her. Holding up a wine bottle, she showed them how much less than a full liter of milk (at twenty-four times the price of milk before the war) they had allowed her for the little one, who fortunately was now in the country, where milk was plentiful. They told her about their life in America, and she told them about her childhood in a village in the Dordogne. They asked if the Germans had gone, and she said no. She had given them their dinner the night before, in their room.

"What a queer household we are!" she exclaimed, rolling her eyes in the direction of Mme Cestre's room. "Nobody speaks anybody else's language and none of us belong here." But they noticed that she was pleasant and kind to the Germans, and apparently it did not occur to them that she might have any reason to hate them. They did not hate anyone.

The door to Mme Cestre's room was open, and the sounds that came from it this morning were cheerful; those mice, too, were enjoying the fact that the cat was away. The Americans left their door open also, and were aware of jokes and giggling down the hall.

"When we need butter, speak to Mme Emile," Eugène had said, and so Harold went downstairs and found her having a cup of coffee at her big round table. She rose and shook hands with him and he took out his wallet and explained what he had come for. While she was in the next room he looked at the copy of *Paris Soir* spread out on the dining table. The police had at last tracked down the gangster Pierrot-le-Fou. He had been surprised in the bed of his mistress, Catherine. The dim photograph showed a young man with a beard. Reading on, Harold was reminded of the fire in Pontorson. No doubt the preparations had been just as extensive and thorough, and it was a mere detail that the gangster had got away. Mme Emile returned with a pound of black-market butter, which she wrapped in the very page he had been reading, and since her conscience seemed perfectly clear, his did not bother him, though he supposed they could both have been put in jail for this transaction.

Shortly afterward, he went off to pick up their passports and the military permit to enter Austria, and when he returned at two o'clock, he found Barbara half frantic over a telephone call from Mme Straus-Muguet. "I didn't want to answer," she said, "but I was afraid it might be you. I thought you might be trying to reach me, for some reason. I tried to persuade her to call back, but she said she was going out, and she *made* me take the message!"

What Barbara thought Mme Straus had said was that they were to meet her on the steps of the Madeleine at five.

They left the apartment at four, and took a taxi to the bank, where they picked up their mail from home. Then they wandered through the neighborhood, going in and out of shops, and at a quarter of five they took up their stand at the top of the flight of stone steps that led up to the great open door of the church. For the next twenty minutes they looked expectantly at everybody who went in or out and at every figure that might turn out to be Mme Straus-Muguet approaching through the bicycle traffic. The more they looked for her, the less certain they were of what she looked like. Suddenly Barbara let out a cry; her umbrella was no longer on her arm. She distinctly remembered starting out with it, from the apartment, and she was fairly certain she had felt the weight of the umbrella on her arm as she stepped out of the taxi. She could not remember for sure but she thought she had laid it down in the china shop, in order to examine a piece of porcelain.

They left the steps of the Madeleine, crossed through the traffic to the shop, and went in. The clerk Barbara spoke to was not the one Harold had wanted her to ask. No umbrella had been found; also, the clerk was not interested in lost umbrellas. As they left the shop, he said: "Don't worry about it. You can buy another umbrella."

"Not like this one," she said. The umbrella was for traveling, folded compactly into a third the usual length, and could be tucked away in a suitcase. "If only we'd gone to the Rodin Museum this afternoon, as we were intending to," she said. "I'd never have lost it there."

He went back to the Madeleine and waited another quarter of an hour while she walked the length of the rue Royale, looking mournfully in shop windows and trying to remember a place, a moment, when she had put her umbrella down, meaning to pick it up right away. . . .

"I'm sure I left it in the china shop," she said, when she rejoined him.

"It's probably in that little room at the back, hidden away, this very minute. . . ."

He led her through the bicycle traffic to a table on the sidewalk in front of Larue's and there, keeping one eye on the steps of the church, they had a Tom Collins. It was possible, they agreed, that Barbara had misunderstood and that Mme Straus might have been waiting (poor old thing!) on the steps of some other public monument. Or it could have been another day that they were supposed to meet her.

"But if it turns out that I did get it right and that she's stood us up, then let's not bother any more with her," Barbara said. "We have so little time in Paris, and there is so much that we want to do and see, and I have a feeling that she will engulf us."

"We've already said we'd have dinner with her and go to the theater, tomorrow night."

"If she knows so many people, why does she bother with two Americans? She may be making a play for us because we're foreigners and don't know any better."

"To what end?"

"Oh, I don't know!" Barbara exclaimed. "I don't like it here! Should we go?"

She was always depressed and irritated with herself when she lost something—as if the lost object had abandoned her deliberately, for a very good reason.

The waiter brought the check, and while they were waiting for change, Harold said: "She may call this evening."

They crossed the street one last time, to make sure that their eyes hadn't played tricks on them. There were several middle-aged and elderly women waiting on the steps of the Madeleine, any one of whom could have explained the true meaning of resignation, but Mme Straus-Muguet was not among them.

That night, when they walked into the apartment at about a quarter of eleven, after dinner and another movie and a very pleasant walk home, the first thing they saw was that the mail on the hall table was gone. The study door was closed.

"Oh *why* couldn't he have stayed!" Barbara whispered, behind the closed door of their room. "It was so nice here without him. We were all so happy."

Chapter 16

"ALIX SENT YOU HER LOVE," Eugène said when he joined them at breakfast.

He did not explain why he had not stayed in the country, or describe the wedding. They were all three more silent than usual. The armchair, creaking and creaking, carried the whole burden of conversation. It had come down to Eugène from his great-great-grandfather. In a formal age that admired orators, military strategists, devout politicians, and worldly ecclesiastics, Jean-Marie Philippe Raucourt, fourth Count de Boisgaillard, had been merely a sensible, taciturn, unambitious man. He lived in a dangerous time, but, having bought his way into the King's army, he quickly bought his way out again and put up with the King's displeasure. He avoided houses where people were dying of smallpox and let no doctor into his own. He made a politic marriage and was impatient with those people who prided themselves on their understanding of the passions. He had children both in and out of wedlock, escaped the guillotine, noticed that there were ways of flattering the First Consul, and died at the age of fifty-two, in secure possession of his estates. His son, Eugène's great-grandfather, was a Peer and Marshal of France under the Restoration. Eugène's grandfather was an aesthete, and his taste was the taste of his time. He collected grandiose allegorical paintings and houses to hang them in, married late in life, and corresponded with Liszt and Clara Schumann. His oldest son, Eugène's uncle, had a taste for litigation. The once valuable family estates were now heavily mortgaged and no good to anyone, and the house at Mamers stood empty. But scattered over the whole of France were the possessions of the fourth Count de Boisgaillard—beds and tables and armchairs (including this one), brocades, paintings, diaries, letters, books, firearms—and through these objects he continued, though so long dead, to exert an influence in the direction of order, restraint, the middle ground, the golden mean. But even he had to give way and became merely a name, a genealogical link, one of thousands, when the telephone started ringing. Seeing Eugène in his study, with his hat on the back of his head and the call going on and on in spite of his impatience and the air of distraction that increased each time he glanced over his shoulder at the clock, one would have said that there was no end to it; that it was a species of blackmail. The telephone seemed to know when he left the apartment. Once he was out the front door, it never rang again all day.

At nine o'clock, Mme Emile brought up the morning's mail, and Eugène, leafing through it, took out a letter and handed it to Harold, who ripped the envelope open and read the letter standing in the hall:

Petite Barbara Chérie
Petit Harold Chéri

I am a shabby friend for failing to keep my word yesterday evening, and not coming to the rendezvous! But a violent storm prevented me, and no taxi in the rain. I was obliged to mingle my tears with those of the sky. Forgive me, then, petits amis chéris. . . . Yes, I say "chéris," for a long long chain of tenderness will unite me to you always! It is with a mother's heart that I love you both! My white hairs didn't frighten you when we met at "Beaumesnil," and at once I felt that a very sincere sympathy was about to be established between us. This has happened by the grace of God, for your dear presence has given back to me my twentieth year and the sweetness of my youth, during which I was so happy! . . . but after! . . . so unhappy! May these lines bring you the assurance of my great and warm tenderness, mes enfants chéris. Je vous embrasse tous deux. Votre vieille amie qui vous aime tant—

Straus-Muguet

This evening on the stroke of 8h½ if possible.

He put the letter in the envelope and the envelope in his pocket, and said: "Did you ever hear of a restaurant called L'Etoile du Nord?"

"Yes," Eugène said.

"What is it like?"

"It's a rather night-clubby place. Why do you ask?"

"We're having dinner there this evening, with Mme Straus-Muguet."

Eugène let out a low whistle of surprise.

"Is it expensive?"

"Very."

"Then perhaps we shouldn't go," Harold said.

"If she couldn't afford it, she wouldn't have invited you," Eugène said. "I have been making inquiries about her, and it seems that the people she says she knows definitely do not know her."

Harold hesitated, and then said: "But why? Why should she pretend that she knows people she doesn't know?"

Eugène shrugged.

"Is she a social climber?" Harold asked.

"It is more a matter of psychology."

"What do you mean?"

"Elle est un peu maniaque," Eugène said.

He went into the study to read his mail, and Harold was left with an uncomfortable choice: he could believe someone he did not like but who had probably no reason to lie, or someone he liked very much, whose behavior in the present instance . . .

He took her letter out and read it again carefully. Mme Straus's hair was not white but mouse-colored, and though the sky had been gray yesterday afternoon, it was no grayer than usual, and not a drop of rain had fallen on the steps of the Madeleine.

When he and Barbara went out to do some errands, they saw that a lot more of the rolling metal shutters that were always pulled down over the store fronts at night had not been raised this morning, and in each case there was a note tacked up on the door frame or the door of the shop explaining that it would be closed for the "vacances." Every day for the last three days it had been like this. Paris seemed to be withdrawing piecemeal from the world. At first it didn't matter, except that it made the streets look shabby. But then suddenly it did matter. There were certain shops they had come to know and to enjoy using. And they could not leave Harold's flannel trousers at the cleaners, though it was open this morning, because it would be closed by Monday. The fruit and vegetable store where they had gone every day, for a melon or lettuce or tomatoes, closed without warning. Half the shops in the neighborhood were closed, and they had to wander far afield to get what they needed.

Shortly after they got home, there was a knock on their door, and when Barbara opened it, there stood the three Berliners in a row. They had come to say good-by. Herr Rothenberg and the one whose ears stuck out were going home. The one with the pink glasses had managed to get himself sent to a conference in Switzerland. There was something chilling in their manner that had not been there before; now that they were on the point of returning to Germany, they seemed to have become much more German. When they had finished thanking the Americans for their kindness, they took advantage of this opportunity to register with these two citizens of one of the countries that were now occupying the Fatherland their annoyance at being made a political football between the United States and the U.S.S.R.

And the war? Harold asked silently as they shook hands. *And the Jews?*

And then he was ashamed of himself, because what did he really know about them or what the last ten years had been like for them? Herr Doerffer and Herr Rothenberg and Herr Darmstadt were in all probability the merest shadow of true Prussian aggressiveness, and its reflection in them was undoubtedly something they were not aware of and couldn't help, any more than he could help disliking them for being German. And feeling as he did, it would have been better—more honest—if he had not acted as if his feelings toward them were wholly kind. They carried away a false impression of what Americans were like, and he was left with a feeling of his own falseness.

As THEY STEPPED OUT OF THE TAXI at eight thirty Saturday evening, they saw a frail ardent figure in a tailored suit, waiting on a street corner with an air of intense conspiratorial expectancy. She's missed her calling, Harold thought as he was paying the driver; we should be spies meeting in Lisbon, and recognizing each other by the seersucker suit and the little heart encrusted with diamonds.

Mme Straus embraced Barbara and then Harold, and taking each of them by the arm, she guided them anxiously through traffic and up a narrow street. With little asides, endearments, irrelevancies, smiling and squeezing their hands, she caught them up in her own excitement. The restaurant was air-conditioned, the décor was nautical; the whole look of the place was familiar but not French; it belonged in New York, in the West Fifties.

They were shown to a table and the waiter offered a huge menu, which Mme Straus waved away. From her purse she extracted a scrap of paper on which she had written the dinner that—with their approval—she would order for them: a consommé, broiled chicken, dessert and coffee. They agreed that before the theater one doesn't want to stuff.

When the matter of the wine had been disposed of, she made them change seats so that Barbara was sitting beside her ("close to me") and Harold was across the table ("where I can see you"). She demanded that they tell her everything they had seen and done in Paris, all that had happened at the château after her departure.

Barbara described—but cautiously—their pleasure in staying in Mme Cestre's apartment, and added that they had grown fond of Mme de Boisgaillard.

"An angel!" Mme Straus-Muguet agreed. "And Monsieur also. But I do not care for *her*. She is not *gentille*. . . ." They understood that she meant Mme Viénot.

"Do you know anything about M. Viénot?" Harold asked. "Is he dead? Why is his name never mentioned?"

Mme Straus did not know for sure, but she thought it was— She tapped her forehead with her forefinger.

"Maniaque?" Harold asked.

She nodded, and complimented them both on the great strides they had made in speaking and understanding French.

Under her close questioning, he began to tell her, hesitantly at first and then detail by detail, the curious situation they had let themselves in for by accepting the invitation to stay in Mme Cestre's apartment. No one could have been more sane in her comments than Mme Straus, or more sympathetic and understanding, as he described Eugène's moods and how they themselves were of two minds about everything. A few words and it was all clear to her. She had found herself, at some time or another, in just such a dilemma, and there was, in her opinion, nothing more trying, or more difficult to feel one's way through. But what a pity that things should have turned out for them in this fashion, when it needn't have been like that at all!

Having found someone who understood their ambiguous situation, and did not blame them for getting into it, they found that it could now be dismissed, and it took its place, for the first time, in the general scheme of things; they could see that it was not after all very serious. Mme Straus was so patient and encouraging that they both spoke better than they ever had before, and she was so eager to hear all they had to tell her and so delighted with their remarks about Paris that she made them feel like children on a spree with an indulgent aunt who was ready to grant every wish that might occur to them, and whose only pleasure while she was with them was in making life happy and full of surprises. This after living under the same roof with kindness that was not kind, consideration that had no reason or explanation, a friend who behaved like an enemy or vice versa —it would be hard to say which. And she herself spoke so distinctly, in a vocabulary that offered no difficulty and that at moments made it seem as if they were all three speaking English.

Mme Straus was dissatisfied with the consommé and sent it back to the kitchen. The rest of the dinner was excellent and so was the wine. As Harold sat watching her, utterly charmed by her conversation and by her, he thought: She's a child and she isn't a child. She knows things a child doesn't know, and yet every day is Bastille Day, and at seventy she is still saying *Ah!* as the fountains rise higher and higher and skyrockets explode.

While they were waiting for their dessert, Mme Straus's goddaughter came over to the table, with her husband. They were introduced to Harold and Barbara, and shook hands and spoke a few words in English. The man shook hands again and left. Mme Straus's goddaughter was in her late thirties, and looked as if she must at some time have worked in a beauty parlor. Harold found himself wondering on what basis godparents are chosen in France. It also struck him that there was something patronizing—or at least distant—in the way she spoke to Mme Straus. Though Mme Straus appeared to rejoice in seeing her goddaughter again, was full of praise for the food, for the service, and delighted that the restaurant was so crowded with patrons, the blonde woman had, actually, nothing to say to her.

When they had finished their coffee, Mme Straus summoned the waiter, was horrified at the sight of Harold's billfold, and insisted on paying the sizable check. She hurried them out of the restaurant and into a taxi, and they arrived, by a series of narrow, confusing back streets, at the theater, which was in an alley. Mme Straus inquired at the box office for their tickets. There was a wait of some duration and just as Harold was beginning to grow alarmed for her the tickets were found. They went in and took their seats, far back under the balcony of a small shabby theater, with twelve or fifteen rows of empty seats between them and the stage.

Mme Straus took off her coat and her fur, and gave them to Barbara to hold for her. Then she gave Harold a small pasteboard box tied with yellow string and Barbara her umbrella, and sat back ready to enjoy the play. With this performance, she explained, the theater was closing for the month of August, so that the company could present the same play in Deauville. Pointing to the package in Harold's lap, she said that she had bought some beautiful peaches to present to her friend when they went backstage; Mme Mailly was passionately fond of fruit. He held the carton carefully. Peaches were expensive in France that summer.

Only a few of the empty seats had been claimed by the time the house lights dimmed and went out. Mme Straus leaned toward Barbara in the dark and whispered: "When you are presented to Mme Mailly, remember to ask for her autograph."

The curtain rose upon a flimsy comedy of backstage bickering and intrigue. The star, a Junoesque and very handsome woman, entered to applause, halfway through the first scene. She played herself—Mme Marguerite Mailly, who in the play as in life had been induced to leave the Comédie Française in order to act in something outside the classic repertory. The playwright had also written a part for himself into the play—the actress's husband, from whom she was estranged. Their domestic difficulties were too complicated and epigrammatic for Harold to follow, and the seats were very hard, but in the third act Mme Mailly was given a chance to deliver—on an offstage stage—one of the great passionate soliloquies of Racine. An actor held the greenroom curtain back, and the entire cast of the play listened devoutly. So did the audience. The voice offstage was evidence enough of the pleasure the Americans had been deprived of when Mme Mailly decided to forsake the classics. It was magnificent—full of color, variety, and pathos. The single long speech rose up out of its mediocre setting as a tidal wave might emerge from a duck pond, flooding the flat landscape, sweeping pigsties, chicken coops, barns, houses, trees, and people to destruction.

The play never recovered from this offstage effect, but the actress's son was allowed to marry the ingénue and there was a reconciliation between the playwright and Mme Mailly, who, Harold realized as she advanced to the apron and took a series of solo curtain calls, was simply too large for the stage she acted on. The effect was like a puppet show when you have unconsciously adjusted your sense of scale to conform with small mechanical actors and at the end a giant head emerges from the wings, the head of the human manipulator, producing a momentary surprise.

The lights went on. Mme Straus, delighted with the comedy, gathered up her fur, her umbrella, her coat, and the present of fruit. She spoke to an usher, who pointed out the little door through which they must go to find themselves backstage. They went to it, and then through a corridor and up a flight of stairs to a hallway with four or five doors opening off it and one very bright light bulb dangling by its cord from the ceiling. Mme Straus whispered to Harold: "Don't forget to tell her you admire her poetry. You can tell her in English. She speaks your language beautifully."

Four people had followed them up the stairs. Mme Straus knocked on the door of the star's dressing room, and the remarkable voice answered peremptorily: "Don't come in!"

Mme Straus turned to Harold and Barbara and smiled, as if this were exactly the effect she had intended to produce.

More people, friends of the cast, came up the stairway. The little hall grew crowded and hot. The playwright came out, wearing a silk dressing gown, his face still covered with grease paint, and was surrounded and congratulated on his double accomplishment. Mme Straus knocked once more, timidly, and this time the voice said: "Who is it?"

"It's me," Mme Straus said.

"Who?" the voice demanded, in a tone of mounting irritation.

"It's your friend, chérie."

"Who?"

"Straus-Muguet."

"Will you please wait. . . ." The voice this time was shocking.

Harold looked at Mme Straus, who was no longer confident and happy, and then at Barbara, who avoided his glance. All he wanted was to push past the crowd and sneak down the stairs while there was still time. But Mme Straus-Muguet waited and they had no choice but to wait with her until the door opened and the actress, large as Gulliver, bore down upon them. She nodded coldly to Mme Straus and looked around for other friends who had come backstage to congratulate her. There were none. Barbara and Harold were presented to her, and she acknowledged the introduction with enough politeness for Barbara to feel that she could offer her program and Mme Straus's fountain pen. The actress signed her name with a flourish, under her silhouette on the first page. When Harold told her that they had read her poems, she smiled for the first time, quite cordially.

Mme Straus tore the string off the pasteboard carton and presented it open to her friend, so that Mme Mailly could see what it contained.

"No, thank you," Mme Mailly said. And when Mme Straus like a blind suppliant continued to show her peaches, the actress said impatiently: "I do not care for any fruit." Her manner was that of a person cornered by some nuisance of an old woman with whom she had had, in the past and through no fault of her own, a slight acquaintance, under circumstances that in no way justified this intrusion and imposition on her good nature. All this Harold could have understood and perhaps accepted, since it took place in France, if it hadn't been for one thing: in his raincoat pocket at that moment were two volumes of sonnets, and on the flyleaf of one of them the actress had written: "To my dear friend, Mme Straus-Muguet, whose sublime character and patient fortitude, as we walked side by side in the kingdom of Death, I shall never cease to remember and be grateful for. . . ."

In the end, Mme Mailly was prevailed upon to hold the pasteboard box, though nothing could induce her to realize that it was a present. The stairs were spiral and treacherous, requiring all their attention as they made their way down them cautiously. The passageway at the foot of the stairs was now pitch dark. By the time they found an outer door and emerged into the summer night, Mme Straus had had time to rally her forces. She took Barbara's arm and the three of them walked to the corner and up the avenue de Wagram, in search of a taxi. No one mentioned the incident backstage. Instead, they spoke of how clever and amusing the play had been. As they parted at the taxi stand, Harold gave Mme Straus the two books that were in his coat pocket, and she said: "I'm glad you remembered to ask for her autograph. You must preserve it carefully."

On Sunday morning, Eugène showed his membership card at the gate in the stockade around the swimming pool in the Bois de Boulogne. Turning to Harold, he asked for their passports.

"You have to have a passport to go swimming?" Harold asked in amazement.

"I cannot get you into the Club without them," Eugène said patiently.

"I don't have them. I'm so sorry, but it never occurred to me to bring them. In America . . ."

With the same persistence that he had employed when he was trying to arrange for food and lodging for the Berliners, Eugène now applied himself to persuading the woman attendant that it was all right to let his American guests past the gate. The attendant believed that rules are not made to be broken, and the rule of the Racing Club was that no foreigner was to be admitted without proof of his foreignness. There are dozens of ways of saying no in French and she went through the list with visible satisfaction. Eugène, discouraged, turned to Harold and said: "It appears that we will have to drive home and get your passports."

"But the gasoline— Couldn't we just wait here while you go in and have a swim?" Harold asked, and then he started to apologize all over again for causing so much trouble.

"I will try one last time," Eugène said, and, leaving them outside the gate, he went in and was gone for a quarter of an hour. When he came back he brought with him an official of the Club, who told the attendant that it was all right to admit M. de Boisgaillard's guests.

Harold and Barbara followed Eugène into a pavilion where the dressing rooms were. There they separated, to meet again outside by the pools, in their bathing suits. Though he had seen French bathing slips at Dinard, Harold was astonished all over again. They concealed far less than a fig leaf would have, and the only possible conclusion you could draw was that in France it is all right to have sexual organs; people are supposed to have them. Even so, the result was not what one might have expected.

I: *Leo and Virgo*

The men and women around him, standing or lying on canvas mats and big towels or swimming in the two pools, were not lightened and made happier by their nakedness, the way people are when they walk around their bedroom without any clothes on, or the way children or lovers are. Standing by herself at the shallow end of one of the pools was a woman with a body like a statue by Praxiteles, but the two young men who were standing near her looked straight past her, discontented with everything but what they themselves exposed. It was very dreamlike.

Having argued energetically for half an hour to get Harold and Barbara into the Club, Eugène stretched out in a reclining chair, closed his eyes, and ignored them. Sitting on the edge of the pool with his feet in the water, Harold thought: So this is where he comes every afternoon. . . . What does he come here for? The weather was not really hot. And what about his job? And what about Alix? Did she know that this was how he spent his free hours?

From time to time, Eugène swam, or Harold and Barbara dived into the deeper pool and swam. But though they were sometimes in the water at the same time, Eugène didn't swim with them or even exchange remarks with them. Nothing in the world, it seemed—no power of earth, air, or water—could make up to him for the fact that he had had to go to the Allégrets' dressy party in a tweed jacket.

The sun came and went, behind a thin veil of clouds. Harold was not quite warm. He offered Barbara his towel and she wouldn't take it, so he sat with it around his shoulders and looked at the people around him and thought that this was a place that, left to himself, he would never have succeeded in imagining, and that the world must be full of such surprises.

Barbara went into the pool once more, and this time Harold stayed behind. Instinct had told him that something was trying to break through Eugène's studied indifference. Instinct was wrong, apparently. Eugène's eyes stayed closed, in spite of all there was to stare at, and he said nothing. Barbara came back from the pool, and Harold saw that she was cold and suggested that she go in and dress. "In a minute," she said. He tried to make her take his bath towel and again she refused. He looked at Eugène and thought: *He's waiting for someone or something. . . .*

Suddenly the eyelids opened. Eugène looked around him mildly and asked: "How well do you know George Ireland?"

"I know his parents very well, George hardly at all," Harold said. "Why?"

"I thought you might be friends."

"There is a considerable difference in our ages."

"Oh?" Eugène said. And then: "Have you had enough swimming, or would you like to stay a little longer? I do not think the sun is coming out any more."

"It's up to you," Harold said. "If you want to stay, we'll go in and get dressed and wait for you."

"I am quite ready," Eugène said.

They drove home to the apartment, and Barbara made lunch for them. They ate sitting around the teacart in the bedroom. Eugène congratulated Barbara on her mastery of the French omelet, and she flushed with pleasure. "It's the stove," she said. "They don't have stoves like that in America."

The swimming and the food made them drowsy and relaxed. The silences were no longer uncomfortable. Without any animation in his voice, almost as if he were talking about people they didn't know, Eugène began to talk about Beaumesnil and how important it was that the château remain in the family, at whatever cost. When his daughter came of age and was ready to be introduced to society, the property at Brenodville must be there, a visible part of her background. Seeing it now, he said, they could have no idea of what it was like before the war. He himself had not seen it then, but he had seen other houses like it, and knew, from stories Alix had told him, what it used to be like in her childhood.

The Americans had the feeling, as they excused themselves to dress and keep an appointment with Mme Straus, that Eugène was reluctant to let them go, and would have spent the rest of the day in their company. The last two days he had been quite easy with them, most of the time, but they couldn't stop thinking that they shouldn't be here in the apartment at all, feeling the way they did about him. Against their better judgment, they had come here when they knew that they ought to have gone to a hotel. Tempted by the convenience and the space, and by the game of pretending that they were living in Paris, not just tourists, they had stayed on—paying a certain price, naturally. During those times when they were with Eugène, they avoided meeting his eyes, or when they did look directly at him, it was with a carefully prepared caution that demonstrated, alas, how easily he could have got through to them if he had only tried.

AT FIVE O'CLOCK THAT AFTERNOON, while Barbara waited in a taxi, Harold went into the convent in Auteuil and explained to the nun who sat in the concierge's glass cage that Mme Straus-Muguet was expecting them. He assumed that men were not permitted any farther, and that they would all three go out for tea. The nun got up from her desk and led him down a corridor and into a large room with crimson plush draperies, a black and white marble floor, too many mirrors, and very ugly furniture. There she left him. He stood in the middle of the room and looked all around without finding a single object that suggested Mme Straus's taste or personality. Surprised, he sat down on a little gilt ballroom chair and waited for her to appear. He felt relieved in one respect; the room was so large that in all probability they didn't need to worry for fear Mme Straus couldn't afford to entertain them at an expensive restaurant.

It was at least five minutes before she appeared. She greeted him warmly and, as he started to sit down again, explained that they were going to take tea upstairs in her chamber; this room was the public reception room of the convent. He picked up his hat, went outside, paid the taxi driver, and brought Barbara back in with him. The rest of the building turned out to be bare, underfurnished, and institutional. Mme Straus led them up so many flights of stairs that she had to stop once or twice, gasping, to regain her breath. Harold stopped worrying about her financial condition and began to worry about her heart. It *couldn't* be good for a woman of her age to climb so much every day.

"I am very near to heaven," she said with a wan smile, as they arrived on the top floor of the building. They went down a long corridor to her room, which was barely large enough to accommodate a bed, a desk, a small round table and, crowded in together, three small straight chairs. The window overlooked the convent garden, and opening off the room there was a cabinet de toilette, the walls of which were covered with photographs. Mme Straus opened the door of her clothes closet and brought out a box of pastries. Then she went into the cabinet de toilette and came out with goblets and a bottle of champagne. There being no ice buckets in the convent, she had tried to chill the champagne by setting it in a washbasin of cold water.

They drank to each other, and then Mme Straus, lifting her glass, said: "To your travels!" And then nobody said anything.

Barbara asked the name of a crisp sweet pastry.

"Palmiers," Mme Straus said—from their palm-leafed shape—and apologized because there were no more of them. She opened a drawer of the desk and brought out two presents wrapped in tissue paper. But before she allowed them to open their gifts, she made Barbara read aloud the note that accompanied them: "Mes amis chéris, before we part I want you to have a souvenir of France and of a new friend, but one who has loved you from the beginning. Jolie Barbara, in wearing these clips give a thought to the one who offers them. Harold, smoke a cigarette each day so that the smoke will come here to rejoin me."

The Americans were embarrassed by the note and by the fact

that they had not thought to bring Mme Straus a present, but she sat back with the innocent complacency of an author who has enjoyed the sound of his own words, and did not appear to find anything lacking to the occasion.

Barbara put the mother-of-pearl clips on her dress, which wasn't the kind of dress you wear clips with, and so they looked large and conspicuous. Harold emptied a pack of cigarettes into the leather case that was Mme Straus's gift to him. He never carried a cigarette case, and this one was bulky besides. He hoped his face looked sufficiently pleased.

He and Barbara stood in the door of the cabinet de toilette while Mme Straus showed them the framed photographs on the walls of that tiny room—her dead son, full-faced and smiling; and again with his wife and children; various nieces and goddaughters, including the one they had met the night before; and another, very pretty girl who was a member of the corps de ballet at the Opéra. The last photograph that Mme Straus pointed out was of her daughter, who did not look in the least like her. The old woman said, with her face suddenly grave: "A great egoist! Her heart is closed to all tenderness for her mother. She refuses to see me, and replies to my communications through her lawyer."

After a rather painful silence, Harold asked: "Was your son like you?"

"But exactly!" she exclaimed. "We were alike in every respect. His death was a blow from which I have never recovered."

Harold turned and looked at the picture of him. So pleasure-loving, so affectionate, so full of jokes and surprises that were all buried with him.

When they sat down again, she showed them a small oval photograph of herself at the age of three, in a party dress, kneeling, and with her elbows on the back of a round brocade chair. A sober, proud child, with her bangs frizzed, she was looking straight at the click of the shutter. Mme Straus explained that in her infancy she had been called "Minou." Barbara expressed such pleasure in the faded photograph that Mme Straus took it to her desk, wrote "Minou à trois ans" across the bottom, and presented it to her. Then she asked Harold to bring out from under the bed the pile of books he would find there. He got down on his hands and knees, reached under, and began fishing them out: Mme Mailly's verses, the memoirs of General Weygand in two big volumes handsomely bound, and, last of all, the plays of Edmond Rostand, volume after volume. The two books of verse were passed from hand to hand and admired, as if Harold and Barbara had never seen them before. The General's memoirs had an inscription on the flyleaf and looked highly valued but unread. Mme Straus explained that she had enjoyed Rostand's friendship during a prolonged stay in the South of France. Each volume was inscribed to the playwright's charming companion, Mme Straus-Muguet; and Mme Straus described to Harold and Barbara the moonlit garden in which the books were presented to her, on a beautiful spring night shortly before the First World War. "These are my treasures," she said, "which I have no place to keep but under the bed."

When the books were returned to their place of safekeeping, they went downstairs and walked in the garden. It was a gray day, and from the rear the convent looked dreary and like a nursing home. The only other person in the garden was a young woman who was sitting on a bench reading a newspaper. As they approached, Mme Straus explained that it was one of her dearest friends, a charming Swedish girl. They were presented to her, and the Swedish girl acknowledged the introduction blankly and went on reading her newspaper.

They sat down on a bench in the far end of the garden, but after a minute or two the chill in the evening air made them get up and walk again. Barbara suggested that Mme Straus come out and have dinner with them. There was a little restaurant nearby, Mme Straus said, very plain and simple, where she often went. The food was excellent, and she was sure they would find it agreeable.

I: *Leo and Virgo*

The restaurant was dirty, and they sat under a harsh, white overhead light. The waitress, whom Mme Straus addressed by her Christian name, was brusque with her, and the food was not good. They were all three talked out.

On the way back to the convent, Mme Straus saw a lighted pastry shop, rushed in, bought all the palmiers there were, and presented them to Barbara. Still not satisfied with what she had given the Americans, she opened her purse while they were standing on a street corner waiting for their bus and took out two religious stamps that were printed on white tissue paper. She gave one to Harold and the other to Barbara. The design was Byzantine—the Virgin and the Christ child, with two tiny angels hovering like birds, one on either side of the Virgin's rounded shoulders. The icon from which the design was taken was in a church in Rome, Mme Straus said, where they must go and pray for her. Meanwhile, the stamps, through their miraculous efficacy, would conduct her two dear children safely on their journey and bring them back to her in September.

Chapter 17

On the fourth of September, with their faces pressed to the window of the San Remo–Nice motorbus, they saw a little harbor surrounded by cliffs. They saw the masts of fishing boats. They saw a bathing beach. They turned their heads and saw, on the other side of the road, a small three-story hotel. "Since we don't have any hotel reservation in Nice," he said, "what about staying here?" She nodded, and, rising from his seat, he pulled the bell cord. The bus came to a stop on the brow of the next hill, and the driver, handing the suitcases down to Harold, said: "Monsieur, that was a very good idea you just had."

The small hotel could accommodate them, and sent a busboy back with Harold to help with the luggage. When Harold tipped him, he also asked if the tip was sufficient, and the boy looked at him the way people do at someone who is obviously running a fever. Then, serene and amused, he smiled, and said: "Mais oui." In Beaulieu nobody worried about anything.

Very soon Harold and Barbara stopped worrying also. Right after breakfast, they went across the road to the beach. They read for a while, and then they stretched out on the sand and surrendered themselves to the sun. When it grew hot they swam, with their eyes open so that they could watch their shadows on the sandy floor of the harbor. Barbara walked slowly up the beach and back again, searching for tiny pieces of broken china which the salt waves had rounded and faded and made velvet to the touch. She was collecting them, and she kept sorting over her collection, comparing and discarding, saving only the best of these treasures that no one else cared about. Harold sat watching her and eavesdropping. At first the other people on the beach thought Barbara had lost something: a ring, perhaps. And one of the life guards offered his help. When they found out that it was only an obsession, they paid no more attention to her searching. They did not even make jokes about it. If Harold grew tired of looking at sunbathers, he looked at the cliffs, or at the sails on the horizon. Or he got up and went into the water.

By noon they were ravenous. After a long heavy nap they got dressed, yawning, and went out again. They walked the streets of Beaulieu, stopping in front of shop windows or to stare at the huge, empty Hôtel Bristol. They found a café that sold American cigarettes. They bought fruit in an open-air market. They went to the English tea shop. They had a quick swim before dinner. In the evening they sat in a canvas tent on the beach, drinking vermouth and dancing, or watching the hotel chambermaids dancing with each other or with the life guards, to a three-piece band that played "Maria de Bahia" and "La Vie en Rose." Or they walked, under a canopy of stars, with the warm sea wind accompanying them like an inquisitive dog. Now and then they stopped to smell some garden that they could not see: box and oleander, bay leaves, night-blooming stock.

One afternoon they took a bus into Nice to see what they were missing. Half an hour after they had stepped off the bus they were on their way back to Beaulieu. Nice was like Miami, they decided, without ever having been to Miami.

They walked all the way around Cap Ferrat. Behind one of the high, discolored stucco walls was the villa of Somerset Maugham; behind which was the question. Instead of becoming friends with Somerset Maugham, they took up with a couple fifteen years older than they were—a cousin of Mme la Patronne and his English wife. The four of them climbed the Moyenne Corniche and saw Old Eze; lingered in the dining room of the Hôtel Frisia, drinking brandy and Benedictine; went to Monte Carlo and saw the botanical gardens. In the Casino at Beaulieu, Barbara won four hundred francs at roulette, and a life of gambling opened before her.

On all the telephone poles there were posters announcing a Grand Entertainment under the Auspices of the Jeunesse de Beaulieu. Harold and Barbara went. Nothing could have kept them away. The Grand Entertainment was in a big striped circus tent. The little boy from the carnival in Tours came and sat at their table—or if it was not that exact same little boy, it was one just like him, his twin, his double. They supplied him with confetti and serpentines and admiration, and he supplied them with family life. The orchestra played "Maria de Bahia" and "La Vie en Rose." Fathers danced with their two-year-old daughters tirelessly. At midnight the little boy's real mother claimed him. Harold and Barbara stayed till the end, dancing. When they rang the bell of their hotel at two o'clock in the morning, the busboy let them in, his eyes pink with sleep, his good night unreproachful. He was their friend. So was the single waiter in the dining room. Also the chambermaids, and—but in a more reserved fashion—Mme la Patronne.

Their hotel room was small and bare but it looked out over the harbor. Undressing for bed, Harold would step out onto their balcony in his bathrobe, see the lanterns hanging from the masts of fishing boats, hear God knows what mermaid singing, and reach for his bathing slip. At night the water was full of phosphorescence. They slept the sleep of stones. The man in the camel's-hair coat could not find them. Those faint lines in her forehead, put there prematurely by riddles at three a.m., by curtains that did not hang straight in the dark, by faults there was no correcting, disappeared. With his lungs full of sea air, he held himself straighter. "I feel the way I ought to have felt when I was seventeen and didn't," he said. Their skin grew darker and darker. Their faces bloomed. The very bed they made love on was like a South Sea Island.

They should never have left Beaulieu, but they did; after ten days, he went and got bus tickets, and she packed their suitcases, and he went downstairs and paid the bill, and early the next morning they stood in the road, waiting for the bus to Marseilles. It is impossible to say why people put so little value on complete happiness.

They arrived at Marseilles at five o'clock in the evening. The city was plastered with posters advertising the annual industrial fair, and they were turned away from one hotel after another. They decided that the situation was hopeless, and Harold told the taxi driver to take them to the railway station. The next train to anywhere left at seven thirty a.m. They drove back into the center of town and tried more places. While Harold was standing on the sidewalk, wondering where to go next, a man came up to him and handed him a card with the name of a hotel on it. Harold showed the card to the taxi driver, who tore it up. Though they had no place to stay, they had a friend; the driver had taken them under his protection; their troubles were his. He remained patient and optimistic. After another hour and a half, Harold dipped a pen into an inkwell and signed the register of the Hôtel Splendide. It had a hole right down through the center of the building, because the elevator shaft was being rebuilt. The lobby was full of bricks and mortar and scaffolding, and their room was up five flights and expensive, but they knew how lucky they were to have a roof over their heads. And besides, this time tomorrow they would be in Paris.

They went for a walk before dinner and found the Old Port, but whatever was picturesque had been obliterated by the repeated bombings. They saw some sailboats along an esplanade that could have been anywhere, and left that in favor of a broad busy boulevard with shops. After a few blocks they turned back. As a rule, the men who turned to stare at Barbara Rhodes in public places were generally of a romantic disposition or else old enough to be her father. Even more than her appearance, her voice attracted and disturbed them, reminding them of what they themselves had been like at her age, or throwing them headlong into an imaginary conversation with her, or making them wonder whether in giving the whole of their affection to one woman they had settled for less than they might have got if they had had the courage and the patience to go on looking. But this was not true here. In the eyes that were turned toward her, there was no recognition of who she was but only of the one simple use that she could be put to.

Harold had the name of a restaurant, and the shortest way to it was an alley so dark and sinister-looking that they hesitated to enter it, but it was only two blocks long and they could see a well-lighted street at the other end, and so they started on, and midway down the alley encountered a scene that made their knees weak—five gendarmes struggling to subdue a filthy, frightened, ten-year-old boy. At the corner they came upon the restaurant, brightly lighted, old-fashioned, glittering, clean. The waiters were in dinner jackets, and the food was the best they had had in Europe. They managed to relegate to the warehouse of remembered dreams what they had just seen in the alley; also the look of considered violence in faces they did not ever want to see again.

THE PORTER who carried their heavy luggage through the Gare Montparnasse informed them that there was a taxi strike in Paris. He put the luggage down at the street entrance, and pointed to the entrance to the Métro, directly across the street. "If you'll just help me get these down into the station," Harold said. The porter was not permitted to go outside the railway station, and left them stranded in the midst of their seven pieces of luggage. Though they had left the two largest suitcases here in Paris with the American Express, during their travels they had acquired two more that were almost as big. Harold considered moving the luggage in stages and found that he didn't have the courage to do this. Somewhere—in Italy or Austria or the South of France—he had lost contact with absolutes, and he was now afraid to take chances where the odds were too great. While they stood there helplessly at the top of a broad flight of stone steps, discussing what to do, a tall, princely man with a leather strap over his shoulder came up to them and offered his services.

"Yes," Harold said gratefully, "we do need you. If you'll just help me get the suitcases across the street and down into the Métro—" and the man said: "No, monsieur, I will go with you all the way to your hotel."

He draped himself with the two heaviest suitcases, using his strap, and then picked up three more. Harold shouldered the dufflebag, and Barbara took the dressing case, and they made their way through the bicycles and down the stairs. While they stood waiting for a train, the Frenchman explained that he was not a porter by profession; he worked in a warehouse. He had been laid off, the day before, and he had a family to support, and so he had come to the railway station, hoping to pick up a little money. At this moment, he said, there were a great many people in Paris in his circumstances.

At his back there was a poster that read, incongruously: *L'Invitation au Château.* Harold thought of Beaumesnil. Then, turning, he looked up into the man's eyes and saw that they were full of sadness.

Each day, the Frenchman said, things got a little worse, and they were going to continue to get worse. The only hope was that General de Gaulle would come back into power.

"Do you really think that?" Harold said, concerned that a man of this kind, so decent and self-respecting, so courteous, so willing to take on somebody else's heavy suitcases while weighted down by his own burdens, should have lost all faith in democracy.

They talked politics all the way to the Concorde station, and made their way up the steps and across the rue de Rivoli and past the Crillon and down the narrow, dark, rue Boissy d'Anglas. In the lobby of the Hôtel Vouillemont, the Frenchman divested himself of the suitcases, and Harold paid him, and shook hands with him, and thanked him, and thought: *It isn't right to let him go like this when he is in trouble,* but did let him go, nevertheless, and turned to the concierge's desk, thinking that their own troubles were over, and learned that they were just beginning. They had wired ahead for a reservation but the concierge was not happy to see them. The delegates to the General Assembly of the United Nations, the secretarial staff, the delegates' families and servants—some three thousand people—had descended on Paris the day before, and the Hôtel Vouillemont was full; all the hotels were full. How long did monsieur expect to stay? . . . Ah no. Decidedly no. They could stay here until they had found other accommodation, but the sooner they did this the better.

So, instead of unpacking their suitcases and hanging up their clothes and having a long hot bath and deciding where to have dinner their first night back in Paris, they went out into the street and started looking for a hotel that would take them for five weeks. Avoiding the Crillon and places like it that they knew they couldn't afford, they went up the rue du Mont-Thabor and then along the rue de Castiglione. They would have been happy to stay in the Place Vendôme but there did not seem to be any hotels there. They continued along the rue Danielle Casanova and turned back by way of the rue St. Roch. Nobody wanted them. If only they'd thought to arrange this in July. If they'd only been able to imagine what it would be like . . . But in July they could have stayed anywhere.

Early the next morning, they started out again.

Harold removed his hat and with a pleasant smile said: "Bonjour, madame. Nous désirons une chambre pour deux personnes . . . pour un mois . . . avec un—"

"Ah, monsieur, je regrette beaucoup, mais il n'y a rien." The patronne's face reflected satisfaction in refusing something to somebody who wanted it so badly.

"Rien du tout?"

"Rien du tout," she said firmly.

He did not really expect a different answer, though it was possible that the answer would be different. Once he had been refused, nothing was at stake, and he used the rest of the conversation to practice speaking French. Within the narrow limits of this situation, he was becoming almost fluent. He even tried to do something about his accent.

"Mais la prochaine semaine, peut-être?"

"La semaine prochaine non plus, monsieur."

"C'est bien dommage."

He glanced around the lobby and at the empty dining room and at the glass roof over their heads. Then he considered the patronne herself—the interesting hair-do, the flinty eyes, the tight mouth, the gold fleur-de-lys pin that had no doubt belonged to her mother, the incorruptible self-approval. She was as well worth studying as any historical monument, and seemed to be made of roughly the same material.

"C'est un très joli hôtel," he said, and smiled experimentally, to see whether just this once the conversation could be put on a personal or even a sexual basis. All such confusions are, of course, purely Anglo-Saxon; the patronne was not susceptible. He might as well have tried to charm one of her half-dozen telephone directories.

"Nous aurions été très contents ici," he said, with a certain pride in the fact that he was using the conditional past tense.

"Ah, monsieur, je regrette infiniment qu'il n'y a rien. L'O.N.U., vous savez."

"Oui, oui, l'O.N.U." He raised his hat politely. "Merci, madame."

"De rien, monsieur." The voice was almost kind.

"Nothing?" Barbara asked, when he got outside. She was standing in front of a shop window.

"Nothing. This one would have been perfect." Then he studied the shop window. "That chair," he said.

"I was looking at it too."

"It would probably cost too much to ship it home, but we could ask, anyway." He put his hand to the door latch. The door was locked.

They started on down the street, looking for the word "hôtel." The weather was sunny and warm. Paris was beautiful.

In the middle of the morning, they sat down at a table under an awning on a busy street, ordered café filtre, and stretched their aching legs. Barbara opened her purse and took out the mail that they had picked up at the bank but not taken the time to read. They divided the letters between them. It was not a very good place to read. The noise was nerve-racking. Every time a big truck passed, the chairs and tables and their two coffee cups shook.

"Here's a letter from the Robertsons," she said.

"Are they still here?" he asked, looking up from his letter with interest.

Among the American tourists whom the Austrian government had billeted at a country inn outside Salzburg because the hotels in town were full of military personnel there was an American couple of the same age as Harold and Barbara and so much like them that at first the two couples carefully avoided each other. But when day after day they ate lunch at the same table and swam in the same lake and took the same crowded bus into Salzburg, it became more and more difficult and finally absurd not to compare notes on what they had heard or were going to hear. The Robertsons had no hotel reservations in Venice, and so Harold told them where he and Barbara were staying. And when they got to Venice they were welcomed in the hotel lobby by the Robertsons, who had already been there two days and showed them the way to the Piazza San Marco. With the mail that was handed to Harold at the American Express in Rome there was a note from Steve Robertson: he and Nancy were so sorry to miss them, and they must be sure and go to the Etruscan Museum and the outdoor opera at the Baths of Caracalla. The note that Barbara now passed across the table contained the name and telephone number of the Robertsons' hotel in Paris.

He finished reading the mail that was scattered over the table and then said suddenly: "I don't think we are going to find anything."

"What will we do?"

"I don't know," he said. He signaled to the waiter that he was ready to pay the check. "Close our suitcases and go home, I guess."

After lunch they started out again. There was only one small hotel in the neighborhood of the Place Redouté and it was full. Rien, monsieur. Je regrette beaucoup. They tried the Hôtel Bourgogne et Montana, the Hôtel Florida, the Hôtel Continental. They tried the Hôtel Scribe, and the Hôtel Métropolitain, and the Hôtel Madison. The Hôtel Louvre, the Hôtel Oxford et Cambridge, the Hôtel France et Choiseul . . . Rien, monsieur. Je n'ai rien . . . rien du tout . . . pas une seule chambre pour deux personnes avec salle de bains, pas de grand lit . . . Absolument rien . . . And all the while in his wallet there was that calling card, which he had saved as a souvenir. Used properly, the card of M. Carrère would have got them into any hotel in Paris, no matter how crowded. He never once thought of it.

From their room in the Hôtel Vouillemont, Harold called the Robertsons' hotel. The voice that answered said: "Ne quittez pas," and then after several minutes he heard another voice that was like an American flag waving in the breeze. "Dusty? How wonderful! You must come right over! It's our last night in Paris, we're taking the boat train in the morning, and what could be more perfect?"

The Robertsons' hotel was on the other side of the river, in the rue de l'Université, and as Harold and Barbara walked up the street from the bus stop, they saw Steve coming to meet them. He was smiling, and he embraced them both and said: "Paris is marvelous!"

"If you have a place to lay your head," Harold said.

They told him about the trouble they had been having, and he said: "Let's go talk to the proprietor of our hotel. We're leaving in the morning. I'm sure you can have our room. You'll love it there, and it's dirt cheap." The proprietor said that he would be happy to let them have the Robertsons' room, but for one night only. So they went on upstairs.

"Oh, it's just marvelous!" Nancy said as she kissed them. "We've had the most marvelous two weeks. I know it's a terrible thing to say but neither of us want to go home. We're both heartsick at the thought of leaving Paris. Wasn't Rome wonderful!"

The Robertsons had friends who were living here and spoke perfect French and had initiated them into the pleasures of the Left Bank. They took Barbara and Harold off to have dinner at a place they knew about, where the proprietor gave the women he admired a little green metal souvenir frog, sometimes with a lewd compliment. He was considered a character. The restaurant was full of students, and Harold and Barbara felt they were on the other side of the moon from the Place Redouté, where they belonged.

Saturday morning, Harold came down in the elevator alone, and, avoiding the reproachful look of the concierge as he passed through the lobby on his way to the street door, went to the Cunard Line office to see if their return passage could be changed to an earlier date, and was told that they were fortunate to be leaving as soon as the middle of October; the earliest open sailing was December first.

"I think it's a sign," Barbara said.

"We might as well take what we have," he said. "While we have it."

They got into a taxi and went back to the Left Bank and fanned out through the neighborhood of St. Germain-des-Prés—the rue Jacob, the rue de l'Université, the rue des Saints Pères, the rue des Beaux-Arts . . . The story was always the same. Their feet ached, their eyes saw nothing but the swinging hotel sign far up the street. Harold had tried to get Barbara to stay in their room while he walked the streets, but she insisted on keeping him company.

At one o'clock she said: "I'm hungry," and he said: "Shall we try one more?" The concierge was eating his lunch when they walked into the hotel lobby. The smell of beef casserole pierced the Americans to the heart. It was the essence of everything French, and it wasn't for them.

When they returned to their hotel, the concierge called to Harold. Expecting the worst, he crossed the lobby to the desk. The concierge handed him a letter and Harold recognized Steve Robertson's tiny, precise handwriting. Inside there was an advertisement clipped from that morning's Paris *Herald*. The Hôtel Paris-Dinard, in the rue Cassette, had a vacancy—a room with a bath.

THEY MOVED across the river the first thing Sunday morning, and by lunchtime their suitcases were unpacked and stored away under the bed, their clothes were hanging in the armoire, the washbasin in the bathroom was full of soaking nylon, the towel racks were full, the guidebooks were set out on the rickety little table by the window, and they had all but forgotten about that monotonous dialogue between the possessor and the dispossessed, which began: "Nous désirons une chambre pour deux personnes . . ."

The hotel was very quiet, there were no other Americans staying there, and they were delighted with the room and the view from their window. They were up high, in the treetops, and could see through the green leaves the greener dome of a church. They looked down into a walled garden directly across the street from the hotel. The room was not large, but it was not too small, and it was clean and quiet and had a double bed and a bathroom adjoining it, and it was not expensive. Fortune is never halfhearted when it decides to reverse itself.

The green dome was in their guidebooks; it was the Church of the Ancient Convent of the Carmelites. During the Reign of Terror, a hundred and sixteen priests had had their throats cut on the church steps, and every morning, in the darkness and the cold just before dawn, Harold was wakened by a bell tolling, so loud and so near that it made his heart race wildly. Barbara slept through it. Leo is sleepy at night and easily wakened in the morning; the opposite is true of Virgo.

When the bell stopped tolling, he drifted off. Three hours later the big breakfast tray was deposited on their laps, before they were wholly awake or decently clothed. Though white flour was illegal, by paying extra they could have, with their coffee, croissants made of white flour. They were still warm from the bakery oven. Through the open window came the massed voices of school children in the closed garden, so like the sound of noisy birds. After they had finished their breakfast they fell asleep again, and when they woke, the street was quiet; the children had been swallowed up by the school. At recess time they reappeared, but the racket was never again so vivid during the rest of the day.

The owner of the hotel sat at a high desk in the lobby, behind his ledger, and nodded remotely to them as they came and went. If they turned right when they emerged from the hotel, they came to a street of religious-statuary shops, which took them into the Place St. Sulpice, with its fountain and plane trees and heavy baroque church. If they turned left, they came to the rue

Vaugirard, which was busier, and if they turned left again, they eventually came to the Palais du Luxembourg and the gardens. Sitting on iron chairs a few feet away from the basin where the children sailed their boats, they read or looked at the faces—narrow, unhandsome compared to the Italian faces they had left behind, but intense, nervously alive. Or they got up and walked, past the palace, between the flower beds, down one of the formal avenues.

In an alley off the Place St. Sulpice they found the perfect restaurant, and they went there every day, for lunch or dinner or both. Harold held the door open for Barbara, and they were greeted as they came in—by madame behind her desk and then by monsieur with his hands full of plates—and went on into the back room, where they usually sat at the same table in order to be served by a waiter called Pierre, who took exquisite care of them and smiled at them as if he were their affectionate older brother. Here in this small square room, eating was as simple and as delightful as picking wildflowers in a wood. They had artichokes and pâté en croûte, green peas and green beans from somebody's garden, and French-fried potatoes that were rushed to their table from the kitchen. They had little steaks with Béarnaise sauce, and pheasant, and roast duck, and sweetbreads, and calf's liver, and brains, and venison. They had raspberries and pears and fraises des bois and strawberry tarts, and sometimes with their dessert Pierre smuggled them whipped cream. They drank Mâcon blanc or Mâcon rouge. They ate and drank with rapture, and, strangely, grew thinner and thinner.

Though there were always people in the Place St. Sulpice, they almost never saw anybody in the rue Cassette. It had not always been so quiet. Walking home one day they saw there wasn't a single house that didn't have pockmarks that could only have been made by machine-gun bullets in the summer of 1944.

They learned to use the buses, so that they could see the upper world of Paris when they went out, instead of the underworld of the Métro. They also walked—down the rue Vaugirard to the

Odéon and then down the rue de l'Odéon to the boulevard St. Germain; down the boulevard St. Germain to the Place St. Germain-des-Prés. Over and over, as if this were a form of memorizing, they walked in the rue Bonaparte and the rue Jacob, in the rue Dauphine and the rue du Cherche-Midi, in the rue Cardinale and the Carrefour de l'Odéon, in the rue des Ciseaux and the rue des Saints Pères, in the boulevard St. Germain and the boulevard Raspail.

In their hurry to move into a hotel that wanted them, they neglected to leave behind their new address. Their first piece of mail, forwarded by the bank, was a letter from Mme Straus-Muguet:

Sunday

Dear Little Friends:

What a disappointment! I passed by your hotel a little while ago and you had taken flight this very morning. But where? And how to rejoin you? Have you returned to the country? In short, a word guiding me, I beg of you, for I am leaving for Sarthe for six days, and I had so much hoped to spend this past week with you. Well, that's life! But your affectionate Minou is so sorry not to see you, and fondly embraces you both!

Straus-Muguet

Harold called the convent in Auteuil, and was told that Mme Straus-Muguet had left. Barbara wrote and told her where they were, and that they would be here until the nineteenth of October. She also wrote to Alix, who answered immediately, inviting them down to the country for the week end.

"Do you think that means we're to pay or are we really invited?" he said.

"I don't know. Do you want to go? I'd just as soon."

"No," he said. "I don't want to leave Paris."

They heard a gala performance of *Boris Godounov* at the Opéra, with the original Bakst settings and costumes. On a rainy night they got into a taxi and drove to the Opéra Comique. The house was sold out but there were folding seats. Blocking the center aisle, and only now and then wondering what would happen if a fire broke out, they heard *Les Contes d'Hoffman.*

They went to the movies, they went to the marionette theater in the Champs-Elysées. They went to the Grand Guignol. They went to the Cirque Médrano.

"What I like about living in Paris," he said, "is planning ahead very carefully, so that every day you can do something or see something that you wouldn't do if you weren't here."

"That isn't what *I* like," Barbara said. "What I like is *not* to plan ahead, but just see what happens. Couldn't we do that for a change?"

"All right," he said. But his heart sank at the thought of leaving anything to chance. The days would pass, would be frittered away, and suddenly their five weeks in Paris would be used up and they wouldn't have seen or done half the things they meant to. He managed to forget what she had said. He waited impatiently for each new issue of *La Semaine de Paris* to appear on the kiosks, and when it did, he studied it as if he were going to have to pass an examination in the week's plays, concerts, and movies. They did not understand one word in fifty of Montherlant's *La Reine Morte*, and during the first intermission he rushed out into the lobby to buy a program; but they were in France, the rest of the audience did not need a résumé of the plot, the program was not helpful.

At Cocteau's *Les Parents Terribles* the old woman who opened the door of their box for them came back while the play was going on and tried to oust them from their seats in order to put somebody else in them. With one eye on the stage—the mother was in bed with a cold, the grown son was kneeling on the bed, he accused, she admitted to remorse, incest was in the air—Harold fought off the ouvreuse. They were in their right seats, and indignation made him as eloquent as a Frenchman would have been in these circumstances. But by the time the enemy had retired and he was free to turn his attention to the play, the remarkable love scene was over.

Barbara went off by herself one morning, while he stayed home and wrote letters. When she came back, she reported that she had found a store with wonderful cooking utensils—just the kind of thin skillets that were in Mme Cestre's kitchen and that she had been looking for for years.

"I would have bought them," she said, "except that I decided they would take up too much room in the luggage. . . . Now I'm sorry I didn't."

"Where was this shop?" he asked, reaching for his hat.

She didn't know. "But I can find my way back to it," she said.

It was a virtuoso performance, up one street and down the next, across squares and through alleys, beyond the sixth arrondissement and well into the fifth. At last they came on the shop she was searching for. They bought four skillets, a nutmeg grater, a salad basket, some cooking spoons, a copper match box to hang beside the stove, and a paring knife. In the next street, they came upon a bookshop with old children's books and Victorian cardboard toy theaters. They bought the book of children's songs with illustrations by Boutet de Monvel that was in the bookcase of the red room at Beaumesnil. While Barbara was trying to decide between the settings for *La belle au bois dormant* and *Cendrillon,* he said suddenly: "Where did Sabine sleep while we were occupying her room?"

"In the back part of the house, probably. Why?"

"Or one of those dreary attic rooms," he said. "It's funny we never thought about it at the time. Do you think she minded our being in her room?"

That evening while Barbara was dressing, he gave M. le Patron the number of the apartment in the rue Malène and waited beside the bed, with the telephone held to his ear. The phone rang and rang. But she's too thin, he thought, watching her straighten the seam of her stockings. She isn't getting enough rest. . . .

Reaching into the armoire, she began pushing her dresses

along the rod. She could hardly bear to put any of them on any more.

"Mme Viénot's affectionate manner with you I took at the time to be disingenuous," he said. "Looking back, I think that it wasn't."

The cotton print dress she had bought in Rome was out of season. The brown, should she wear, with a green corduroy jacket? Or the lavender-blue?

"I think she really did like us. And that we totally misjudged her character," he said.

She chose the brown, which had a square neck and no sleeves, and so required the green jacket. "We didn't misjudge her character."

"How do you know?"

"From one or two remarks that Alix made."

"They do not answer," M. le Patron said.

In her letter Alix had said that she would be coming back to Paris soon, but a week passed, and then two, and there was still no answer when they called the apartment in the rue Malène. One morning they made a pilgrimage to the Place Redouté and stood looking affectionately around at the granite monument, the church, the tables piled on top of each other in front of the café, the barber shop. Standing in the rue Malène, they saw that all the windows of Mme Cestre's apartment were closed, and the shutters as well. "Shall we go in and ask when they are coming back?" Barbara said.

Mme Emile shook hands cordially but had no news. They were all away, she said. Monsieur also. She did not know when they were returning.

"Do you think she wrote and the letter got lost in the mails?" Barbara asked as they were walking toward the bus corner.

"I don't know," he said. "I don't think so. Perhaps their feelings were hurt that we didn't accept the invitation to come down to the country."

"We should have gone," Barbara said with conviction.

"But then we would have had to leave Paris."

"What do you think really happened?"

"You mean the 'drame'? They lost their money."

"But how?" Barbara said.

"There are only about half a dozen ways that a family that has money can lose it. They can run through it—"

"I don't think they did."

"Neither do I," he said. "Or they can lose it through inflation—which could have happened, because the franc used to be twenty to the dollar before the war. But then what about the drama? Maybe they were swindled out of it."

"Not Mme Viénot, surely."

"Well, something," he said.

SUMMER DEPARTED without their noticing exactly when this happened. Fall was equally beautiful. It was still warm in the daytime. The leaves were turning yellow outside their window. He started wearing pajamas because the nights were cold. So was their room when they got up in the morning. Soon, even in the middle of the day it was cool in the shade, and they kept crossing the street to walk in the sun. They discovered the Marché St. Germain, and wandered up and down the aisles looking with surprise at the wild game and enjoying the color and fragrance and appetizingness of the fruit and vegetables. They walked all the way down the rue de Varennes, and saw the Rodin Museum and Napoleon's tomb. They took a bus to the Jardin des Plantes and walked there. They took the Métro to the Bois de Vincennes. Walking along the Left Bank of the Seine in the late afternoon, they examined the bookstalls, but with less interest than they had shown in the shabby merchandise in the avenue de Grammont in Tours. The apparatus of rejection was fatigued; they only looked now at what there was some possibility of their wanting, and the bookstalls were too picked-over.

Coming home on the top of a bus just as the lights were turned on in the shops along the Boulevard St. Germain, they saw a china shop, and got off the bus and went inside and bought two small ash trays of white porcelain, in the shape of an elm and a maple leaf.

Barbara bought gloves in the rue de Rivoli, and in a little shop in the rue St. Honoré she found a moss-green velours hat with a white ostrich feather that curled charmingly against her cheek. It was too small, and after the clerk had stretched it Barbara knew suddenly that it was not right. It was too costumy. But the clerk and Harold both begged her to take it, and so, against her better judgment, she did.

He was looking for the complete correspondence of Flaubert, in nine volumes, and this was not easy to find and gave him an excuse to stop in every bookstore they came to.

In a little alley off the rue Jacob they saw a small house with a plaque on it: *Ici est mort Racine*. Across the door of a butcher shop in the rue Vaugirard they saw a deer hanging head down, with a sign pinned to its fur: *Will be cut up on Thursday*.

They took the train to Versailles, and walked all the way around the palace and then a little way into the park, looking for the path to the Petit Trianon. They couldn't find it, but came instead upon a fountain with a reclining goddess whose beautiful vacant face was turned to the sky. Leaves came drifting down and settled on the surface of the pool and sailed around the statue like little boats. For the few minutes that they stood looking at the fountain, they were released from the tyranny of his wristwatch and the calendar; there was no time but the time of statues, which seems to be eternity, though of course they age, too, and become pitted, lose a foot or a hand, lichen grows in the folds of their drapery, their features become blurred, and what they are a statue of nobody knows any longer.

Finding themselves in the street where Jean Allégret lived, they stopped and rang his bell. There was no answer. Harold left a note for him, in the mailbox. There was no answer to that, either.

Passing through the Place St. Sulpice on their way home, they raised their eyes to the lighted windows and wondered about the people who lived there. As far as they could see, nobody wondered about them.

The woman who had helped Barbara write those two mildly misleading letters to Mme Viénot had also given Harold the name and telephone number of two old friends from the period when she and her husband were living in Paris. One was a banker. She had not heard anything from him for a long time and she was worried about him. The other was her doctor. Both men were cultivated and responsive and just the sort of people Harold and Barbara would enjoy knowing. Harold called the Hanover Bank and learned that the banker was dead. Then he telephoned the doctor, and the doctor thanked him for giving him news of his friends in America and hung up. Harold looked at the telephone oddly, as if it must in some way be to blame. As for their own French friends, he had been conscious for some time of how completely absent they were—Alix, Sabine, Eugène, Jean Allégret, Mme Straus. Not one word from any of them.

Though they were very happy in Paris, they were aware that a shadow hung over the city. The words "crise" and "grève" appeared in the newspaper headlines day after day. The taxi strike had lasted two weeks. One day the Métro was closed, because of a strike. Two days later, to save coal, the electric utilities shut off all power for twelve hours, and as a result the elevator in their hotel did not run and their favorite restaurant was lit by acetylene lamps. Tension and uncertainty were reflected in the faces they saw in the streets.

They made one more attempt to find the château with the green lawn in front of it—they went to Fontainebleau. They enjoyed seeing the apartment of Mme de Maintenon and Napoleon's little bathtub, and from across the water the château did look like a fairy-tale palace, but not the right one. It was too large, and it was not white.

When they got back to their hotel, M. le Patron handed them a letter. Mme Straus-Muguet's handwriting dashed all the way across the face of the envelope, which was postmarked *Sarthe:*

> My dear little friends, what contretemps all along the line, since I miss you at every turn! Because of the beautiful weather I have not had the courage to remain in Paris, and here I am in paradise! Sun, flowers, and the dear nuns, who are so good to me! But let us put an end to this game of hide-and-seek. I must return to Paris on Thursday, the fourteenth, but if it is necessary I shall advance the date of my return in order to see you. What are the sorties, plays, operas that will be performed on these dates, and what would you like to see? Find this out in *La Semaine* or from the billboards, and write me at once if between the fifteenth and your departure there is to be a Wednesday soirée de ballet, for I will then write immediately to Paris to the Opéra. If I return on Sunday—the eleventh that would be—is that better for you? Have you still many things to do before the final departure? And from where do you sail? And on what boat? Behind all these questions, my dear children, is only the desire to please you and see you again before the complete separation that will be so hard for me to bear. . . . I will continue to write to your present hotel, and do not change without telling me. What have you done up to this moment that was delightful and interesting? I so much wanted to show you all the beautiful things—but you have already seen many of them! . . . Au revoir, dear little friends. I clasp you to my heart, both of you, and embrace you with all my tenderness—the tenderness of a friend and of a mother.
>
> Madame Minou
Straus-Muguet
October 4

THERE WAS NO BALLET between the twelfth and the nineteenth, and so Harold got seats for *le Roi d'Ys* instead. He wrote to Mme Straus that they had seats for the opera for the fourteenth of October and were looking forward to her return. Also that they were enjoying Paris very much, and that on Sunday they were going to Chartres for the day.

Chartres was wonderful; it was one of the high points of their whole trip. There was no streetcar line, just as Mme Viénot had said, and so no little church at the end of it, but they got off the train and found that it was only a short walk to the cathedral from the station. To their surprise, in the whole immense interior there was no one. The greatest architectural monument of the Middle Ages seemed to be there just for them. The church was as quiet as the thoughts it gave rise to. They stood and looked at the stained-glass prophets, at the two great rose windows, at the forest of stone pillars, at the dim, vaulted ceiling, at a little side altar with lighted candles on it. They felt in the presence of some vast act of understanding. When they spoke, it was in whispers. Their breathing, their heartbeat, seemed to be affected.

They climbed one of the towers, and saw what everybody in Chartres was doing. Then they went down and had a very good lunch in a little upstairs restaurant, where they were the only patrons, and walked through the old part of town until dusk. They went back to the cathedral, and walked all the way around it, and came upon the little vegetable garden in the rear; like every other house in Chartres, it had its own potager. This time, when they went inside, there was no light at all in the sky, and it was a gray evening, besides. The stained-glass windows were still glorious, still blazing with their own color and their own light.

I: *Leo and Virgo*

"NOTHING FROM ALIX?"

"Nothing," he said, and sat down on the edge of the bed, ripped open an envelope, and commenced reading a long letter from Mme Straus-Muguet.

"What does she say?" Barbara asked when he turned the first page.

"I'll start at the beginning: '*Sunday . . . Mes petits enfants chéris, I am sad at heart at the thought that you are going to leave France without my being able to find you again—*' "

"No! She's not coming?"

" '*—and embrace you with all my heart. But it is impossible*' —underlined—'*for me to return the fourteenth donc pas d'opéra le R.*'—whatever that means."

"Let me see," she said, looking over his shoulder. " '*Therefore not of the opera le Roi d'Ys*' . . . But she said for you to get tickets. What will we do with the extra one?"

"Take Sabine," he said, "if she's here by then. '. . . *but there is at Mans a charity fête for "the work of the prisons" of my dear Dominicans, of which I occupy myself so much. It takes place Sunday the seventeenth and Monday the eighteenth, and it will be only after the twentieth that I will be returning! . . . And to say that during eight days in August I was alone in Paris! Then my poor dears, understand my true chagrin at not seeing you again, and just see how all the events are against us! Of more I was*'— Is that right?"

"Let me see . . . '*de plus j'étais à une heure de Chartres . . . all the more since I was only one hour from Chartres and it was there that I would have been able to join you . . .*' "

He continued: " '*And you would have passed the*' . . . or '*we*' would. Her handwriting is really terrible. '. . . *passed the day together. You would even have been able to come to Mans, city so interesting, superb cathedral! That all that is lacking, my God, and to say that in this moment (nine o'clock in the morning) when I am writing you, you are perhaps at Chartres.*

But where to find you? . . . Little friends, it is necessary to combler mon chagrin'—what's 'combler'?"

"You'll have to look it up," Barbara said. "The dictionary is in my purse."

The dictionary was not in the purse but in the desk drawer.

" 'Combler' means 'to fill up,' 'to overload,' 'to heap,' " he said. " '. . . *it is necessary to try to heap my sorrows by a kindness on your part. It is of yourselves to make photographs, tous les deux ensemble, and to send me your photo with dédicace—dedication—underneath. 19 rue de la Source, that will be a great joy for me, and at Paris there are such good photographers. Make inquiries about them and*'—it could be 'épanchez.' "

"Exaucez," Barbara said, and read from the dictionary.

" 'Exaucer: to grant, give ear to, answer the prayer of someone.' "

" '. . . *grant the prayer that I make of you. You will be thus with me, in my chamber that you know, and I will look at you each day, and that will be to me a great happiness. . . . Thank you in advance! . . . I am enchanted that you are going to the Opéra to hear Le Roi d'Ys—so beautiful, so well sung, such beautiful music. But to avoid making the queue at the location*'—the box office, I guess she means—'*do this: go take your two places at the Opéra at the office of the disection—*' "

"That can't be right," Barbara interrupted.

" '. . . *direction*,' then. '*Boulevard Haussman. Enter by the large door which is in back of the Opéra. On entering, at right you will see the concierge, M. Ferari. He will point out the office of M. Decerf or his secretary Nelle*'—no, Mlle.—'*Simone cela de ma part. Both are my friends, and you will have immediately two good places à la corbeille*'—But we have the seats already, and it took exactly ten minutes in line at the box office, and they're the best seats in the opera house . . . '*where it is necessary to be to see all, salle et scène. I'm writing to M. Decerf by this same courier to reserve you two places, and it is Wednesday morning at eleven o'clock that it is necessary to go there to take them. In this fashion all will go well and I will be tranquil about you. Servez-vous de mon nom dans tout l'Opéra et à tout le monde. . . . In mounting to the premier étage, to the office of M. Decerf (they speak English, both of them) speak to M. Georges, on arriving, de ma part. He will lead you to M. Decerf. I hope I have explained sufficiently the march to follow to arrive à bien, and to all make my good compliments. . . . On your arrival in New York I pray you to write me immediately to tell me your voyage is well passed. Such is my hope, and above all do not leave alone in France your Maman Minou, who loves you so much and has so many regrets. But "noblesse oblige" says the proverb, and to the title of president I owe to be at my post. I will send you tomorrow the book of Bethanie Fontanelle's work of the prisons. Perhaps they will go one day to America. I know the* Mauretania, *splendid boat, and I am going to make the crossing with you—in my thoughts. Et voilà, mes petits amis . . . a long letter that you are going to find too long, perhaps, but I was desirous of writing to you. An idea comes to me: if you have the time Saturday or Sunday to come to Le Mans, a train toward eight o'clock in the morning brings you here at eleven. We will lunch together, and that evening a train takes you to Paris, arriving at nine o'clock.'* That makes seven hours on the train. '*Mais c'est peut-être grosse fatigue pour vous. Anyway, at need you may telegraph me at Arnage, Straus, Sarthe. Au revoir, au revoir, mes chéris, je vous embrasse de tout mon cour et vous aime tendrement. . . . Madame Minou.*' "

He closed the window, and the cries from the school yard became remote.

"Chartres isn't a very big place," Barbara said thoughtfully. "And there is only one thing that people go there to see. She could probably have found us all right, if she had come. But anyway, I'm not going to Le Mans."

"The trains may not even be running," he said. "There is a railroad strike about to begin at any minute. We might get there and not be able to get back. Also, I never wanted to hear *Le Roi d'Ys*. I wanted to hear *Louise* and they aren't giving it this week. *Le Roi d'Ys* was entirely Mme Straus's idea."

"I can't bear it!" Barbara exclaimed. "It's so sad. '*Use my name all through the Opéra, and to everybody. . . .*' "

THE BOOK on the prison work of the Dominican nuns did not arrive, and neither did Harold search out the office of M. Decerf and tell him they already had three tickets for *Le Roi d'Ys*. He could not believe that Mme Straus had written to the manager of the Paris Opéra, any more than he could believe that after a stay of three weeks in Arnage she was in charge of a charity bazaar in Le Mans; or that it is possible for it to rain on the sixteenth arrondissement of Paris and not on the eighth. As the gypsy fortuneteller could have told him, this was perhaps not wise. The only safe thing, if you have an ingenuous nature, is to believe everything that anybody says.

In spite of his constant concern that she dress warmly enough, Barbara caught a cold. They were both showing signs of a general tiredness, of the working out of the law of diminishing returns. There were still days when they enjoyed themselves as keenly as they had in the beginning, but the enjoyment was never quite complete; they enjoyed some things and not others; they couldn't any more throw themselves on each day as if it were a spear. Also, their appetite was beginning to fail. They found that once a day was all they could stand to eat in the little restaurant in the alley off the Place St. Sulpice. They bought bread and cheese and a bottle of wine, and ate lunch in their room, and at dinnertime were embarrassed by the welcome they received when they walked into the back room of the restaurant. Or they avoided going there at all.

Sometimes he dreamed in French. He found, at last, the complete correspondence of Flaubert. In a shop in the Place St.

Sulpice he saw a beautiful book of photographs of houses on the Ile St. Louis, but it cost twenty dollars and he did not buy it. Their American Express checkbook was very thin, and he had begun to worry about whether they were going to come out even.

Barbara saw a silk blouse in the window of a shop in the rue Royale, and they went inside, but she shook her head when the clerk told her the price. The clerk suggested that, since they were Americans, all they had to do was get their dollars changed on the black market and then the blouse would be less expensive, but Harold delivered a speech. "Madame," he said, "j'aime la France et je ne prends pas avantage du marché noir." The clerk shook hands with him and with tears in her eyes said: "Monsieur, il n'y a pas beaucoup." But she didn't reduce the price of the blouse.

Barbara's cold got worse, and she had to go to bed with it. Harold stopped at the desk and asked if her meals could be sent up to her until she was feeling better. The hotel no longer served meals, but M. le Patron and his wife ate in the empty dining room, and so he knew that what he was asking for was possible, though it meant making an exception. One of the ways of dividing the human race is between those people who are eager to make an exception and those who consider that nothing is more dangerous and wrong. M. le Patron brusquely refused.

Burning with anger, Harold started off to see what could be done in the neighborhood. Their restaurant was too far away; the food would be stone-cold by the time he got back with it; and so he tried a bistro that was just around the corner, in the rue Vaugirard, and the bartender sent him home with bread and cheese and a covered bowl of soup from the pot-au-feu. It was just the kind of food she had been longing for. After that, he ate in the bistro and then took her supper home to her. Shopping for fruit, he discovered a little hole-in-the-wall where the peaches were wrapped in cotton and where he and the proprietress and her grown daughter discussed seriously which pear madame should eat today and which she should save till tomorrow.

He kept calling the apartment in the rue Malène and there was never any answer. It was hard not to feel that there had been a concerted action, a conspiracy, and that the French, realizing that he and Barbara had got in, where foreigners are not supposed to be, had simply put their heads together and decided that the time had come to push them out. It was not true, of course, but that was what it felt like. And it wasn't wholly not true. Why, for example, didn't Alix write to them? She knew they were only going to be here eight days longer, and still no word came from her; no message of any kind. Was she going to let them go back to America without even saying good-by?

The next morning, as if someone at the bank were playing a joke on them, there was a letter, but it was from Berlin, not Brenodville. It was an old letter that had followed them all around Europe:

> Dear Mr. Rhodes:
>
> A few days before, we returned to Berlin, only our friend Hans got clear his journey to Switzerland at the consulate in Baden-Baden. And now I want to thank you and Mrs. Rhodes once more, also in the name of my wife and of my children. You can't imagine how they enjoyed the oranges and the chocolate and the fishes in oil and the bananes, etc; many of these things they never saw before. They begged me to send you their thanks and their greetings and a snapshot also "that the friendly uncle and the friendly aunt from America may see how we look." (I beg your pardon if the expression "aunt" in U.S.A. is less usual than in Germany for a friend of little children.)
>
> In Paris I was glad that I could report you over the circumstances under which we are living and working. But I am afraid that we saw one side only of the problem. We came from a poor and exhausted country into a town that seemed

to be rich and nearly untouched by the war. And personally we were in a rather painful situation. So it could happen that we grew more bitter and more pessimist than it is our kind.

We told you from the little food rations—but we did not speak from all the men and women who try to get a little harvest out of each square foot bottom round the houses or on the public places. We did not speak from the thousands who leave Berlin each week end trying to get food on the land, who are hanging on the footboards or on the buffers of the railway or wandering along the roads with potatoes or corn or fruit. We did not speak from all those who are working every day in spite of want of food or clothes or tools. And we did not speak from the most important fact, from all the women who supply their husbands and their children and know to make something out of a minimum of food and electricity and gas, and only a small part of all these women is accustomed to such manner of living by their youth.

To me it seems to be the greatest danger in Germany: on the one side the necessity to live under rather primitive conditions—on the other side the attempts of an ideology to make proletarians out of the whole people with the aim to prepare it for the rule of communisme. A people within such a great need is always in the danger to loose his character, to become unsteady. And the enticement from the other side is very dangerous.

And another point seems important to me: there are two forms of democracy in Germany, the one of the western powers, the other of communisme in the strange form of "Volksdemokratie." It is not necessary to speak about this second form, but also the first is not what we need. The western democracy may be good for the western countries. Also the German people wants to bear the whole responsibility for his government, but it is not prepared to do so. It is very dangerous to put it into a problem that it cannot solve. Our people needs some decades of political education (but it does not need instructors which try to feed it with their own ideas and ideologies) and in the meantime it ought to get a strong governent of experts assisted by a parliament with consultative rights only. German political parties incline to grow dogmatical and intolerant and radical—even democratical parties—and it is necessary to diminish their influence in administration and legislative and, later on, specially in foreign affairs.

I am sure that my opinion is very different from the opinion of the most Germans but I don't believe in the miracle of the majority.

Dear Mr. Rhodes, I suppose you are smiling a little about my manner of torturing your language, but I am sure that you hear what I want to say and that you will not be inconvenienced by the outside appearance.

May I ask you for giving my respects to Mrs. Rhodes?

Would you allow me to write you then and now.

Always your faithfully
Stefan Doerffer.

"Let's see the picture of the children," Barbara said when he had finished reading the letter to her.

The children were about four and six. Both were blond and sturdy. The little girl looked like a doll, the boy reminded Harold of those fat Salzburgers whose proud stomachs preceded them and whose wives followed two steps behind, carrying the luggage. It was partly the little boy's costume—he had on what looked like a cheap version of Bavarian lederhosen—and partly his sullen expression, which might have been nothing more than the light the picture was taken by or a trick of the camera, but it made him look like a Storm Trooper in the small size. The children's feet were partly covered by a large square block of building stone. It could have been ruins or a neglected back yard. The little boy's hands made it clear that he was only a child and that there was no telling what kind of German he would be when he grew up.

"I don't feel like being their uncle," Harold said as he put the letter back in its envelope. " 'A strong government of experts, assisted by a parliament with consultative rights only . . .' It's all beyond me. It depresses me."

"Why should it depress you?" Barbara said. "It's a truthful letter."

"But they haven't learned anything—anything at all. He feels sorry for the German women but not a word about the others, all over the world. Not a word about who started it. Not a word about the Jews."

"What can he say? They're dead. Maybe he doesn't speak about it because he can't bear to."

"He could say he was sorry."

"Maybe. But you aren't a Jew. What right have you to ask for or receive an apology in their name? And how do you know they would accept his apology if he said it? I wouldn't—not if it was my relatives that were sent to the gas chambers."

"I don't know," he said sadly. "I don't know anything. All I know is I'm tired, and I guess I'm ready to go home."

She looked at him, to see if he really meant it. He didn't. But she was ready to go home, and had been for some time. In Beaulieu her period was five days late. This disappointment she was not able to leave behind her in the South of France. She woke to it every morning, and it confronted her in the bathroom mirror when she washed her face. For his sake she concealed the weight on her heart and did not allow herself so much as a sigh. But more and more her pleasure was becoming second-hand, the reflection of his.

Chapter 18

JUST WHEN they had got used to the idea that they had been cast out, and had managed to accept it philosophically, they discovered that they were not cast out; there had been no change in the way that the French felt about them.

Sabine was the first to call. Harold asked about Alix, and Sabine said that they were back too—they had all come up from the country together.

And while he was out doing an errand, Alix called and asked them to tea on Monday.

"What did she sound like?" he asked.

"Herself," Barbara said.

"You didn't hear anything in her voice that might indicate she was hurt or anything?"

"No. She was just affectionate, as always."

"Perhaps we imagined it," he said. "It will be so nice to see them and the apartment again. Did she say Eugène would be there?"

"She said he wouldn't be there."

The next morning, Barbara heard him say: " 'My dear little friends, do not come to Le Mans,' " and called out from the bathroom, where she was brushing her teeth: "It's too far!"

"Nobody's going to Le Mans," he said, and doubled over with laughter.

"Then what are you talking about?"

"Mme Straus. She's coming after all. Just listen: '*Tuesday . . . Mes petits amis chéris, Do not come to LeMans*'—underlined—'*It is I who will arrive in Paris Saturday evening, Gare Montparnasse, at six o'clock. I have arranged all in order to see you . . .*'"

In the same mail, there was an invitation from Jean Allégret, who had been in the country, and had just returned to Paris and found their note, and was inviting them to have dinner with him at his club on Friday.

"Do you want to?" Barbara asked dubiously.

"It might be interesting," Harold said.

His pajamas had split up the back and, later that morning, he went out to buy a new pair. When he came back, he showed them to her and said: "Look—they're made of parachute cloth."

"Not really?"

"So the clerk said. I guess they don't have anything else. Anyway, something wonderful happened. I asked him if they weren't too large and he looked at me and said no, they were the normal size. . . . In France *I'm* the normal size. *Not* football players. The first time in my life anybody has ever said that. . . . It's so beautiful out. No matter which direction you look. The clerk was the normal size too. Everything in France is normal. It doesn't seem possible that Tuesday morning we're going to get on a train and— Except that maybe we won't. The railway strike is supposed to start Monday or Tuesday."

"What will we do if there are no trains?"

"There probably will be," he said.

"Would you like to stay?"

"A few days longer, you mean?"

"No, for good."

"We can't," he said soberly. "There is no way that it is possible, or reasonable. And besides, they tried that, in the twenties, and it didn't work. In the end they all had to come home."

He read in *La Semaine de Paris* the plays that were to be

performed at the Comédie Française and the Odéon, the movies, the concerts, for the first three days after they would be gone. Like a man sentenced to execution, he had a sudden stabbing vision of the world as it would be without him. The day after they left, there was to be a performance of *Louise* at the Comique.

And he was haunted by that book he felt he shouldn't buy—the book of photographs of the old houses on the Ile St. Louis. And by the Ile St. Louis itself. Every time he went across the river, there it was, in plain sight, just beyond the Ile de la Cité. He kept trying to get there, and instead he found himself going to the American Express, getting a haircut, cashing traveler's checks, standing at the counter at the Cunard Line. These errands all seemed to take more time than they would have at home, and time—time running out—was what he kept having to deal with.

It did not interest him to wonder if he could stay, if there was after all some way of arranging this, because he did not want to stay here as an observer, an outsider, an expatriate; he was too proud to do that. He wanted to possess the thing he loved. He wanted to be a Frenchman.

When he got home in the late afternoon, a group of school boys would be having choir practice out of doors under the trees in the school yard. There was no music teacher—only an older boy with a pitch pipe—and the singing that rose from the walled garden was so beautiful that it made him hold his head in his hands. This and other experiences like it (the one-ring circus on the outskirts of Florence; the big searchlight from the terrace of Winkler's Café picking out a baroque church, which they then ran through the streets to, and then moving on to a palace, and then to a fountain—all the churches and palaces and fountains of Salzburg, bathed in lavender-blue light; the grandiose Tiepolo drawn in white chalk on the pavement of the Via Ventidue Marzo in Venice by a sixteen-year-old boy out of another century, who began his work at eight in the morning and finished at four in the afternoon and was rewarded with a hatful of lira notes; arriving in Venice at midnight, leaving Pisa at six in the morning, taking an afternoon nap in Rome, eating ice cream under a canvas awning by the Lake of Geneva during a downpour; the view from the Campanile at Siena in full sunshine—a medieval city constructed on the plan of a rose; the little restaurant on a jetty in San Remo, where they ate dinner peering out through the rain at the masts of fishing boats; the carnival in Tours, the Grand Entertainment in Beaulieu, dinner at Iznard, dinner at Doney's, the dinner with Sabine at Le Vert Gallant, just before they left for Switzerland, with the river only a few yards from their table, and with their vision concentrated by the candle flame until they saw only their own three faces, talking about what they believed, what they thought, what they felt—so intently that they did not know exactly when it got dark or even at what point the tables all around them were taken by other diners. And so on, and so on) —these ecstatic memories were, he thought, what made the lines in his face, and why he had lost so much weight. He felt that he was slowly being diminished by the succession of experiences that he had responded to with his whole heart and that seemed to represent something that belonged to him, and that he had not had, and, not having, had been starved for all his life, without knowing it. He was being diminished as people are always diminished who are racked with love, and that it was for a place and not a person was immaterial.

JEAN ALLÉGRET'S CLUB was in a little narrow street behind the Chamber of Deputies, and they did not allow enough time to get there from their hotel, and had trouble finding it, and when they walked into the courtyard, half an hour late, Jean Allégret was standing on the steps of the building. They felt that he felt that in not being punctual they had been guilty of rudeness, and so the evening began stiffly. Through dinner, they talked about Austria and Italy, and he talked about his farm—about how the people he was living with—the two old gardeners who had been in the family for fifty years—were sick, and would have to go, since they could not help him any longer, and he did not know who he would find to do his cooking, for he could not do it himself; and about the water system, which would be running at the end of the month; and about his efforts to bring a few improvements to his little village. There was no doctor or chemist nearer than four miles, and he had decided that there must be a dispensary. With the help of the men and boys of the place, he had fixed up an old uninhabited house, and got two nuns to come there, and provided them with supplies. The money they needed for this had been raised through benefits—plays given by boys and girls, bicycle races, that sort of thing; and a few days ago they had celebrated the hundredth case treated there. In his spare time he had been drawing, doing sketches of rabbits, pheasants, wild ducks, stags, wild boars, or of people working in the fields or going to market. Someday, perhaps, he would publish some of them in a book.

The club was an army-officer's club, and he had done murals for it, which he showed them after dinner. Looking at the people around them, they thought: This is not at all the sort of place Americans usually see. . . . Neither was it very interesting. Then they sat down again and, over a glass of brandy, went on talking. But something was missing from the conversation. There were moments when they had to work to make it go. Why does it have to go, Harold wondered. *Because it went before* was the answer. His eyes came to rest on one figure after another at the nearby tables—the neat blond mustache, the trim military carriage, the look of cold pride.

He heard Barbara saying: "They gave Gluck's *Orpheus* in the Riding Academy, and there was a wonderful moment. The canvas roof was rolled back without our knowing it, and as Orpheus emerged from the Underworld we saw the lights of Salzburg. . . ."

Jean Allégret nodded politely, and Harold thought: Has she left out something? The music, of course. The most important part of all.

"*Orpheus* is a beautiful opera," he said, but Jean Allégret's expression did not change.

There is something he's not saying, Harold thought, and that's why the evening has gone this way. Instead of listening, he watched Jean Allégret's face. It told him nothing, and he decided that, as so often happened, he was imagining things that did not really exist.

"In the mountains," Jean Allégret was saying, "the political struggle and all the unsolved problems of modern life belong to a tiny lost spot over there in the evening fog, miles away in the bottom of the valley . . . the last village. We slept in any deserted hut or rolled up in our blankets in a hole between rocks. Our only concern was the direction of the winds, the colors of the sunset, the fog climbing from the valley, the bucks always on the top of the following peak . . ."

"My older brother loved to hunt," Harold said.

Jean Allégret turned and looked at him with interest.

"He took me rabbit hunting with him when I was about eight years old. It was winter, and very cold, and there was deep snow on the ground. I still remember it vividly. We got up at five o'clock in the morning, to go hunting, and he missed three rabbits in a row. I think it flustered him, having me there watching him. And he swore. And then we went home."

It seemed hardly worth putting beside a shooting expedition in the Pyrenees, but Harold, too, was holding something back, and it was: *I never had a gun. I never wanted one. I always thought I couldn't bear to kill anything. But once when we were staying in the country—this was after Barbara and I were married—there was a rabbit in the garden every day, and it was doing a lot of damage, and I killed it with a borrowed shotgun, and I didn't feel anything. People are so often mistaken about themselves. . . .*

Though they were close enough to have reached out and touched each other (and it would perhaps have been better if they had) the broad Atlantic Ocean lay between them. That first conversation, under the full moon, had been so personal and direct that it left no way open for increasing intimacy, and so they had reverted; they had become an aristocratic Frenchman and an American tourist.

Outside on the steps of the building, they thanked Jean Allégret for a very pleasant evening, and shook hands, and at the last possible moment the brandy brushed Harold's hesitations aside and spoke for him: "There were no brown-eyed people in Austria."

"Why not?" Jean Allégret said.

"You know why not," Harold said solemnly.

"Yes, I'm afraid I do," Jean Allégret said, after a moment.

"I kept looking for them everywhere. All dead. No brown-eyed people left. Terrible!" And then: "It was all right before, and now it isn't. . . . Home, I'm talking about . . . not Austria. I didn't know about any other place. Or any other kind of people. I didn't have to make comparisons. I will never be intact again."

"In the modern world," Jean Allégret said gently, "nobody is intact. It is only an illusion. When you are home, you will forget about what it is like here. And be happy, as you were before."

"No I won't!"

"Well, you will be busy, anyway," Jean Allégret said, looking into Harold's eyes, the same person, suddenly, that he had been on that moon-flooded terrace in the Touraine. Having reached each other at last, they shook hands once more, and Jean Allégret said: "If you come back to France one day, come and spend a few days with me."

⚜ ⚜
⚜

I: *Leo and Virgo*

WITH SABINE they did not feel any constraint. She came to their hotel on Saturday evening, and they took her to the restaurant in the alley off the Place St. Sulpice. She had a job, she told them. She was going to work for an elderly man who published lithographic reproductions of paintings and some art books. The salary was a little less than she had been earning at *La Femme Elégante*, but it was work that she would enjoy doing, she liked the man she would be working for, and perhaps it might lead to something better, in time. The job was to start on the first of November, and she had come up to Paris a few days early.

She was wearing the same white silk blouse and straight skirt that she invariably wore. Doesn't she have any other clothes, Harold wondered. But it turned out to be one of those things men don't understand; the white silk blouse was beautifully tailored, Barbara said later, and right for any occasion.

There were no awkward silences, because they never ran out of things to say. The few things Sabine told them about herself were only a beginning of all there was to tell, and each time they were with her they felt they knew her a little better. But there was something elusive about her. The silvery voice that was just right for telling stories and the faintly mysterious smile, though charming in themselves, were also barriers. It is possible to see the color of flowers by moonlight, but you can never quite read a book.

While Pierre was changing the plates, Harold said suddenly: "Would you like to hear a ghost story? . . . In Marseilles, all the hotels were full, because of a big fair of some kind, and we went to one after another, and finally one that the taxi driver had never heard of, and he didn't even think it was a hotel, but it was listed in the Michelin, so I made him stop there and I got out and went inside. There was no hotel sign, and when I opened the door and walked in off the street, there wasn't any lobby either. Nothing but a spiral stairway. I decided the lobby must be one flight up. On the second floor there was a landing, but no doors led from it. So I went on, and while I was climbing the stairs I heard footsteps."

"This is not a true story?" Sabine said. "You are inventing it just to please me?"

"No, no, it all happened. . . . Someone was climbing the stairs ahead of me. I called out and there was no answer. I stood still and listened. The footsteps continued, and I felt the hair rise on the back of my neck. I went a little farther, and when there were still no doors, I stopped again. This time there wasn't any sound. My heart was pounding. I could feel somebody up there waiting for me to climb the last few steps. I turned and ran all the way down the stairs and burst through the doorway into the open air. . . . What was it, do you think? Was it really a hotel?"

"I think it was a nightmare," Sabine said.

"But I was wide awake."

"One is, sometimes," she said, and he thought of the drama that had happened in her family. He had a feeling that if he leaned forward at that moment and asked: "What *did* happen?" she would tell them. But the next course arrived, and put an end to the possibility.

Sabine said to Barbara: "Where did you find your little heart?"

The little heart was of crystal, bound with a thin band of gold, and Barbara had noticed it in the window of an antique shop in Toulon, during the noon bus stop. "It wasn't very expensive," she said. "Do you think it's a child's locket? Do you think I shouldn't wear it?"

"No, it's charming," Sabine said. "And perfectly all right to wear."

"Do you remember," Barbara said, "that little diamond heart that Mme Straus always wore?"

They began to talk about the gloves and scarves and purses in the window of Hermès, and he picked up his fork and started eating.

After dinner they walked through the square and back to the

hotel, and sat on the big bed, leaning against the headboard or the footboard, with their legs tucked under them, talking, until eleven thirty. He knew that Sabine liked Barbara, and had always liked her, but as he was walking her to the Métro station he realized with surprise that she liked him too. She could not say so, directly and simply, as Alix said such things; it came out, instead, in her voice, in the way she listened to his account of their last days in Paris, and how queer he felt about going home. It was something he had been refusing to think about, but apparently he had been carrying the full weight of it around, because now that he had spoken to somebody about it, he felt lighter. He had the feeling that, no matter what he told her, she would get it right; she wouldn't go off with a totally wrong idea of what he was feeling or thinking.

He was going to take her all the way to her door but she wouldn't let him. At the entrance to the Métro, they stopped and he started to say good-by, under a street lamp, and she said: "I will be at my aunt's house on Monday."

"Oh, that's good," he exclaimed. "Then I won't say good-by. . . . I keep trying to get to the Ile St. Louis. It's as if my life depended on it. As if I *must* see it. And every day something keeps me from going there. What is it like?"

"From the Ile St. Louis there is a beautiful view of the back of Notre Dame," she said. "Voltaire lived there for a while. So did Bossuet. And Théophile Gautier, and Baudelaire, and Daumier. In the Ile St. Louis you feel the past around you, more than anywhere else in Paris. The houses are very old, and the streets are so silent. Perhaps you will go there tomorrow. . . ."

HE SUGGESTED to Mme Straus, over the telephone on Sunday morning, that she take a taxi directly to their hotel, and she said

Mon dieu, she would be taking the bus, and that they should meet her at one o'clock in front of the church of St. Germain-des-Prés, which was only five minutes' walk from where they were staying.

Barbara was still dressing when the time came to start out to meet her, and since Mme Straus was usually prompt and they did not want to keep her waiting outside on a damp, raw day, he went on ahead. As he crossed the boulevard St. Germain, he saw standing in front of the church a figure that could have been Mme Straus; he wasn't sure until he had reached the sidewalk that it wasn't. In the two months since they had seen her, her face had grown dim in his mind. The old woman at the foot of the church steps was poorly dressed, and when he got closer to her, he saw she had a cigar box in her hand. The purpose of the cigar box became clear when people began to pour out of the church at the conclusion of the service. Harold stood in a doorway where he could keep an eye on the buses arriving from Auteuil and from across the river. One bus after another arrived, stopped, people got off and other people got on, but still no Mme Straus.

The beggarwoman was also not having much luck. About one person in fifty, he calculated. He found himself judging the people who came out of the church solely in relation to her. Those who gave her something were nice, were good, were kind. Those who ignored her outstretched box, or were annoyed, or raised their eyebrows, or just didn't see her, he disliked. He watched a young woman who was helping an older woman down the steps—mother and daughter, they must be. So like Alix, he thought. The young woman didn't notice the box at first, and then when she did see it, she immediately smiled at the old woman, stopped, opened her purse—all in such a way that there could be no questioning her sincerity and goodness of heart. As for the others, perhaps they had been stopped by too many beggars, or knew the old woman was a fraud, or just didn't have ten francs to spare.

I: *Leo and Virgo*

He kept expecting the old woman to come over to him, and she did finally. She came over and spoke to him—a rushing speech full of bitterness and sly derision at the churchgoers—that much was clear—though most of it he could not understand. He looked at her and listened, and smiled, and didn't say anything, thinking that she must know by his clothes that he was an American, and waiting for her to present the box. She didn't, and so he didn't put his hand in his pocket and draw out his folded French money. Something more personal was happening between them. Either he was serving her well enough by listening so intently to what she said, or else she recognized in him a character somehow on the same footing with her—a beggar holding out his hand for something if not for money, a fraud, a professional cheat of some kind, at odds with society and living off it, a blackmailer, a thief—somebody the police are interested in, or if not the police then the charity organizations. . . . A poor blind tourist, that's what he was.

While he was listening, his eyes recorded the arrival of Mme Straus-Muguet. She stepped down to the cobblestones from the back platform of a bus, and as he went toward her, looking at her clothes—her fur piece, her jaunty hat with a feather, her lorgnette swinging by its black ribbon—he wondered how he could, even at a distance, have mistaken the old beggar woman with the cigar box and a grievance against society for their faithful, indomitable, confusing friend.

Her voice, her greeting, her enthusiasm, the pressure on his arm were all affectionate and unchanged. She could not bear to leave the vicinity of such a famous church, the oldest church in Paris, without going inside for a moment. They stood in the hushed empty interior, looking down the nave at the altar and the stained-glass windows, and then they came out again. As they were crossing the street, she said that she knew the quarter well. Her sister had an apartment in the boulevard Raspail, and as a child she had lived in the rue Madame, a block from their hotel.

"But you are thin!" she exclaimed.

"Too much aesthetic excitement," he said jokingly, and she said: "You must eat more!"

Barbara was waiting for them in the rue des Canettes. Mme Straus kissed her, admired Barbara's new hat, and then, turning, perceived that she knew the restaurant; she had dined here before, with satisfaction. As they walked in, monsieur and madame bowed and smiled respectfully at Mme Straus and then approvingly at Harold and Barbara for having at last got themselves a sponsor. Pierre led them to their regular table, and recommended the pâté en croûte. Mme Straus ordered potage instead. The restaurant was unusually crowded, and the waiters were very busy. Though Barbara had explained to Mme Straus that Pierre was their friend, she called "Garçon!" loudly. And when he left what he was doing and came over to their table, she complained because the pommes de terre frites weren't hot. He hurried them away and came back with more that had just been taken from the spider. She continued to be condescending to him, but as if she were acting for Harold and Barbara—as if this were one more lesson they ought to learn. He kept his temper but something passed between them, an exchange of irritable glances and cutting phrases that the Americans could not follow and that made them uneasy. They felt left out. Pierre and Mme Straus were like two members of the same family who know each other's sore spots and can't resist aggravating them. As Pierre hurried off to bring the coffee filters, Mme Straus assured them that their friend was an intelligent boy. And a few minutes later, when Harold got up and went into the front room to pay the check, Pierre stopped, on his way past, and remarked gravely (but kindly, as if what he was about to say was dictated solely by concern for them): "Your guest—that old lady—is not what she pretends to be. The girl you brought yesterday—*she's* the real thing."

After lunch they walked in the square, and Mme Straus pointed out that the fountain, which they had never really looked at before, was in commemoration of Bossuet, Fénelon,

Massillon, and Fléchier—the four great bishops who should have been but were not made cardinals. "How they must have hated each other!" she exclaimed merrily.

Barbara took a snapshot of Harold and Mme Straus standing in front of the fountain, and then they walked to their hotel. She approved of their room and of the view, and asked how much they paid. She considered seriously the possibility of taking a room here. She was in mortal terror lest the nuns raise the price of her small chamber among the roses, in which case she could no longer afford to stay there.

They left the hotel and wandered up the rue Vaugirard to the Luxembourg Gardens, and walked up and down looking at the flower beds, the people, the Medici fountain, the balloon man, the children sailing their boats in the shallow basin. A gas-filled balloon escaped, and they followed it with their eyes. Since we last saw her, Harold thought, there has been a change—if not in her then in her circumstances.

Mme Straus kept looking at her wrist watch, and at five o'clock she hurried them out of the Gardens and up the street to a tea shop, where she had arranged for her grandson Edouard to meet them. Edouard was seventeen and in school; he was studying to be an engineer, Mme Straus said, and he had only one desire—to come to America.

After so big a lunch, they had no appetite. Barbara crumbled but did not eat her cupcake. Harold slowly got his tea and three cakes down. Edouard did not appear. Mme Straus sat with her back to the wall and glanced frequently at the doorway. Conversation died a dull death. There was no one at the surrounding tables, and the air was lifeless. The tea made them feel too warm. Done in by so much walking and talking, or by Edouard's failure to show up for the tea party, Mme Straus reached out for her special talent, and for the first time in their experience it was not there. She sat, silent and apparently distracted by private thoughts. She roused herself and said how disappointed Edouard would be, not to make their acquaintance. Something must have happened, of a serious nature; nothing else would account for his absence. And a few minutes later she considered the possibility that he had gone to the cinema with friends. Harold found himself wondering whether it is possible to read the mind of someone who is thinking in a language you don't understand. What he was thinking, and did not want Mme Straus to guess that he was thinking, was: Does Edouard exist? And if there really is an Edouard, does he regard his grandmother with the same impatience and undisguised contempt as the celebrated actress, her friend, to whom she is so devoted?

Mme Straus called for the check, and either misread the amount or absent-mindedly failed to put down enough to pay for the tea and cakes and *service*. The waitress pointed out the mistake, and while it was being rectified, Harold looked the other way, for fear he would see more than Mme Straus intended them to see.

They parted from her at dusk. She announced that she was coming to the boat train on Tuesday, to see them off. As they stood on a corner of the boulevard St. Germain, waiting for the bus, she pointed out the Cluny Museum to them, and was shocked that they hadn't heard of it.

The bus came and she got on it and went up the curving steps. Waving to them from the top of the bus, she was swept away.

"Do you think he forgot?" Barbara asked as they started on down the street.

"I don't even think he exists," Harold said. "But does *she*, is the question. You don't think she is something we made up?"

"No, she exists."

They crossed over, so that she could look in the window of a shoe shop.

"So courageous," he said. "Always taking life at the flood. . . . But what is she going to do—Who or what can she turn to, now that the flood has become a trickle?"

I: *Leo and Virgo*

THE LAST DAY was very strange. He had hoped that there would be time to go to the Ile St. Louis in the morning, and instead he found himself on the top of a bus going down the rue Bonaparte with another suitcase to leave at the steamship office. The sun was shining, the air was cool, and there was a kind of brilliance over everything. The bus turned left and then right and went over the Pont du Carrousel, and as he looked up and down the river, the sadness that he had managed to hold at arm's length for the last four days took possession of him.

The bus went through the south gate of the Louvre and out into the sunshine again and stopped to take on passengers. The whole of the heart of Paris lay before him—the palace, the geometrical flower beds, the long perspective down the gardens, which had been green when he came and were now autumn-colored, the people walking or bicycling, the triumphal arch, the green statues, the white gravel, the grass, the clouds coming over from the Left Bank in a procession. Looking at it now, so hard that it made his eyes burn and ache, he knew in his heart that what he loved was here, and only for the people who lived here; it wasn't anywhere else. *I cannot leave!* he cried out silently to the old buildings and the brightness in the air, to the yellow leaves on the trees, and to the shine that was over everything. *I cannot bear it that all this will be here and I will not be. . . . I might as well die. . . .*

AT NOON they turned into the rue des Canettes for the last time. When Harold had finished ordering, he made a little farewell speech to Pierre and, after the waiter had gone off to the kitchen, thought: How foolish of me. . . . What does he care whether we love France or not? . . . But then, though they had asked for Perrier water, Pierre brought three wine glasses and a bottle of Mâcon rouge. First he assured them that the wine would not be on their bill, and then he opened the bottle ceremoniously, filled their two glasses, and poured a little wine into his. They raised their glasses and drank to each other, and to the voyage, and to the future of France. Pierre went on about his work, but from time to time he returned, with their next course or merely to stand a moment talking to them. They dallied over lunch; they had a second and then a third cup of coffee. They were the last clients to leave the restaurant, and the wine had made them half drunk, as usual. They shook hands with Pierre and said good-by. They stopped to shake hands with the other waiter, Louis, and again, in the front room with Monsieur and Madame, who wished them bon voyage. As they stepped out into the street, they heard someone calling to them and turned around. It was Pierre. He had shed his waiter's coat and he drew them into the restaurant across the street, to have a cognac with him. Then they had another round, on Harold, and before he and Barbara could get away, Louis joined them, as jealous as a younger brother, insisting that they have a cognac with him. Harold said no, saw the look of hurt on both men's faces, and said: "Why not?"

Pierre went off, and came back a few minutes later with his wife, who worked in a nearby department store. The two women talked to each other, in English. They had one last round, and shook hands, and said good-by, and the Americans promised to come back soon.

They got into a taxi and went to the bank. With the floor tilting dangerously under him, Harold stood in line and grinned foolishly at the teller who counted out his money.

To clear their heads, they rode to the Place Redouté on the top of a bus, and they were able to walk straight by the time they stopped to shake hands with Mme Emile, on their way into the building.

"Are you all right?" Barbara asked as they stepped into the elevator.

"Yes. How about you?"

"I'm all right," she said. "But we probably smell to high heaven of all that we've been drinking."

"It can't be helped," he said, and pressed the button.

Alix was just the same, and they were very happy to see her, but the apartment was different. With the shutters thrown back in the drawing room, it was much lighter and brighter and more cheerful.

Shortly after they arrived, Mme Viénot came in, with Sabine, and took possession of the conversation. While she sat listening, Barbara had a question uppermost in her mind, and it was why didn't Mme Viénot or Alix or Mme Cestre mention the soap? Didn't it ever arrive? Or weren't they as pleased with it as she had thought they would be?

Harold was telling how they couldn't find the Simone Martinis in Siena and finally gave up and climbed the bell tower of the very building the paintings were in, without knowing it. When he finishes I'll ask them, she thought, but she didn't because by that time she had another worry on her mind: what if Françoise should show Alix the stockings she had given her, which were the same kind that Barbara had presented to Alix and Mme Cestre and Mme Viénot in the country, and that they had been so pleased with. She wished now the stockings had been of a better quality. She had economized on them, but she could not explain this without bringing in the fact that they were to give to the chambermaids in hotels in place of a tip.

"You must excuse me," Alix said. "I am going to get the tea things."

"Can I help?" Barbara asked, but Alix did not hear her, and so she sat back in her chair. The thing she had hoped was that she would have one last look at the kitchen. It was very queer, having to act like a guest in a place where they were so much at home. Neither Alix nor Mme Cestre made any reference to the fact that she and Harold had spent ten days in this apartment. One would almost have thought that they didn't know it. Or that it hadn't really happened.

Speaking very distinctly, Harold said to Mme Cestre: "In Italy I saw with my own eyes how fast the earth is turning. We went to hear *Traviata.* It was out of doors—it was in the Baths of Caracalla—and during the second act the moon came up so fast that it was almost alarming to watch. Within five minutes from the time it appeared above the ruins it was high up in the sky."

"You saw St. Peter's? And the Vatican?" Mme Viénot asked.

Right after she had finished her tea, she rose and shook hands with her sister, and then with Barbara and Harold. In the hall she presented her cheek to Alix to be kissed, and said: "Good-by, my dear. I'll call you tomorrow afternoon, before I leave for the country. . . . I won't say good-by now, M. Rhodes. I am seeing someone off on the boat train tomorrow—a cousin who is going to America on the *Mauretania* with you."

"You think the boat train will be running?" he asked.

"For your sake, I hope it is," Mme Viénot said. "You must be quite anxious."

"I have a present for you," Sabine said as she was shaking hands with them. "I am making you a drawing, but it isn't quite finished."

"We'd love to have one of your drawings," Barbara said.

"Maman will bring it to the train tomorrow."

When she and Mme Viénot had left, the others sat down again, and the Americans waited until a polite interval had passed before they too got up to go.

Mme Cestre told them that she had been at Le Bourget when Lindbergh's plane appeared out of the sky.

"You were in that vast crowd?" Harold said.

"Yes. It was very thrilling," she said. "I will never forget it. I was quite close to him as they carried him from the field."

Harold thought he heard someone moving around in the study, and looked at Alix, to see if she too had heard it. She said: "I also have a present for you." She opened a door of the secretary and took out a small flat package wrapped in tissue paper and tied with a white ribbon. This present gave Barbara a chance to ask about the soap.

"I should have thanked you," Alix said. "Oh dear, you will think we are not very grateful. We thought it might be from you. But there are also some other people, cousins who are now traveling in America, who could have sent it, and so I was afraid to speak about it. . . . Mummy, you were right. It was Barbara —that is, it was Barbara's mother who sent us the beautiful package of soap!"

On their way out of the building, they shook hands one last time with Mme Emile, who wished them bon voyage, and when they were outside in the street, Barbara opened the little package. It was a book—a charming little edition of Flaubert's *Un Coeur Simple* with hand-colored illustrations. On the flyleaf, Alix had written their names and her name and the date and the words: "Really with all my love."

"Wasn't that nice of her," Barbara said. And then, as they were crossing the square: "What about dinner?"

"Are you hungry?" he asked.

She shook her head. "There was somebody in the study."

"I know," he said. "Eugène."

"You think?"

"Who else."

"Françoise, maybe."

"What would she be doing in there?"

"I don't know. Do you feel like walking?" she asked.

"All right. . . . He gave me four Swiss francs, to buy sugar for him in Switzerland. I didn't do it."

"Why not?"

"It would have been a lot of trouble, and it turned out that we didn't have much time. Also, I didn't feel like doing it."

"Do you still have the money?" she asked.

"Yes. It's not very much. About a dollar. I guess we can forget about it."

They turned and took one last look at the granite monument.

"Do you think there was something going on that we didn't know about?" he said.

"Like what?"

"That's just it, I have no idea what."

"If you mean the 'drama' that—"

"I don't mean the 'drama.' That was two or three years ago. I mean right now, this summer."

"There would be no reason for them to tell us if there was," she said thoughtfully.

"No," he agreed.

"You think they're all right? You don't think they're in any kind of serious trouble, all of them?"

"Maybe not all of them. Maybe just Alix and Eugène. It would explain a lot of things. The way he was with us. And why they stayed in the country so long. I don't suppose we'll ever know what it was."

"Then you think there was something?"

"Yes," he said.

"So do I."

"Even when we thought we were on the inside," he said, "we weren't really. Inside, outside, it's nothing but a state of mind, I guess. . . . Except that if you love people, you can't help wanting to—"

"Alix is having another baby."

He took her hand as they walked along but said nothing. He was not sure at this moment what her feelings were, and he did not want to say something that would make her cry in the street.

They skipped dinner entirely and instead took the Métro halfway across Paris to a movie theater that was showing *Le Diable au Corps*. Harold wanted to see it, and they had missed it when they were here in the summer, and it had not been showing anywhere since they got back. In America it would be cut.

They were half an hour early, and walked up and down, rather than go in and sit in an empty theater. Over the ticket booth there was an electric bell that rang insistently and continuously; the whole street was filled with the sound. They looked at all the shop windows on both sides of the street. He glanced at his wrist watch. It was still twenty minutes before it would be time to go inside, and at the thought of twenty minutes more of that dreadful ringing, and then the hocus-pocus and the delay that always went on in French movie theaters, and people passing through the aisles selling candy, while they waited and waited for the picture to begin, he suddenly stopped, swallowed hard, and, taking Barbara's arm, said: "Let's go home. I can't stand that sound. . . . And even if we do wait, I won't be able to enjoy the movie. I've had all I can manage. I'm through. I can't take in any more."

THEY ARRIVED at the Gare St. Lazare, with their hand luggage, an hour early. The boat train was running. It was due to leave at eleven ten, and they would get to Cherbourg about five. They walked down the platform, looking for their carriage and compartment, and found it. Barbara waited in the train, while Harold walked up and down outside. Magazine and fruit vendors had come to see them off, and a flower girl whose pushcart was covered with bouquets of violets, but there was no sign of Mme Straus. Minute after minute passed. The platform grew crowded. There was a sense of growing excitement. Harold wandered in and out among the porters and the passengers, who, standing in little groups along the track, were nearly all Americans. For the first time in four months it didn't require any effort on his part to overhear scraps of conversation. He didn't like what he heard. The voices of his compatriots were loud, and what they said seemed silly beyond endurance. It was like having home thrown at him.

At three minutes of eleven, he gave up all hope of finding Mme Straus in the crowd that was milling around on the platform and started back to their coach, telling himself that it didn't matter that she had failed to come. It wasn't so much that she was insincere as that she loved to arouse expectations it wasn't always convenient or even possible to satisfy, when the time came. . . . Only it did matter, he thought, still searching for her among the faces. Now that they were leaving, he wanted some one person out of a whole country that they had loved on first sight and never stopped loving—he wanted somebody to be aware of the fact that they were leaving, and come to say good-by.

At the steps of their carriage he took one last look around and saw her, talking agitatedly to one of the train guards. He was close enough that he could hear her asking the guard to point out the carriage of M. and Mme Rhodes. The guard shrugged. Harold went up to her and took hold of her elbow, and she cried: "Ah, chéri!" and kissed him.

She had been delayed. She thought that she would never find them in the crowd.

Barbara saw Mme Straus from the train window and came out onto the platform. Mme Straus kissed her and then presented her with a farewell gift, a pasteboard box containing palmiers. "They're to eat on the train," she said.

Edouard's mother had been taken ill on Sunday afternoon and he couldn't leave her. He was sorry to have missed them.

She wanted to see their compartment, so they mounted the steps and went down the corridor and showed her their reserved seats and their luggage, safely stowed away on the overhead rack.

"By the window," she said approvingly. "Now that I have it firmly in mind, I can go with you." She squeezed their hands in both of hers.

They went outside again and stood talking together on the platform. Mme Viénot appeared out of the crowd, with a boutonniere for Barbara. "From the garden at Beaumesnil," she said. She and Mme Straus greeted each other with the comic cordiality of two women who understand the full extent of their mutual dislike and are not concerned about it. Then, turning to Barbara and Harold, she said: "Sabine had something that she wanted me to bring you—a drawing. But she didn't get it finished in time. She said to tell you that she would be mailing it to you. I saw it. It is quite charming. It is of the old houses on the Ile St. Louis. . . . Au revoir, my dears. Have a good trip home."

She went off to rejoin her cousin.

The train guards called out a warning, and Mme Straus embraced them both one last time and urged them back on the train. When they sat down, she was at the window, dabbing her eyes with a tiny white handkerchief. They tried to carry on a conversation in pantomime.

She said something but they couldn't hear what it was. Harold said something back and she shook her head, to show that she didn't understand. They got up and went down the corridor to the end of the car. The door was still open. Mme Straus was there waiting, with the tears running down her cheeks. They leaned down and touched her hands, as the train began to move. For reasons that there was now no chance of their knowing, she clung to them, hurrying along beside the slowly moving train, waving to them, calling good-by. When she could no longer find them among the other heads and waving arms they could see her, still waving her crumpled handkerchief, old, forsaken, left in her own sad city, where the people she knew did not know her, and her stories were not believed even when they were true.

Part II

Some Explanations

Chapter 19

IS THAT ALL?

Yes, that's all.

But what about the mysteries?

You mean the "drama" that Mme Viénot didn't tell Harold Rhodes about?

And where M. Viénot was.

Oh, that.

And why Hector Gagny didn't go up to Paris with the Americans. And why Alix didn't say good-by to them at the station. And why the actress was so harsh with poor Mme Straus-Muguet, when they went backstage. And why that woman who kept the fruit and vegetable shop—Mme Michot—was so curious about what was going on at the château.

I don't know that any of those things very much matters. They are details. You don't enjoy drawing your own conclusions about them?

Yes, but then I like to know if the conclusions I have come to are the right ones.

How can they not be when everything that happens happens for so many different reasons? But if you really want to know why something happened, if explanations are what you care about, it is usually possible to come up with one. If necessary, it can be fabricated. Hector Gagny didn't go up to Paris on Bastille

Day because Mme Carrère invited him to go driving with them, and he was perfectly happy to put off his departure until the next day. And the reason that Mme Michot was so curious is that her only daughter was married and had left home, and M. Michot had left home, too, years before, in a crowded box car bound for the German border, and there had been no word from him since. It is only natural that, having to live with an unanswered question of this kind, she should occupy her mind with other questions instead. . . . But if you concentrate on details, you lose sight of the whole. The Americans fell in love with France, the way Americans are always doing, and they had the experience of knowing some French people but not knowing them very well. They didn't speak French, which made it difficult, and they were paying guests, and the situation of the paying guest is peculiar. It has in it something of the nature of an occupation by force. Once they were home, they quickly forgot a good many of the people they met abroad and the places they stayed in, but this experience with a French family, and the château, and the apartment in Paris, they couldn't forget. Hearing the blast that departing liners give as they turn in the Hudson River, Harold Rhodes raised his head and listened for a repetition of the sound. For those few seconds his face was deeply melancholy. And he took a real hatred—briefly—to an old and likable friend whose work made it possible for him to live in Paris. Neither of these things needs explaining. As for those that do, when you explain away a mystery, all you do is make room for another.

Even so. If you don't mind.

No, I don't mind. It's just a question of where to begin.

Begin with the drama.

Which one?

Were there two?

There was a drama that occurred several years before the Americans came to stay at the château, and there was another, several years after. One was a tragedy, the other was a farce.

II: *Some Explanations*

They don't belong together, except as everything that happens to somebody, or to a single family, belongs together. In that case, though, there is no question of why anything happened, but only what happened, and what happened then, and what happened after that—all of it worth looking at, as a moral and a visual spectacle.

Well, what happened to the money, then?

That's the first drama. You're sure you want to hear about it? . . . "Somebody will tell us," Harold said, and sure enough somebody did. A cousin turned up, in New York, and called Mrs. Ireland, who invited her to lunch. She was the same age as Sabine and Alix, but a rather plain girl, and talkative. And what she talked about was the sudden change in the situation of the family at Beaumesnil. She said that shortly after the war ended, M. Viénot sold all the securities that Mme Bonenfant had been left by her husband, who was a very rich man, and bought shares in a Peruvian gold mine. The stocks and bonds he disposed of were sound, and the gold mine proved to be a swindle.

Then he was a crook?

It may have been nothing more than a mistake in judgment. . . . The cousin said that he himself profited by the transaction, but then she may not have got the facts straight. People seldom do.

But how could he have profited by reducing his wife's family from affluence to genteel poverty? It doesn't make any sense.

No, it doesn't, does it? Neither did his explanations. So Mme Viénot left him and went to live with her mother. But quite recently Barbara had a letter from Sabine in which she said that her mother and father were living in Oran, and Beaumesnil was closed. So they must have gone back together again.

The day young George Ireland arrived to spend the summer, M. Viénot turned up at the château, in an Italian sports car, with a blonde on the seat beside him. She was young, George said. And pretty. They were invited to stay for lunch, and they did, and drove back to Paris that night.

How extraordinary.

After which Mme Viénot communicated with him only through her lawyer, but Sabine continued to see her father, and so did her sister. The family could only suppose that his reason had been affected, what he did was so out of character, so unlike the man he had always been. And since Mme Bonenfant had always loved him like a son, she particularly clung to this explanation of his disastrous behavior. But there were certain signs they ought to have paid attention to. He had begun to wear less conservative clothes. He drove his car recklessly, was inattentive and irritable, sighed in his sleep, and showed a preference for the company of young people. He had even ceased to look like the man he used to be. These changes were gradual, of course, and they saw him with the eyes of habit.

So much for the tragedy. The second drama, the farce, began when two men appeared at the door one day and asked to speak to Mme Viénot. They said that they had heard in the village that she took guests and they wanted to stay at the château. Mme Viénot said that surely the person who told them this also told them that she only took guests who came to her with a proper introduction. They said they'd be back in an hour with a proper introduction and Mme Viénot said that she was sorry they had had this long walk for nothing, and shut the door on them. After lunch, at the moment when Thérèse should have appeared in the drawing room with the coffee tray, she appeared without the coffee tray, and informed Mme Viénot that the cook wanted to speak to her. This was unprecedented, and Mme Viénot foresaw, as she excused herself, that on the cook's face too there would be a look of fright.

This was Mme Foëcy?

This was a different cook. Mme Foëcy was there only that summer. She was not in the habit of staying very long in any one establishment. . . . The same two men had turned up at the kitchen door, it seems, and asked for something to eat. The cook gave them a sandwich but wouldn't let them come inside. They wanted her to leave the kitchen window open that night, so they could get into the house. She threatened to call out for help, and so they left. That same afternoon, at teatime, Mme Viénot saw the gardener hovering in the vicinity of the drawing room windows.

As soon as she could, she slipped outside. The gardener was in a state of excitement. He too had had a visit, and the two men said that there was a treasure hidden somewhere in the house.

No!

Gold bullion. Left by the Germans, because they didn't have the means or the time to take it with them.

And was it true?

It is true that there was such a rumor in the village. The same story was told of other country houses after the war, and probably had its origin in a folk tale. The story varied, according to who told it. Sometimes the treasure was buried in the garden, in the dead of night. Sometimes it was hidden inside the walls. Great importance was attached to the fact that no member of Mme Bonenfant's family had ever denied this story, but actually it had never reached their ears.

The gardener told the men he would help them. He agreed to leave a cellar window open for them, but not that night. It was not a good time, he said; the house was full of people. And if they'd wait until there was no one here but the women, their chances would be better. They decided upon a signal, and as soon as the two men were off the property, the gardener came to find Mme Viénot.

Then what happened?

She went to the police, and together they worked out a plan. The only men in the house, Eugène and Mme Viénot's son-in-law, Jean-Claude Lahovary, were to leave as conspicuously as possible in Eugène's car and come back after dark, on foot. The gardener would hang the lantern in the potting shed—the signal that had been agreed upon—and the police would be nearby, waiting for a telephone call saying that the robbers were actually inside the house. It was all very melodramatic and like a British spy movie, except for one characteristically French touch. When the police cars came up the drive, they were blowing their sirens.

So the robbers got away?

No, they were caught. They must not have heard the sirens. Or else they were confused, or couldn't find their way out of the house in the dark. They were convicted of housebreaking, and sentenced to a term in jail. At the trial it came out that one of them had had some education; he had been a government clerk. Later, in the woods back of Beaumesnil, somebody found the remains of a campfire, and it was assumed that the robbers hid out there, while they were waiting for the signal.

What an amazing story.

Yes, isn't it. What would you like to know about next?

I think I'd like to know about Eugène—why he acted the way he did. Was he in the study, the day the Americans came to say good-by?

Of course.

And Alix knew that he was there?

Her hearing was excellent. It was her mother who suffered from deafness. There was no one Eugène could not make love him if he chose to, but he blew hot and cold about people. He blew hot and they mistook it for friendship; he blew cold and they had to learn, in self-defense, to despise him. This deadly, monotonous pattern did not occur with his wife. In spite of his belief that married people change and grow less fond of one another with time, this did not happen in his case. Their marriage had its ups and downs, like all marriages, but it did not become absent-minded or perfunctory. Would you like to see them sleeping together?

Well, I don't know that I—

It's quite all right. No trouble at all. The workshirt hanging across the attic window has been replaced by a potted geranium, and the Prodigal Son is gone. Someone, unable to stand the sight of so much raw emotion any longer, took it down and put it away in a closet. If you look closely, you will see that the fauteuil that belonged to Eugène's great-great-grandfather has been mended. The dresses and skirts in the armoires throughout the apartment are of a different length, and Alix and Eugène have three children now. But certain things are the same: the church bell, the rays of the star arriving and departing simultaneously, and whoever it is that at daybreak comes through the rue Malène and silently searches through the garbage cans for edible peelings, cheese rinds, moldy bread, good rags, diamond rings, broken objects that can be mended, shoes with holes in their soles, paper, string, and other treasures often found in just such refuse by old men and women with the will to live. The sky, growing lighter, says: *What is being but being different, night from day, the earth from the air, the way things were from the way things are?* The newspaper lying in the gutter announces that a turning point has been reached in the tide of human affairs, and the swallows, skimming the rooftops—

I've really had enough of those swallows.

For some reason, I never grow tired of them. The swallows, in their quick summarizing trip over the rooftops prove conclusively that there *is* no point of turning, because turning is all there is—constant, never-ending patterns of turning.

The shutters are open, the awnings are rolled. Alix and Eugène are sleeping with their backs turned to each other but touching. When she moves in her sleep, his body accommodates itself to the change without waking. Now they are facing each other. Of his forearm, shoulder, and cheek he makes a soft warm box for her head. Over her bent knees he extends protectively a relaxed weightless leg. Shortly afterward they turn away from each other. In their marriage also there is no real resting place; one partner may dominate, may circumscribe, the actions of the other, briefly, but nothing is fixed, nothing is final.

His moods—what were they all about?

Those recurring periods of melancholy, of a kind of darkness of the soul, had nothing to do with her.

What did they have to do with?

Money, chiefly. Money that is lost becomes a kind of magic mirror in which the deprived person sees himself always in the distorted landscape of what might have been. When they were living in Marseilles, Eugène did not think about money, largely because everyone else was poor also. But in Paris he was reminded continually that his father had always lived in a certain way, and so had his grandfather, and he would have liked to live in the same way himself and he couldn't, and never would be able to, because they have made no provision for him to do this.

Shouldn't they have?

Perhaps.

Then why didn't they?

Life was beautiful, and they thought it couldn't go on being this way—about this they were quite right—and in any case it would have meant sacrificing their pleasures and they needed their pleasures; they needed all of them. His father's desk was a mosaic of unpaid bills, which he never disturbed. When he wanted to write a letter, he used his wife's desk.

What about Alix? Did she mind it that they were poor?

Not for herself. But she listened carefully to what Eugène had to say about rich young men like Jean Allégret and René Simon, and what she perceived was that it was not the money itself but that he felt the loss of it had cast a shadow over their lives so dense that they could not be seen. They were no longer part of the world. They did not move among people who counted. They might as well be the children of shopkeepers.

It would have been better if she had not made him give up his work among the poor in Marseilles.

She didn't. That was only Mme Viénot's idea of what happened. Since he had renounced his spiritual vocation in order to marry her, she was prepared to give up everything for his sake, but unfortunately it turned out that he did not really have a spiritual vocation. If he had, he would not have taken it so to heart when the men he was trying to educate failed him by falling asleep over the books he lent them, or by getting drunk and beating their wives, or simply by not understanding what it was that he wanted from them. Two or three years later, he threw himself into politics in the same high-minded way. He dedicated every free moment to working for the M.R.P.—the Mouvement Républicain Populaire, the Catholic reform party. Then he decided that all political efforts were futile, and found himself once more committed to nothing, nothing to cling to, no foothold, and totally outside the life around him. And though he was patient—no one was ever more patient—he was not always easy to live with. Or pleasant to people. Anyone in trouble could count on his help, and the telephone rang incessantly, but he had no friends. If he met someone he liked, someone who interested him, he was intensely curious, direct, personal, and charming. And then, his curiosity satisfied, he was simply not interested any more. The friends of his school days called up, made arrangements to see him, were startled by what they found, and didn't return.

That painful train journey, do you remember? the time he went up to Paris with Sabine and the Americans? What really happened?

He had quarreled with Alix on the way to the station, just as the Americans thought, and the quarrel was about them. After a few days of staying in the apartment by himself, he had found that he liked being alone, and he was sorry he had invited them. On the way to the station he proposed to Alix that she tell the Americans that it was not convenient to have them stay in the apartment at this time, and she refused. He said he would tell them himself, then, and she said that she could at least not be present when he did. After she left him, he decided that instead of telling the Americans outright that he didn't want them, he could make them understand, from his behavior, that he had changed his mind about having them.

And they didn't understand.

No, they did understand, and started to go to the Hôtel Vouillemont. But in the Métro, when they tried to leave him, he changed his mind again. For a moment, he felt something like affection for them. He continued to teeter in this fashion, between liking and not liking them, the whole period of their stay in the apartment.

But why did he act the way he did? Was it because Barbara did not dance with him? She really should have. It was inexcusable, her refusing to dance with him at the Allégrets' party.

She would have danced with him, except that he was so sullen when he asked her. But that wasn't why he changed.

Was it something Harold did?

It was something he was, I think.

What was he?

A young man with a beautiful wife and the money to spend four months traveling in Europe. An American. A man with a future, and no shadow across his present life.

But that isn't what his life was like.

No, but that's what it looked like, from the outside.

It was also wrong of them, very wrong, not to accept Alix's invitation to come down to the country for the week end. And not to call on M. and Mme Carrère, after M. Carrère had given Harold his card, was—

True. Perfectly true. Their behavior doesn't stand careful inspection. But on the other hand, you must remember that they were tourists. This is not the way they behaved when they were at home. And it is one thing to hand out gold stars to children for remembering to brush their teeth and another to pass moral judgment on adult behavior. So much depends on the circumstances.

In short, it is something you don't feel like going into. Very well, what happened to Hector Gagny?

He divorced his wife, and married a woman with a half-grown boy, and she made him very happy. I always felt that his first wife was more—but she was impossible, as a wife. Or at least as a wife for him. The little boy in the carnival is grown up now and has a half interest in the merry-go-round. The gypsy fortuneteller dealt herself the ace of spades. Anybody or anything else you'd like to know about?

That drawing Sabine was going to send to the Americans. Did it ever arrive?

Yes, it arrived, about a month after Harold and Barbara got home, and with it was a rather touching letter, written the day they took the boat train:

> Here is the little drawing promised, I hope it will not oblige you to lengthen your list for the douane!— Thanks still for all your kindness— You don't know what it meant for me, nor what both of you meant to me—. It's difficult to explain specially in English—. I think you represent like Aunt Mathilde and Alix an atmosphere *kind,* gay and harmonious, where everything is in its real place. And seeing you was a sort of rest through the roughness of existence, a bit like putting on fairy shoes.
>
> Perhaps did you guess there was, a few years ago, a sad drama in our family. Since then many things changed, and I lived in one place and then in another—missing baddly that sort of atmosphere I just described. That's why perhaps I bored you a bit like Mme Straus, in trying to see you often— I am very sorry if I did. But you know: qu'il est encore plus difficile de diriger ses bons mouvements que ses mauvais, car, contrairement à ces derniers on ne peut jamais prévoir exactement leur résultat. En tout cas sachez que vous m'avez fait grand plaisir. . . .

It is so curious how, in the history of a family, you have one drastic change after another, all in a period of two or three years, and then for a long long time afterward no change at all. Sabine continued to live now in this place and now in that. The one place where she was always welcome at any time, and for as long as she cared to stay there, the apartment in the rue Malène, she would not make use of. But she turned up fairly often, and stayed just long enough to take her bearings by what she found there. "You will stay and eat with us?" Mme Cestre would say, but she did not urge her. And a few minutes later, Alix would say: "Françoise has set a place for you. . . . Well, come and sit down with us anyway," and Françoise waited and when the others were halfway through dinner she brought in a plate of soup, which Sabine allowed to grow cold in front of her, and then absent-mindedly ate. And then she went home—only it wasn't home she went to but the apartment of a cousin or an uncle or an old school friend of her grandmother's; and the bed she slept in was only a few feet away from an armoire that was crammed with somebody else's clothes.

But the family stood by her. And people were kind; very kind. ("Such a pleasure to have you, dear child"—until the end of the month, when this large room overlooking the avenue Friedland would be required for a granddaughter whose parents were traveling in Italy, and who was therefore coming here for the school holidays.) And Sabine was still invited to the larger parties, but when she went, wearing the one dress she had that was suitable, what she read on the faces of older women—friends of her mother or her grandmother, women she had known all her life—was: "It is a pity that things turned out the way they did, but you do understand, don't you, that you are no longer a suitable match for any of the young men in our family?"

And did she mind?

The way children mind a bruise or a fall. She cried sometimes, afterward, but she did not mind deeply. She did not want the kind of life that a "brilliant" marriage would have opened up to her. And the waters did not close over her head, though there was every reason to think that they would. Or perhaps there wasn't every reason to think that. It all depends on how you look at things. She did have talent; it was merely slow in revealing itself. And failure—real failure—has a way of passing over slight, pale, idealistic girls with observant eyes and a high domed forehead, in favor of some victim who is too fortunate and whose undoing therefore offers a chance for contrast and irony. You know those marvelous windows in Paris?

In the Sainte Chapelle, you mean? And the rose windows of Notre Dame?

No. They're marvelous too, God knows. But I meant the windows of the shops in the rue St. Honoré and the place Vendôme. She had a talent for designing window displays that were original and had humor and appealed to the Parisian mind. For example, she did a small hospital scene, in which the doctor and the patient in bed and the nurses were all perfume bottles dressed up like people. It created a small stir. She worked very hard, but her work was valued. The hours were long, and sometimes she overtaxed her strength. The family worried about her lungs. But she was well paid. And happy in her work. And she did not have to go to a fortuneteller because Eugène had a way of sardonically announcing the future. It was a gift the family stood in some fear of. "Would you like to know what is going to happen to Sabine?" he demanded one day. "She is going to be introduced to a man without any papers. Of good family, but dispossessed; a refugee. And he will not become a French citizen because he is a patriot and cannot bring himself to renounce his Polish, or Hungarian, or Spanish citizenship, and therefore, even though he speaks without an accent, and is educated, and has a first-class mind, he cannot even get a job teaching school. And Sabine, unequipped as she is, is going to take care of him, and they are going to marry, and her mother will never accept him or forgive her. . . ."

His name was Frédéric. His father was a well-to-do banker in——. In the fall of 1939, when the sky was full of German planes day after day, the house Frédéric grew up in, along with whole blocks of other houses, was destroyed by a bomb. The family was in the country when this happened. The caretaker was killed, but no one else. Then the Russians came, and they were allowed to keep one room in that enormous country place, and Frédéric's father arranged for him to escape in a Norwegian fishing vessel. Or perhaps it was on foot, across the border, with a handful of other frightened people. His father remained, to avoid the confiscations of his property, and his mother would not leave his father. For a year and a half, Frédéric lived in the Belleville quarter of Paris. Would you like to see him the way he was at that time? He is stretched out on a bed, in an ugly furnished room that he shares with a waiter in a café in the rue de Menilmentant. He is fully dressed, except for his bare feet, which are thin and aristocratic. The bulb in the unshaded ceiling fixture is not strong enough to bother his eyes. The one window is open to the night. The soft rain fills the alleyway outside with small sounds, sounds that are all but musical, and he is quite happy, though the walls are mildewed and the bedclothes need airing and the sheets are not clean and shortly he will have to get up and spend the rest of the night on the stone floor. He turns on his back, and with his hands clasped under his head, he thinks: *She is hearing this rain. . . .*

The girl who hid out from the Gestapo in Mme Cestre's apartment had brought him to a party where Sabine was, and he saw her home from the party, but she could not, of course, ask him in. One of the ways by which Ferdinand and Miranda are to be distinguished from all commonplace lovers is that, along with Prospero, Ariel, and Calaban, they have no island. It has sunk beneath the sea. Sometimes Frédéric and Sabine meet in an English tea room that is one flight up and rather exposed to the street, but there is one table that is private, behind a huge chart of the human hand showing the lines of the head and the heart, and the mountains of Venus, Jupiter, Saturn, the Sun, Mercury, and Mars. Also the swellings of the palmar faces of the five fingers, indicative of (beginning with the thumb) the logical faculty and the will; materialism, law and order, idealism; humanity, system, intelligence; truth, economy, energy; goodness, prudence, reflectiveness. When the weather permits, the lovers meet on the terrace in front of the Jeu de Paume.

This time, she arrives first. She goes up that little flight of marble steps and crosses the packed dirt to where there are two empty iron chairs. It is a beautiful evening. There are pink clouds against a nearly white sky. Shortly afterward he comes. There is a greenish pallor to his skin. His hands are beautiful and expressive. And he is just her height and just her age, and he speaks French without an accent. His suit is threadbare, but so are most people's suits in France at this time. The part of the terrace they are sitting in now is like the prow of a ship. They look down at the bicycles and motorcars and taxis that come over the bridge and disappear into the delta of wide and narrow streets that flows into the Place de la Concorde. He says: "You are looking at the hole in my shoe?"

"I was looking at your ankle," she says.

"You don't like it?" he says anxiously. "It is the wrong kind of ankle?"

"I was thinking I would like to draw it."

"I was afraid you thought it looked Polish," he says. (Or Hungarian. Or Spanish. I forget which he was.)

They see that the old woman who collects rent for the chairs is coming toward them. He digs down in his coat pocket and produces a five-franc note. Wrinkled and dirty and sad, the old woman gives him his change and moves on.

"You have never thought of committing suicide?" he asks after a time.

She shakes her head.

"I think I used to be in love with death," he says. "I sat in a cold room on an unmade bed with the barrel of a loaded revolver in my mouth, counting to . . . the number varied. Sometimes it was three, sometimes it was seven, and sometimes it was ten."

Farther along the balustrade, the old woman has got into an altercation with a middle-aged couple, and the altercation is being carried on in two languages.

"I was not in any particular trouble, and one is supposed to want to live. . . . What are they saying? They speak too fast for me."

"The man is saying that in America it does not cost anything to sit down in a public park."

"And is he indignant?"

"Very."

"Good," Frédéric says, nodding. "I have hated that old woman for a year and a half. And is she giving him as good as she is taking?"

"Yes, but he does not speak French, and she does not understand English."

"Too bad, too bad. Shall we go and translate for him? With a little help from us, it may become an international incident—the start of the war between the United States and the U.S.S.R." He starts to rise, and she puts a hand on his wrist, restraining him.

A few minutes later, he turns to her and says: "You are going to your aunt's?"

She nods. "You could come too. She has told me to bring you. And you would like them."

"I'm sure I would."

And then, after an interval, in a toneless voice, he says: "I must not keep you."

She gets up from her chair and walks with him to the head of the stairs. In the sky the two colors are now reversed. The clouds are white, and the sky they float in is pink. As they shake hands he does not say: "Will you marry me?" but this question hangs in the air between them, and is why she looks troubled and why he steps out into the traffic like a sleepwalker. Oblivious of the horns and shouts of angry drivers, he arrives safely at the other side. She stands watching him until he passes the Crillon and is hidden by a crowd of people who are waiting in a circle around the red carpet, hoping to see the King of Persia.

Would you like to know about the King of Persia?

II: *Some Explanations*

Not particularly. What I would like to know is the name of that white château with the green lawn in front of it that Barbara Rhodes was always looking for.

One time when Eugène and Sabine were going down to the country together, there was a picture, behind glass, in their compartment. Eugène was furious at her because she had given her seat to an old woman who was sitting on her suitcase in the corridor, and so had made him sit next to a stranger. Or perhaps it was because the old woman was large and crowded him in his corner. Or it might not have been that at all, but something that had nothing to do with her that was making him cold and abstracted. Ultimately the cause of his black moods declared itself, but first you had the mood in its pure state, without any explanation. She stood in the corridor for a while, looking at the landscape that unreeled itself alongside the train, and when the old woman got off at Orléans, she went back into the compartment. She was eager for the trip to be over. The compartment was airless and cramped. With her head against the seat back she sat watching the sunset and noting the signs that meant she was nearing the country of her childhood. She found herself staring at the photograph opposite her. It was of a white château that looked like a castle in a fairy tale. Was it Sully, she wondered. Or Luynes? Or Chantilly? There was a metal tag on the frame, but it was tarnished and could not be read.

You don't know what château it was?

There is every reason to be grateful that these losses do occur, that every once in a while something that is listed in the inventory turns up missing. Otherwise people couldn't move for the clutter that they make around themselves.

I do not take such a charitable view of Eugène's behavior as you seem to. Many people have had to live with disappointment and still not—

He was also capable of acts of renunciation and of generosity that were saintlike. We all have these contradictions in our natures. . . . In the family they were accustomed to his moods and did not take them seriously. There was a time when Alix thought that their life might go differently (though not necessarily better)—that he had reached a turning point of some kind. His dark mood had lasted longer than usual, and one morning she sat up in bed and looked at him, and was frightened. What he looked like was a drowned man.

It was a Saturday, so he did not go to his office. And suddenly, in the middle of the morning, she missed him. She went through the apartment, glancing in the baby's room, then in their bedroom, then in the dressing room. The bathroom door was open. She turned and went back down the hall. He must have gone out. But why did he go out without telling her where he was going? And how could he have done it so quietly, so that she didn't hear either the study door open or the front door close. Unless he didn't want her to know that he was going out. She had a sudden vision of him ill, having fainted in the toilet. She opened the door of that little room. It was empty.

"Eugène?" she said anxiously, and at that moment the front door closed. She turned around in surprise.

There was still time to stop him, to ask where he was going. When she opened the front door, she heard the sound of feet descending the stairs and, leaning far over the banister, caught a glimpse of his head and shoulders, which were hidden immediately afterward by a turn in the staircase.

"Eugène!" she called, and, loud and frightened though her voice sounded in her own ears, he still did not stop. The footsteps reiterated his firm intention never to stop until he had arrived at a place where she could not reach him. When they changed from the muffled sound made by the stair carpet to the harsh clatter of heels on a marble floor, she turned and hurried back into the apartment, through the hall, through the drawing room, and out onto the balcony, where she was just in time to see him emerge from the building and start up the sidewalk. She tried to pitch her voice so that only he would hear her calling him, and a man on the other side of the street looked up and Eugène did not. He went right on walking.

Step by step, with him, she hurried along the balcony to the corner of the building, where she could look down on the granite monument and the cobblestone square. Hidden by trees briefly, Eugène was now visible again, crossing a street. There was a taxi waiting, but he did not step into it. He kept on walking, past the café, past the entrance to the Métro, past the barbershop, past the trousered legs standing publicly in the midst of the odor that used to make her feel sick as a child. Again he was hidden by trees. Again she saw him, as he skirted a sidewalk meeting of two old friends. He crossed another ray of the star, and then changed his direction slightly, and she perceived that the church steps was his destination. There, in the gray morning light, one of the priests (Father Quinot, or Father Ferron?) stood with his hands behind his back, benevolently nodding and answering the parting remarks of a woman in black.

The image that Alix now saw before her eyes—of Eugène on his knees in the confessional—was only the beginning, she knew. More was required. Much more. The heart that was now ready to surrender itself was not simple. There would be intellectual doubts, arguments with Father Quinot, with Father Ferron, appointments with the bishop, a period of retreat from her and from the world, in some religious house, where no one could reach him, while he examined his faith for flaws. Proof would be submitted to him from the writings of St. Thomas, St. Gregory, St. Bonaventure. And when he returned to her, with the saints shielding him so that each time she put out her hand she touched the garment of a saint, his mind would be full of new knowledge of how men *know*, how the angels *know*, how God in his infinite being becomes all *knowledge* and all *knowledge* is a *knowledge* of Him.

This being true, clear, and obvious even to a slow mind like hers, a person given to looking apprehensively at mirrors and clocks, and there being also no way of joining him on his knees (though there were two stalls in the mahagony confessional, the most that was given to Father Quinot or Father Ferron to accomplish would be to listen to their alternating confession, not their joint one)—this being true, she would not go down and wait for him in the street, as she longed to do, even though it be hours from now, past midnight, or morning, before he reappeared. She would stay where she was, and when he came home she would try not to distract him, or to seem to lay the slightest claim upon his attention or his feelings, in order that . . .

Each of the woman's parting remarks seemed to give rise to another, and as Eugène drew closer, Alix thought: *What if she doesn't stop talking in time?* For Eugène would not wait. He was much too proud to stand publicly waiting, even to speak to the priest. "Oh, please," she said, under her breath. The woman turned her head, as if this supplication had been heard. But then she remembered something else that she wanted to say, and Eugène kept on going, and disappeared down the steps of the Métro.

Shortly after this, he went to see M. Carrère, who was exceedingly kind. Eugène outlined his situation to him, and M. Carrère asked if Eugène had any objection to working for an American firm that he was connected with through his son. "The job would be over there?" Eugène asked, and M. Carrère said: "No, here. I assume that Mme de Boisgaillard would not want to live so far from her mother. Suppose I arrange for an interview?"

The interview went well, and after an hour's talk, Eugène was asked to come back the next day, which he did. They made him an offer, and he accepted it.

A few nights later, when Mme Viénot went in to say good night to her mother, Mme Bonenfant said: "I wonder if Eugène will be happy working for an American firm. He doesn't speak any English."

II: *Some Explanations*

"If it is like other foreign firms that have a branch in Paris, the personnel will be largely French," Mme Viénot said. "I have heard of this one, as it happens. In America they make frigidaires. Sewing machines. Typewriters. That sort of thing."

"It doesn't sound very intellectual," Mme Bonenfant said. "Are you sure that you understood correctly."

"Quite sure, Maman. . . . In France, the firm manufactures only machine guns."

M. and Mme Carrère never came back to the château. They found another quiet country house that was more comfortable and closer to Paris. But from time to time, when Mme Viénot went into the post office, she was handed a letter that was addressed to him. The letters no doubt contained a request of some sort; for money, for advice, for the use of his name. And how it was answered might change the lives of she did not like to think how many people. In any case, the letter had to be forwarded, and it gave her acute pleasure to think that he would recognize her handwriting on the envelope.

Hector Gagny never came back either, with his new wife. But Mme Straus came at least once a year. Her summer was a round of visits. For a woman past seventy, without a place of her own in which to entertain, with neither wealth nor much social distinction, she received a great many invitations—many more than she could accept. And if the friends who were so eager to have her come and stay with them did not always invite her back, there were always new acquaintances who responded to her gaiety, opened their hearts to her, and—for a while at least—adjusted the salutation of their letters to conform with the rapidly increasing tenderness of hers.

A blank space in her calendar between the end of June and the middle of September meant a brief stay at Beaumesnil. She was at the château just after the affair of the robbers, and she brought two friends with her, a M. and Mme Mégille. Monsieur was a member of the permanent staff of the Institut Océanographique, and very distinguished. And since he had been brought up in the country he did not mind the fact that there was no electricity.

They never found that short circuit?

Oh yes. This was a piece of foolishness on Mme Viénot's part. You won't believe it, but she could not get that gold bullion out of her mind. She induced the priest at Coulanges to come and go all through the house with her, holding a forked stick. There was one place where it responded violently, and in opening up the wall the gardener sawed through the main electric-light cable.

But surely Mme Viénot was too intelligent to believe that—

Yes, she did. Mme Viénot is the Life Force, with dyed hair and too much rouge, and the Life Force always believes. Defeated, flat on her back, she waved her arms and legs like a beetle, and in a little while she was walking around again.

Every novel ought to have a heroine, and she is the heroine of this one. She is a wonderful woman—how wonderful probably no one knows, except an American woman she met only once, on a train journey—a woman who, curiously enough, knew Barbara and Harold Rhodes, though only slightly. The two women opened their hearts to each other, as women sometimes do on a train or sharing a table in the tea room of a department store, and they have continued to write to each other afterward, long letters full of things they do not tell anyone else.

What Mme Viénot did the summer Barbara and Harold were with her was miraculous. She had nothing whatever to work with, and bad servants, and somehow she kept up the tone of the establishment and provided meals that were admirable. Singlehanded, she saved the château. It would have gone for back taxes if she had not done what she did. No one else in the family could have saved it. As a person, Mme Cestre was more sympathetic, perhaps, but she was an invalid, and introspective. And the men . . .

What about the men?

II: *Some Explanations*

Well, what about them?

I guess you're right. Go on with what you were saying.

Once more they dined by candlelight. When they went up to bed, they were handed kerosene lamps at the foot of the stairs. There was no writing desk in Mme Straus's room, and so, sitting up in bed, she used a book to write on. Her hair was in two braids and her reading glasses were resting far down on the bridge of her nose. She wrote rapidly, with no trace of a quaver:

> . . . Maman Minou finds that she has been a long time without news of her dear American children. The last letter from Harold, written in English, was translated for me by a friend, but tonight I am not in Paris. I beg him not to be vexed with me. Can he not find, at his office, a good-natured comrade who knows how to read French and will translate this letter into English? But my dear friend, why this sudden change? Your old letters, and those of dear Barbara, were perfectly written. It makes me wonder whether you perhaps no longer wish to correspond with poor Minou in France.

The fountain pen stopped. The old eyes went on a voyage round the room, searching for something to say (one does not create an atmosphere of concert pitch out of accusations of neglect) and came to rest on a large stain in the wallpaper:

> Your presence surrounds me here. I go looking for you, and find my friends occupying your room. I put flowers there for them but Oh miracle! the moment the flowers are in their vase, they fly off toward you. Take them, then, my dears, and may their perfume spread around you. Here it is gray, cheerless, cold. The surroundings are agreeable, even so. M. and Mme Mégille are charming. Sabine pleases me very much. The lady of the manor dolls herself up for each new arrival. So droll! Alix is adorable. She is going off to visit cousins in Toulon next week. I shall miss her. Have you pretty concerts and plays to see? In this moment when we are in summer, are you not in winter? And at the hour when I am writing to you—eleven o'clock at night—your hour of the omelette, the good odor of which I smell even here?

She thought the United States was in South America?

Apparently. Some people have no sense of geography.— The letter ended:

> Life is rather difficult here, but I am so eager to obey our dear President Pinay, whom we admire so much, that all becomes easy. Your dear images still have a place in my little chamber, which you know. Pray for your old Maman Minou, who embraces you with all her loving heart.
>
> Antoinette Straus-Muguet
>
> Please put the date and the year of your letters. Thank you.

Why didn't they answer her letters? It isn't like them.

I'll get around to that in a minute. One thing at a time. She blew the lamp out—

We have to hear about the lamp?

Yes. And settled herself between the damp sheets. And it was at that moment that the odor of kerosene brought back to her something priceless, a house she had not seen for half a century.

The youngest of a large family, she had all through her childhood been the charming excitable plaything of older brothers and sisters. When evening came, so did Charles and Emma and Andrée and Edouard and Lucienne and Maurice and Marguerite and Anna. They gathered in the nursery to assist in putting Minou to bed, invented new games when her head hung like a heavy flower on its stalk, and, as they peeled her clothes off over her head, cried: "Skin the rabbit! Don't let the little white bunny get away." "Stop her!" "Catch her, somebody!" And when she escaped from them, they tracked her down with all the cruelty of love, and carried her on their shoulders around the nursery, a laughing overexcited child with too bright eyes and a flushed face and a nature that was too highstrung and delicate to be playing such games at the end of the day.

All dead, the pursuers; long dead; leaving her no choice but to pursue.

As for the Americans, it was much harder to think in French when they were not in France. They had to sit down with a

French-English dictionary and a French grammar, and it took half a day to answer one of Mme Straus's letters, and they were leading a busy life. Also, he hated to write letters. He used to wait for days before he opened a letter from Mme Straus, because of his shame at not having answered the last one. But they did answer some of the letters. They did not altogether lose touch with her.

Quite apart from the effort it took, and the fact that year after year the friendship had nothing to feed on, her letters to them were really very strange. ("The monsieur who is at Fifth Avenue is not my relative, but my niece is flying over soon, on business for the house, of which she is administrator, director, in place of her dead husband. She will be, *alone*, in our confidence, but see you, become acquainted with you, speak to you of Maman Minou. You will see how nice she is. Answer her telephone calls above everything. She will give you news of me, and fresh news . . .) None of the people she said were coming to America and that Harold and Barbara could expect to hear from ever turned up. And there was one frantic, only half-legible letter, which they had to take to the friend who had lived in the Monceau quarter, to translate for them. She found it distrait, full of idioms that she had never seen and that she didn't believe existed. The letter was about money. Mme Straus' income, with inflation, was no longer adequate to meet her needs. Her daughter had refused to do anything for her, and Mme Straus was afraid that she would be put out of the convent. In the next letter it appeared that this crisis had passed: Mme Straus-Muguet's children, to whom her notary had made a demand, had finally understood that it was their duty to help her. "Forgive me," she wrote, "for boring you with all my miseries, but you are all my consolation." Her letters were full of intimations of increasing frailty and age, and continually asked when they were coming back to France. At last they were able to write her that they were coming, in the spring of 1953, and she wrote back: "If Heaven wills it that I have not already departed for my great journey, it will be with arms wide open that I will receive you. . . ."

And was she there to receive them?

They went first to England, and had two weeks of flawless weather. The English countryside was like the Book of Hours, and they loved London. They arrived in Paris on May Day Eve, and by nightfall they were in the Forest of Fontainebleau, in a rented car, on their way south. They spent the night in Sens, and in the morning everyone they saw carried a little nosegay of muguets. After their other trip, they enrolled in the Berlitz, and spent one winter conscientiously studying French. Though that was years ago now, it did seem that their French had improved.

The boy learns to swim in winter, William James said, and to skate in summer.

From Provence, Barbara wrote to Mme Straus that they would be in Paris by the end of the second week in May. When they were settled in—someone had told them about a small hotel whose windows overlooked the gardens of the Palais-Royal—Harold telephoned, and the person who answered seemed uncertain of whether Mme Straus could come to the telephone. The stairs have become too much for her, he thought. There was another of those interminable waits, during which he had a chance to reflect. Five years is a long time, and to try and pick up the threads again, with people they hardly knew, and with the additional barrier of language . . . But they couldn't not call, either. . . .

Mme Straus's voice was just the same, and she seemed to be quite free of the doubts that troubled him. They settled it that she would come to their hotel at seven that evening.

At quarter after six, as they were crossing the Place du Palais-Royal, Barbara said: "Aren't we going to have an apéritif?"

They had only five weeks altogether, for England and France, and there was never a time, it seemed, when they could sit in front of a sidewalk café, as they used to do before, and watch the people. They were both tired from walking, and he very much wanted a bath before dinner, but he decided that with luck they could do it, in spite of the crowd of people occupying the tables of that particular café, and the overworked waiter. They did it, but without pleasure, because he kept looking at his watch. They hurried through the gardens, congratulating themselves on the fact that it was still only twenty minutes of seven—just time enough to get upstairs and bathe and dress and be ready for Mme Straus.

"You have company," Mme la Patronne said as they walked into the hotel. "A lady." There was a note of disapproval in her voice. "She has been waiting since six o'clock."

The Americans looked at each other with dismay. "You go on upstairs," he said, and hurried down the hall to the little parlor where Mme Straus was waiting, with two small parcels on the sofa beside her. His first impression was that she looked younger. Could he have misjudged her age? She kissed him on both cheeks, and told him how well he looked. They sat down and he began to tell her about Provence. Then there was an awkward pause in the conversation, and to dispell it they asked the questions people ask, meeting after years. When Barbara came in, he started to leave the room, intending to go upstairs and at least wash his face and hands, but Mme Straus stopped him. It was the moment for the presentation of the gifts, and again they were dismayed that they had not thought to bring anything for her. They were also dismayed at her gifts—a paper flower for Barbara, a white scarf for Harold that had either lain in a drawer too long or else was of so shoddy a quality that it bore no relation to any man's evening scarf he had ever seen. Mme Straus had learned to make paper flowers—as a game, she said, and to amuse herself. "Oeillet," she said, resuming her role of language professor, and Barbara pinned the pink carnation on her dark violet-colored coat, where it looked very pretty, if a trifle strange.

They left the hotel intending to have dinner at a restaurant in the rue de Montpensier, but it was closed that night, and so Mme Straus led them across the Place du Théâtre-Français, to a restaurant where, she assured them, she was well known and the food and wine were excellent. It was noisy and crowded; the maître d'hôtel received Mme Straus coldly, but at least the waiter knew her and was friendly. "He is like a son to me," she said, as they sat down.

There were a dozen restaurants in the neighborhood where the food was better, and Harold blamed himself for not insisting that they go to some place more suited to a long-delayed reunion, but Mme Straus seemed quite happy. Nobody had very much to say.

The Vienna Opera was paying a visit to Paris, and during dinner he explained that he had three tickets for *The Magic Flute*. She said: "Quelle joie!" and then: "Where are they?" He told her and she exclaimed: "But we won't be able to see the stage!"

The tickets had cost five times what tickets for the Opéra usually cost, and were the most he felt he could afford. He said: "They're in the center," and she seemed satisfied. And would they arrange for her to stay at their hotel that night, since the doors of her convent were closed at nine o'clock?

Arm in arm, they walked to the bus stop, and waving from the back of the bus, she was swept away.

"It isn't the same, is it?" he said, as they were walking back to their hotel.

"We're not the same," Barbara said. "She took one look at us and saw that the jig was up."

"Too bad."

"If you hadn't got tickets for the opera—"

"I know. Well, one more evening won't kill us."

Harold found that Mme Straus could stay at their hotel the night of the opera, and when she arrived—again an hour early—she was delighted with her room. "It's just right for a jeune fille," she said, laughing. And did Barbara have a coat she could wear? And wouldn't it be better if they had dinner in the same place, because the service was so prompt, and above all they didn't want to be late.

When they arrived at the Opéra, she introduced them to the tall man in evening clothes who was taking tickets, and they were introduced again on the stairs, to an ouvreuse or someone like that. They climbed and climbed and eventually arrived at their tier, which was above the "basket." Their seats were in the first row and they had a clear view of the stage and the stage was not too far away. Mme Straus arranged her coat and offered Harold and Barbara some candy. Stuffed with food and wine, they said no, and she took some herself and then seized their hands affectionately. She made them lean far forward so that she could point out to them, in the tier just below, the two center front-row seats that her father and mother had always occupied. She regretted that *Les Indes Galantes* was not being performed during their stay in Paris. A marvelous spectacle.

The Magic Flute was also something of a spectacle, and the soprano who sang the role of Pamina had a very beautiful voice.

Harold had failed to get a program and so they didn't know who it was. In the middle of the first act, he became aware of Mme Straus's restlessness. At last she leaned toward him and whispered that this opera was always sung at the Comique; that it did not belong on so large a stage. The Opéra was more suited to *Aida*. She found the singing acceptable but the opera itself did not greatly interest her. Did he know *Aida?* It was her favorite. Again she pressed the little bag of candy on him in the dark, and he suddenly remembered the strange behavior of Mme Marguerite Mailly, when they went backstage after her play. A few minutes later, hearing the rustle of the little bag again coming toward him, he was close to hating Mme Straus-Muguet himself. They left their seats between the acts, and as they walked through the marble corridors, he noticed a curious thing: because their French had improved, Mme Straus understood what they were saying, but not always what they meant, and when they explained, it only added to the misunderstanding. Wherever her quick intuitive mind was, it wasn't on them.

After the performance, she insisted that they go across the street, as her guests, and have something to eat. Harold and Barbara drank a bottle of Perrier water, and Mme Straus had a large ham sandwich.

"I am always hungry," she confessed.

Worn out with the effort of keeping up the form of an affectionate relationship that had lost its substance, they sat and looked at the people around them. Mme Straus borrowed the souvenir program of a young woman at the next table, and they learned the name of the soprano with the beautiful voice: Irmgard Seefried. Then Mme Straus brought up the matter of when they would see her next. Barbara said gently that they were only going to be in Paris a few more days, and that this was their last evening with her.

"Ah, but chérie, just one time! After five years!"

"Two times," Barbara said, and Mme Straus smiled. She was not hurt, it seemed, but only pretending.

They said good night on the stairs of the little hotel, and the Americans went off early the next morning, to Chartres; they wanted to see the cathedral again. When they got back to the hotel, Mme Straus had gone, leaving instructions about when they were to telephone her. There were several telephone calls during the next two days and in the end they found themselves having lunch with her, in that same impossible restaurant. She took from her purse a postcard she had just received from her daughter, who was traveling in Switzerland. It was simple and affectionate—just such a card as any daughter might have sent her mother from a trip, and Mme Straus seemed to have forgotten that they knew anything about her daughter that wasn't complimentary.

At the end of the meal, Mme Straus asked for the *addition*, and Harold, partly out of concern for her but much more out of a deep desire to get to the bottom of things, reached for his wallet. In the short time that remained, perhaps it was possible to discover the simple unsentimentalized truth. At the risk of being crass and of hurting her feelings, he insisted on paying for the luncheon she had invited them to, and, smiling indulgently, she let him. So I could have paid for all the other times, he thought. And should have.

"Now what would you like to do?" she asked. "What would you like to see? Do you like looking at paintings and old furniture?"

They got into a taxi and drove to the shop of a cousin of Mme Straus's husband. It was a decorator's shop, and the taste it reflected was not their taste, in furniture or in objets d'art. Finding nothing else that she could admire, Barbara pretended to an interest in a Chinese luster tea set. "You like it?" Mme Straus said. "It is charming, I agree." She could not be prevented from calling a salesman and asking the price—three hundred thousand francs. Mme Straus whispered; "I will speak to them, and tell them you are my rich American friends." She giggled. "Because of me, they will give you a prix d'ami."

Barbara said that the tea set was much too expensive. As she turned away, her short violet-colored coat swept one of the cups out of its saucer. With a lunge Harold caught it in mid-air.

They went upstairs and looked at what they were told were Raphaels. "Copies," Harold said, committed now to his disagreeable experiment. "And not necessarily copies of a painting by Raphael."

The salesman did not disagree, or seem offended. Seeing that they were not interested in what he showed them, he asked what painters they did like.

"Vuillard and Bonnard," Harold said.

They were shown a small, uninteresting Bonnard and told that there were more in the shop if they would like to see them. Harold shook his head. It was tug of war, with Mme Straus endeavoring to give her husband's cousin the impression that

Harold and Barbara were rich American collectors and might buy anything, and Harold and Barbara trying just as hard to convey the truth.

Mme Straus started to leave the shop with them, and then hesitated. "I have some business to discuss with monsieur upstairs," she said, and kissed them, and said good-by, and perhaps she would come to the airport.

In the taxi Harold said: "Is that the explanation? All this elaborate scheming so she can get her commission?"

"No," Barbara said. "I don't really think it is that. . . . I think it is more likely something she thought of on the spur of the moment. A role she performed just for the pleasure of performing it. But I kept thinking all the time we were with her, there is something about her manner and her voice. I couldn't place it until we were in that shop. She is like the women in stores who try to sell you something. Whatever she is, or whoever she was, she knows that world. I think that's why Pierre disapproved of our being with her. . . . But it is the young she likes. Now that we are no longer young, it isn't worth her while to enchant us."

The other reunions were not disappointing. They liked Sabine's husband, and she was exactly as they remembered her. It was as if they had bicycled home in the moonlight from the Allégrets' party the night before. She did not even look any older. The questions she asked were the right questions. They could convey to her in a phrase, a word, the thing that needed to be said. She is all eyes and forehead, Harold thought, looking at her. But what he was most aware of was how completely she took in what they said to her, so that talking to her was not like talking to anybody else. Walking to her door from the restaurant where they had had dinner, he heard their four voices, all proceeding happily like a quartet for strings. Allegro, andante, etc. While he was telling Frédéric about an experience with some gypsies outside the walls of Aigues-Mortes, she began to tell Barbara about the robbers. Harold stopped talking to listen.

Then, turning to Frédéric, he asked: "She's not making this up?" and Frédéric said: "No, no, it all happened," and Harold said: "I guess when anything is that strange you can be sure it happened." Looking up at the lamplit underside of the leaves of the chestnut trees, he thought: We're in Paris, I am not dreaming that we are in Paris. . . .

The next day, they met Eugène and Alix for lunch, and that too was easy and pleasant. Eugène spoke English, which made a difference. And he was in a genial mood. Their eyes had no trouble meeting his. They did not have to make conversation out of passing the sugar back and forth. *We're not the same, are we?* they all three agreed silently, and after that he treated them and they treated him with simple courtesy. And unwittingly, Harold saw, they had pleased Eugène by inviting him to this restaurant. He informed them that Napoleon used to play chess here, and that the décor was unchanged since that time. With its red curtains, its red plush, it was exactly right, and what a classical restaurant should look like. . . . He enjoyed his lunch as well. And the wine was of his choosing. He was sardonic only once, with the waiter, who urged them a shade too insistently to have strawberries.

After lunch they strolled through the gardens of the Palais-Royal, and Barbara took a picture of the three others, standing in front of the spray of a fountain. When Eugène left to go back to his office, Alix said, somewhat to their surprise, that, yes, she would like to go and see the rose garden at Bagatelle with them. In appearance she was totally changed. She was not an unconfident young woman with a baby; she was a stylish Parisian matron. Her hair was cut short, in a way that was becoming to her. Her black suit had the tailoring of Paris, and what made them instantly at ease and happy with her was that she didn't pretend she wasn't pleased with it. "All my life I've wanted a black suit," she said, when Barbara spoke of it. If she understood the meaning of pretense, she did not understand the need for it. It had no part in her nature. We thought all these years that we remembered her, Harold said to himself—her voice, her face, how nice she is, how much we liked being with her. But all we had, actually, was a dim recollection of those things. And it didn't even include the most important fact about her—that she would never under any circumstances turn away from the presence of love, happy or unhappy.

Because she was wearing a tight skirt, they stopped off first at the apartment in the rue Malène, and Barbara and Harold saw Alix's children, who were charming, and had a visit with Mme Cestre while Alix was changing her clothes. At Bagatelle, something awaited them—a red brick wall almost a hundred feet long, and trained against it were climbing roses and white and blue clematis, demonstrating their cousinship. Both flowers were at the very perfection of their blooming period. It was one more ecstatic experience, to put with the lavender-blue searchlight, the rainy night in San Remo, the one-ring circus, and the medieval city that was enclosed in itself like a rose. Sitting on a bench, with the wall in front of them, Alix talked about her present life. All that Harold remembered afterward was the one sentence: "I don't mind doing the washing and ironing, or anything else, so long as I don't have to sit with them in the park." It reduced the Atlantic Ocean to a puddle, and he began to tell her about their efforts to adopt a child. Then they looked at the roses some more. And then they made their way to a bus stop, and back into the city. She got off first, and they waved until they couldn't see her any longer. They saw her once more after that. Sabine had a party for them, an evening party, and invited Alix and Eugène and also her sister and brother-in-law.

The man who looked like an acrobat but wasn't?

He was a performer. Their instinct about him was right. But his performance was intellectual; he balanced budgets in the air. He had changed so in five years that they didn't recognize him. He didn't refer to the evening they had spent together, and they didn't remember until afterward who he was.

And Sabine was different, Harold suddenly realized. In one

respect she had changed. That strange suggestion of an unprovoked or unrelated amusement was not there any longer. Was this because it was now safe to be serious? In any case, she was happy.

Feeling that the party was for them, they tried too hard, and didn't really enjoy themselves, but it didn't matter; they had already reached the people they wanted to reach. Including that waiter, Joseph.

Pierre, you said his name was.

His name was Joseph, but they didn't know it. The patron's name being Joseph also, he called himself Pierre, to avoid confusion. But his name was really Joseph. The simplest things are often not what they seem. . . . The restaurant in the alley off the Place St. Sulpice had gone downhill. The patron had taken to drink, and their friend was now working in a brasserie on the boulevard St. Germain. The first time they stopped in, he was off duty. They left a message—that they would be back two days later. They almost didn't go back. Though they had exchanged Christmas cards with him faithfully, would they have anything to say to him? It didn't seem at all likely. When they walked in, there he was, and he saw them and smiled, and they knew that they didn't have to have anything to say to him. They loved him. They had always loved him.

He led them to a table and they asked him what to order and he told them, just as he used to do; but when Harold asked him to bring three glasses with the bottle of wine, he shook his head and said warningly, as to a younger brother: "This is a serious restaurant." He stood by their table, talking to them while they ate, or left them to go look after another table and then returned to pick up where they had left off. They found they had too much to say to him. When they left, they promised to meet him at noon on Sunday—for an apéritif, they assumed. On Sunday, the four of them—Joseph's wife was there beside him—sat for a while in front of the brasserie, watching the people who passed, and talking quietly, and when the Americans got up to go, they discovered that they had been invited to lunch, in Joseph's apartment, seven flights up, in the rue des Ciseaux. It was a tiny apartment, with two rooms, and only two windows. But out of each they could see a church tower, Joseph's wife showed them. And they could hear the bells. She confessed to Barbara that they greatly regretted not having children, and that all their affection should be heaped on a canary. It was wrong, but they could not help it. And Barbara explained that at home they had a gray cat to whom they gave too much affection also. The canary's name was Fifi, and all that love it had no right to poured back out of its throat, and remarks were frequently addressed to it from the lunch table. Lunch went on for hours. Joseph had cooked it himself, that morning and the day before, and they saw that there is, in France, a kind of hospitality that cannot be paid for and that is so lavish one can only bow one's head in the presence of it. They drank pernod, timidly, before they began to eat. They drank a great deal of wine during lunch. They drank brandy after they stopped eating. From time to time there were toasts. Raising his glass drunkenly, Harold exclaimed: "A Fifi!" and a few minutes later Joseph pushed his chair back and said: "A nos amis, à nos amours!" The Americans were just barely able to get down the stairs.

Side by side with what happens, the friendship that unexpectedly comes into full flower, there is always, of course, the one that could and does not. Among the clients of the little restaurant in the rue de Montpensier there was a tall interesting-looking man, in his late forties, and his two barely grown sons. The father usually arrived first, and the sons joined him, one at a time. In their greeting there was so much undisguised affection that the Americans found them a pleasure to watch. But who were they, and where was the boys' mother? Was she ill? Was she dead? And why, in France, did they eat in a restaurant instead of at home? Like a fruit hanging ripe on the bough, the acquaintance was ready to begin. All it needed was a word, a smile, a small accident, and they would all five have been eating together.

If they had been on shipboard, for instance—but they were not on shipboard.

And who were they? Were they aware of the Americans?

Of course. How could they not be? The Americans went to a movie that was on the other side of Paris, and when the lights came on, there sitting in the row ahead of them were the father and his two sons. It was all Harold could do not to speak to them. . . . Though their story is interesting, and offers some curious parallels, I don't think I'd better go into it here.

The Americans continued to see things, and to be moved by what they saw, and to love France. During the few days they were in Paris, there was an illumination of Gothic and Renaissance sculpture at the Louvre, and a beautiful exhibition of medieval stained-glass windows, at the Musée des Arts Décoratifs.

And Mme Viénot?

They didn't see her. And neither did they try to see Jean Allégret. They were afraid it would be pushing their luck too far, and also they were in Paris such a short time, and there were so many things they wanted to see and do. They saw a school children's matinee of *Phèdre* at the Comédie Française and a revival of *Ciboulette* at the Comique. Harold got up one morning at daybreak and wandered through the streets and markets of Les Halles. Coming home with his arms full of flowers, he stopped and stared at an old woman who was asleep with her cheek pressed against the pavement. His eyes, traveling upward, saw a street sign: rue des Bons Enfants. The scene remained intact in his mind afterward, like a vision; like something he had learned.

Did they adopt a child?

No. It is not easy, and before they had managed to do it, Barbara became pregnant. It was as if someone in authority had said Since you are now ready and willing to bring up anybody's child, you may as well bring up your own. . . . So strange, life is. Why people do not go around in a continual state of surprise is beyond me. In the foyer of the Musée Guimet, Barbara saw a Khmer head—very large it was, and one side of the face seemed to be considering closely, from the broadest possible point of view, all human experience; the expression of the other half was inward-looking, concerned with only one fact, one final mystery.

Those people whose windows look out on the gardens of the Palais-Royal know that though the palace is built of stone it is not gray but takes its color from the color of the sky, which varies according to the time of day. In the early morning, at daybreak, it is lavender-blue. In the evening it is sometimes flamingo-colored. If you walk along the rue La Feuillade shortly after five o'clock in the morning, you will come to a bakery that is below the street level, and the smell of freshly baked bread is enough to break your heart. And if you stand late at night on the Pont des Arts, you will find yourself in the eighteenth century. The lights in the houses along the Quai Malaquais and the Quai de Conti are reflected in the river, and the reflections elongate as if they were trying to turn into Japanese lanterns. The Louvre by moonlight is a palace, not an art gallery. And if you go there in the daytime you must search out the little stairway that leads up to a series of rooms where you can buy, for very little money, engravings of American flowers—the jack-in-the-pulpit, the May apple, the windflower—that were made from specimens collected by missionaries and voyageurs in the time of Louis XIV. At the flower market there is a moss rose that is pale pink with a deeper pink center, and you will walk between trenches of roses and peonies that are piled like cordwood. And though not every day is beautiful (sometimes it is cold, sometimes it is raining) there will be days when the light in the sky is such that you wonder if—

I know, I know. Everybody feels that way about Paris. London is beautiful too. So is Rome. So, for that matter, is New York. The world is full of beautiful cities. What interests me is

Mme Viénot. It is a pity that they did not bother to see her.

She was in the country. But just because the Americans didn't see her is no sign we can't. . . . It is a Tuesday. The sky in Touraine is a beautiful, clear, morning-glory blue. She wheels her bicycle from the kitchen entryway, mounts it, and rides out of the courtyard. The gardener and his wife and boy are stacking the hay in the park in front of the house, and a M. Lundqvist is leaning out of the window of Sabine's room. He waves to her cheerfully, and she waves back.

She stops to talk to the gardener, who is optimistic about the hay but thinks it is time they had rain; otherwise there will be no fodder for the cows, and the price of butter will go sky-high, where everything else is already.

Halfway down the drive she turns and looks back over her shoulder. The front of the house, with its steep gables, box hedge, raked gravel terrace, and stone balustrade, says: "If one can only sustain the conventions, one is in turn sustained by them . . ." Reassured, she rides on. She is going to haggle with the farmer, five miles away, who supplies her with cream and butter and the plain but admirable cheese of the locality. When she looks back a second time, the trees have closed in and the château is lost from sight. But it can be seen again from the public road, across the fields—a large, conspicuous white-stone house, the only house of this size for several miles around.

M. and Mme Bonenfant celebrated their son's coming of age here, and the marriages of their two daughters, and of one of their granddaughters. Like all well-loved, well-cared for, hospitable, happy houses, the Château Beaumesnil gives off a high polish, a mellowed sense of order, of the comfort that is felt by the eye and not the behind of the beholder. A stranger walking into the house for the first time is aware of the rich texture of sounds and silences. The rugs seem to have an affinity for the floor they lie on. The sofas and chairs announce: "We will never allow ourselves to be separated under any circumstances." "This is rightness," the house says. "This is what a house should be; and to have to live anywhere else is the worst of all possible misfortunes."

The village is just the same—or practically. M. Canourgue's stock is now on open shelves instead of under the counter or in the back room. There is a clock in the railway station, and the station itself is finished. Though the travel posters have been changed and the timetables are for the year 1953, the same four men are seated on the terrace of the Café de la Gare.

The village is proud of its first family, and also of the fact that the old lady chose to throw in her lot with theirs. Mme Bonenfant is eighty-eight now, and suffers from forgetfulness. Far too often she cannot find her handkerchief or the letter she had in her hand only a moment ago. On her good days she enjoys the quickness and clarity of mind that she has always had. She is witty, she charms everyone, she is like an ivory chess queen. On her bad days chère Maman sits with her twisted old hands in her lap, quiet and sad, and sometimes not really there; not anywhere. It bothers her that she cannot remember how many great-grandchildren she has, and she says to Sabine: "Was that before your dear father died?" and realizes from the look of horror that this question gives rise to that she has confused a son-in-law who is dead with one who is very much alive. She leaves the house only to go to Mass on Sunday, or to the potager with her wicker garden basket and shears. She is still beautiful, as a flower stalk with its seed pod open and empty or a tattered oak leaf is beautiful. The potager never ceases to trouble her, because ever since the war the fruit trees, flowers, and vegetables have been mingled in a way that is not traditional. And terrible things have happened to the scarecrow. "Look at me!" he cries. "Look what has happened to me!" Mme Bonenfant, snipping away at the sweet-pea stems, answers calmly: "To me also. All experience is impoverishing. A great deal is taken away, a little is given in return. Patience is obligatory—the patient acceptance of much that is unacceptable."

II: *Some Explanations*

Now it is evening, but not evening of the same day. The house is damp, and it has been raining since early morning. There are no guests at the moment. With her poor circulation Mme Bonenfant feels the cold, and so sometimes even in summer a small fire is lit for her in the Franklin stove in the petit salon. Mme Viénot is sitting at the desk, going over her accounts. Alix is on the divan. And Mme Bonenfant is going through a box of old letters.

"This is what the world used to be like," she says suddenly. "It is a letter from my father to his sister in Paris. 'The two young people'—Suzanne and Philippe, he is referring to—'evinced a delicate fondness for each other that we ought to be informed of. . . .' "

"And were they informed of it?" Alix asks.

"Yes. Shortly afterward," Mme Bonenfant says, and goes on reading to herself. When she finishes the letter, she puts it back in its envelope and drops it into the fire. The paper bursts into flame, the pale-brown ink turns darker for a few seconds and then this particular link with the remote past is gray ashes, and even the ashes are consumed.

"But surely you aren't destroying old letters!" Mme Viénot exclaims.

"When I am gone, who will be interested in reading them?" Mme Bonenfant says.

"*I* am interested," Mme Viénot says indignantly. "We all are. I have implored you—I implore you now—not to burn family letters."

"You didn't know any of the people," Mme Bonenfant says with finality, as though Mme Viénot were still a child.

Though she is very old, and tired, and forgetful, she is still the head of the family.

Now suppose I pass my hand over the crystal ball twice. What do we see? The furniture is under dust covers, the shutters are closed, the grass is not cut in the park, the potager is a tangle of weeds and briers. Sometimes in the night there are footsteps on the gravel terrace in front of the house, but no one lies in bed with a wildly beating heart, hearing them. All the rooms of the house are quiet except the third-floor room at the head of the stairs. The shutters here have come loose; they must not have been fastened securely. At some time, the ornamental shield has been removed from the fireplace, and occasionally there is a downdraft that redistributes the dust. Wasps beat against the windowpanes. In the night the shutters creak, the black-out paper flaps softly, the room grows cold. The mirrors recall long-forgotten images: the Germans; the young American couple; M. Lundqvist; Mme Viénot as a girl, expectant and vulnerable. Moonlight comes and goes. The mirrors remember the poor frightened squirrel that got in and could not get out. And in the hall at the foot of the stairs—this is really very strange—the grandfather's clock chimes again and again, though there is nobody to wind it.

You are not asking me to believe that?

No. The wheels turn, revealing (but in the dark, and to nobody) the exact hour of the day or night when footsteps are heard on the gravel. The children on their teeter-totter on the clock face are not afraid. They go right on recording the procession of seconds. Time is their only concern: the relentless thieving that nobody pays any attention to; or if they have become aware of it, they try not to think about it.

If you are of a certain temperament, you do think about it, anyway. You think about it much too much, until the sense of deprivation becomes intolerable and you resort to the Lost-and-Found Office, where, by an espèce de miracle, everything has been turned in, everything is the way it used to be. It requires only a second to throw open the shutters and remove the dust covers and air out musty rooms. "Do, do, l'enfant, do . . ." Alix sings, pushing the second-hand baby carriage back and forth under the shade of the Lebanon cedar, until Annette lets go of her thumb and falls fast asleep. The departure is as abrupt as if she had stepped into a little boat. The baby carriage has become a familiar sight on the roads around the château. Propped up on a fat pillow, the fat baby stares at the barking dog, at M. Fleury when he drives past in his noisy camion, at the little boy, Alix's friend, who has now fully mastered the art of riding a bicycle and rides round and round the baby carriage, sometimes not using his hands. Watching Alix go off down the driveway, Mme Viénot is sometimes tempted to say to her sister: "She does not look happy," but it is not the kind of remark one shouts into a hearing aid, if one can avoid it, and also, Mme Viénot reflects, it is quite possible that Mathilde's daughters do not confide in her, either.

During the daytime, Sabine reads or draws. She makes drawings of grasses and leaves and fruit from the garden. She makes a drawing of the two rain-stained statues, with the house in the background. Mme Viénot observes that no letters come for her, and that she does not seem to expect any. There is a note from a cousin, and Sabine leaves it unopened on the table in her room for three days. The sound of her voice coming from her grandmother's room is cheerful, but that is perhaps nothing more than the effect chère Maman has on her, on everybody. Mme Bonenfant arranges bouquets in the manner of Fantin-Latour, who is her favorite painter, in the hope that Sabine will be tempted to paint them. Sabine draws the children instead.

For the second week in a row, Eugène does not come down from Paris. Neither does he write, though Alix writes to him. In the evenings, Mme Viénot works at her desk in the petit salon. The two girls sit side by side on the ottoman, sharing the same pool of lamplight. Alix is knitting a sweater for the baby, Sabine is reading *Gone With the Wind* in French, Mme Bonenfant and Mme Cestre face each other across the little round table, with the *diamonoes* spread out on the green baize cloth. If she plays with anyone else, Mme Bonenfant finds that the game tires her. But Mme Cestre, far from being impatient with her mother when it takes her so long to decide where to place her counter, does not even notice, and has to be reminded that it is now her turn. The evenings pass very much as they did during the war, except that everybody is a little older, trucks do not come and go in the courtyard all night, and the only male in the house is a little boy of four, who shows no signs of ever becoming a professional soldier.

When they have all gone up to bed, the grandfather's clock in the downstairs hall chimes eleven fifteen and eleven thirty and a quarter of twelve and midnight.

Hearing the clock strike, Mme Viénot gets up from her desk, where she is writing a letter, and goes into the room across the hall. Mme Bonenfant is sitting up in bed, and when Mme Viénot takes the book from her hands, she sees that her mother has been reading Bossuet's funeral oration on the Grand Condé. The white bedspread is lying on a chair, neatly folded. The room's slight odor of camphor and old age Mme Viénot has long since become accustomed to. Mme Bonenfant removes her spectacles, folds them, and puts them on the night table, beside the photograph of her dead son.

Mme Viénot takes away the pillows at her mother's back, and the old woman lies flat in the huge double bed, as she will lie before very long in her grave. Is she afraid, Mme Viénot wonders. Does she ever think about dying?

There is little or no point in asking. Her mother would not consider this a proper subject for conversation. Actually, there are a good many subjects that chère Maman, close as she is to the end of her life, does not care to speak of. To question her about the past, to try to get at her secrets, is merely to provoke a smile or an irrelevant remark.

As she opens the window a few inches, Mme Viénot suddenly remembers how when she was a child her mother, smelling of wood violets, used to come and say good night to her. If one only lives long enough, every situation is repeated. . . .

Back in her own room, she undresses and puts on her nightgown and the dark-red wrapper, which is worn at the cuffs, she notices. Seated at the dressing table, she digs her fingers into a jar of cleansing cream and, having wiped away powder and rouge, confronts the gray underface. She and it have arrived at a working agreement: the underface, tragic, sincere, irrevocably middle-aged, is not to show itself until late at night when everyone is in bed. And in return for this discreet forbearance, Mme Viénot on her part is ready to acknowledge that the face she now sees in the mirror is hers.

She goes over to the desk and takes up the letter where she left off. When it is finished, she puts it in its envelope, licks the flap, seals it, and puts it with several other letters, all written since she came upstairs. The pile of letters represents the future, which can no more be trusted to take care of itself than the present can (though experience has demonstrated that there is a limit, a point beyond which effort cannot go, and many things happen, good and bad, that are simply the work of chance).

She begins a new letter. After a moment her pen stops moving, and she listens to the still house. Again there is a creaking sound, but it is in the walls, not in the passage outside her door. The pen moves on again, like a machine. Mme Viénot is waiting for Sabine to come and say good night. The poor child must be disheartened at losing her job with *La Femme Elégante,* and it is indeed a pity, but such things happen, and she is prepared to offer comfort, reassurance, the indisputable truth that what seems like misfortune is often a blessing in disguise. She glances impatiently at her wrist watch, and sees that it is quarter of one. She writes two more letters, even so. Her acquaintance, now that she no longer lives in Paris, shows a tendency to forget her unless prodded regularly with letters and small attentions. Paying guests, when they leave, cannot be counted on to remember indefinitely what an agreeable time they have had, and so may fail to return or fail to send other clients. A note, covering one page and part of the next, serves to remind them, if it is a question of someone's searching out a pleasant, well-situated, wholly proper establishment, that they know just the place—a handsome country house about two hundred kilometers from Paris and not far from Blois.

Mme Viénot takes off the red dressing gown and puts it over the back of a chair, gets into bed, and opens the book on her bedside table. She reads a few lines and then turns out the light. It is time that Sabine learned to be more thoughtful of others.

Stretched out flat, she discovers how tired she is, and for a moment or two she passes directly into that stage of conscious dreaming that precedes sleep. Between dreams, she reflects that the younger generation has very little affection for Beaumesnil. It is important only to Eugène.

The telephone rings, and when Mme Viénot answers it, she hears the voice of Mme Carrère. Monsieur has had a slight relapse—nothing serious, but the doctors think it would be advisable for him to be in the country, where there is absolute quiet, in a place that did him so much good before. They arrive that afternoon by car, and find their old rooms waiting for them. "You will want to rest after your long drive," Mme Viénot says. "Thérèse will bring you a can of hot water immediately. Then you need not be disturbed until dinnertime." And closing the door behind her, she passes happily over the border into sleep, but the ratching, scratching sound draws her back into consciousness. The sound continues at irregular intervals. A squirrel or a fieldmouse, she tells herself. Or a rat.

After half an hour she sits up in bed, turns on the light, props the pillows behind her back. With a sigh at not being able to go to sleep when she so much needs a good night's rest, she reaches for the book. It is the memoirs of Father Robert, an early nineteenth-century Jesuit missionary, who lived among the Chinese, and was close to God. Mme Viénot puts what happened to him, his harsh but beautifully dedicated life, between her and all silences, all creaking noises, all failures, all searching for answers that cannot be found.

Harvill Paperbacks are published by

THE HARVILL PRESS

1 Giuseppe Tomasi di Lampedusa *The Leopard*
2 Boris Pasternak *Doctor Zhivago*
3 Aleksandr Solzhenitsyn *The Gulag Archipelago*
4 Jonathan Raban *Soft City*
5 Alan Ross *Blindfold Games*
7 Vasily Grossman *Forever Flowing*
8 Peter Levi *The Frontiers of Paradise*
9 Ernst Pawel *The Nightmare of Reason*
10 Patrick O'Brian *Joseph Banks*
11 Mikhail Bulgakov *The Master and Margarita*
12 Leonid Borodin *Partings*
13 Salvatore Satta *The Day of Judgment*
14 Peter Matthiessen *At Play in the Fields of the Lord*
15 Aleksandr Solzhenitsyn *The First Circle*
16 Homer, trans. by Robert Fitzgerald *The Odyssey*
18 Peter Matthiessen *The Cloud Forest*
19 Theodore Zeldin *The French*
20 Georges Perec *Life A User's Manual*
21 Nicholas Gage *Eleni*
22 Evgenia Ginzburg *Into the Whirlwind*
23 Evgenia Ginzburg *Within the Whirlwind*
24 Mikhail Bulgakov *The Heart of a Dog*
25 Vincent Cronin *Louis and Antoinette*
26 Alan Ross *The Bandit on the Billiard Table*
27 Fyodor Dostoyevsky *The Double*
28 Alan Ross *Time was Away*
29 Peter Matthiessen *Under the Mountain Wall*
30 Peter Matthiessen *The Snow Leopard*
31 Peter Matthiessen *Far Tortuga*
32 Jorge Amado *Shepherds of the Night*
33 Jorge Amado *The Violent Land*
34 Jorge Amado *Tent of Miracles*
35 Torgny Lindgren *Bathsheba*
36 Antaeus *Journals, Notebooks & Diaries*
37 Edmonde Charles-Roux *Chanel*
38 Nadezhda Mandelstam *Hope Against Hope*
39 Nadezhda Mandelstam *Hope Abandoned*
40 Raymond Carver *Elephant and Other Stories*
41 Vincent Cronin *Catherine, Empress of All the Russias*
42 Federico de Roberto *The Viceroys*
43 Yashar Kemal *The Wind from the Plain*
44 Yashar Kemal *Iron Earth, Copper Sky*
45 Yashar Kemal *The Undying Grass*
46 Georges Perec *W or the Memory of Childhood*
47 Antaeus *On Nature*
48 Roy Fuller *The Strange and the Good*
49 Anna Akhmatova *Selected Poems*
50 Mikhail Bulgakov *The White Guard*
51 Lydia Chukovskaya *Sofia Petrovna*
52 Alan Ross *Coastwise Lights*
53 Boris Pasternak *Poems 1955–1959* and *An Essay in Autobiography*
54 Marta Morazzoni *Girl in a Turban*
55 Eduardo Mendoza *City of Marvels*
56 Michael O'Neill *The Stripped Bed*
57 Antaeus *Literature as Pleasure*
58 Margarete Buber-Neumann *Milena*
59 Torgny Lindgren *Merab's Beauty*
60 Jaan Kaplinski *The Same Sea in Us All*
61 Mikhail Bulgakov *A Country Doctor's Notebook*
62 Vincent Cronin *Louis XIV*
63 David Gilmour *The Last Leopard*
64 Leo Perutz *The Marquis of Bolibar*
65 Claudio Magris *Danube*
66 Jorge Amado *Home is the Sailor*
67 Richard Ford *Wildlife*
68 Aleksandr Solzhenitsyn *One Day in the Life of Ivan Denisovich*
69 Andrei Bitov *Pushkin House*
70 Yashar Kemal *Memed, My Hawk*
71 Raymond Carver *A New Path to the Waterfall*
72 Peter Matthiessen *On the River Styx*
73 Ernst Pawel *The Labyrinth of Exile*
74 John Clive *Not by Fact Alone*
75 Osip Mandelstam *Stone*
76 Elias Khoury *Little Mountain*
77 Osip Mandelstam *The Collected Critical Prose and Letters*
78 Edward Hoagland *Heart's Desire*
79 Mikhail Bulgakov *Black Snow*
80 Evgeny Pasternak *Boris Pasternak: The Tragic Years 1930–60*
81 Leonid Borodin *The Third Truth*
82 Michael Hulse *Eating Strawberries in the Necropolis*
83 Antaeus *Jubilee Edition*
84 Robert Hughes *Nothing if not Critical*
85 Aleksandr Solzhenitsyn *Rebuilding Russia*
86 Yury Dombrovsky *The Keeper of Antiquities*
87 Mikhail Bulgakov *Diaboliad*
88 Penelope Fitzgerald *The Knox Brothers*
89 Oleg Chukhontsev *Dissonant Voices: The New Russian Fiction*
90 Peter Levi *The Hill of Kronos*
91 Henry Green *Living*
92 Gesualdo Bufalino *Night's Lies*
93 Peter Matthiessen *Partisans*
94 Georges Perec *Things* and *A Man Asleep*
95 C. K. Stead *The Death of the Body*
96 Leo Perutz *By Night under the Stone Bridge*
97 Henry Green *Caught*
98 Lars Gustafsson *The Death of a Beekeeper*
99 Ismail Kadare *Broken April*
100 Peter Matthiessen *In the Spirit of Crazy Horse*
101 Yashar Kemal *To Crush the Serpent*
102 Elspeth Huxley *Nine Faces of Kenya*
103 Jacques Presser *The Night of the Girondists*
104 Julien Gracq *A Balcony in the Forest*
105 Henry Green *Loving*
106 Jaan Kaplinski *The Wandering Border*
107 William Watson *The Last of the Templars*
108 Penelope Fitzgerald *Charlotte Mew and her Friends*
110 Gustaw Herling *The Island*
111 Marguerite Yourcenar *Anna, Soror…*
112 Dominic Cooper *Men at Axlir*
113 Vincent Cronin *The Golden Honeycomb*
114 Aleksandr Kushner *Apollo in the Snow*
115 Antaeus *Plays in One Act*
116 Vasily Grossman *Life and Fate*
117 Mikhail Bulgakov *Manuscripts Don't Burn*
118 C. K. Stead *Sister Hollywood*
119 José Saramago *The Year of the Death of Ricardo Reis*
120 Gesualdo Bufalino *Blind Argus*
121 Peter Matthiessen *African Silences*
122 Leonid Borodin *The Story of a Strange Time*
123 Raymond Carver *No Heroics, Please*
124 Jean Strouse *Alice James*
125 Javier Marías *All Souls*
126 Henry Green *Nothing*
127 Marguerite Yourcenar *Coup de Grâce*
128 Patrick Modiano *Honeymoon*
129 Georges Perec *"53 Days"*
130 Ferdinand Mount (ed.) *Communism*
131 John Gross (ed.) *The Modern Movement*
132 Leonardo Sciascia *The Knight and Death*
133 Eduardo Mendoza *The Truth about the Savolta Case*
134 Leo Perutz *Little Apple*
135 Ismail Kadare *The Palace of Dreams*

136 Vitaliano Brancati *The Lost Years*
137 Jean Rouaud *Fields of Glory*
138 Adina Blady Szwajger *I Remember Nothing More*
139 Marguerite Yourcenar *Alexis*
140 Robert Hughes *Barcelona*
141 Paul Durcan *A Snail in My Prime*
142 Evgeny Popov *The Soul of a Patriot*
143 Richard Hughes *A High Wind in Jamaica*
144 Lars Gustafsson *A Tiler's Afternoon*
145 José Saramago *The Gospel according to Jesus Christ*
146 Leonardo Sciascia *The Council of Egypt*
147 Henry Green *Blindness*
149 Vitaliano Brancati *Bell'Antonio*
150 *Leopard II: Turning the Page*
151 Virgil *Aeneid*
152 Jaan Kross *The Czar's Madman*
153 Julien Gracq *The Opposing Shore*
154 Leo Perutz *The Swedish Cavalier*
155 Andrei Bitov *A Captive of the Caucasus*
156 Henry Green *Surviving*
157 Raymond Carver *Where I'm Calling from*
158 Ingmar Bergman *The Best Intentions*
159 Raymond Carver *Short Cuts*
160 Cees Nooteboom *The Following Story*
161 Leonardo Sciascia *Death of an Inquisitor*
162 Torgny Lindgren *Light*
163 Marguerite Yourcenar *Zeno of Bruges*
164 Antonio Tabucchi *Requiem*
165 Richard Hughes *The Fox in the Attic*
166 Russell Page *The Education of a Gardener*
167 Ivo Andrić *The Bridge over the Drina*
168 Marta Morazzoni *His Mother's House*
169 Jesus Moncada *The Towpath*
170 Gesualdo Bufalino *The Keeper of Ruins*
171 Peter Matthiessen *The Tree where Man was Born*
172 Peter Matthiessen *Blue Meridian*
173 Ismail Kadare *The Concert*
174 Ingmar Bergman *Sunday's Child*
175 Robert Hughes *Culture of Complaint*
177 Milos Tsernianski *Migrations*
178 Patrick O'Brian *Picasso*
179 Georges Perec *A Void*
180 *Leopard III: Frontiers*
181 Raymond Carver *Fires*
182 Leo Perutz *The Master of the Day of Judgment*
183 Torgny Lindgren *In Praise of Truth*
184 Javier Marias *A Heart so White*
185 José Saramago *The Stone Raft*
186 Jaan Kross *Professor Martens' Departure*
187 Jaan Kross *The Conspiracy*
188 Viktoria Schweitzer *Tsvetaeva*
189 Cees Nooteboom *In the Dutch Mountains*
190 Leonardo Sciascia *Candido*
191 Gjertrud Schnackenberg *A Gilded Lapse of Time*
192 Yi Mun-yol *The Poet*
193 Richard Hughes *The Wooden Shepherdess*
194 Marguerite Yourcenar *A Coin in Nine Hands*
195 Giuseppe Tomasi di Lampedusa *The Siren and Selected Writings*
196 Vasily Grossman *Life and Fate*
197 Lidiya Ginzburg *Blockade Diary*
198 Israel Metter *The Fifth Corner of the Room*
199 Claudio Margris *A Different Sea*
200 Andrei Platonov *The Foundation Pit*
201 Aleksandr Solzhenitsyn *The Russian Question*
202 David Bellos Georges Perec: *A Life in Words*
203 Carmen Martín Gaite *Variable Cloud*
204 Raymond Carver *Will You Please Be Quiet, Please?*
205 Paul Durcan *O Westport in the Light of Asia Minor*
206 Paul Durcan *The Berlin Wall Café*
207 C. K. Stead *All Visitors Ashore*
208 Cees Nooteboom *Rituals*
209 Jean Giono *The Horseman on the Roof*
210 Henry Green *Party Going*
211 Ismail Kadare *The Pyramid*
212 Ivo Andrić *Bosnian Chronicle*
213 William Watson *The Knight on the Bridge*
214 José Saramago *The History of the Siege of Lisbon*
215 Rex Warner *The Aerodrome*
216 Georges Perec *Three by Perec*
217 W. G. Sebald *The Emigrants*
218 Slobodan Selenić *Premeditated Murder*
219 Octavio Paz *The Double Flame: Essays on Love & Eroticism*
220 Evgeny Popov *Merrymaking in Old Russia*
221 Leo Perutz *Turlupin*
222 Javier Marías *Tomorrow in the Battle Think on Me*
223 Vladimir Arsenijević *In the Hold*
224 Daniele del Giudice *Take-off*
225 Jaan Kaplinski *Through the Forest*
226 Raymond Carver *What We Talk about When We Talk about Love*
227 Ingmar Bergman *Private Confessions*
228 Aleksandr Solzhenitsyn *Invisible Allies*
229 James Hanley *The Last Voyage & Other Stories*
230 Henry Green *Concluding*
231 Vitaly Shentalinsky *The KGB's Literary Archives*
232 William Maxwell *So Long, See You Tomorrow*
233 William Maxwell *All the Days and Nights*
234 Yury Dombrovsky *The Faculty of Useless Knowledge*
235 Monika Fagerholm *Wonderful Women by the Water*
236 Jacqueline Harpman *The Mistress of Silence*
237 Alan Garner *The Voice that Thunders*
238 *Leopard IV: Bearing Witness*
239 Richard Pipes *The Russian Revolution 1899–1919*
240 Richard Pipes *Russia Under the Bolshevik Regime 1919–1924*
241 Andrey Platonov *The Return and Other Stories*
242 Ismail Kadare *The File on H*
243 Sebastiano Vassalli *The Swan*
244 Thomas Brussig *Heroes Like Us*
245 Raymond Carver *All of Us: The Collected Poems*
246 Ramond Carver *Cathedral*
247 José Saramago *Blindness*
248 José Saramago *Baltasar & Blimunda*
250 Julio Cortázar *Bestiary and the Selected Stories*
251 Mayra Montero *You, Darkness*
252 Octavio Paz *India: Essays*
253 Jean Giono *Angelo*
254 Lars Gustafsson *The Tale of a Dog*
255 Carmen Martín Gaite *The Farewell Angel*
256 William Maxwell *Time Will Darken It*
257 Jean Echenoz *Lake*
258 Henry Green *Back*
259 Henry Green *Doting*
260 Anita Brookner *Soundings*
261 Bernardo Atxaga *The Lone Woman*
262 William Maxwell *The Folded Leaf*
263 Halldór Laxness *Independent People*
264 Jacqueline Harpman *Orlanda*
265 Gesualdo Bufalino *The Plague-Spreader's Tale*
266 *The Paris Review* Interviews: *Women Writers at Work*
267 *The Paris Review* Interviews: *Beat Writers at Work*
268 Javier Marías *When I Was Mortal*
269 José Saramago *All the Names*
270 James Hanley *The Ocean*
271 William Maxwell *The Château*
272 Ismail Kadare *The General of the Dead Army*

For the full list of titles please write to:
The Harvill Press,
2 Aztec Row, Berners Road
London N1 0PW
enclosing a stamped self-addressed envelope

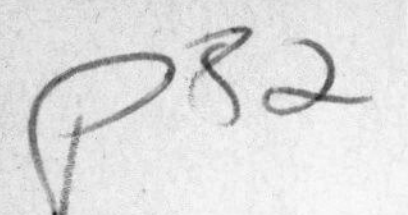